About the Author

After a successful career over nearly thirty years in the corporate world, based mostly in London, Andrew Pratt now lives and writes in Prague, Czech Republic.

One of Us Lied is his third book in the Honza crime series. The previous books in the series are: *In the Heart of Prague (Honza Book 1)*, published in 2021, and *Head to Head (Honza Book 2)*, published in 2022.

More information on the author and the Honza series can be found at www.thehonzaseries.com.

One of Us Lied

Andrew Pratt

One of Us Lied

Olympia Publishers
London

www.olympiapublishers.com
OLYMPIA PAPERBACK EDITION

A CIP catalogue record for this title is
available from the British Library.

ISBN: 978-1-80439-245-4

This is a work of fiction.
Names, characters, places and incidents originate from the writer's
imagination. Any resemblance to actual persons, living or dead, is
purely coincidental.

First Published in 2023

Olympia Publishers
Tallis House
2 Tallis Street
London
EC4Y 0AB

Printed in Great Britain

Dedication

This book is dedicated to my wonderful daughters,
Laura and Emily.

Acknowledgements

Thank you to my dear friends, Nick White and Dominic Jennings, for supporting me through the process of writing this novel. Your unconditional support, suggestions for improvement, and also enthusiasm to read through drafts were so helpful to rounding the story and the characters.

Emma Hall and Paul McCarthy also read through the final draft and helped me refine the murder mystery element of the book. Thank you for your invaluable feedback. Thank you also to Věra Colbecková for reading through the final version, spotting uncorrected spelling mistakes and grammatical errors.

My biggest supporter is however my partner, Pavla. This series would not be possible without you, both because of the support you have given me, but also because you remain the inspiration for writing about Prague. Love you, or as we say in Czech: Miluju tě.

1

The Pull of the River

Sunday, 21ˢᵗ June 2010

Jonny stood on the balcony of his new apartment, leaning forward on the rail and taking in the calming scene along the River Vltava. The early evening sun was starting to slip away behind the buildings on the rising ground of the opposite bank. A boat trip full of tourists chugged past, towards the iconic Charles Bridge, the faint sound of jazz music carrying to him on the gentle breeze.

Since arriving in Prague three months before, he'd become enthralled with the odd-shaped roof terraces and balconies fitted in amongst the stunning architecture of the historic city. But he'd never for one minute imagined himself living in such an apartment. The instructions to the letting agent had been simple: a comfortable two bedroom apartment with a central location to allow him to continue exploring his adopted home. The initial annoyance at being dragged to see a third floor apartment in Prague 4 was quickly overcome by the sense of space of the recently renovated, glass-fronted building and the spell of the ever-changing light reflecting off the surface of the water. Only two days after moving in, the balcony had quickly become his favourite place: sitting outside for breakfast, reading the newspaper to the sound of water flowing in the background, and enjoying the sunset with a drink and background music.

The sound of approaching footsteps on the wooden floorboards made him turn. Ivana stepped onto the balcony, her summer dress and beaded belt swishing with the movement of her hips. She picked up her glass of white wine and joined him standing at the rail, her free hand gently caressing the base of his back.

Instead of turning back to his new window view, he stayed watching her as she nuzzled her shoulder into his and looked out onto the slapping waves on the river. Watching her move always managed to mesmerise him, stopping him in his tracks and leaving him momentarily flummoxed. Her lightness of foot seemed to carry her over the ground effortlessly, her bohemian-style clothes twirling in tune to her graceful movements. Even watching her head move across the dinner table was entrancing: her long brown hair pulled up to expose her slender neck, the dangling long, white gold earrings swaying hypnotically like the flame of a candle.

"Honza, stop it! You're doing it again."

She turned to face him. The stern look on her face was undermined by the hint of a smile around her eyes.

Jonny chuckled. During the early stages of their relationship her swift change in tone had concerned him; he was never quite sure how to react. But now he knew to always be himself, surf the waves of emotion and wait for her returning smile. That was the person she fell for, and the one easiest for him to be.

"I was just thinking what a lovely weekend it's been."

She held his gaze, her features softening with the setting sun. "Yes it was." She leaned into him and, raising herself on tiptoes, kissed him gently on the lips.

Jonny picked up the wine bottle from the table, expertly

refilling their glasses. He raised his glass. "Na zdraví."

"Na zdraví," she repeated, starting to raise the glass to her lips.

Jonny quickly intercepted the move, gently catching the upward movement of her arm. "To us!"

"Yes." She smiled, tilting her head slightly. "To us."

They clinked glasses, eyes locked on each other, and sipped the wine in silent celebration.

The journey to this point in their relationship hadn't been all smooth sailing. The stress of a detective's life had threatened to destabilise the early stages of their union, the shock of his demanding work-life balance was initially too much for Ivana to cope with. The search for Jonny's Czech family in Prague had been their saviour. Discovering the existence of his mother's extended family, and finding the half-sister he never knew existed, had provided the opportunity for them to explore something new as a couple; the diversion had allowed them time to enjoy the emotional journey together, and in the process see the positives in each other with fresh eyes.

After Jonny had helped solve the high profile double murder of British man Alex Corbet and his new partner, Yulia Ivanova, his work life had settled into a manageable routine. Through his new role as consultant to the Czech police, he'd established a protocol for mentoring new and upcoming detectives, and provided guidance on the development of police procedures to integrate the use of new technology. His friend and boss, Felix Mikeš, shielded Jonny from the unwanted exposure to the higher echelons of the Czech Police or the media. Mikeš enjoyed the attention and only demanded Jonny attend one meeting with the Police Commissioner, requested to put a face to the hot, new name in town. Jonny missed the buzz sometimes, but knew he'd gained the right balance. Plus, he knew from experience that a murder was always just around the corner.

For the first time in his life, Jonny had uninterrupted weekends, allowing Ivana to continue in her quest to show him interesting parts of the Czech Republic. The highlights had been trips to Český Krumlov and Pilsen, the latter including an unforgettable tour of the famous Pilsner Urquell brewery. The most enjoyable times however were relaxed, long weekends with his new family. Getting to know his half-sister, Lenka, and her husband, Miloš, was a joy, and added so much depth and colour to the memories of his late mother. The fact that their daughter, Lucie Dvořáková, was coincidentally also the sergeant in Mikeš' Serious Crime and Homicide department only served to make the link to his new adopted city extra special.

Despite the serenity of the new phase in his life, Jonny had been deeply aware that there was a decision looming. He'd initially landed in Prague as a tourist, renting the spare attic room in Ivana's top floor apartment. Whilst she'd been flexible from the beginning, giving him the freedom of her apartment, she was also fiercely independent. He was effectively living out of a suitcase, his belongings remaining behind in London. There was also the matter of privacy when his teenage daughter, Charlotte, came to visit him over the summer.

The matter came to a head one evening when Jonny had wanted to listen to some music. Bob Dylan had become an integral part of his life from his early twenties and he felt the absence almost physically if a few days went by without some time alone with the bard. He'd loved sharing his favourite songs and their history with Ivana, but his personal listening experience was different – and he missed it. Laying on the bed in the spare room, listening to his iPod through headphones, his craving had been initially sated. But, the iPod battery had suddenly failed. In ripping off his headphones, the iPod fell to the floor and suffered a heavy fall. Recharging proved useless; the drop had been fatal and the unit was beyond repair. Jonny had sat on the bed in the spare room in despair, feeling lost and yearning for his complete vinyl collection back in the UK.

Jonny had raised the subject with trepidation over dinner the following evening, unsure how to explain exactly what he was feeling, or how to move forward.

Ivana had understood immediately, leaning over the table to take his hand. "Honza, you need to get your own apartment."

When he'd dithered, unsure of the effect on their still young relationship, she'd resolved all his doubts. "Well, what else did you think was going to happen? These last few months were always going to be our honeymoon period. I'll help you find a nice apartment, and we can stay over with each other as much as we want... It's probably the real start to our relationship."

The next month had been hectic. After the apartment was found, Jonny went back to the UK. He tidied up his own London flat to rent out and made plans to move his belongings abroad. The shiny, glass-fronted apartment in Prague felt like a new beginning and so he threw out a lot of old clothes as well as any personal items that he hadn't used in the previous few years. A fresh start. Only his extensive vinyl collection and catalogue of CDs, including every Bob Dylan album released, were spared the cull, along with his precious sound system, put together as quality separate units over the years. Personal items kept from his mother were also packaged up, along with the urn of her ashes he'd kept, not knowing what to do with them. Although his mother had left Prague, her birthplace, under a cloud, he knew it was now time to take her back.

15

The enormity of everything that had happened to him since arriving in Prague in March only hit home when he fully explained the journey to Charlotte. Their relationship had been strained since the divorce from her mother, built on his failures to attend important events such as parents' evenings and generally be the father figure she wanted or needed. His defence was always that he hadn't had a father figure himself – his own father having left at an early age – but he knew it was a lame excuse. Charlotte's excitement about Prague and his new life had left him slightly dazed but looking forward to the future. Perhaps now that she was developing into a young adult, keen to learn about the world, he'd be better positioned to have a closer relationship with her.

Jonny glanced out across the river as a small craft sped past before turning back to Ivana. "Thank you so much for helping me move in."

"Honza, it was fun. The pizza and champagne was very classy."

They smiled together at the memory.

"Mind you, I still can't believe how many records and CDs you have. They wouldn't fit in my apartment!"

Jonny laughed but decided against trying to defend his obsession.

"Thanks also for the female touches," he quickly added, looking through the open French doors at the fresh flowers on the dining table, potted plants positioned around the room, and knick-knacks Ivana had bought for the apartment. "You know what I'm like. I'd have bought a few small cactuses and that would have been it."

"I understand you British call it a Man's Cave."

He laughed again.

"All we need to sort out is the spare bedroom for when Charlotte comes to stay," she said. "I'll have a look for a nice duvet and some sheets. When is she coming?"

"Mid-July. She's finishing her exams now, and then going away with her mum at the start of the holidays."

Ivana looked at her watch and gulped down the last of her wine. "I need to get going – got to get ready for work tomorrow."

"Really?" Jonny looked at his watch. "When will I see you this week?" he asked, a hint of hesitancy in his voice.

"Well, I think you should take a few days to get used to your new apartment. Then we've got dinner on Wednesday."

"Dinner?"

She rolled her eyes. "Dinner for your name day. Remember?"

"Ivana, we've talked about this—"

"Too late arguing now, it's already organised. You're half-Czech and custom dictates that you must celebrate your name day. It's tradition. Just think, on Wednesday you'll be celebrating for the first time with every other Czech man that is called Jan, or nicknamed Honza."

"I suppose—"

"It's like your second birthday!" She kissed him on the lips before he could speak again, picked up the empty wine bottle and walked back inside the apartment.

Jonny watched her walk away, smiling to himself. His gaze remained fixed on her as she found her fabric handbag and bustled around the living room collecting up her scattered belongings, in the process picking up a thin summer scarf and wrapping it around her neck. He turned back to the pull of the river, knowing at that moment he was more contented than he could remember for a very long time.

17

Once Ivana had left, Jonny poured himself a single malt and selected Bob Dylan's album *Highway 61 Revisited*. After carefully dropping the needle on the edge of the spinning record, he settled back in the reclining chair and nestled the whisky glass in his hands. The subtle hiss from the stylus was soon replaced by the opening drum snare and swirling organ of 'Like a Rolling Stone'. Now he felt completely at home.

2

Meet the Neighbours

The iconic song was not even finished before Jonny heard a loud, chiming sound. His initial thought was that something was wrong with the connection to the speakers, so he started to lean forward in the chair ready to check the connections at the back of the stereo unit. When the chime sounded again, this time more pronounced and persistent, he realised it was coming from the front door of his new apartment.

He laughed to himself, believing it to be a returning Ivana. She had proved herself to be extremely scatty over the time they'd been together; the running joke between them was that she always forgot something, only to drag him back to her apartment and then force them to rush to avoid being late for their engagement. She's probably already lost the key I only gave her yesterday, he thought.

Without thinking, he opened the door to find Chief Warrant Officer Felix Mikeš standing on the other side, a wide cat-like grin spread across his face. Standing respectfully behind him was his deputy, Chief Sergeant Marek Boukal.

"Ahoj, Honza!" Mikeš shook Jonny's hand and walked straight into the apartment without being invited. "You have a very swanky apartment here, my friend."

Jonny looked at Boukal and rolled his eyes. "Ahoj, Marek. Come in."

"Ahoj. Thank you."

Boukal stepped tentatively into the apartment as Mikeš set off to explore every corner of the living space.

Mikeš was one of those characters who polarised opinion on first meeting. Most people came to love him, even if they'd initially been put off by his energetic and seemingly brash, assuming style. Jonny had been no different. During the initial interviews on The Old Town Square Murder, when he'd been a potential witness despite only having just landed in Prague for a holiday, Mikeš had been almost overpowering. He'd identified Jonny as a fellow detective, unilaterally claimed a new friend and nicknamed him 'Honza'. All within thirty minutes. But Mikeš' effervescent character had quickly rubbed off on Jonny and now they were close friends, as well as colleagues. Mikeš' celebrity status as probably the most successful DCI equivalent in Czech history followed him everywhere, but Jonny thought about him more as an emotional, older brother.

Mikeš also looked the part. His trademark pressed, tweed three-piece suit was always paired with a colourful shirt and tie combination, this day's selection being sky blue with bold, white spots on the tie. His ever-present wide-brimmed hat and black cane completed the signature outfit, the tip of the cane lightly tapping the wooden floorboards as he walked the perimeter of the living room.

"Very nice, my friend," Mikeš concluded, nodding his head in appreciation. "I think you'll be very happy here. I can feel it."

"Of course, all the nice touches came from Ivana. Plants and I don't usually get on well together, but she's promised to show me how to care for them."

Mikeš seemed only to be half listening. "So, Honza, we're the same now."

Jonny looked confused. He turned to Boukal for help, but just received a shrug of the shoulders in response.

"What do you mean, Felix?"

"Well, we're both in relationships with women we love, but we are living apart from them."

"Felix, I've explained it to you already—"

"Yes, yes…" Mikeš insisted. "But, it's still the same."

"This is like a restart in our relationship," Jonny started to explain again. "Everything's fine between us, but it's the best move for our relationship right now. We couldn't have carried on with me being her tenant. Ivana can rent her attic room out again, and we can stay with each other as much as we want. I'm sure we'll end up living together again at some point in the future."

"Maybe, maybe not." Mikeš had an impish grin on his face, knowing he was stirring trouble. "This could be the new way forward – the best of both worlds."

As was often the case when Mikeš was in full flow, passion overflowing, Jonny was nonplussed, stumped for words. His usual role in their friendship, including their unlikely detective teaming, was the voice of reason: calm, assured and logical. But, his track record in matters of the heart was not exemplary, unlike his police career, and so his silence on this occasion was more in hope that the conversation would move on quickly.

Mikeš' long-term relationship with Pathologist Ella Králová had been a source of confusion to Jonny from the start. Their marriage had failed, but they still clearly loved each other and dated on almost a weekly basis despite living apart: they were together, definitely a couple, but committed to having separate homes. The thought had never crossed Jonny's mind that he and Mikeš were now in the same situation.

"What's the fascination with vinyl, Honza?"

Thankful for the distraction, Jonny turned to see Boukal holding the sleeve of *Highway 61 Revisited* and watching the record circling under the clear, plastic turntable cover.

"You're just too young to appreciate it, Marek," Jonny answered quickly, moving over to put his arm around his protégé in a fatherly fashion. "This is how music was designed to be listened to. It makes for a very personal experience."

Boukal smiled sarcastically, unconvinced, making Jonny feel his age – a father figure. But, that was what *his* role was in many ways. Mikeš was an unpredictable boss: caring but also impatient and full of quirky ways. Jonny had agreed to take on the role of Boukal's mentor and the initial results had been pleasing for everyone involved. Boukal had risen through the ranks quickly during his short police career, and had the raw skills required of a detective. Jonny had just focused on honing Boukal's skills further, trying to get him to think the way a criminal would.

One lesson already successfully delivered involved upgrading Boukal's sense of how to dress for the job. When Jonny had first met Boukal, he'd most often looked like he'd slept in his suit and shirt. After Boukal had physically apprehended the murderer of Alex Corbet and Yulia Ivanova, earning him a bravery award from the Police Commissioner, Jonny had frogmarched him to the tailors where he'd been fitted with two new suits, five new shirts and a matching set of ties. To Jonny's amazement, the new look had been mostly maintained, although he'd had to show the young detective how to knot his tie properly on more than one occasion.

Jonny and Boukal followed Mikeš onto the balcony. "Great view," Mikeš remarked. "This part of the river doesn't get as much credit as it deserves. The focus is always on the stretch further down because of Charles Bridge and the old town."

"That's why I like it," Jonny commented. "It feels like a private, uninterrupted view."

Silence descended as they all watched the small crafts pass by, the resulting waves lapping against the shore.

"Hang on," Jonny exclaimed, a puzzled look creeping over his face. "It's Sunday evening. What are you both doing dressed up for work?"

"Finally he notices," Mikeš stated, unblinkingly. "I thought that love had started to dull your powers of deduction."

Jonny laughed, accepting the jibe. "So, what's the story?"

"Well, the first part of the answer is that we've got a busy week ahead. Marek has his bravery award, plus we have a few holidays in the team. I thought it would be a good idea to get ahead before the week officially starts."

"And the second part?" Jonny prompted.

"We wanted to come and visit you in your stylish, new apartment."

Jonny looked at Mikeš, trying to read him. "No, that's not it. What's the real reason?"

"Fair cop, guv," Mikeš replied quickly, smiling and holding his arms up in submission.

"Felix!"

"The Police Commissioner has personally asked me to investigate a matter relating to someone he knows. You know, these old school networks of people with influence really annoy me—"

"But, why here?"

"They live upstairs," Mikeš stated, matter-of-factly.

Jonny shook his head, rolling his eyes. "I told you, trouble follows me around."

It was Mikeš' turn to laugh. "My friend, don't take it so personally. It's almost certainly nothing. Michal Polák runs a prominent start-up company in Prague. He's become a bit of a star in Prague society, with his pretty wife on his arm and his wide circle of influential friends."

"Has someone been murdered?"

"No, nothing like that," Mikeš confirmed. "But, it seems he's received some threatening messages. And, now the Police Commissioner is involved." He rolled his eyes dramatically. "We have no option but to check out the story."

"But, people in the public eye always get crank messages," Jonny stated. "It's almost expected."

Mikeš sighed heavily. "I told you, Michal Polák knows a lot of people in high places…"

"Why do you need me?" Jonny enquired. "I know nothing about the celebrity circles in Prague."

"He's Slovakian, but his wife is American. The business operates by speaking English day-to-day. I'd like you to meet them. You might spot something that neither Marek nor I pick up in the conversation."

Jonny shrugged his shoulders in acceptance.

"Let's meet the neighbours," Mikeš boomed, slapping Jonny on the back.

***

They took the stairs. Mikeš led the way with his bouncing strides up the steps, weaving past the lift entrances on the floor landings and appealing city views through the full-length glass windows at each turn of the staircase.

Mikeš' energy amazed Jonny. Despite being close to

retirement age, Mikeš was still full of life and outpaced Jonny on their frequent walks around the city. After taking early retirement from the Metropolitan Police, Jonny had felt himself slowly losing his fitness, feeling the tiredness in his limbs after a day's work. Mikeš had made it his mission to get his new friend in shape, even threatening to enter them both in a 10k run around the city at night in the coming autumn.

The top floor landing of the apartment building was open and light, affording bird's eye views in both directions: over the city centre and the river. The starkness of the brightly painted walls and marbled tiles was balanced by large, potted plants, giving the feel of an atrium. Jonny had only travelled up the first three floors during his short residence, mostly carrying boxes to and from the lift, but now he appreciated the full elegance of the entrance hall area. He also suddenly realised that whilst the other floors, including his, branched out into two apartments – one two bedroom like his, the other three bedroom – this penthouse apartment took up the whole floor.

Boukal stepped forward to press the bell.

Mikeš mistook Jonny's scrutiny of the surroundings. "I don't like these people either."

The apartment door was opened by a radiant, slim lady in her early thirties. Her wavy blonde hair framed a beautiful smile, full of openness and welcome. She wore a knee-length summer dress, white with printed flowers, with matching red shoes. Her makeup was perfectly applied, bold but matching her vibrancy.

"Mrs Poláková, I am Chief Sergeant Marek Boukal. We have come to speak to your husband."

"Yes, yes. Please come in. And, please call me Amy." Her American accent was softened by years of living abroad.

She opened the door fully and beckoned them inside.

Mikeš stepped through the doorway and offered Amy his hand. "Madam, I am Chief Warrant Officer Felix Mikeš. I think we met last year at a function before the opera."

"Yes, indeed. You are very welcome, Felix. My husband is expecting you."

Mikeš waved Jonny forward. "This is Jonathan Fox. He's a consultant working with the Czech Police." He leaned in towards Amy, cupping his hand around his mouth in exaggerated fashion. "He was a top detective in the Metropolitan Police in London. And, the good news for you is that he's moved in downstairs." He winked at her to seal the secret.

"Oh, how delightful. We must tell Michal."

Jonny stepped forward and extended his hand. Well used to Mikeš' antics, he decided to play it straight. "Very pleased to meet you, Amy."

Holding her hand and looking into her eyes, he was able to fleetingly study her beauty close up. The proportion and balance of her facial features were flawless, almost mesmerising. If asked at that very moment, he'd have been hard pressed to recall a woman he'd met over his life who was more naturally beautiful.

Boukal closed the apartment door and followed the others through the hall into the expansive living room, Amy leading from the front.

The apartment was simply decorated, the finish contemporary and sophisticated; the home design utilised the available space and prevailing light to maximum effect. The walls were adorned by modern paintings, expertly positioned and expensively framed for attention, interspersed by floor-standing, abstract sculptures on waist-height plinths. The dark brown leather sofas, floor lamps and finery of the curtains softened the art gallery effect, but it was clear the room was less for living, more for hosting and showing off. Jonny found it hard to believe he was living in the same building, only two floors below.

The open French doors led onto a spacious terrace providing uninterrupted views towards Prague old town: Charles Bridge was just visible in the distance, before the bend in the river. An outside seating area was the centrepiece of the decked terrace, surrounded by a neatly, pruned hedgerow, providing protective fencing and additional privacy.

A well-groomed, handsome man sat on a large sofa, totally engrossed in the pages of a Sunday newspaper. His tall frame spilled over the low sofa, his knees raised higher than the seat cushions. Like his wife, he also seemed dressed for an occasion, wearing a designer open-neck shirt, chinos and suede, brown shoes.

"Darling, the police are here for you," Amy called out.

Michal Polák folded away the newspaper quickly and stood to receive his guests. His welcoming smile was genuine, matching his wife's, but the frown on his forehead hinted at preoccupied thoughts from his weekend reading.

"Felix, how are you?" Michal shook hands with Mikeš. "It must be, let me see... yes, it must be a year since we last saw you."

Amy had naturally moved to Michal's side, completing the striking husband and wife pairing.

"That is correct," Mikeš confirmed firmly. "The Police Commissioner sends his regards."

Michal laughed nervously. "Yes, yes..." he stuttered in reply, flicking his thick mop of dark hair. "I'm sorry to drag you out here on a Sunday. It's just that the business takes up so much of my time during the week. Doesn't it, darling?"

"Absolutely," Amy replied positively, full of smiles as she

27

turned to Mikeš. "Sometimes, Felix, I hardly see him Monday to Friday."

"Anyway," Michal continued, keen to explain, "I took the liberty of speaking to the Commissioner. I hope you don't mind. We've been at a charity function today, but I knew we had a free evening, and—"

"Let me introduce Jonathan Fox. He's a top British detective and is providing consultancy to my team… as supported by the Commissioner." Mikeš smiled ironically. "And, also my deputy, Marek Boukal."

Michal extended his hand to Jonny and they shook.

"Mr Fox, I've heard a lot about you," Michal started diplomatically. "It is nice to put a face to the name. Please…" He indicated for them to sit down on the opposite sofa.

"And, he's also now your neighbour!" Mikeš stated boldly, enjoying the ambush.

Despite enjoying Mikeš' eccentric behaviour and odd conversation in most situations, Jonny had learned to step in early to control introductions and ensure cordial ongoing relations. Being the foreigner in the city, his view of people wasn't tarnished by the history of politics over the last decade or so.

"Firstly, please call me Honza – everyone does. And, yes, I moved into an apartment on the third floor on Friday. It is very nice here—"

"You must come to one of our evening parties," Amy exclaimed, clapping her hands excitedly. Whilst her reaction was intentionally girlish, she retained an air of authority in the male company through the sureness of her natural looks and her privileged background.

"Thank you, I would like that," Jonny replied graciously. "But, maybe, given that it is Sunday evening, you should explain the reason why you called us here."

Mikeš nudged Jonny's elbow discreetly next to him, holding back his developing wry smile.

"Yes, of course," Michal complied. "This is what we wanted to ask for your advice on." He took a creased piece of paper out of his trouser pocket, unfolded it and placed it on the low table between the sofas.

Mikeš picked up the piece of A4 paper with a printed message on it. "ONE OF US LIED," he read aloud.

"We received this through the post yesterday," Michal confirmed. "But, it's not the first message like this we've received. They've also become more frequent in the last few weeks."

Jonny inched forward on the sofa, now interested. He took the paper from Mikeš and studied the words more carefully. "Do you have any idea what the message is about?"

Michal shook his head. "Absolutely no idea. We initially just thought it was a crank, someone looking for attention. Many businesses or celebrities get followers who are obsessed with them. We've heard of many such cases amongst our circle of friends, haven't we, darling?"

Amy nodded vigorously in support of her husband. "You've had crackpot calls to the business before, but they all stopped quite quickly. This one seems different…"

"In what way?" Jonny asked Michal when it was clear his wife wasn't going to elaborate.

"Well, it is always the same message and the way it is written seems, I don't know, sort of personal and threatening. We're now receiving one message per day, sometimes more, so the level of potential threat seems to be escalating."

Mikeš sighed heavily. "The message isn't exactly

threatening."

Amy took her husband's hand. Jonny could see they were a close, supportive, couple, but he also detected an element of show intended for the detectives in front of them – playing to the audience.

"When you say 'we'," Jonny continued, "are you talking about you and your wife?"

"No, no," Michal answered. "I believe this is all aimed at me and the other directors of the business. We have all received the same message."

"Always the exact same wording?"

"Yes."

"And, the 'us' in the message?" Jonny prompted.

Michal shook his head slowly. "Sorry, no idea. Your guess is as good as mine. Obviously, the business has competitors, both here in the Czech Republic and abroad, but the rivalry with these companies is mostly good-natured."

"Any disgruntled ex-employees?"

"The company has grown quickly, especially over the early years. There have definitely been a few unhappy leavers over this time, but I cannot think of anyone who has a sufficient grudge to try to hound us with a campaign like this."

Jonny looked at the letter again, turning it over in his hands, a thoughtful frown developing on his forehead.

Boukal lifted his head from writing in his notepad. "Mr Polák, has anything strange happened to you or any of the other directors recently? In fact, to anyone working at the business? Maybe something small that appeared insignificant at the time. Something that could be linked to the person who sent this message."

"To be honest, we didn't really take it seriously until last week. We had just laughed about it. But, once we realised we'd all received multiple messages over the week, at least one per day between us, we sat down and talked about it on Friday. We asked ourselves the exact same question, but couldn't think of anything that has happened out of the ordinary. Also, none of our other senior managers have received messages." Michal shrugged his shoulders. "I'm sorry, I know that's not very helpful…"

Just as Boukal opened his mouth, ready to ask a follow-up question, Mikeš exhaled deeply to stop him continuing. An uncomfortable silence descended.

Mikeš shifted in his seat, clearly losing patience with the situation. He took his pocket watch out from his waistcoat and flipped the cover open. "We understand your predicament and will take any threat seriously," he said to Michal, unable to stay quiet any longer. "But, you must understand that nothing illegal seems to have taken place. This message is just a statement of supposed facts, an opinion, nothing more at this stage. We don't even know who it is really aimed at."

"What about the business?" Michal pleaded. "We are a celebrated, home-grown success story in Prague, one that the Czech government is proud of. We have our ten year anniversary coming up soon and we've even been—"

"Mr Polák, I appreciate that," Mikeš snapped, "but quite frankly the business is not my primary concern."

Jonny held out the letter, now folded compactly into a smaller size. "This letter seems to fold up into the size of an envelope."

"It arrived in the post yesterday morning," Amy answered cheerily, keen to maintain a cordial atmosphere.

"So, the person who sent this knows your home address?" Jonny suggested.

"Yes," Michal confirmed. "Some messages were sent by email to my work email address, some by post here, and also to the office. It's been the same for the three other directors."

Jonny turned to Mikeš. "That puts a slightly different complexion on the situation."

"Complexion?" Mikeš looked confused.

"What I mean is that the person who's sending the messages is making it very personal. And, with the increase in the frequency of the messages, maybe something is about to happen?"

"But, what can we do about it?" Mikeš huffed. "At the moment, a crime hasn't been committed."

"Michal, do you still have the envelope from yesterday?" Jonny continued, unabated. "Maybe also some of the other messages you've received?"

"Only the envelope from yesterday," he confirmed. "We didn't keep the others. I threw them away."

Amy got up from the sofa. "I'll get it." She strode briskly from the terrace into the living room, her walk both majestic and beguiling in equal measure.

"Do you still have the emails?" Boukal enquired.

"I'm sure we've deleted most of the early ones, but I've definitely still got the recent emails. We can also probably retrieve the deleted emails from the server."

Amy returned with the envelope, full of smiles, and handed it to Jonny.

"At this stage, all we can really do is check the letter and envelope for fingerprints, and maybe also try to trace the IP address of the computer from which the messages were sent," Jonny stated. "But, even if we did find out who's behind it, all we can really do is interview them and warn them to stop."

"That would be very useful," Michal replied warmly, smiling at his wife.

"In the meantime, I suggest you make a list of anybody who might resent you or your business' success," Jonny added.

"It could be a long list," Mikeš murmured under his breath.

Michal looked at his wife again, raising his eyebrows slightly.

"We'll do that," Michal confirmed to Jonny. "Thank you, Mr Fox."

"Yes, thank you, Honza," Amy echoed, smiling brightly at her guests. "And, thank you all for coming to help my husband with this delicate matter. We both really appreciate it."

"I think we're done here," Mikeš blurted out, clearly still irate.

3

Suggestive Behaviour

Monday, 22nd June 2010

After having had a few weeks off to sort out his personal situation, it was time to get back to work.

Being unexpectedly drawn into a murder investigation on his holiday only months before had made Jonny realise how much he'd missed the mental challenge of chasing criminals. The lingering doubts that had festered after his last, bad case in London, leading to taking the early retirement on offer, were now a past memory; he knew his destiny was to be a detective. Being central to solving a couple of high profile murder cases in Prague had left him reinvigorated. With a settled base in Prague established, he was now looking forward to working amongst Mikeš' team again, getting his hands dirty on a new case.

Waking early though, full of good intentions, his early morning routine had felt oddly unsettling. The layout of his new apartment was not yet familiar and nothing appeared to be where he thought he'd put it after unpacking: the trousers he'd intended to wear were finally discovered in the newly-bought washing bin, whilst he was unable to find his favourite pair of brown shoes anywhere.

He also missed not waking up with Ivana, and found his mind wandering, trying to guess what she was doing. Worries also started to surface about whether he'd made the right decision. They'd slept together in the same bed almost every night since their first date, except for his time in the UK, and had become more intimate than any relationship he could remember. She was far more independent than him, and less prone to reflection or doubt, but he knew she also treasured their natural comfort with each other. Of course, she was still liable to get frustrated with his dithering or the poor management of his work-life balance – her Slavic temperament showing little tolerance – but any issue was usually quick to dissipate.

Breakfast on the balcony helped, the calmness of the river contrasting with the distant sounds of the early morning rush hour. Drinking his coffee and plotting his walk to the police station in Prague 1, he reflected on Mikeš' annoyance the evening before. They both had deep resentment of anyone playing power politics, especially within the police hierarchy, but Mikeš' patience seemed equally thin with the Czech celebrity circle. Mikeš had previously described it to Jonny as a closed shop, but his suspicion was that his friend's anger ran deeper, and was personal.

As they'd descended the inner staircase from the penthouse apartment the night before, Jonny had invited Mikeš and Boukal back to his own apartment out of courtesy. Although he'd been relieved when the offer was declined, Mikeš' vehement outburst had surprised him, "Honza, you don't understand these people. They are just out to take what they can. They use people like you and me, and then they spit them out!" With that, Mikeš had bounded down the remaining floors, leaving Boukal only able to shrug his shoulders in acceptance and scamper after his boss.

Jonny had intrinsically never liked these type of people either; they took for granted that you were there to serve them, and never considered the impact of their actions or words on others. But, he'd come to tolerate them, even use them to his own benefit on a few investigations. Mostly though, he just tried to ignore them. He wanted his sole focus to be on catching the perpetrators of serious crimes – nothing else mattered to him.

With breakfast finished, he took a jacket from his wardrobe and headed for the door. He looked at his watch, eight a.m. A swift walk into the centre, and he'd be in the office by just after eight thirty a.m. Not too early, and not too late.

Locking the door, he heard someone approaching up the stairs behind him.

"Honza!"

He turned to see Amy Poláková's infectious smile beaming back at him.

"Good morning, Amy. Is everything okay?"

"Yes, of course," she said with a flirtatious tilt of her head. "I was just coming to see you."

"Right…" he stammered, not sure how to respond.

She laughed softly, seeing his apprehension. "To give you this, silly." She waved an envelope in front of him, grasping it carefully between her long fingernails in the opposite corner to the stamp. "I just checked the mailbox downstairs and I think we have another letter. I recognise the writing. I didn't want to open it in case it compromised any evidence."

"Right…" he repeated, caught off guard.

The reason for his fluster was Amy's choice of clothing. She wore a low-cut sport vest, displaying an ample cleavage, and high-cut Lycra shorts leaving little to the imagination. The sparseness of material left her stomach exposed from below her breastbone to her lower abdomen.

"I'm off running." She ran on the spot to support her claim, the soles of her running shoes squeaking against the marble tiles in the hallway. "I like to run 5k every morning. Good for the mind and the body. I've done my stretching, now I'm ready to go."

Despite the distraction of the bare skin on show, Jonny's attention was caught more by how naturally beautiful she was. The previous evening she'd been dressed up elegantly after a social engagement, but now she was kitted out solely for sport: her blonde hair was unpretentiously pulled back in a simple ponytail and she wore no makeup. The effect however was the same. Her cheekbones were prominent, and her face was perfectly balanced with strong features, especially the shape of her eyes, nose and mouth. Whereas the dress had disguised her body, he could now see that her womanly shape and limbs were equally well proportioned. She had the body of a model, one that men and women looked at equally, whether in admiration, jealousy or lust.

"Yes, of course…" he managed in response, still stumbling over the right words.

"I know what you're thinking," she replied, sighing in mock annoyance. "Michal is always telling me off for wearing so few clothes when I go running. I think he's worried that someone is going to kidnap me." She laughed gently. "But, as I always say: if you've got it, why not flaunt it?"

She opened her arms wide, putting her body on full show for him.

"Yes… well…"

She smiled, enjoying his discomfiture.

"Well done on the letter," he spluttered, keen to get back on safe ground. "Here, let me take it." He pulled down the sleeve of his jacket and took the envelope carefully with the material covering his fingers.

"Michal and I are so pleased you're looking into this matter for us." Her large eyes shone brightly at him. "It's been worrying us terribly."

"Don't worry. I'll let you know what we find out."

"Thank you, Honza. Well, I suppose I'd better get going." She blew him a kiss, waved suggestively, and skipped to the top of the staircase.

"And, don't forget to pop up to see me sometimes," she called back. "I'm always in. Well, apart from going out for lunch... and, of course, drinks in the evening."

He stood holding the envelope as Amy headed down the stairs, the echo of her footsteps fading as she reached the ground floor and exited the building.

***

Jonny dashed back into the apartment, bagged the envelope in a small, plastic food bag from the kitchen, and left for the police station immediately.

Amy Poláková's appearance at his door, half-dressed and unreservedly flaunting her body, had unnerved him slightly. He was a naturally private person and, although always polite and friendly, his strong preference was to maintain a safe distance from his neighbours. But, it wasn't just that. He couldn't help feel that Amy had another motive for her visit; whilst there was the valid reason of another letter arriving in the post, she seemed to have enjoyed the staging of their meeting and his resulting shock a little bit too much for his liking.

The walk alongside the riverbank before cutting through the cobbled streets into the old town cleared his head. He rationalised the situation with Michal and Amy as solely work, deciding to ignore her suggestive behaviour. But, he knew it would be wise to head off any greater attempts at friendship from either of them; he didn't want Amy concocting plans to pull him in their social circle.

After picking up a caffe latte from his favourite café, and briefly catching up with his friend Luka, the café owner, Jonny strolled across Old Town Square. Despite venturing further and further afield in his exploration of Prague and the Czech Republic, the famous square was still his favourite place. The space was the perfect size to be busy but peaceful at the same time, and provided an immersive cloak of history over him for the time it took to amble across the cobble stones.

Jonny strode into the station full of purpose, being warmly greeted by all the police staff, from the officers on the front desk to the detective team working away in the second floor open plan office. Calls of "Ahoj, Honza", followed him, many staff not even aware of his full name but instantly recognising the foreign detective. Mikeš' sponsorship had ensured he'd been treated with respect from the start, but successfully solving two recent murder cases had enhanced his reputation.

Boukal and Mikeš' sergeant, Lucie Dvořáková, were in the glass-fronted Incident Room – Mikeš' control centre – in the corner of the floor. It looked like a typical Monday morning of administrative tasks: both were busy sorting out the files of case paperwork and rearranging the story boards of the completed and on-going investigations. Jonny couldn't help smiling to himself, realising how important these people had become to him in such a short period of time.

When Jonny thought of everything the proverbial hand of fate had delivered to him in return for a simple holiday to Prague, it was hard for him to get his head around it all. Of course, he'd been curious about the city from his mother's past, but being warmly welcomed into the team like a long-lost colleague by Mikeš had felt like a new start. He'd felt wanted again, possibly for the first time since the early years of his marriage.

This would have been enough on its own, certainly surpassing any expectations he'd had beforehand. But, then he'd discovered that Dvořáková was part of his family. *His niece.* Jonny's search for his lost Czech family, facilitated by Ivana's friend, had revealed Dvořáková's mother as his half-sister – the daughter his mother had given birth to before she'd left Prague, never to return. As an only child (or so he'd thought), he'd always believed himself slightly unlucky. But, this luck had definitely changed. Yes, he had good reason to be thankful for everything Prague had given to him so far.

"Ahoj, Lucie. Ahoj, Marek. I see you're busy."

Boukal and Dvořáková paused their tasks to greet him.

"How's the new apartment?" Dvořáková asked.

"Really great, thanks. I need to arrange a time for you to come over with your mum and dad."

"That would be nice," she replied. "I'm looking forward to the British cooking you've promised us."

"Don't set your expectations too high." Jonny chuckled. "My mother used to cook me mostly Czech dishes when I was younger, but I never paid much attention to the recipes. My speciality is a Sunday Roast – a classic British dish."

Boukal and Dvořáková laughed.

"You'll need to tell me a Sunday when you know you'll be free."

"Sounds great, but you might struggle to get some of the ingredients here," Dvořáková remarked.

"All under control." Jonny tapped the side of his nose. "I've brought from the UK all I need to make a great stuffing. I've also got some cranberry sauce. The rest are fresh ingredients you can buy anywhere."

"This talk is making me hungry," Boukal exclaimed.

"How's the study going for your detective exam?" Jonny asked Dvořáková.

"Not bad. I'm happy with all the procedural aspects of the role and I've completed all the example papers with good scores. But, I suppose I'm slightly worried about the free format questions, when they provide example crimes to analyse. What if I miss something important?"

"Don't worry." Jonny dismissed her concern with a wave of his hand. "I think your detective instincts are strong. But, if you like, I can set you a question to make you think. One from my catalogue of murders solved in the UK."

She smiled at him. "Thanks, Honza."

Jonny turned to look at the whiteboards around the room. "I see you're updating the list of open cases. Anything interesting?"

Boukal shook his head. "The good people of Prague are all behaving themselves at the moment. The big focus is still trying to break the money laundering operation controlled by the owners of the dodgy clubs in the city. But, if things don't improve, we're going to be back on the beat soon, helping old people cross the road."

Jonny laughed heartily. "Marek, you are starting to get a British sense of humour."

"It's all your fault," Dvořáková joked.

"Where's Felix?" Jonny asked.

"He's gone to update the Police Commissioner after your meeting with Michal Polák yesterday. He wasn't in a good mood this morning."

41

"Yes, the Prague socialites seem to get right under his nose," Jonny commented. "But, I have an interesting addition to what we were told last night." He took the plastic bag out of his jacket pocket and waved it in front of them.

"Another letter?" Boukal enquired.

"Yes," Jonny confirmed. "I'm hoping we might be able to get some prints from this one. Amy Poláková passed it directly to me after finding it in her mailbox this morning."

Dvořáková passed him a pair of plastic gloves and laid a large sheet of white paper on the table. Jonny slowly took the envelope out of the bag and slit open the top of the envelope using a small biro. He slid his hand inside and pulled out the folded piece of A4 paper.

Boukal and Dvořáková crowded either side of him as he unfolded the paper.

"It's different," Boukal exclaimed.

Jonny studied the paper, a frown developing on his brow as he processed the information. Finally, he read the new message aloud, "ONE OF US WILL DIE."

"So, Michal Polák was right about the increasing threat," Boukal stated, looking at Jonny.

"Could be…" he replied, puckering his lips in concentration. "And, I suppose we could have an interesting case now. But, first we need to find a body, and then determine whether a crime has actually been committed."

4

The End of the Line

They didn't have to wait long.

Dvořáková was in the process of bagging up the newly received letter and its envelope to send to forensics when Mikeš burst into the Incident Room in a whirl of energy. His animated face, eyes wide with adrenaline, and urgent, pumping arms indicated important news of some kind. The day's choice of a blood red shirt and tie combination to complement his customary tweed suit only added to the anticipated level of severity.

"A dead body has been found on the metro," he declared. "We need to get down there as quickly as we can."

Mikeš saw Jonny, Boukal and Dvořáková all looking inquisitively at each other. "What is it?"

"Felix, you need to have a look at this," Jonny suggested, pointing to the bagged letter on the table.

"Can't it wait, Honza? The metro line is currently suspended and I'm under pressure to investigate so they can restart the service. Actually, you should come along. I'd appreciate a fresh set of eyes—"

"This could be important," Jonny stated firmly.

Having already learned to trust Jonny's proven instinct of what was vital information, Mikeš shuffled over to the table. "ONE OF US WILL DIE," he read out loud. "Where has this come from?"

"Amy Poláková gave it to me before I left my apartment this morning. The letter arrived in the post, addressed to her husband."

Mikeš studied the message again, a quizzical frown developing across his forehead. "What do you think it means?"

"I don't know." Jonny shrugged. "I only opened the letter when I arrived here. When she gave it to me, I just assumed it would be the same as all the others. But, this just seems too much of a coincidence—"

"And, you don't believe in coincidence," Mikeš added glumly.

"Exactly. If the dead body on the metro is in anyway connected to Michal Polák or his wife then we definitely have got a case to investigate."

"These people!" Mikeš shook his head in anger. "They make my skin creep."

"Just keep an open mind," Jonny said, patting Mikeš on the shoulder gently. "Let's check out this dead body and take it from there."

***

Boukal needed no invitation to put his foot down. The black, unmarked Skoda Superb shot around the cobbled streets of the old town like a pinball, across the river and into the Letenský tunnel. Picking up speed, the car weaved around the tail lights of other vehicles in the murky light of the tunnel, the siren and flashing lights creating space to pass down the middle of the two lanes. Exiting the tunnel, Boukal broke a red light and swung the car sharp left, around the Ministry of Interior building, joining a main road heading out of the city centre. The morning rush hour traffic was still heavy so Boukal avoided any hold-ups by following the tram tracks running through the middle of the dual carriageway, criss-crossing the tracks to overtake at tram stops.

Jonny had been first introduced to Boukal's prowess as a junior racing car champion during The Old Town Square Murder. Despite hating every moment of every journey in the speeding car, he'd come to accept them as an unavoidable part of working in Mikeš' detective team. He was sat in the back seat as normal, tightly holding onto the dangling door handle, the blood draining from his face as the car violently veered from side to side like a dodgem ride. Mikeš by contrast was relaxed, unaffected by the speed or the jerky ride, turning from the passenger seat to brief Jonny on the body found and the suburb of Prague they were travelling through.

"The dead body was found at the Dejvická metro station on the A Line. It's the station at the end of the line. They are in the process of building an extension, closer to the airport, but it won't be finished for a few years."

"Do we know the identity of the dead person yet?" Jonny managed to ask whilst being slammed sideways into the rear car door.

"No. The metro staff have been told to secure the area and suspend the line, but I've given strict instructions not to search the body until we get there. I don't want anyone interfering with potential forensic evidence. Ella has been notified and should be on her way."

"Is there any evidence of foul play?"

A puzzled frown developed across Mikeš' face. "Foul play?"

"Sorry, we use this term in the UK Police to mean criminal or violent behaviour. Strange term, I know. I mean, is there any sign of blood on the victim? Or maybe a weapon close by?"

"No, nothing obvious like that," Mikeš confirmed. "But, it does look suspicious. We've had a couple of incidents on the metro over the past few years, but mostly involving homeless or drunk people late at night. This seems different. It's a man in his thirties, smartly dressed. He was sitting in his seat, hunched forward – like he was asleep. A bike was also in the carriage, close to where he was sitting, but we don't know if it belongs to him."

"Are you sure he's dead?"

"Yes. One of the station staff felt his neck and there was no pulse. The body was still warm." Mikeš checked his pocket watch. "The body was found just before eight forty-five a.m, so about twenty minutes ago."

Jonny nodded and turned to watch the blur of the urban scenery seemingly running in fast forward past the car windows, his hand still holding tightly onto the strap. This outer part of the city was mostly unknown to him: the only familiarity he had with the area came from a trip to the Dejvická Farmers' Market with Ivana and a couple of taxi rides from the city centre to the airport and back again.

With a lack of familiarity to focus on, and wishing to be out of the car as soon as possible, he found himself zoning out. His thoughts wandered to Michal Polák and his wife, Amy. There were coincidences looming all over the initial stages of this case (if it was a case at all), including his very recent arrival in the building they lived in and the sudden request to the Police Commissioner. His instinct told him that whatever had happened, and the reasons why, would be complicated and messy. He rolled his eyes; a case was what he'd almost wished for – something to get his teeth into – but the prospect of unravelling secrets amongst a circle of socialites, with their elevated opinions of themselves, was not something to look forward to. He'd had his fill of the London elite over the last decade.

Boukal brought the car to a screaming stop. Mikeš and Boukal jumped out from the front of the car, immediately consulting with the uniform officers standing guard outside one of the subway entrances to the metro station.

Jonny took his time, wanting to regain his composure. He unwrapped his hand, now red and blotchy, from the door handle, and shook it gently to help restore the blood flow. After dusting off his blue jacket and beige chinos, he opened the rear passenger car door and stepped out into the sunlight.

The station entrance was a busy scene. Two parked police cars with flashing lights had blocked one lane of the road into the city and police tape was blocking public entry into the station. The other entrances to the metro, positioned around Victory Square, were also sealed off. A small group of people were gathered awaiting further information: flustered travellers seeking news on the resumption of the service as well as nosey locals attempting to find out what had happened. An approaching tram was announced by the driver ringing his bell. Seeing that the tram was travelling down the hill towards the city centre, many of the commuters hurriedly crossed the busy road to the tram stop in the central reservation; although slower and less comfortable, the tram was their most direct alternative route to get to work.

"Honza!"

Jonny turned on hearing his shouted name. Mikeš was entering the police cordon and waving at him to follow.

The foyer of the station was eerily quiet. Without passengers to absorb the sound, his footsteps echoed loudly on the concrete floor as he strode over the station concourse, past the ticket zone entrance, to the top of the escalator. On his first journeys on the metro, Jonny had been fascinated by how fast the escalators moved, but this descent to the platforms on the level below was dominated by the surrounding emptiness; only Mikeš and Boukal were visible in the large space, about twenty rungs ahead of him on the escalator.

"Bit sluggish today, my friend," Mikeš boomed, putting his arm around Jonny's shoulder when he arrived at the bottom.

Jonny remained silent, only rolling his eyes slightly.

The platform area was a hive of activity by comparison. Only one train was in the station: the neighbouring platform for travelling in the opposite direction was empty. Station staff and the train driver were grouped together, talking animatedly, being marshalled by two uniform police officers. The forensics team had arrived and were setting up base, stepping into their sterilised uniforms of white hooded suits, face masks, plastic gloves and shoe covers. Suitcases of equipment were open on the platform, full of apparatus to log and gather evidence. One member of the team was taking photographs of the platform and the outside of the metro train.

Mikeš spoke briefly to one of the uniform officers then beckoned Jonny towards the train carriage at the end of the platform. Boukal remained behind to talk with the group of potential witnesses.

Dr Králová was inside the carriage, pensively bent over the dead man in her protective clothing. Her stance was instantly recognisable, even though her face was not visible: the white suit could not hide her slim, agile frame, only the absence of her medium length hair seeming irregular. She had the inquisitive body position that only a doctor would take, carefully studying the physical state of the man in front of her, and seemingly impervious to the photographer who was now dancing around her taking photos of the potential murder scene.

Mikeš and Jonny stood in the carriage and watched as Králová used an extendable, metal pointer to carefully lift open the man's jacket and pull out his wallet.

"Hello, dear," Mikeš said softly from behind her.

Králová turned round abruptly. "I've made it to the crime scene before you again, Felix. You must be getting slow in your old age." She winked at Jonny. "Ahoj, Honza."

"Ahoj, Ella," Jonny greeted her. "Any early signs to indicate what has happened here?"

"Not you as well." She rolled her eyes in jest. "That's what Felix always asks me before I've even had a chance to examine the crime scene."

Mikeš smiled in relief, glad not to be the only one in his ex-wife's bad books.

"I've been here less than five minutes myself," Králová confirmed. "All I can tell you is that he's definitely dead."

"Sorry," Jonny apologised. "It was wrong of me to ask so bluntly. It's just that although we don't know who this man is yet, I have a horrible feeling that we're going to find out that he's connected to someone we spoke to only yesterday."

"Who's that?" Králová asked, looking interested now.

"Michal Polák," Mikeš answered, his tone flat.

"Really?" She paused to take in the information. "I haven't met him, but I've obviously read all about him in the gossip columns. He's become quite a star with his pretty wife on his arm."

"Indeed."

All eyes were now on the wallet in Králová's gloved hands. She opened it slowly and slid out a few bank and credit cards before finding what she was looking for. Holding an identification card in her hand, she read aloud the details, "Mr David Farrell. Chief Technology Officer at Midakati Limited."

"That's the company Michal Polák is CEO of," Mikeš declared.

"CTO..." Jonny pondered. "David Farrell must have been a senior manager with a job title like that, if not one of the directors. I suppose our next stop has to be a visit to the head office of the business. And, then his next of kin."

"It would help if we knew at least something about what has happened to David Farrell," Mikeš stated, smiling hopefully at Králová.

All attention turned to the dead man. The body was slumped forward in the seat at the end of the row, just as if he'd been caught dozing on his daily commute to work. The mid-length brown hair flopped forward, masking any facial features. The man's dress attire was smart casual: a designer jacket with different coloured lapels, open-neck white shirt, jeans and dark shoes. A black leather rucksack was still over his shoulders, wedged between his back and the upright of the train seat. The peculiar aspect of the otherwise almost normal scene before them, was the half-eaten banana the man had been eating and was still holding tightly in his hand; the skin of the banana had been peeled back and two or three bites taken.

"Has he been poisoned?" Jonny posed, pointing at the fruit.

"I can't be sure," Králová replied. "I will need to run further tests. But, I've checked his mouth already and he seems to have suffered some internal bleeding – there is blood in his mouth and on his lips. There are also a few drops of blood on his jeans." She lifted the flaps of the man's jacket to show Mikeš and Jonny, both bending in closer to see. "What I don't understand is where the internal injuries have come from…" Her whispered voice trailed off as she set about examining the body more closely.

Mikeš and Jonny stepped back, almost bumping into the photographer who was still snapping away. Whilst they were impatient to find out the cause of death, they knew this part of the pathological process could not be rushed; accuracy was the number one priority, and Dr Králová was in total control of the timeline.

As crime scenes went this one was mild: calm and peaceful. Jonny's abhorrence to the usual gory scene, with the accompanying blood, had developed early in his police career, and he'd never been able to shake it off. Only by being careful to make sure he wasn't first on the scene, and insisting on being thoroughly briefed beforehand, had he been able to manage over the years, protecting against the natural reflex in his stomach. He loved being a detective, chasing down criminals, but he'd happily leave the crime scenes and autopsies to others, working solely from reports and photographs if allowed to.

Boukal bounded up to them. "I've spoken to the metro staff and unfortunately none of them had much to add to what we already know. The train reached the end of the line and the doors were opened. The driver walked the length of the train, checking inside each carriage and closing the doors one by one. He saw the man when he entered the last carriage. He called out to him, but there was no answer: the man remained leaning forward in his seat. The driver then went to shake him and realised something serious was wrong, so he raised the alarm immediately. All the other passengers had left the station by then so there were no witnesses to talk to."

"Weren't there passengers on the other platform waiting for the return journey?" Jonny asked.

"Almost certainly. But the train left the station, heading back to the city centre, before the alarm was raised. If this train had been clear, it would have been the next train to go back to the centre: they would have driven it into the tunnel and then reversed it back onto the other platform."

"Makes sense."

"The metro stations all have CCTV, inside the concourse and also at platform level," Boukal added. "We'll be able to check the CCTV for this station and all the other stations down the line."

Jonny looked around the carriage. "Any idea why he would be in the last carriage?"

"Probably because of his bike," Mikeš explained. "There is always more room on the end carriages. Mothers with prams, and people with bikes or mobility scooters tend to use it."

"Found it!" Králová announced loudly.

She held the man's right shoulder in both hands, bending him forward slightly. The three detectives crowded around her.

"He has a knife of some sort stuck in the middle of his back. The blade looks thin and sharp. It isn't, however, protruding from his front so it must only be about twenty or twenty-five centimetres long. My guess is that the knife has punctured his heart and probably also his lungs. He would have died almost instantly."

Jonny and Mikeš exchanged a concerned look. The only sound was the continual clicking of the camera.

"Did he die here?" Jonny muttered. "I mean, where is the—"

"The blood?" Králová was now enjoying the drama of her revelation. She carefully moved the dead man's body further forward. The detectives craned their necks to get a good view behind. "He has bled out from the wound in his back, and the fabric seat has absorbed all the blood."

Jonny was suddenly overcome by the odd sensation of not being sure of his own feet. He felt nauseous, the bile rising in his throat. He lurched backwards and started to gag, his hand raised protectively over his mouth. Knowing he had to get away immediately, he turned and staggered out of the carriage, along the platform and to the escalator in the desperate search for fresh air.

5

The Big Boss

The entrance to the head office was grander than Jonny was expecting: a modern, glass building fronted by an impressive courtyard with healthy shrubbery framing the approach. Cobbled pathways led up from the road and car park, parting at the small fountain in the middle of the garden. A large, imposing sign announcing the business – 'Midakati Ltd' – stood just outside the revolving doors into the building.

Mikeš took off his hat and led the way to the reception desk, announcing himself and asking for Michal Polák. His manner was brusque, clearly irritated by the course of events since the Police Commissioner's intervention over the weekend.

The receptionist led them to the waiting area. "Mr Polák will be with you shortly. Would you like a drink? Maybe a tea or—"

"Tell him this is urgent," Mikeš barked in response. "If he's not down in three minutes we will go up to find him."

A look of alarm in her eyes, the receptionist glanced quickly at Jonny, seeking help. Getting none, she scurried back behind the reception desk to make the urgent phone call.

When Mikeš and Boukal had emerged from the metro station to find Jonny still pale-faced but recovering, Mikeš was already in a rage. Jonny was expecting to be ribbed for his hasty and, some would say unprofessional, disappearance from the crime scene, but Mikeš' attention was directed elsewhere. The focus of his anger was clear as he'd shouted out "These bloody people!" on the short walk back to the car. The thunder hadn't dissipated during the drive to the Midakati head office, Mikeš' frequent cursing breaking the strained silence. Jonny knew Mikeš would eventually calm down and return to the fray with a renewed positive attitude. Until then, he'd have to wait for a better time to be asking pertinent questions about the reasons for Mikeš' vehement loathing of Michal Polák and his social circle.

The ground floor of the head office was as impressive as the approach to the building. The reception area, including the space for waiting, was modern in design but also what any visitor would expect. The opposite side of the entrance was however notably different. The space seemed to have been designed as a breakout area for staff, but also allowed glass rooms for more formal meetings. The dominant feature was a raised grassed area for sitting on. Around it was stationed garden furniture: an array of wooden tables and chairs creating a picnic area. There were even deck chairs placed on an area of sand, facing out of the front glass window. On the far side was a table tennis table, table football, a garden chess set, along with a variety of other outdoor games. To complement the scene, the walls had been painted to reflect an autumnal day, the sun peeping through the clouds and the leaves turning shades of orange and red on the trees. Posters adjourned the walls promoting soundbites from the company's mission statements and commitment to the treatment of its staff.

Michal Polák strode through the security barriers towards them, beaming a welcoming smile. His business casual uniform was almost the same as the previous evening: a light blue, designer shirt complementing his grey trousers and black shoes. Being in his business environment seemed to give him greater stature, accentuated by his height.

"Gentlemen, welcome to Midakati. I hope you are enjoying the slightly different approach we have taken to designing a head office—"

"Do you know where David Farrell is?" Mikeš interrupted, his tone harsh.

"Well, I'm sorry…" Michal scanned the detectives' faces, searching for an insight into the reason behind the question. "I'm due to see David later, but I've been in a meeting since eight this morning. What's this all about?"

"We found David Farrell dead this morning," Mikeš added firmly. "Presumed murdered."

"What?" Michal's eyes bulged and his face fell. As his jaw slackened, his mouth hung open in shock. Eventually he ran his hands through his thick hair and shook his head as if attempting to shake away a bad thought. "Is this a joke?"

"I can assure you this is not a joke," Mikeš asserted, anger rising in his face. "We are not comedians. We *are* police detectives."

"Yes, but…" Michal's voice trailed off. He looked towards Jonny in hope, his eyes pleading for some sort of contradiction to the news he'd just been given.

"Mr Farrell was found dead on the metro this morning, and the working assumption is that he was murdered," Jonny confirmed. "At this stage, we know nothing more. That's why we have come straight to see you. Is there somewhere private we can talk? You have an office?"

Michal's hand rubbed over his face in anguish. "Yes, yes…" he managed.

Jonny guided Michal gently by his upper arm and led him back to reception and through the security barriers to the lifts. Exiting at the third and top floor, Michal pointed towards his office and they led him into the glass bowl, and safely onto the soft seating in the corner. Boukal hung behind to explain what was happening to Michal's executive assistant, and to ask for refreshments.

"This can't be happening," Michal muttered as the detectives seated themselves around him. Sitting hunched forward in his seat, he suddenly looked broken, his air of authority lost with the terrible news.

Mikeš put his hat and cane down on the small table in a clear grab for territory.

"Michal, we all realise this is a shock for you," Jonny started, "but we need to act quickly. That's why we have come straight to see you."

Michal nodded his head slowly, absorbing the information.

His assistant entered the office and put four glasses and a bottle of water on the table. Boukal poured and Michal took a long gulp of the drink.

"Is this related to the messages we've been receiving? You know, the one I showed you last night?"

"We don't know," Jonny confirmed. "But, at this stage it has to be our working assumption."

"Well..." Boukal started, but stopped immediately when Jonny shot him a hard stare.

"What is it?" Michal asked, looking between the detectives inquisitively.

"Nothing for now," Jonny explained. "We want to come back later today and interview you formally. We also want to talk to all the other directors. But, right now, to get started, I have a few simple questions for you."

Michal ran his hands through his hair again. "Sure."

"Have you received any further emails this morning or over

the weekend?" Jonny enquired.

"There was nothing over the weekend, but I haven't yet checked all my emails this morning. As I explained, I've been in a meeting."

"Understood, but can you and the other directors please check your emails before we come back later. We will also need access to your IT Team. Chief Sergeant Boukal will be our contact point."

"No problem," Michal assured them.

"Can I also clarify something?" Jonny persisted. "Was David Farrell a director?"

"Yes."

"Had he received the same messages by email, and by post to his home address? Like you and the others?"

"Yes. On Friday, David told us that he was going to investigate the emails. That's when we all got together and decided we had to do something about the situation."

Jonny raised his eyebrows. "Had he found out anything?"

"I don't know. I was going to ask him today."

"Was David late today?" Jonny prompted. "It's just that I notice many people in Prague seem to start work early."

Michal shook his head. "He was never an early starter. In truth, he tended to come and go as he pleased. David was a bit of a free spirit, never liked being pinned down."

"Okay, thanks. Can you tell me about the business?"

"Right," Michal replied, scratching his head. "Maybe if I start talking and you guys can ask questions about anything you want to know."

"Take your time," Jonny encouraged.

Michal took a deep breath. "We formed the company right after university. It was the classic case of friends having a business idea to get rich. But, somehow our idea worked out."

"Were you all friends at university?"

"Yes. We all met in the first year whilst living in halls of residence, but then we shared a student house in the second and third years. David was the technical one and was always full of ideas. He studied engineering, but was a top computer programmer in his own right. Karel Vaněk studied business management with me. He was a process guy, a natural for the role of Chief Operating Officer. The last original director of the business was Titus Arnold: he is the Marketing Director."

"But you became the big boss – the Chief Executive Officer," Jonny stated. "Why was that?"

Michal shrugged nonchalantly. "It just seemed to happen. I was always quite organised."

"You just said: the last original director of the business," Jonny stated. "What do you mean by that?"

"Oh right, yes. Well, the other person who shared our house was Freddie Pedersen. Clever guy who was studying accountancy. He didn't believe in our business idea, thought the financials were rubbish. Actually, he was probably right at the time." Michal chuckled gently at the memory. "Anyway, he decided to join one of the top consultancy firms after university, and travelled the world working with large corporate clients. But, I like to work with people I know and trust, and eventually, I managed to get him to come back to Prague and join us as Chief Financial Officer."

"You are quite persuasive, Mr Polák," Mikeš declared in a sarcastic tone, edging forward in his seat.

"I like to think it's because people want to work for me." Michal smiled sanctimoniously.

Michal's assistant entered the office carrying a tray with a coffee pot and mugs. She looked between the men, sensing the heavy atmosphere in the room. Continuing in silence, she placed the items on the small table between the sofas and poured coffee into each mug. She backed away discreetly, looking at her boss in case there were any further instructions.

"Thank you, Olga," Michal said. "Please cancel all my meetings for the day. I'll brief you when I've finished this meeting."

Boukal leaned forward in his seat, sensing a lull in the conversation. "Mr Polák, we need to organise formal interviews for you and the other directors. At this stage, the interviews can be held here because nobody is under suspicion: we are just trying to get background information on recent events in David Farrell's life. But, we will be recording the interviews just in case we need to return to them at some point later in the investigation."

Michal remained silent, but nodded.

"We will also need to take DNA and fingerprint samples from all the directors, including you," Boukal added. "Can I suggest we come back at midday?"

"My assistant will organise that." Michal wiped his brow and drank the rest of the water in his glass. "But, can I ask that you be as discreet as possible. We still have a business to run."

Mikeš snorted and sat back hard on the sofa. "One of your friends and fellow directors has been killed, and you ask us to be discreet!"

"I am not thinking of myself," Michal replied quickly, now clearly rattled. "We have over one hundred people working in this building. It is their livelihoods. Of course they need to be informed about what has happened, but I also think they should be protected so there isn't widespread panic."

Mikeš stood up for effect and grabbed his hat and cane. "We

60

will decide who to interview and how the interviews will be conducted…"

He turned to Jonny. "Honza, I'll be waiting outside."

"Why is he so abrasive?" Michal asked Jonny once Mikeš had left the office and crossed to the lifts.

"Chief Sergeant Boukal will tell you how good a detective Chief Warrant Officer Mikeš is, perhaps the most celebrated detective there has ever been in the Czech Republic," Jonny answered firmly. "I also admire him greatly. His first priority is always solving the crime and catching the criminals. He hates anyone or anything standing in the way of justice." He paused for effect. "And, I am totally with him on this. Finding out what happened to David Farrell, and apprehending the person or persons that murdered him, is all that matters to us."

"Please don't misunderstand me," Michal replied. "I also want you to catch whoever did this horrible thing to David. He was my friend first and foremost. I will get all the staff together for a briefing in the next hour. All I was trying to say was—"

"Mr Polák," Jonny interrupted, raising his hand. "You do what you have to do, it is not really of interest to us. Just make sure that all the directors are here at midday for the interviews we have requested. The only other information I need from you at this stage concerns David's next of kin. Is he married?"

"Yes… well, he was. They've been separated for about a year. Zoe still lives in their apartment in Prague 2, but David rents another apartment close to the city centre. My assistant can give you the addresses."

"Thank you. Do you have Zoe's mobile number?"

"Yes." Michal took out his smartphone and found the contact, showing the number to Boukal.

"Please do not contact Zoe before we get a chance to speak

61

to her," Jonny requested. "This is a murder investigation now and we will manage all the communications with friends and family."

"I understand."

Jonny rose from his seat and started to move towards the door. Boukal followed.

"Last thing," Jonny said. "Have you managed to compile a list of the people or other companies that might hold a grudge against you or your business?"

"No," Michal answered tentatively. "There really hasn't been much time."

"Well, I suggest you find time to focus on the list before we speak again at midday. It might be the key to catching the person who murdered your friend."

Jonny turned on his heel and left the office. Boukal followed, closing the door behind them, leaving Michal looking lost, sitting alone on the sofa in his large office.

6

Gentle Soul

If the conversation with Michal Polák hadn't maddened Mikeš enough, the call from the Police Commissioner clearly tipped him over the edge. The journey back to the city centre was dominated by Mikeš' grumbling from the front seat, his wiry frame bursting with energy to get out of the car and take his frustration out on something.

"I told him it was a murder investigation, and that we would manage the communications with David Farrell's family and friends from this point," Jonny said, feeling the need to explain.

"Michal called the Commissioner straight away…" Mikeš shook his head vigorously. "These people all think they're above the law and can do whatever they want."

Boukal had remained silent for the journey so far, focused on expertly manoeuvring the car through the lighter, mid-morning traffic. "To be fair to him though," he started hesitantly, eyes fixed on the road ahead, "he hasn't actually ignored our request. He knew the Police Commissioner already and was probably just calling to update him."

"Marek is right—" Jonny began.

"Of course," Mikeš jumped in, "but I'll bet you a lot of money the Commissioner will now be keen to stress to me how important it is for us to tread carefully and not upset the day-to-day running of the business." He dramatically turned to Jonny in the back seat. "Am I right, Honza?"

"Yes. Sadly, you're probably spot on."

"Don't go shaking the apple tree," Mikeš mimicked the Commissioner, using heavily accentuated English.

Jonny laughed. "Very good, Felix. But the saying is: don't upset the apple cart."

"Whatever…" Mikeš turned in his seat to face forward, waving his hand to dismiss the merit of the correction.

The emotional rollercoaster of working with Mikeš was always entertaining, if frustrating at times. Jonny was used to being the principal detective in his previous jobs in the UK Police: the person leading from the front and making all the decisions. But, whilst he'd enjoyed the responsibility, and had thrived in the role, it had also been a lonely place sometimes. His new consultant role was a big change but gave him the right balance for what he needed at this stage in his life, including working alongside and developing other people. But, whether he liked it or not, Mikeš was the emotional heartbeat of the team – and their detective partnership.

"Marek, I also wanted to explain why I cut you off in the meeting just now," Jonny said. "Amy Poláková gave me the latest letter in an unopened envelope this morning. Until we have further information, we have to presume that we are the only people that know about the 'ONE OF US WILL DIE' message."

"I guessed that," Boukal replied, nodding as he drove. "Sorry, I wasn't thinking."

"No problem. At the moment, it feels to me like we're being led. Everything since yesterday, when we visited Michal and Amy, seems to have been scripted like a play and we've had no option but to play our part. We need to find a way to start leading this murder investigation, and the message is the only thing we have at the moment that might give us the upper hand."

"Good thinking, Honza," Mikeš declared, still staring forward. "We can't let these people twist us around their little fingers."

***

After dropping Mikeš at the Prague Police Headquarters in the city centre, Boukal drove them to the address provided by Michal Polák's assistant. Jonny recognised the route through the residential area in Prague 2, it being close to Ivana's apartment, where he'd lived for the previous three months.

The address they were looking for was on the street U Havlíčkových sadů, in the middle of a row of beautifully preserved buildings lining the top edge of one of his favourite parks, Havlíčkovy sady. The frontages were all newly painted, the contrasting pastel pinks, pale blues and lime greens lining up to create a restrained rainbow effect. The fascia of each of the four or five floor buildings had its own unique architectural style, with different porticos and balustrades at each level, but still blending in seamlessly with its neighbours.

Boukal approached the building entrance and pressed the intercom. After a respectful length of time with no answer, he pressed the buzzer again.

"Can I help you?"

Jonny turned to see a woman pushing a buggy in which a small boy was asleep. She had stopped close to them, the buggy positioned ready to be lifted up the steps. The woman had bright features, her long strawberry blonde hair and freckles matching her white, green and orange flowery dress.

"Do you live here, Madam?" Jonny asked.

"Yes. Who are you looking for?"

Jonny flashed his badge. "We are looking for Zoe Farrell. Do you know if she's in?"

"I'm Zoe," the woman replied, a concerned look on her face. "What's happened?"

"I am Jonathan Fox, a consultant with the Czech Police. And, this is Marek Boukal, Chief Sergeant. I think it would be better if we spoke inside."

Zoe hesitated momentarily, and stepped forward to open the grand front door. Jonny let Zoe lead the way, but stayed close to help her manoeuvre the buggy up the steps and into the entrance hall. The lift was too small for all of them so Boukal offered to take the stairs.

Jonny was all too familiar with these difficult situations. Telling a spouse, partner or close family member about the murder of a loved one was second only to gory crime scenes on the list of aspects of the job he'd choose to avoid if he could. However, whilst the reports and photographs from a crime scene were sometimes enough to work from, he would never miss seeing the physical reaction to the terrible news. He knew from experience that he had the knack to interpret responses or the surroundings of the situation; often a stray word, or a fleeting sign of pleasure, had provided him with an idea, or even a significant clue, to eventually crack the case.

"Is this your son?" he asked, breaking the suffocating silence.

"Yes." She looked down lovingly at her child. "I like to take him to the park in the morning. He's a big boy for his age and has so much energy. The playground is about the only thing that really tires him out."

The lift stopped and the automated voice announced their

arrival at the top floor. Boukal was waiting outside the lift, panting from his exertions.

Zoe opened the apartment door and led the way into the living room. She indicated for Jonny and Boukal to sit on the sofa whilst she positioned the buggy in the hall so she could keep an eye on her sleeping son.

The room was expensively decorated but appeared on first impression to be designed more for display than for living. The leather sofas were standard, plush and comfy, but the surrounding décor hinted at a strong African influence. The ivory, embossed wallpaper provided a plain backdrop for numerous artefacts positioned around the walls. Jonny was no art expert but he could easily identify traditional head sculptures, wooden carvings, and textiles hanging on the wall alongside night-time landscape paintings. Pride of place was taken by a pear-shaped bronze casting of a roped pot, sitting alone atop a wooden cabinet in the middle of the facing wall. The views of the green tops of the park trees from the penthouse apartment windows offered a real-life distraction away from what was otherwise a dark and serious room.

Zoe sat down on the opposite sofa, noticing Jonny surveying the room. "I spent a few years in Nigeria and fell in love with the art. I'm a bit of a collector now, but unfortunately it's not very child friendly."

Jonny nodded but did not answer, knowing the reason for their visit was burning a hole in the awkward atmosphere.

"Mrs Farrell—"

"Please call me Zoe."

"Zoe, I'm sorry to have to inform you that your husband, David Farrell, was found dead this morning. At this stage, we are treating it as murder."

She took a sharp intake of breath, letting out a high-pitched noise, and lifted her hands instinctively to her face. Jonny and Boukal waited.

"What happened to him?" she asked after composing herself.

"We are still waiting for the results of the autopsy, but he was found dead on the metro at Dejvická."

"Are you sure it's David?"

"We found identification on him, but we do need to have his body formally identified. He also had a red bike with him."

Zoe nodded in recognition. "That bike was his pride and joy. He went everywhere on it."

Boukal shuffled forward in his seat. "Mrs Farrell, would you be able to identify the body for us? I can pick you up by car later, and then return you back here. It will probably take one hour in total." He placed his business card on the coffee table between them.

"Yes, of course." She shook her head in disbelief, wiping her nose with her hand. "I'll need to talk to my neighbour first, but I'll call you later."

"Thank you. I'll go and get you a glass of water." Boukal walked out of the living room, carefully stepping around the child asleep in the buggy, and headed for the kitchen.

"This is a very distressing situation," Jonny began, "but can I ask you a few questions? The more information we have early on after a crime like this, the more chance we have of catching whoever did it."

"Sure. But… I just can't believe it. I only saw him yesterday. He seemed fine." She again covered her face with her hands and lowered her head slightly.

Jonny waited; he could see her reaction was genuine and that she was upset. Sounds of cupboards opening and closing could

68

be heard from the kitchen.

"We have spoken with Michal Polák…" Jonny started. He scanned her face, but she did not react. "He told us that you have been separated from David for a while."

"Yes. David moved out last year… It was the beginning of the year, so about eighteen months ago. I love him dearly, and we are… sorry, we were still friends. But, he was impossible to live with. He was so clever, Mr Fox, he wasn't like other people. He became lost in his work, closed away. The closest I can get to explaining it is to say it was like living with a mad scientist."

"Had he changed over the past few years?"

"He'd become worse. The pressure on him was enormous. He was the ideas man in the business: he'd invented the original prototype for the product that the business was founded on. But, he didn't really have a coping mechanism, like say Michal, or the others. David was an engineer at heart and just wanted to work on his inventions. Instead, he got pulled into meetings, sales pitches, all that stuff, and he hated it. It nearly pushed him over the edge a few times."

"Are you implying he was suicidal?"

Zoe shook her head. "No, it was never that bad. But, he did have a few bouts of depression and was on medication to control his mood swings."

"That is useful. Thank you."

Boukal entered the room and placed a glass of water on the table in front of Zoe. "I could only find a bottle of sparkling water in the fridge. I hope that's okay."

"You sound British to me. Is that right?" Jonny asked Zoe.

"Yes, I'm originally from Gloucestershire, not far from Bristol. David was Irish, from Cork. We met here at university in Prague and were together for just over ten years."

69

Jonny hesitated, writing in his notebook. "I'm sorry to ask you this, but I assume your son is from your marriage to David?"

"Of course," she replied, her tone suddenly becoming stern. She looked offended.

"Look, I'm sorry." Jonny held his hands up in apology. "That was insensitive of me. The last thing I want to do is offend you at a time like this. I'm just looking to confirm the facts so we can find out who did this to your husband."

"Liam is three. He thought the world of his father, and David thought the world of him." She wiped her nose again. "He is going to be devastated."

"Thank you," Jonny said sincerely, maintaining eye contact with her. "And, Zoe, do you work?"

"Yes, I have my own Press Relations agency. I work from home mostly, so it works well with Liam. I have good neighbours, and most of the time they can look after him if I need to go out to meet a client."

"When was the last time you saw David?" Jonny enquired gently.

"Yesterday." She wiped her nose with her hand again. Boukal rose from the sofa and left the living room again, returning quickly with a box of tissues. "Thank you," Zoe said, blowing her nose and dapping her eyes.

"David picked Liam up late afternoon, at three p.m," Zoe continued. "Then I went to David's apartment about six p.m to pick him up. It was a usual routine for Sunday, but David was slightly later picking Liam up yesterday because he had to go to an event with Michal. David could be very distracted with his work, but he never missed time with Liam."

"Did you notice anything wrong? Maybe how David was behaving?"

Zoe dabbed her nose as she considered the question. "Nothing springs to mind. He actually seemed to be having a good day. I know I just said that he could get very down, but David seemed at his happiest when he was spending time with Liam."

"You didn't notice anything unusual at his apartment?"

A stifled smile crossed her face. "That would be difficult, Mr Fox. David's apartment was always so messy. It was so awful his cleaner resigned recently. Luckily, we'd managed to find him a replacement last week. I always tried to help him by doing some cleaning when I went over to pick Liam up. I'd clean around the bathroom, and especially the kitchen: wash the dishes, clean the work surface, and even sort out his clothes for the washing machine. The kitchen was a potential health hazard so I used to clean it as thoroughly as I could."

"Did he mention the messages that he and Michal had been receiving?"

"Yes. David told me to ignore them, just put them in the bin."

"You received them as well? Here, at your apartment?"

"Yes," she confirmed. "David said it was just some nutcase trying to threaten the business."

"You threw them all away?"

"Yes." She shrugged her shoulders. "They were getting on my nerves."

"Can you remember what was written on the message?"

"The messages were always the same: 'ONE OF US LIED'."

Jonny looked up from his notebook. "Did you receive another message today?"

"No. I didn't receive a letter today." Zoe looked confused. "Is it connected to what happened to David?"

71

"We don't know at the moment. But, we're treating it as suspicious. I want to find out who sent the messages and why."

"David told me to ignore them," she repeated, anxiety creeping into her voice.

"There is nothing you could have done," Jonny reassured her. "We will do everything we can to find out what has happened."

Zoe blew her nose and put her head in her hands.

"We will need to interview you again, more formally this time," Jonny continued. "You're not under suspicion at all, but we'd like to probe a bit further into David's life recently, and it seems to me that you're most likely to know what was happening to him. You might even be able to corroborate the details we find out from talking to other people."

She looked up and nodded, looking tired and drawn.

"Can you also try to remember if anything odd happened in the past few weeks? Particularly concerning the messages. Also, maybe you can think of someone who held a grudge against David…"

Zoe shook her head, dismissing the suggestion. "Everyone liked him. He was a worrier, and lived on his nerves, but he was such a gentle soul."

7

Window onto the World

Next stop was David Farrell's apartment. And, this time it was Jonny setting the pace. Whilst Boukal was finalising the logistics with Zoe Farrell for the later interview and identification of the body, Jonny was anxiously waiting on the landing, holding open the lift door. Down on the ground floor, he marched out of the building and, to Boukal's surprise, was standing next to the passenger door before the car was even unlocked.

Jonny always took pride in giving time to the victim's family and friends, but this had to be balanced against catching the murderer. Everything that had happened so far gave him the distinct feeling that they'd arrived late to the party. Or, maybe they'd been intentionally invited late to the party? Usually he could frame a murder investigation in his head, needing only to solve the riddle of motive, opportunity and method. But, this case was different. He just couldn't get the parameters clear in his head – nothing made sense yet. The only way he knew was to push on, working harder and faster, to cover the ground as quickly as possible and find a way to at least complete the outside edge of the jigsaw puzzle.

"Zoe Farrell gave me her set of keys for David Farrell's apartment," Boukal said as he drove off.

"Good. It will also stop her going over there, tidying up…"

"You don't seem convinced that her reaction was genuine."

73

"It's not that." Jonny hesitated, forming the words. "She was upset and surprised, I could see that. It's just that every time I asked a question that got close to her husband, or their relationship, she got defensive and started to speak about him in glowing terms. She was trying to make it sound like they were a perfect couple, the only problem being his work. It didn't make complete sense to me."

"She was definitely upset, but I noticed that she didn't cry," Boukal stated.

"Not everybody does. Sometimes the shock numbs the reactions, and the tears come later. But, there's definitely more to their story, especially why they were living apart."

Boukal focused on the road, speeding around the busy Náměstí Míru square, heading towards the city centre. He turned to Jonny as they waited at a red traffic light. "I noticed you were more direct than usual when asking about her son."

"Yes, that was a bit naughty of me." Jonny grinned. "It's not really my usual style, but the opportunity just presented itself to dig deeper without being too rude. The question definitely got under her skin. It could be nothing. Maybe she's just defensive about it because other people ask her the same question. But, it's another reason to probe into this supposed happy family."

The remainder of the short journey was quiet, both deep in their own thoughts. Boukal followed the main road down towards the river, turned right and followed a small maze of cobbled streets before eventually parking in the street Jungmannova, running parallel to the bottom of Wenceslas Square.

Dvořáková was waiting for them outside the building, standing proud in her police uniform and hat.

"Ahoj, Lucie," Jonny greeted her. "How's everything at the crime scene?"

"Forensics have taken the body away for examination, and the metro service has been restarted. Felix is slightly more relaxed now that the immediate pressure is off."

A concerned look crept over Jonny's face. "Did they have enough time to complete a thorough forensic examination?"

"They took the metro train out of service. It was driven to the depot and the forensic team are examining it there."

After explaining she also had a set of keys, found on David Farrell's dead body, they entered the building and followed the maze of steps and corridors to the annexe at the back of the building. They took the lift to the fourth floor. After handing out the plastic gloves, Dvořáková opened the door to an explosion of light.

The apartment had clearly been built as an adjunct to the existing building, the overall effect being that the living space was hanging in mid-air over the park – a window onto the world below. Whilst only about twenty-five square metres in size, the expansive light made the room feel bigger.

"And, I thought my apartment was swanky," Jonny exclaimed.

They stepped into the main room and closed the door. The wall opposite the entrance was effectively one large window, the large pieces of glass only separated by thin metal panels, providing an almost uninterrupted view over the inner city park, Františkánská zahrada. The helicopter view from the apartment showed people milling around the paths segregated by a hedgerow maze, beds of rose bushes and a small fountain. The children's playground on the far side of the park provided the action in an otherwise tranquil scene; a sea of small heads bobbed around as the young children energetically ran from one outdoor activity to another.

Dvořáková set out to check the rest of the apartment, whilst Jonny and Boukal walked the main room.

Zoe Farrell had been right – the apartment was messy. Loose papers were strewn over the floor, casual clothes were scattered on the large sofa, and a plate and cutlery from the previous evening's meal had been left on the wooden floor next to the armchair. The main room was minimalistic in design, purposeful, so as not to detract from the view, but the unintended effect of the clutter was to make the room look unkempt.

"All clear," Dvořáková shouted from an adjoining room.

After pacing around the living room and searching down the back of the sofa, Boukal walked down the hall. "I'll check the bedrooms."

Jonny sat down on the armchair and took in the view. This was definitely the best seat in the house, he thought, the slightly worn material on the cushions supporting the supposition. He tried to place himself in David Farrell's position, sitting in the chair late on Sunday evening before the week ahead. A laptop charger, still plugged into a socket, laid curled on the floor, next to a laser printer. The plain pages of A4 were on the other side of the armchair, an untidy pile of papers with unstructured, scribbled notes across them in pen. A single envelope was also on the floor with the papers.

Dvořáková walked back into the living area.

"Lucie, have we secured David Farrell's laptop?" Jonny asked, still seated.

"Yes, it was in the front compartment of his rucksack," she confirmed. "It is still with forensics, but they know to pass it on to the technical team once they are finished with it. I'll obviously check up to make sure they get it."

Jonny nodded. "It's just that I'm pretty sure he'll have been working on his laptop here last night. It would be useful to know what he was working on before he was murdered this morning."

Leaning forward in the armchair, he took photos of the original position of the scattered papers on the floor with his smartphone. Picking up each paper in turn, he studied the writing on both sides and took more photographs. Nothing seemed to grab him, but the handwriting was not easy to read; there were more numbers than words, limiting his chance of understanding. He placed the papers back on the floor where he'd found them.

He picked up the envelope. Turning it in his hand, he could see it was sealed but there was no writing on the outside. After taking a photo of the envelope from various angles, he carefully opened the envelope using a pen from his jacket. The envelope was empty. That's odd, he thought. Maybe he just intended to use it as notepaper but forgot. He placed the envelope back on the floor with the papers.

Boukal walked back into the main room. "I heard you talking about the laptop. I plan to speak to the IT Team when we go back to Midakati later. It will be a lot easier to search the laptop if we know the software configuration and they can reset the passwords."

"Did you see anything unusual in the other rooms?" Jonny asked them.

Dvořáková shook her head.

"The only thing that struck me as strange," Boukal began, "is that there's very little sign of a child coming here regularly. There's one blanket in what looks like the spare bedroom, but nothing else: no toys, no clothes in the drawers or wardrobes, and no child's plate or cutlery…" He shrugged his shoulders.

"That is strange," Jonny commented. "But, Zoe Farrell did say that she picked her son up from David's apartment yesterday.

She might just give David enough clothes and food for the day. I suppose Liam is still only three. Maybe he's too young to be sleeping overnight."

Jonny picked up the pile of loose papers. "What do you make of these?" he asked Boukal. "They mean absolutely nothing to me."

Boukal flicked through the papers. "It doesn't make sense to me either. Some of the strings of letters and numbers look like IP addresses, but I can't be sure."

"I never know what they are…"

"They are unique identifiers for a device, like a laptop or tablet, on a network."

"So, it could just be part of his work?"

"Yes, it could," Boukal confirmed. "I assume he's responsible for all IT matters at the company. But, it does seem a low level of detail for him to be getting involved in. Maybe it's part of his own investigation into who was sending the messages by email."

"Right," Jonny acknowledged. "Can you make sure the technical team know about them when they check over the laptop?"

"Sure."

"By the way," Dvořáková intervened, "I requested details of the recent activity on David Farrell's phone from the mobile phone provider before I left the station. We might get the results later, but more likely tomorrow morning. It was a company phone so I let the Personnel Manager at Midakati know out of courtesy. She told me that Michal Polák has let all the staff know about David Farrell. He first gathered all the staff at head office together for an announcement and then sent out a brief message by email. The Personnel manager was also very keen for me to understand that this shouldn't have a detrimental effect—"

"…on the business," Jonny finished her sentence, exaggerating the words for effect. "Yes, we had enough of that from Michal Polák earlier."

"Right," Dvořáková muttered. "Maybe that's why Felix is so angry."

Jonny looked directly at her. "What do you mean, Lucie?"

"Well, it was a few years ago now," she started, "but a high profile businessman was found dead in Prague. It was all over the newspapers, and the saga ran for a long time."

"But, what's the connection to Felix?"

"Felix was investigating the death with Josef Liška, who was his partner at the time. I was a young Constable, only recently joined. I just remember Felix stomping around the station and mimicking someone with almost the exact same words. It was obviously in Czech, but the same meaning: Make sure the business isn't affected. Something similar to that. It was one of my first cases, I remember it vividly. Felix was in a bad mood for weeks."

"What happened?" Jonny prompted.

"There was huge pressure to wrap up the case quickly, and Felix felt we were not given the time or resources to investigate the leads we had. The death was recorded as suicide in the end, but rather suspiciously the business was taken over less than a year later."

"I remember that case," Boukal remarked. "I was working outside Prague then, but it was all over the news. The media claimed there was a cover-up."

"Interesting," Jonny said. "Makes sense why Felix is so rattled – it's probably bringing back bad memories. He has a great sense of justice. It's one of the things I really like about him."

Working for Mikeš was clearly tough at times and Jonny had sympathy for some of the team, Boukal and Dvořáková included, who were sometimes on the end of his overbearing, old school management methods. But, the admiration and respect for Mikeš from his staff always shone through, even in the darker moments when everyone was under pressure.

"Let's have a quick look around the apartment," Jonny said, walking off down the short hall.

The main bedroom was next to the living room, and also benefitted from a floor-to-ceiling view over the park. The double bed was unmade, the duvet crumpled up in a loose ball, with underwear and t-shirts littered around the wooden floor. Jonny searched amongst the bed linen and opened the wardrobe doors of the fitted units around the bed. He rummaged through the hanging clothes, sliding his hand inside the pockets of jackets, and bent down to rifle through the shoes and small boxes at the base of the units. Next, he moved closer to the bed and opened the top drawer of the bedside unit. After a close inspection of the contents, he turned to Boukal and Dvořáková with his eyes wide in interest. He took a photo of the open drawer using his phone before lifting out a brown bottle of pills.

"What are these?" Jonny held out the bottle to Dvořáková.

She took the bottle and studied the label. "They look like anti-depressants to me. On prescription, the pharmacy's details are printed here."

He checked the other drawers on either side of the bed, finding only socks, boxer shorts and spare cables.

Jonny walked out of the bedroom, Boukal and Dvořáková parting to let him across the hall into the bathroom.

"Pretty clean," he said. "It looks like his wife cleaned it yesterday."

Opening the bathroom cabinet he found two more bottles of pills. "And these?" He took a photo of the open cabinet before handing one bottle each to Boukal and Dvořáková.

"Sleeping pills," she said quickly.

"These are also for anxiety, I think," Boukal stated, "but they look quite old from the prescription date." He showed the bottle to Dvořáková and she nodded her agreement.

"Quite a cocktail of pills he has here," Jonny commented, adopting a serious tone. "Just remember, it's always worth taking time to look in all the cupboards and drawers. Don't rush, you never know what you will find in the darkest corners of people's lives."

Boukal and Dvořáková looked at each other, then nodded silently back at Jonny in acceptance of their oversight.

Jonny walked out of the bathroom and into the spare room. The window faced onto a small garden between the main building and the annexe. He searched the single wardrobe and small bedside table, noting the child's blanket on top of the duvet.

The kitchen was in the far corner of the apartment, also facing onto the back. Jonny took his time to check the fridge and kitchen units. One lower cupboard door was partially open showing a washing machine full of dirty clothes. The kitchen table was clear apart from a recent local newspaper, a couple of scientific and engineering magazines, and a small pile of flyers for pizza delivery and removal services.

"The bin has been emptied," Jonny stated, opening the cupboard under the sink.

Standing at the granite work surface he carefully moved the coffee machine, kettle and toaster forward, examining where the surface met the tiles. Noticing something, he bent down and looked closer. "David Farrell has either been baking a cake, or using a fine, white powder for recreational purposes."

He licked his gloved finger and wiped it gently over the surface. After putting the finger to his tongue, he turned to Boukal and Dvořáková with a knowing smile. "Zoe Farrell's cleaning isn't quite as thorough as she claimed." He chuckled. "Her husband's toxicology report is going to make very interesting reading."

8

Interviews – Directors of Midakati Limited

The following is a transcript of the recorded interviews conducted with the directors of Midakati Limited on Monday, twenty-second June 2010. The interviews were conducted at the company's head office in Prague 6.

Present at the interview were Chief Warrant Officer Felix Mikeš (FM), Chief Sergeant Marek Boukal (MB) and Consultant Jonathan Fox (JF).

The interviews were conducted in English, in agreement with all the interviewees.

<u>Michal Polák (MP)</u>

MB: Interview commenced at 12.02. Please state your name for the record.

MP: Michal Polák.

FM: Mr Polák, I would first like to start by explaining the rules for this interview.

MP: I want to help as much as I possibly—

FM: Mr Polák, please listen to what I have to say. If you do not adhere to my rules for these police interviews, they will take a long time and we will all get very frustrated and angry.

MP: I am listening.

FM: I know we are conducting these interviews at your head

office, but this is just so we can conduct them quickly. They are still police interviews. And, they are related to a serious matter – the potential murder of your fellow director, David Farrell, this morning on his way to work. Whilst you are not under any suspicion at this time, we are recording the interviews so that we have them on record. We reserve the right to return to points made in the interviews and/or conduct further interviews at the police station in the city centre.

MP: I understand.

FM: Despite your wish to protect your company at this difficult time, you also need to understand that the business is of absolutely no interest to me. All of the questions in this interview will come from us, and you will answer truthfully and not with the interests of your company in mind. If you do raise the subject of your business – any aspect of it – we will simply stop the discussion and move onto *our* next question. Do you understand?

MP: Yes.

FM: And, finally, if you mention any connections to people you know in the Czech Police, or other well-known people in Prague, we will also simply move on. You are not here to impress us. You are here to answer questions to help *us* find out what happened to David Farrell.

MP: You really don't like me, do you?

FM: What I like or don't like is irrelevant. I am a police detective, and my job is to solve serious crimes that are committed in the city I love.

[Pause]

MP: Can I ask one question of my own?

FM: Just one.

MP: What makes you think that David was murdered?

JF: Michal, you are an intelligent man. You must appreciate that we cannot divulge details of this murder investigation. All I can say at this time is that David Farrell has been found dead and we believe he was murdered.

MP: All I've told the staff is that he was found dead and—

FM: Move on!

JF: Michal, can you please give us a brief overview of how you, David and the other directors met? This is to help us understand the relationships between you all.

MP: Well, as I told you earlier, we all met at university here in Prague. I met David on the first day. He was on the same floor as me in the halls of residence. It was a crazy time, lots of parties, but the group of us became friends over that first year and we all looked for a student house together.

JF: The people in the student house were you, David, Karel Vaněk, Titus Arnold and Frederick Pedersen?

MP: Correct. We were an odd bunch in a big city, but we hit it off. I'm Slovakian, David is from Ireland, Titus from the US, and Freddie (Frederick) is Norwegian. Only Karel was Czech, from Ostrava, but even he'd only been to Prague on school trips before.

JF: Many people stay in contact with friends they lived with at college or university, but it's unusual for all of you to go on to form a business.

MP: Apart from Freddie. As I told you earlier, he went to work for a large consultancy firm and only came to work for the company about three years ago.

JF: So, the primary shareholders were the other four, the ones that started the business together?

MP: Yes. David was a gifted engineer and IT programmer and had created an innovative product design for one of his course projects. I could see the potential benefit of it and convinced the others to work together on creating a business model around it. For the first couple of years we lived in squalid conditions: we had almost no income and effectively lived in one room as we developed the product alongside a business and marketing plan. It was tough, but also a great time. We were all in it together and split the business 25% each way. We were very close and even named the business after us: MI for me, DA for David, KA for Karel, and TI for Titus – Midakati.

JF: Please continue.

MP: We'd given ourselves four years, until we were twenty-five, to make progress. Thankfully we sold the first variant of the system to one client. It was rough and ready but they wanted to trial it. Life was still hard, but at least we had some money coming in. In 2005, we launched the fully packaged suite of services and it really took off. We moved into this head office three years ago. That's when Freddie joined. We needed someone credible on the company board to manage the finances.

JF: What is the business known for?

MP: We provide customised drone services for commercial purposes. Many people think about drones as just being for fun, flying over the park etc. Our drones can be programmed to survey agriculture, inspect solar farms, for the mapping and surveying of large properties or estates, and also aerial photography. The base product is very adaptable, and there isn't really a direct competitor on the market.

JF: What will happen to the company without David around?

MP: It's going to be a big loss, of course. He was a really talented guy. But, in recent years, it wasn't always so easy to have him around, and his contribution had started to reduce over time.

JF: You mean his depression?

MP: Yes, amongst other things. Working in a growing business is like being in a hothouse. He found the pressure difficult to cope with. At times, he's been drinking too much, or taking drugs. Between Zoe (Farrell) and his friends, we thought he'd got past the worst. We built a strong team around him at work to take the pressure off him, and from my perspective he'd been much better this year.

JF: So, you didn't have any recent problems with him?

MP: No. His mood could fluctuate, but David was David. Sometimes he offended other members of staff, especially people who couldn't keep up with his intellect. But, I could deal with that, it was nothing really.

JF: Our sergeant checked the filed company information and Karel Vaněk is no longer listed as a shareholder.

MP: Yes, he left. Back in 2003.

JF: Why was that? I thought you said the business was doing well, even if it was tough going.

MP: He thought the company should be going in a different direction. There was no real issue.

JF: What happened to his 25% holding?

MP: We bought it. I mean the remaining three directors. According to the shareholder agreement he had to give us first refusal if he left. We borrowed some money and bought him out.

JF: So, the three directors now own a third of the company each?

MP: No. We own 25% each. We sold 20% to an investment company in 2007 to raise money for the last stage in the growth of the business, including opening this head office. When Freddie joined the company, we also allowed him to buy 5% of the business: I wanted him to be fully committed and the best way is to own part of the company.

JF: Following our conversation earlier today, did you check if you or any of the other directors had received further messages by email today?

MP: We all checked and none of us received an email today. But, Titus' wife, Elena (Arnold), called and he'd received a message in the post saying 'ONE OF US WILL DIE'. I also phoned Amy (Poláková) and she said we received another letter in the post. Was it the same message?

JF: At this stage in the investigation, I am only able to confirm that we have the letter. Amy gave it to me unopened. We will talk to Titus separately.

MB: When was the last time you saw David?

MP: Yesterday. Amy and I went to an afternoon performance of a prominent youth orchestra in the city. It was the finale of a week-long programme of youth events. It was important for us because the business was the main sponsor. I asked David to come along to show his face. Titus also came along with his wife. I presented an award—

FM: Just answer the question.

MP: Right. David left straight after the first performance, about two thirty or just before. He had to pick up his son. I spoke to him briefly at the reception before the show started. I knew it wasn't his type of thing, but it was important he was there even for a short time. He used to hate coming to these type of events even when he was together with Zoe.

MB: Where was the event?

MP: It was in the Mirror Chapel at Klementinum.

MB: And, you didn't see David again after the performance?

MP: No. I called him later in the evening, to check he was okay and also to agree a few things about the week ahead. He was quite chatty and seemed fine.

MB: What time did you call him?

MP: About nine o'clock. I can check my phone and give you the details after the meeting.

MB: What time did the last performance finish?

MP: About four fifteen, but we had to hang around talking to people. Amy and I probably didn't leave until after five. I wanted to stretch my legs after sitting around for such a long time so we took a walk around the city centre. We walked around the market on Havelská, then around the old town. It was lovely weather so we strolled over Charles Bridge and stopped for a coffee. Then I ordered a taxi back to the apartment. That was about six thirty I think, but I can check the receipt. You must have all arrived at our apartment about an hour later.

MB: After our meeting this morning, did you have a think about people that might have held a grudge against David?

MP: Well, I've written down the names of a couple of companies that might be jealous of our success. They're not exactly in the same sector, but they are all start-up companies. But, we haven't had any major fights with any of these companies. There was certainly no issue just with David.

MB: What about staff at the company?

MP: No. David could be difficult, but I've never known of a major issue with a member of staff. Because I'm sensitive to it, I've always made sure to check with other senior managers and people reporting directly to him.

JF: Can I ask why David was travelling on the metro this morning? Surely he could afford a nice car, or even get a taxi.

MP: David described himself as an environmentalist. He was sensitive to a lot of issues such as climate change, and was also quite involved with green campaigns. He gave money to charities and even convinced me to subscribe to a programme for planting trees across the country.

FM: You haven't answered the question.

MP: Right. He didn't own a car, although he could drive. He went everywhere by bike if he could. In the mornings, he preferred to take the metro to the end of the A Line and then cycle the last fifteen minutes or so to the office. After work, he'd always cycle the whole way back to his apartment, maybe even taking the long way around.

MB: Can you confirm where you were this morning, Mr Polák?

MP: I left the apartment early, about six forty-five, and drove to the office. I was at my desk by seven thirty. My assistant can give you details of my first meeting at eight o'clock.

MB: And, last night?

MP: My wife and I stayed in after you left us.

JF: Michal, this morning we went to David's apartment near Wenceslas Square. It didn't seem particularly lived in; there weren't many personal possessions around.

MP: David was like that. If he had only his laptop he was happy.

JF: Does he own the apartment?

MP: No, he's rented it since he separated from Zoe. Actually the landlord is a friend of mine, he's a film producer—

FM: Right, I've heard enough. This interview is over.

MB: Interview terminated at 12.42.

Titus Arnold (TA)

MB: Interview commenced at 12.53. Please state your name for the record.

TA: Titus Arnold.

JF: Mr Arnold, is it okay to call you Titus?

TA: Yeah, sure.

JF: Titus, we've just had a long interview with Michal about the set-up of the business, David's role, and also recent events.

Rather than going through this again, I'd like to just pick up on a few points that we'd like to understand better.

TA: No problem. Just catch whoever did this. David was a great guy and we were all close friends.

JF: That's actually a good place to start. Titus, can you explain how you all stayed together since university? I'm interested because it is very rare. Even Freddie kept in touch and came back to work with you.

TA: That's all down to Michal. I know he comes across as a control freak, and a bit distant, but he's not really like that. He's very loyal as a friend, and also extremely good at his job. He was always in charge, even when we were drunken students, organising fun events and places to go. It was also Michal that saw the potential in David's project, and kept focus on creating a business from it. And look at what we've now got – a thriving business, hopefully only a few years away from floating on the stock market. We would never have been able to achieve all this without Michal in charge.

JF: But Karel left. Wasn't he one of the core group of friends?

TA: Yes, that was sad.

JF: Why sad?

TA: He committed suicide a few years after leaving us.

JF: What happened to make Karel leave?

TA: There wasn't one event that sparked Karel's departure. But, he and Michal studied business management together and they clashed on many aspects of setting up the company's operational processes. It was fairly easy for David and me: he was focused on the technical and IT side of the prototype, and I was working out the marketing and promotional plan. But Karel and Michal were working together almost all the time and started to have arguments about the direction of the company. Eventually, Karel couldn't take any more, or so he said, and he resigned. We tried to keep in touch, but it was difficult because he wouldn't speak to Michal after he left. David and I met him a few times, but it just wasn't the same: Karel would just talk about Michal non-stop.

JF: We understand Michal, David and you bought Karel's shares. What did Karel do with the money?

TA: After six months or so, we found out that Karel was setting up a similar company. It wasn't exactly a direct competitor, but it was close. It was certainly using some of the core technical design that David created albeit for a slightly different purpose. Unfortunately, he made the classic mistake of spending too much money. He employed some programmers but they weren't in the same league as David, and it just ate up all the cash he had. There wasn't really any communication between us from the point we found out about the business… And, then we found out he'd committed suicide in late 2006.

JF: Did any of you go to the funeral?

TA: No. It was made clear we weren't welcome.

JF: That is a sad story. How did it affect you all?

TA: It was tough. I still sometimes wonder if there was anything we could have done differently to help Karel, but he made his position quite clear.

JF: I would like to ask you now about David. We know he suffered with depression, and also had trouble with alcohol and drugs, but Michal says he was in a much better state this year.

TA: Yes, definitely. David used to confide in me a lot. Michal is our long-standing friend but he's also our boss, so the relationship is not as open as it used to be. David told me he was feeling much better and it showed in his physical appearance. He seemed to have really turned a corner and was coming up with lots of great ideas to develop the product set.

JF: Was he still drinking and taking drugs?

TA: I saw no evidence of it.

JF: Is his past behaviour the reason his marriage to Zoe broke down?

TA: Yes and no. He was always a sensitive soul, and all the things happening in the world used to get him down. But, Zoe wasn't easy to live with either. She was always very opinionated, even when he first met her. David was more flexible so their marriage worked for a while. In truth, I think his drinking and drug-taking really started when their relationship started to get difficult.

JF: David must have appreciated your support during this time.

TA: I would like to take credit, but it was mostly Zoe and Michal. I was more of his confidant. Zoe and Michal organised all the support he needed, from getting him to go to support groups, organising his new apartment when he moved out, and even getting him a cleaner.

JF: I understand you are American. Didn't you ever want to go back?

TA: Not yet. The business kept me here after I graduated, and now I'm married with two children. Maybe in the future...

JF: Is your wife connected to the business in any way?

TA: No. I met my wife outside work. She likes to keep our family life separate, and I also like it that way. It's healthier.

JF: But, you and your wife were at the event on Sunday.

TA: You got me there. There are a couple of events a year where I ask her to come along, and yesterday was one of them. I'm sure you know by now but we were sponsoring the event, and it was in a good cause...

JF: Moving on to the messages you'd all been receiving, did you get emails as well as messages sent by post to your home?

TA: Yes, we all did.

JF: What did you think of them?

TA: I think we all thought it was a scare tactic. But then the intensity increased and we thought we should do something just in case.

JF: So, Michal said that he'd take responsibility for contacting the police?

TA: Yes. But, David called me Sunday evening, after nine. He said he'd been investigating the emails we'd received and he thought he knew who'd sent them.

JF: Did he say anything else?

TA: No. I asked him who he thought it was, but he said he'd prefer to tell me in person. I remember he said he wanted to check something else to be sure.

JF: Didn't you think that was strange?

TA: The whole situation with the messages was weird, as I've already told you. But, I didn't think it was particularly threatening. If David knew something that would help reveal the identity of the sender then I could definitely wait until the next day to find out.

JF: Michal told us that none of the directors received emails with a message over the weekend or today. Is that right?

TA: I didn't receive anything by email. But, I did receive another message by post to my home this morning. My wife called earlier.

JF: This is the message saying 'ONE OF US WILL DIE'?

TA: Yes. She was a bit freaked about it, as you can imagine. Then we heard about David…

JF: Can you please advise her not to touch the letter or the envelope because it is evidence. Chief Sergeant Boukal will make arrangements to collect them later today.

TA: Understood.

JF: Thank you. That's all the questions I have at this stage.

MB: Mr Arnold, can you confirm your movements after the performance yesterday afternoon?

TA: My wife and I stayed until near the end of the event. We mingled with the guests for a while, then I checked with Michal and we left together at about five. We got a taxi from outside the venue, back home to Prague 6 where we live.

MB: Thank you. We may need to confirm this with your wife and the taxi company.

TA: No problem.

JF: Actually, I do have one other question. Did David always have his rucksack with him?

TA: Yes. He was always on his bike, so took his rucksack everywhere. Even to business meetings.

JF: Did he have it at the performance yesterday?

TA: I didn't see it, but he may have left it in the cloakroom. But, he definitely didn't have his bike with him yesterday afternoon because he was going by metro to pick up his son. I know because he told me when we were talking before the performance.

MB: Thank you for taking the time to talk to us. If we have any further questions we will be in contact with you. Interview terminated at 13.22.

Frederick Pedersen (FP)

MB: Interview commenced at 13.28. Please state your name for the record.

FP: Frederick Pedersen, but everyone calls me Freddie.

JF: Freddie, we understand you are the Finance Director of Midakati Ltd.

FP: Chief Financial Officer.

JF: Noted. Why the American job titles?

FP: Michal insists on it. He says it appeals to our market in the US.

JF: Right. Did you receive the same messages as the others, to both your work emails and also in the post to your home address?

FP: Yes.

JF: What did you think?

FP: I thought it was an unhappy ex-employee. I've had experience of these type of situations in many large companies, and usually a legal action follows the messages. The idea is that the company gets scared, or just wants it to go away, so they settle quickly. But, interestingly, there was no follow-up on this one – the emails and letters just kept coming.

JF: Any other thoughts on it? Having more recently joined the business, but also knowing the people involved for a long time, you maybe have a different perspective.

FP: Michal is very quick to lose patience with people and had a reputation as a hire-and-fire CEO for a while—

JF: Like Karel Vaněk?

FP: Not really. I wasn't here at the time, but as I understand it, he wanted to leave and was paid for his shares. It was his choice. What happened after was awful, but I'm not sure the two events are related.

JF: Can you confirm that you didn't receive any further messages by email over the weekend or today?

FP: That is correct.

JF: Did you receive a message by post today?

FP: I don't know. I left my apartment before the post was delivered.

JF: Okay, but can you let us know as soon as you get home today.

Chief Sergeant Boukal will give you his contact details after the interview. And, please do not touch the envelope or letter with your hand. Leave it in the mail box and we will open it.

FP: Sure.

JF: Why did you join the business after such a long time?

FP: Money. Purely money. I'd done well over the last ten years or so, but Michal and the others made me an offer I couldn't refuse. They wanted a finance guy who they could trust, and in return I had the chance to buy some shares which will provide me with a great return if the company hits its targets.

JF: Michal told us you didn't think much of the finances in the early days.

FP: Very true. But, they proved me wrong, didn't they.

JF: Can I ask you about David? He seemed slightly different to the others, maybe more principled but also more trouble.

FP: He was certainly different. At times he was very likeable, but he could quickly turn and be quite argumentative. I remember him like this at university, but since I joined the business he's been even more so. The purity of the product design was most important to him, the finances probably the least important. Michal tells me that David was so committed in the early days, but I don't think he liked the transition to working in a bigger, growing company. He was a computer geek at heart, and a bit of a maverick, bless him.

JF: Were there major issues in the business because of him?

FP: No. I'm probably making it sound much worse than it actually was. He was difficult to keep in line at times, but Michal always managed to do it. David had his fair share of personal issues as well, but he got through it and the business was thriving. I should know, I add up the numbers.

FM: You make Michal Polák sound like an angel.

FP: I'm not sure what you're getting at. He runs an excellent business and is my friend. That's good enough for me.

MB: Mr Pedersen, can you confirm your movements yesterday?

FP: I had a very lazy day after a busy week. I stayed in and cleaned my apartment in the morning, and then met a friend for a drink in the late afternoon.

MB: Where did you go?

FP: Before I answer, can I check what you will do with this information?

MB: We just need to establish an alibi for you, so that we can eliminate you from our enquiries. We will be very discreet.

FP: It's just that the woman I met is quite a famous artist here in Prague. I've known her for a long time. We had some drinks and then went back to my apartment. [Pause] We are not in a relationship as such, but we are close.

MB: It would be useful if you could provide me with her name, where you met, the times, and also your home address.

FP: I will give you all the details after the meeting. Her name is Frida Nilsson. But, please be discreet.

JF: You weren't in contact with David Farrell yesterday?

FP: No.

JF: Out of interest, why weren't you at the orchestra performance yesterday?

FP: I'm just the numbers guy. I leave the schmoozing to Michal and the others.

MB: Can you also confirm your movements this morning?

FP: I drove to the office and arrived just before eight.

MB: Thank you. If we have any further questions we will be in contact with you. Interview terminated at 13.47.

9

In Cold Blood

The Incident Room in the station was studiously quiet. Mikeš was leaning over a desk carefully studying paperwork, wildly signing some pages with a flick of the pen in his hand. Jonny was turning the pages of his notebook, a deep, thoughtful frown stretched across his forehead. Only Dvořáková was active, busily preparing the Murder Board with photos of David Farrell and the spider's web of connections to his estranged wife and the directors of Midakati Ltd.

The exertions of their full-on morning had taken its toll. Jonny's head was spinning with all the information collected in the space of only a few hours; he needed time to think. His body was also feeling the strain, his legs aching from being constantly on the move. The consultant role to the Czech Police was poles apart from his previous DCI role, the daily grind in the Metropolitan Police having been relentless. Now, he had the bonus of a much improved work-life balance, but he knew that he wasn't in the right shape to cope with the peaks of activity; when a new murder case started the pace was intense, providing mental and physical tests. With his apartment now sorted out, he knew he needed to get back on the running machine.

"Where's Katka?" Mikeš boomed, raising his head to look out of the glass office. "I'm starving."

"I did order a late lunch, sir," Dvořáková explained. "It

should be here very soon."

Boukal burst into the room, looking flustered and struggling to hold a file of papers as he closed the door behind him. "What a morning!"

Dvořáková stepped forward to help him, taking the file and placing it on the desk with the other papers from the case.

"Zoe Farrell has confirmed the victim is her husband," Boukal started to explain between gasps. "One of the detective team is driving her back home now. I've arranged the interview with her for four p.m, which gives her time to sort out a babysitter."

"Great work, Marek," Jonny remarked.

"Also, our technical team have now got David Farrell's laptop, and I've put them in contact with the IT Department at Midakati."

Mikeš was only half listening, still flicking the papers in front of him. Suddenly his eyes lit up. An approaching squeaky wheel could be heard faintly through the closed office door. "Here she comes!" he exclaimed. All eyes turned to see Katka pushing her faithful trolley of refreshments towards them. She was wearing her standard housecoat, smiling at the detective team in the open plan office, her spritely step defying her seventy or so years (although nobody claimed to know her true age). Mikeš jumped up and opened the door. He put his arm warmly around Katka's shoulders, squeezing her into him gently. "Ahoj, Katka. Jak se máš?"

"Ahoj, Felix." Katka smiled up at him.

Dvořáková helped Katka unload the trolley of sandwiches, cakes, coffee and bottles of water.

Katka turned to smile at Jonny. "Hello, Honza, how are you?" Her pronunciation of the words was poor, the words hardly discernible.

Mikeš laughed and clapped his hands together. "My friend, Katka has been practising her English for you."

Jonny stood up and walked towards Katka. She shook his extended hand, a slightly embarrassed smile breaking out on her wrinkled face. "Katka, I am very well. Thank you for the sandwiches."

Katka looked confused, clearly not understanding any English other than the words she had learned verbatim. Mikeš came to her rescue, translating Jonny's words into Czech for her. She smiled again, waved goodbye and wheeled her trolley out of the room and back across the floor.

With some food inside them, Mikeš started the meeting. "Right, let's have a recap of where we are on this case. I've got so much information bouncing around in my head, I'm not sure I'm clear what the next steps are."

Boukal stood at the whiteboard, pen in hand, ever-ready to capture the points made.

"My views on Michal Polák are clear for all to see," Mikeš declared with an innocent shrug. "Honza, what do you think? I'm sure you've got a more balanced perspective than me."

"Well, for starters," Jonny began, "I don't like him much either. Titus called him a control freak and that seems about right. He clearly wants everything to be running to his own plan. He also knows a lot of important people, including the Police Commissioner—"

Mikeš scoffed, rolling his eyes, momentarily stopping Jonny.

"But, he does seem to be very good at his job," Jonny continued. "He's been the driving force in harnessing the drone product that David Farrell invented, and he's managed to create a thriving business. Not many people could do that, even if they tried." He looked around the room inviting contradictory viewpoints. "He was also visibly upset when we told him the news about his friend's murder."

"He could be a good actor," Boukal suggested.

"Maybe. He'll certainly have had lots of practice, giving presentations and selling his company's services to important people. But, for the time being, I think we should forget about the individuals involved and just focus on the leads we have. We can't get sidetracked: we're already behind the curve on this case. In my opinion, we should concentrate on building evidence to support possible motives."

"I agree," Mikeš hollered with enthusiasm.

"At the moment, only Zoe and Michal seem to have motive," Jonny suggested. "The one obvious contradiction between the interviews and our findings so far is David's recent drug use. Michal implied that David had been much improved this year – 'past the worst' was the words he used – and this was backed up by Titus. However, I'm pretty sure what I found in David's kitchen will turn out to be cocaine. It is possible that Michal knows about it, and he came to the conclusion that David's habit was going to be an obstacle to the business' future plans. David is the technical genius and will be missed, but maybe Michal's assessment is that they've now got enough technical knowledge in-house to support the company going forward."

"And, what about Zoe?" Boukal asked, scribbling the key points up on the board.

"We need to interview Zoe formally and find out more about what happened to their marriage. She's already said that David was messy and difficult to live with, which appears to be true, but she didn't say anything about drugs. Maybe she needed him out of the way for some reason…"

Jonny tilted his head in a questioning pose, leaving the words hanging in the air.

"The important question to answer is who the 'us' is in all the messages," he continued. "This will help us understand how all of this started in the first place, and hopefully also who's been sending them. The message changed today, to 'ONE OF US WILL DIE', so we know that David is almost certainly part of this group. But, who else?"

"If the 'us' are the group of friends from university, maybe it is connected to Karel Vaněk," Boukal suggested. "It seems they all had a strong friendship for a number of years, but then Karel falls out with Michal Polák, leaves the company and commits suicide a few years later."

"I was wondering about that," Jonny accepted. "But, Freddie Pedersen was quite clear that he doesn't believe the two events are connected. Also, both happened a number of years ago. It would, however, be interesting to find out how much money Karel got paid for the shares he sold."

"What about this new message?" Mikeš prompted. "Zoe Farrell seems to be the only one we know who claims to have received the first messages, but says she didn't receive the changed message today."

"True, but from what I understand, the postal system here in the Czech Republic is about as bad as in the UK," Jonny asserted. "We certainly need to question her about it in the interview, but there must be a possibility that the letter will arrive in the post tomorrow."

Dvořáková shifted in her chair, put her elbows on the table, and leaned her face against her palm in concentration.

"What is it, Lucie?" Mikeš asked.

"Well, sir, the letters received in the post this morning would need to have been posted on Friday. Early Saturday morning at the latest. That means the murder was planned in advance."

"That was going to be my next point," Jonny said. "But, well done, Lucie, that's exactly right. This was definitely premeditated; the messages were all leading up to what happened this morning. David Farrell was murdered in cold blood."

"How would the person who sent the letters know the home addresses of all the friends?" Boukal asked.

"They are all directors of a well-known company, so their home addresses are probably not difficult to track down," Jonny clarified. "The person may also have been following them discreetly. I doubt if any of directors would have suspected anything."

"We need a catalogue of all the messages received, and we need to get some information on the emails," Mikeš stated bluntly. "Urgently!"

"The other thing we shouldn't rule out is that the messages and the murder could have been planned by someone *within* the company," Jonny added. "Maybe not one of the directors, but possibly someone in the next tier of management. Michal has already confessed that David Farrell was not overly well-liked, although he claimed he had it under control. At this stage, I think we should wait to see what the technical team find out about the messages, but we might need to interview other senior management to get a better view. Maybe also members of the product design and IT teams at Midakati: staff that worked directly for David Farrell."

The room went silent suddenly, the only sound being the marker pen squeaking as Boukal wrote on the board. Dvořáková used the opportunity to provide her update.

"I have set up the case files," she said, indicating the ring binders on the table. "David Farrell's phone records, including the tracking of his phone signal, haven't come back yet from the mobile provider, but I'll update you as soon as they do. The technical team have, however, unlocked the phone we found on him. We need to analyse it fully, but it looks like he had four calls on Sunday evening. One call was to Titus Arnold, and another from Michal Polák, both of which we know about from the earlier interviews. David Farrell also made a call to his wife, Zoe Farrell, at approximately seven thirty p.m. All these calls were short, less than four minutes long. There was, however, one other call from a number not in his contacts list. There is no indication at this stage who called him, but the call was at 8.23 p.m and lasted twelve minutes. We are checking through the messages, including the messaging applications he used, but nothing appears suspicious at the moment. The detective team are following up, including trying to identify the unknown caller."

"Interesting," Jonny mused. "My first reaction was that it was perhaps a drug dealer, but twelve minutes is a long time to be talking on the phone."

"We have also started reviewing the CCTV at all the metro stations along the A Line," she continued. "David Farrell has been identified boarding a metro train at Můstek station at 08.27 a.m. As we thought, he has his bicycle with him and he joins the last carriage of the train. The focus is now on analysing the film from the platforms along the line from Můstek to Dejvická. In addition, we will be reviewing the CCTV cameras throughout the Můstek station to see if he was being followed when he started his journey."

"Excellent work, Lucie," Jonny commented.

"I have also organised a team of police officers to be present at the Dejvická station during rush hour tonight. They have posters of David Farrell and will be asking commuters to come forward if they saw him on the metro this morning. I've also planned for the same team to be back at Dejvická station tomorrow morning: many people get the same train to work every day, so hopefully we'll find people who were on the same train as him. I plan to put uniform officers at the bottom of the upward escalator and ask everyone as they go through."

"Just like the ticket collectors." Mikeš laughed at the irony.

"Actually, I was thinking of retracing David Farrell's steps tomorrow morning," Jonny said. "I was planning to get the same metro he took to see if anyone remembers him. My only trouble is the language. Do you fancy a trip, Lucie?"

"Of course."

Mikeš laughed again. "You love your hunting, don't you, Honza."

"You know me well, Felix. We may not discover anything significant, but it helps me get inside the victim's shoes… and hopefully also the murderer's thinking. I mean, why the metro? Obviously, we haven't had the autopsy results yet, but the murderer's modus operandi is very unusual."

"Yes, your weak stomach earlier didn't go unnoticed," Mikeš replied, a wry smile spreading across his face.

Jonny held Mikeš' friendly gaze, trying hard not to laugh himself. "Felix," he began seriously, "I will come to the autopsy with you, but please ask Ella to go easy on me."

Mikeš laughed loud and whacked his friend on the back.

"The final thing to cover is the youth orchestra performance yesterday," Boukal interjected after allowing time for the joke to run its course. "We have established that David Farrell left The Klementinum at 2.27 p.m: he has been picked up on a CCTV camera outside. We are now checking the times that Michal Polák and Titus Arnold, and their respective wives, said they left. After that, we'll be trying to substantiate what they claim they did for the rest of the day. For this we will be checking the CCTV cameras in the city centre, including Old Town Square and Wenceslas Square, as well as checking with the taxi companies they used. We are also in the process of checking Freddie Pedersen's movements on Sunday."

"Check also with the organisers of the event," Jonny suggested. "Michal told us that the business was the main sponsor for the programme of events. Sunday's performance must have been very important for them. It would just be interesting to know if the relationship between Michal, David and Titus was as harmonious as has been claimed."

"Sir," Boukal began, addressing Mikeš with slight hesitancy in his voice. "What about the press release? David Farrell's body has now been formally identified by his wife—"

"The Police Commissioner wants to manage that," Mikeš grumbled, shaking his head animatedly. "I think we'd better wrap this up now... before I get angry again." He paused and took a deep breath. "I want this killer caught quickly, before the powers that be decide to take over even more of *my* murder investigation."

10

Deadly Sharp

The walk from the police station to the morgue at the hospital was well known to Jonny after three months in the city. But, it was still an excursion to look forward to. Not because of where they were going; the morgue was one place he'd happily strike off his list of places to be visited again. No, it was the beauty and grandeur of crossing the old town that made it special. He still found it hard to believe that he was actually working amongst these historic and picturesque surroundings. It was even harder to believe that serious crime happened here.

London would always hold a prominent place in his heart. After chasing criminals around the famous capital city for a long time, he'd come to know the urban sprawl and different feel of its many connected villages. But, somehow, in a very short space of time, Prague had managed to take top spot in his heart. It was not something he could describe easily – it had just happened. London had many famous sights, beautiful architecture and parks, but the dense richness of the historic old town had somehow transfixed him, and was going to be hard to surpass.

Mikeš was striding slightly ahead of Jonny, setting the pace as he liked to do, tapping his cane on the cobble stones in time with their steps. In the middle of the Old Town Square, Mikeš suddenly stopped, took off his hat and lifted his face to the afternoon sun.

"Lovely, isn't it? Makes you glad to be alive."

Jonny smiled, pleased to see his friend back to his eccentric self, the stress caused by the unwarranted dabbling in the murder case supplanted by the pleasant weather. For the time being at least...

At the far end of the square, under the watchful eye of the Jan Hus monument, Mikeš veered right rather than their usual left. Jonny was used to these sudden diversions, and had come to trust and also enjoy the tourist guide side of his new friend.

Turning into the side street V Kolkovně, Mikeš led them past the statue of Franz Kafka in front of the Spanish Synagogue, and through a maze of closely-packed cobbled streets into the Jewish Quarter. The streets were busy with tourists, but maintained a solemn respect despite the heavy footfall. At the bend in the street U Starého Hřbitova, Mikeš stopped outside The Ceremonial Hall. The gravestones of the fifteenth century cemetery were visible through the metal railings. The security guard nodded to Mikeš in recognition as he took off his hat and lowered his head.

"I know we're in the middle of a murder investigation, but it's important to take time to remember," he murmured, almost as a reminder to himself.

Jonny laid an avuncular hand on Mikeš' shoulder as they stood together in a shared tribute.

"I'm sure you know that the old Jewish town is still called Josefov," Mikeš explained. "It has become a symbol for the persecution that the Jewish people have suffered throughout history. The seventy-eight thousand Czech Jewish victims of the Shoah are commemorated at the Pinkas Synagogue... including Franz Kafka's three sisters."

Jonny knew any words would be inadequate. He chose to stand side by side with Mikeš in silent solidarity, both men looking through the railings, deep in their own personal homage.

***

Mikeš was fully back to his effervescent self once they reached the hospital. Jonny shared in the rapturous greetings from the administration staff and nurses as they strode across the wide reception area together and headed off down the corridors towards the morgue.

The relationship between Mikeš and Dr Králová was part of the fabric of the emergency services and they were greeted like celebrities wherever they went. Jonny had initially found it disconcerting to be with either or both of them, his natural inclination being to avoid the limelight if he could. The plain fact was that Mikeš loved the attention, and to work alongside him brought public interest, whether Jonny wanted it or not. In London, he'd played the part of the low profile DCI, head down and only focused on solving crimes. Whilst his new boss still harboured some old school practices in police work, he'd also showed Jonny how important it was to smile and greet people with affection, even if inside he was in knots over the investigation and putting on a show was the last thing he wanted.

Mikeš pressed the buzzer at the entrance to the morgue. One of Dr Králová's assistants opened the secure door.

"Ah, you're here," Králová called out, beckoning them over to the metal examination tables where she was working. "You're just in time."

Jonny and Mikeš picked up plastic gloves from the box on the side and put them on as they walked across the gleaming, sanitised floor tiles.

The naked, dead body of David Farrell was laid out like a

slab on a table, face down. The victim's black rucksack was sitting alone on the next table. Jonny winced at the sight, the surgical instruments glinting threateningly under the overhead lights. The gnawing smell of formaldehyde and cadaverine pervaded the air, the chemicals catching at the back of his throat.

"Remember to go gently on Honza," Mikeš said jokily to Králová, winking at his ex-wife.

"Very funny!" Jonny retorted quickly.

"What happened this morning?" Králová asked.

"Long story, Ella." Jonny sighed at the memory. "My first boss orchestrated a perverse initiation ceremony on me when I first became a detective. I won't go into details, but it involved slicing up a dead body in front of me without any warning. The result is that my stomach has been delicate ever since."

"It might be a good idea for you to come in here for a day. I can take you through everything we do. It might help de-mystify the whole dead person and blood thing."

Mikeš nodded animatedly at Jonny, clearly enjoying seeing his friend squirm.

"That's very kind of you, Ella, and I will have a think about it. But, my gut feeling is that I'm just a bit too far gone for that."

Mikeš laughed. "When we were married, Ella used to bring home all sorts of weird stuff in jars. Seeing a severed finger staring at you from the living room table in the morning was, however, a little bit too much for me. It's one of the good things about living apart now."

Králová whacked her ex-husband on the arm and Mikeš feigned injury.

"I think we'd better get on with the results of the autopsy," Jonny offered.

She moved around to the other side of the table, allowing the men to shuffle in closer in order to get a better view.

"Well, firstly, there is no reason for David Farrell to have died apart from the stab wound to his back. He wasn't particularly fit for a man of only thirty-two, but he had no underlying health issues. As you probably already know, his alcohol consumption over his short adult life was much higher than normal, and there is evidence of drug use, including recently. But, these weren't going to kill him. If he'd stopped or moderated his use of either, he could have gone on to live a normal and full life. Many people drink too much and/or use drugs when they're young, but their organs are able to cope with it."

"Had he taken cocaine recently?" Jonny asked. "Over the weekend?"

"I'll come to that in the toxicology report," Králová said, firmly in control. "First of all, I want to talk about what actually killed him."

Jonny and Mikeš waited with bated breath.

"The stab wound is clear to see." She pointed to a small wound in the middle of the upper back, close to the spine. "The knife was still embedded in him when we found him. The blade is, however, shorter than I initially thought. My first guess was that it was twenty centimetres long, or maybe even slightly longer, but in fact the blade is only fifteen centimetres long. It is also quite narrow, less than two centimetres wide. It is sharp, with a pointed tip and a lacerated edge."

She picked up a pack of photos and passed them across the table. The photo images showed various images of the knife inserted in the dead man's back, covered in blood but still attached to the inside of the rucksack. Jonny felt the bile rise in his throat, but relaxed knowing from experience that he could handle photographs.

"In total, including the handle, the knife is twenty three centimetres long," Králová continued. "It's shaped a little bit like what I would call a dagger, but the design is modern. It has a fixed blade, and a short, black handle. The reason it looks like a dagger is that it has a pronounced cross-guard, separating the handle and the blade. I'll come back to this in a minute. It's cute to look at, but deadly sharp."

"Any thoughts of where the knife comes from," Jonny asked hopefully.

She scoffed at the suggestion. "We've yet to even take the rucksack apart and examine the knife closely. But, it does look newish, so probably a recent model."

"Marek will try to track it down," Mikeš stated.

"What I can confirm is that the knife was firmly secured in place within the back compartment of the rucksack, nearest the shoulder straps. This back compartment is the largest and looks like it has been designed for carrying documents or papers because it has two fabric dividers. The compartment also has an inner pocket for valuables and two small straps for attaching keys, or similar items. Both straps are material but have a metal keychain clasp on the end. The knife was held in place by pushing it through one of the clasps, with the strap forced around the cross-guard to keep it secure. You can see it in this image." She pointed to a photo in Mikeš' hand. "The knife was also pushed through the paper files inside the compartment, including the fabric dividers, to stop it from moving."

Jonny looked at Mikeš. "It doesn't look very professional."

"The person who fixed the knife in the rucksack has probably done it quickly," Králová confirmed, "and has clearly improvised. But, they must have had a clear plan of what they were going to do beforehand: this includes prior knowledge about the rucksack, and also the required position of the knife to kill this young man. It was designed very cleverly so that when he sat down with the rucksack on his back – bam! – the knife would go straight into his back as the compartment was squashed under his weight."

"But, how would the killer know that David Farrell would still be wearing the rucksack when he sat down?" Mikeš looked between Jonny and Králová in confusion.

"Felix, I think that's your job to find out." She smiled warmly at him.

"What else was in the rucksack?" Jonny asked.

"The rucksack is quite big, certainly larger than average, with three compartments," Králová explained, lifting up the rucksack to demonstrate. "You can see the knife, still tied into the back compartment here." She pulled open the rucksack. "The middle compartment seems to have been designed for a computer. There were a few computer connections, two USB memory sticks and a set of small screwdrivers at the bottom. The last compartment on the outside of the rucksack is smaller, and contained just a few personal things like tissues and stuff for his bike. There are a few other pockets on the side, but they were empty."

"Were the zips open?" Jonny enquired. "I was just wondering if anything may have been stolen from him."

"The zips were half open," Králová answered. "We have taken photos which are welcome to look at. I think it is difficult to say. There was certainly nothing obviously wrong. We will, however, check closely for fingerprints and DNA all around the rucksack."

"This seems very odd to me," Mikeš remarked. "Wouldn't

David Farrell have noticed there was a knife sticking in his back through the rucksack?"

"You would think so," she replied, "but the material at the back of the rucksack is quite sturdy. Along with the straps, it provides the back support for the person carrying the rucksack."

Jonny stepped around the body to stand at the dead man's feet. "So, David Farrell gets on the last carriage of the metro train, leans his bike safely against the wall behind the driver position, and sits down in the seat at the end of the row." He paused, careful to pick his words carefully. "Instead of taking off his rucksack, he sits down on the seat and leans back hard. The rucksack is wedged between his back and the seat. The back compartment of the rucksack compresses under the weight, and the knife is forced into his back. The knife renders him unconscious and he collapses forward in his seat."

"It was clearly premeditated," Mikeš concurred, "but how could the killer have been sure he would lean back hard in the seat?"

"It must be someone who either knew him well, or studied his mannerisms very closely," Jonny stated. "The murderer could have followed David Farrell on his way to work to study his habits. Either that, or they knew he always did that when he sat down."

"As I thought earlier today," Králová said firmly, taking back control, "the knife penetrated the aorta and his left lung. The lung damage could have been repaired with surgery. The incision to the main artery, just where it comes out of the left ventricle of the heart, would have killed him in seconds."

"Has the murderer got lucky here?" Jonny posed. "I mean, how could they be sure that the damage caused by the dagger would be fatal?"

"Maybe the killer had a plan to finish him off if that didn't work," Mikeš suggested. "They could have been following him."

"True," Jonny admitted. "The appeal for witnesses tonight and tomorrow morning could be more important than we initially thought. Maybe someone was lurking in the carriage…" His voice tailed off as questions raged in his head.

"If you want my opinion," Králová stated, "I think the murderer knew exactly what they were doing. As we've discussed, this was premeditated. And, with that comes the knowledge that the knife was almost certainly going to kill David Farrell if he sat back hard with his rucksack still on."

Jonny and Mikeš looked at each other, both stumped.

"You asked earlier about what was in the victim's bloodstream," she continued, clearly wanting to move on. "Well, he'd had a drink over the weekend, but the remaining trace of alcohol was low so he couldn't have been drunk. But, he'd taken cocaine in the past twelve hours, and quite a substantial amount. In my estimations, he must have been a regular user judging by the level he ingested: many people wouldn't be able to function on it, let alone be the Chief Technology Officer of a successful company." She looked at her notes. "Oh yes, he'd also taken a sedative, or anxiolytic, and a sleeping pill the previous evening. I'm surprised he got out of bed before midday!"

"That is as I thought," Jonny said. "We found some traces of what I thought was cocaine in his apartment."

"Sounds like he was out of his head most of the time." Mikeš shook his head in disbelief.

"David Farrell's apartment could be the key to this," Jonny declared. "I mean, how would someone get that knife into his rucksack? Ella, I think your team should go over every room in his apartment."

"That's our next stop. I should have the autopsy report completed by the end of the day, including DNA and fingerprint analysis of his clothes, the bike and particularly the rucksack and knife."

"Marek told us he has the laptop now. Did you find any DNA or fingerprints on it?" Jonny asked.

"We found fingerprints but they belonged to David Farrell," she confirmed. "We processed it quickly because of the urgency. Once we've processed the knife, I'll get it over to Marek as well so he can start the search."

"Thank you, my dear," Mikeš replied.

"I'll organise a forensic search of David Farrell's apartment, as we've already discussed, including looking at the papers and envelope that you found."

"Anything else we should know?" Jonny asked.

Králová consulted her clipboard once more. "Only that his last meal was a ready-made macaroni cheese. He'd had sex, or at least ejaculated, in the previous twelve or so hours, but he'd washed this morning so there are no remaining traces to give us anything useful. Oh yes, and there was no poisoning involved – the banana was a banana!"

11

Interview 1 – Zoe Farrell

The following is a transcript of the recorded interview conducted with Zoe Farrell (ZF) on Monday, twenty-second June 2010. The interview was held at the home of Zoe Farrell in Prague 2.

Present at the interview were Chief Sergeant Marek Boukal (MB) and Consultant Jonathan Fox (JF).

The interview was conducted in English, in agreement with the interviewee.

MB: Interview commenced at 15.54. Please state your name for the record.

ZF: Zoe Farrell. Just so you know, some people know me as Zoe Henderson: this is my maiden name, and I have always used it for business purposes.

MB: Thank you. I would also like to explain that the senior detective leading this case is Chief Warrant Officer Felix Mikeš (FM). Unfortunately, he has been called to another meeting relating to this investigation and so cannot attend. Mr Fox and I will however brief him afterwards. Taping the interview is also important because it allows us to refer back to it at a later date if we need to.

ZF: That's fine.

JF: Once again, Zoe, we would like to offer you our condolences for the death of your husband, David Farrell. We appreciate you agreeing to talk to us so soon after hearing the sad news.

ZF: Have you confirmed if he was murdered?

JF: Yes, we believe he was.

ZF: Amy (Poláková) phoned me and told me about the message that Michal (Polák) and the others (directors at Midakati Ltd) received today. It's horrible. Do you know who sent it?

JF: It is still early in our investigation. We are currently following up all the leads we have. It is important we are thorough and do not jump to conclusions.

[Pause]

JF: Zoe, can I ask why Amy called you?

ZF: She just called to make sure I was okay. And, as I've said, she also told me about the message that Titus (Arnold) received at home.

JF: We are investigating that. But, I'd first like to talk about you and David. Some information on how you met, your relationship, and also what happened on Sunday would be very useful to our investigation.

ZF: No problem.

JF: You told us earlier that you and David met at university. Can you tell us how you met?

ZF: It was at a student party in the first year. Amy and Michal were already together by then, and they introduced us. David was shy and it was sometimes difficult to keep the conversation going with him, but I liked him because he was intelligent and didn't talk rubbish. I also liked the long hair he had at the time. He was interesting to talk to, you know, asked me questions about where I'd travelled to, my studies etc. I was a couple of years older than him, and had travelled around Asia and especially Central Africa. He found it fascinating and would always get me talking about my love of African art. To start with, the relationship was purely

119

platonic, but being Irish and English, both studying in Prague, we had perhaps more in common than some of the others and seemed to gravitate towards each other at parties, or down the pub. Mind you, it still took him over six months to properly ask me out: he was that shy. It was nice to do it properly though, not just jump into bed together. By then, it was the start of the second year and he was living in the house with Michal, Titus, Karel (Vaněk) and Freddie (Pedersen).

JF: Did David drink a lot and take drugs when he was at university?

ZF: Has Michal been talking to you?

JF: Michal and Titus both told us that David had significant problems in the past, but that he seemed much improved this year. The toxicology report, however, showed that he had used cocaine very recently, probably over the weekend—

ZF: Well, now you know. What are you asking me for?

JF: Listen, Zoe. I'm sure you've tried hard to cover up his addiction over recent years, but now is not the time to try and deceive us. The truth will come out. Just tell us everything and we will decide what is relevant and what is not.

[Long pause]

ZF: David was not a big drinker at university. He liked a joint, but no more than the rest of us. The trouble came when the business started to grow fast in the mid-2000s. Michal was always destined for the top, and led the company through all the hurdles it faced without batting an eyelid. Titus was similar: he didn't get phased by it at all. But poor David, it was all too much for him. He couldn't handle the pressure. Initially he couldn't sleep, then he started drinking... then, well, it all came crashing down in late 2007. At that point, I realised he needed help.

JF: It seems from what you and everyone else has said that you and Michal were his support system.

ZF: That's right. At first, I was a bit suspicious, thinking that Michal was only interested in maintaining the good image of the company. You know, not wanting investors to see that the technical genius behind the product was falling apart. But, I was wrong...

JF: What do you mean?

ZF: Michal went beyond the call of duty. He showed how much he valued David's friendship over a number of years. He had plenty of opportunities to dump David – and it would have been easy – but he never even thought about it. I used to despair, finding it very difficult to cope at times, but Michal was always in control and sorted out everything that David needed. He got David booked into a clinic, managed his workload for him so his time in the office was limited, helped me change my work so that I could be at home more, even found David a new apartment to live in when we separated. Being honest, I'm not sure what I would have done without his help.

JF: It must have been very difficult for you. I'm assuming this was the main reason that your relationship broke down, the reason that David moved out.

ZF: Yes. All those things I told you earlier about David being withdrawn and not a good communicator were true. They got worse as his stress levels and drinking increased, but I was able to deal with them. But, the drugs... I couldn't cope with that. At the time, Liam was still a baby, but I couldn't have him growing up and seeing his father like that.

JF: I understand completely, I really do. You said earlier that Michal helped you change your work. Can you explain what you mean?

ZF: After finishing university, I worked in a trainee Public Relations role for a global American company based in Prague. After a few years of badgering, Michal convinced me to join Midakati and I set up their PR function, working for Titus in

Marketing. When David was ill, Michal allowed me to work from home and eventually I set up my own business. Initially, I was working exclusively for Midakati, and I still do some work for them, but I have branched out and now do work for a variety of clients.

JF: Thank you for explaining. Back to David, I assume you'd noticed that his drug habit had returned?

ZF: Yes. About three weeks ago, I went to pick up Liam from his apartment. It was either a Saturday or Sunday, I'm not sure which. I was helping to discreetly clear up, as I explained to you, and I found one of his credit cards on the work surface in the kitchen. It was clean, but I still confronted him. He said that he'd been ordering something online in the kitchen and had just left it there. It was a plausible excuse because David is very messy, always forgetting things, often just leaving things where he last used them. But, it made me suspicious. I phoned Michal to tell him and we agreed to keep an eye on him. Over the next few weeks, I popped in unannounced but didn't notice anything. David knew what I was doing, but just laughed, telling me that I was imaging things. But, when I picked Liam up on Sunday, I noticed the cocaine in the kitchen. I hit the roof. I was really angry and told him that he wasn't going to be able to see Liam again until he'd sorted himself out.

JF: If it's any consolation, I agree with you. A child of any age should not be exposed to that.

[Pause]

JF: Zoe, did you empty the kitchen bin in David's apartment?

ZF: Yes, probably. I always did it. Even though I was angry, I still must have done it out of habit.

JF: Where did you put it?

ZF: In one of the bins in the refuse storage on the ground floor. I also took down his bags of plastic bottles and paper for recycling.

JF: Okay, thanks. We talked briefly earlier about the message that people in the business have been receiving recently: the ones that said 'ONE OF US LIED'. We are compiling a register of who received these messages, but we believe David received the same message by email and also by post at his new apartment.

ZF: Yes, I saw the letters there. He showed me. He also told me that he'd received emails with the same wording.

JF: Didn't you think it was strange that you received the message by post to this address as well as David receiving the messages by post to his new apartment?

ZF: Not really. The envelope was always addressed to him, but that was not unusual because I still receive some of his post here.

JF: All the envelopes were definitely addressed to him? Never to you, or to both of you?

ZF: Yes, I'm sure. I talked to David and Michal about them, but they told me not to worry so I just put them in the bin.

JF: The messages always mentioned 'us'. Who do you think they were referring to?

ZF: I just assumed it was about the directors of the company. That's what David, and also Michal, told me.

JF: Did David have any enemies in the company? Or maybe someone that used to work for the company but has now left?

ZF: If he did, I didn't know about it. I'm sure he would have told me. David could be impatient and get shirty about something technical, but he usually apologised and it was all over quickly. He certainly wasn't one to hold grudges over a long period.

JF: Do you remember anything strange happening since David received the first message? Maybe someone following you, or something out of the ordinary in David's apartment when you were over there?

ZF: Sorry, no. I don't recall anything.

JF: Please have a think about this after the interview. Maybe something did happen but you didn't associate it at the time. If you remember anything, however small, please let us know immediately.

ZF: Okay.

MB: Mrs Farrell, can I ask you to step through the events of Sunday: when and what time you saw David? This is to help us piece together the timeline of events.

ZF: David picked Liam up from here (Zoe Farrell's apartment) at about three in the afternoon. It's usually two, after Liam has had lunch, but David had to go to a business event. David told me he was taking Liam to the park so he took Liam's favourite push bike. I stayed in, using the time to clean my apartment and do some preparation work for the week ahead. I went to pick Liam up from David's at six. I know it doesn't sound like a lot of time, but given the circumstances… Anyway, I got there bang on six and everything seemed fine. Liam was happy because David had taken him shopping and bought him a new toy. I left them playing in that amazing living room and went to clean. I cleaned the bathroom, picked up the clothes in the living room and bedroom, put some in the washing machine, then went to tidy up the kitchen. That's when I saw the leftover cocaine. I was fuming. I didn't want to argue in front of Liam, but David could see I was angry. He started pleading with me, but I quickly gathered up Liam's stuff and left. I definitely took the bins down, as I've already said, but I left so quickly I don't think I turned the washing machine on.

MB: What time did you leave?

ZF: About half past six, maybe just after. I usually stay for longer to help out, only because he has a cleaner come in on Monday.

MB: Did you see him again after you left?

ZF: No, but he called me later in the evening, probably about eight. It was after I'd put Liam to bed. He apologised again and said it was a one-off. He wanted to confirm the arrangements to see Liam next weekend, but I told him that I didn't want to talk to him. The call was short. He sent me a message after the call but I didn't respond.

MB: Did you tell anyone else about what happened?

ZF: Only Michal. I called him straight after David called me. I wanted him to know that I'd found cocaine at David's apartment.

JF: What did Michal say?

ZF: He was as disappointed as me. He told me not to worry, said he'd talk to David.

JF: Did you check in David's rucksack when you were at his apartment?

ZF: Yes, I did. I always checked it, but David knew what I was doing. I used the excuse of looking for clothes to be washed, but in fact I was always searching for drink or drugs.

JF: Did you notice anything unusual about the rucksack?

ZF: No.

JF: Titus told us earlier that David took his rucksack everywhere with him.

ZF: Yes, that's right. He preferred to cycle everywhere so a rucksack made sense. Why are you asking about this?

JF: I can't explain right now, but it could be important. Was there anything unusual about the rucksack?

ZF: I don't think so. [Pause] His old one was falling apart, so he bought a new one earlier this year. I remember he was talking about it so much, it got a bit boring in the end. He wanted a certain configuration of pockets for his computer and documents. I don't really remember, but he eventually found one that met his requirements.

JF: Did you buy it with him?

ZF: No. I think he bought it online.

JF: This might also sound like a weird question, but did he have any habits about putting it on or taking it off?

ZF: Yes, he did. He had a weak left shoulder: I think he dislocated it badly when he was young. He had to put the rucksack on carefully, over his left shoulder first.

JF: What about when he took it off?

ZF: The same but in reverse. He used to sit down to put it on and take it off.

JF: So, he wouldn't take it on and off a lot when he was travelling.

ZF: I suppose not. I haven't really thought about that. [Pause] Why are you asking about his rucksack so much?

JF: Don't worry, I'm just trying to understand something. Last question, Zoe, and I am not prying here, but are you in a relationship with anyone else?

ZF: It's okay, I understand why you need to ask. The truth is that I've been so tired looking after David and Liam over the past few years that I've not even thought about it. One of my friends has been pressing me to start online dating, but I haven't got past the information stage. So, sadly not.

MB: After the meeting, I would like to take a DNA and fingerprint sample from you. This is standard procedure.

ZF: No problem.

MB: Thank you again for talking to us so soon after this tragic news. We will of course update you with our progress. If we have any more questions we will let you know. Interview terminated at 16.33.

12

Friends in High Places

The café was his bolthole in Prague. Jonny had discovered it during his first week working with the Czech Police, needing a place of his own to escape to, somewhere with a quiet corner and decent coffee. Although it wasn't exclusively his – he met with Mikeš there often, and had even introduced Boukal and Dvořáková to his secret place – it was the space he felt most comfortable to sit in the corner and ruminate on a murder case. Or, just think about life in general. In London, he'd always had an office door to close, but this was the closest to a 'Do Not Disturb' sign he had in Prague.

The small café had only opened one month before Jonny arrived in the city, and he was proud to have seen it develop into a popular kavárna, as the locals called coffee shops. He'd bonded with Luka, the owner, over this time, both being non-Czechs newly arrived and finding their way in a foreign capital city. Even during busy times, particularly over the lunchtime period, Luka always kept the table in the corner reserved for the detective duo.

Jonny had wanted some time alone to think after the interview with Zoe Farrell. Knowing that Boukal needed to get back to his administrative duties at the police station, he'd taken the opportunity to walk back into the city centre from the suburbs of Prague 2. The summer heat was muggy, the late afternoon sun still high in the sky, so he'd taken off his jacket and swung it over his shoulder. After walking through the busy I. P. Pavlova, past throngs of commuters waiting for trams or darting down the steps of the metro station on their way home, he finally reached the serenity of the old town. Even when busy with cars, delivery vans or people milling around, the narrow cobbled streets still managed to block out the outside world and maintain the ebb and flow of modern life with equanimity.

His first reaction on arriving at the café was to scan the space. He knew it was selfish of him, but he wanted a relaxing environment, not groups of tourists and their surrounding noise. Thankfully, less than half the tables were taken and his usual corner table was free.

"Ahoj, Luka."

Luka turned from the large expresso machine. "Ahoj, Honza, how's the new apartment?"

"You know, I'd nearly forgotten about that," Jonny chuckled. "New major investigation today. All hands to the pump, as we say in the UK."

"Yes, I heard about it on the news. I expect you need your usual cappuccino to wind down and think."

"You know me so well." Jonny laughed and turned to walk away.

"By the way, there was someone here earlier asking for you."

"Me?"

"Yes. He asked for you by name."

Jonny's face was etched with surprise. "Did he give a name or leave a message?"

Luka shook his head. "I asked him, but he said it would be better to talk to you in person."

"Interesting. Especially as I hardly know anyone in Prague."

"Yes, but you've made quite a name for yourself after

solving those recent murders."

Jonny ignored the compliment. "What did he look like?"

"Average height and build. Brown hair. Looked more like a student type, probably only in his mid to late twenties."

"Any distinguishing features?"

Luka shrugged his shoulders. "Not really. Average guy."

"Is that it? You wouldn't make a very good policeman."

"Hang on," Luka said, clearly playing back the interaction in his head. "He had a faded brown leather satchel slung over his shoulder. Yes, that's right. That's what made me think he was a student. The flap was open and he had files and papers sticking out the top."

"That's better." Jonny winked in recognition of the improved description. "Thanks, Luka."

Once seated at his corner table, Jonny set about attempting to digest all the information gained over his fast-paced, first day back at work. The starting point was the chosen method to murder David Farrell. Whilst he knew Dr Králová might yet throw more light on the assembly of the knife in the rucksack, he couldn't help conclude that it was either incredibly amateurish or there was a message hidden in the murderer's MO. Then there was the dynamic between David Farrell and his estranged wife, Zoe Farrell, to consider—

"Honza!"

Jonny's quiet contemplation was smashed by Mikeš' ostentatious entrance. Everyone in the café turned to watch the eccentric older gentleman striding between the tables, pointing his cane in Jonny's direction as if he'd caught a naughty schoolboy playing truant.

"I knew I'd find you here," Mikeš boomed, taking off his hat and placing it on one of the spare chairs along with his faithful cane. "You're a creature of habit, my friend. After being away on holiday, I just knew you'd find time to come to the café on your first day back."

"Guilty as charged," Jonny put his hands up, grinning.

Mikeš hesitated, processing the unfamiliar phrase. "Yes, yes… very funny, Honza. I must remember this saying. I can use it with Ella: she's always telling me off."

They laughed, settling back into their favourite time spent together.

"How was the Police Commissioner?"

Mikeš shook his head in disappointment. "He doesn't get it. He keeps telling me that it is *his* job to manage the perception of the police within the general community, as well as the Prague aristocracy. And, *my* job is to catch criminals. So, when a person, or a business, gets threatened or murdered, it is vital that *he's* kept informed so that *he* can manage the communications with all the community leaders and key stakeholders."

"I've heard that speech before," Jonny concurred. "Different words, of course, but fundamentally the same. The 'community' part is of very little meaning in my experience. It's just a cover for being able to keep his powerful friends informed of what's going on."

"Exactly! But it still makes me very angry. Actually, very, very angry."

"What happened on this old case?" Jonny probed, sensing an opening. "Lucie gave me the headlines…"

"Lucie?" Mikeš looked confused. "Well, yes, I suppose she would have just started when it all happened." He stalled, his face recalling the frustration of the time. "Quite simply, it was a cover-up, but I couldn't do anything about it. A well-known businessman was found dead, and the initial signs were that it was suicide. But, there was nothing in his life to indicate he was going to take his own life: he had a wife and a daughter, his business was doing well, and he liked to look after himself and keep fit. I know these aren't proof that it wasn't suicide, but my early investigation into his death uncovered nothing to support the theory that he would take his own life. There was a note found by his body, but even his wife thought it was suspicious: the note read as if he'd been forced to write it. I took my reservations to the Police Commissioner – the previous one, now retired – but he told me to wrap up the case quickly. As you'd expect, I ignored him and set about digging deeper. I found a witness who told me they'd seen two men walking into the woods on the outskirts of Prague the evening he didn't return home, also the place where he was found hanged the next day. The Commissioner went mad with me, accused me of making the police look stupid when, to me, it was clear that something wasn't quite right. He immediately closed down the case. There was definitely an outside influence, I could feel it."

"Friends in high places?"

"Something like that." Mikeš sighed heavily. "I had no further authorisation to investigate what happened. Of course, I still looked into the case in my spare time, but I didn't get anywhere. A case like that needs manpower – it can't be solved single-handedly. I thought about resigning, but I knew I couldn't do it. I felt terrible for a long time. I regret that I let him and his family down... I still do."

"All we can do is focus on our job *now*, Felix." Jonny reached over and patted Mikeš' forearm across the table. "I know you regret it, but nobody can rewrite the past. We have to focus on the present. Our job is to catch criminals. And, we're bloody good at it!"

Mikeš roared with laughter, banging the table in glee.

Luka approached the table carrying the coffees. "Here we are, gentlemen. Two cappuccinos."

"Luka told me that someone came in here earlier looking for me," Jonny remarked.

"Really?" Mikeš commented. "Another admirer?"

"Don't start…" Jonny replied, waving away the suggestion.

"How's Lucie?" Luka asked Jonny.

Jonny and Mikeš looked at each other, and then turned in a slow, synchronised movement to gaze up at Luka. Just two small words had brought out their serious faces: the protective nature of her uncle, and also her boss.

"I was just… you know, just wondering if you're going to bring her in here again," Luka stammered.

"I brought Lucie here the day I found out the results of my Czech family tree," Jonny explained to Mikeš. "It seems that she made quite an impression on Luka."

Luka's cheeks flushed with embarrassment. "I'd… I'd better get back to the counter," he mumbled, scampering back across the café floor, wiping his hands earnestly on the apron tied around his waist.

Jonny leaned in, closer to Mikeš. "Actually, Lucie was asking after Luka the other day."

"Well, well. Maybe the summer months are bringing the flutters of young love in the warm wind. First, you and Ivana… and maybe now Lucie as well."

"Very poetic, Felix."

"I have my moments, Honza." Mikeš winked across the table and took a sip of his coffee.

The natural banter between the detectives was what made their friendship so special to Jonny. He'd had a small number of friends in the past, most now more associates than real friends. But, right from the start, Mikeš had opened up to him, demanding in return that Jonny did the same. The direct approach had taken him by surprise, not being something he was used to or felt natural with. Mikeš was the type of person who got under your skin immediately and there was no halfway house – you either loved him or loathed him. Jonny's initial reaction was reticence, wanting to sit back and see what materialised, but Mikeš' zealous approach and commitment to their friendship had shown no respect for convention. Now, he only felt thankful for what had happened. Meeting Ivana and getting back into police work were key parts of his improved outlook on life, but Mikeš seemed somehow to be the catalyst for everything that had followed.

"Getting back to this murder case, Honza," Mikeš declared loudly. "What's your instinct telling you?"

"I was just going through my notes when you arrived. I haven't had much time to think about it, but I keep coming back to the messages. The key is going to be establishing who has been sending them and for what reason. I mean, why send multiple messages over a number of weeks saying one of the group has lied, then change the message to say that one of them will die and quickly murder David Farrell?" Jonny locked Mikeš' concentrated stare with a puzzled look. "Either something has happened to force the quick change, or this was all planned in advance."

"I feel this is going to be another complex case… and a nightmare to solve," Mikeš stated with a sigh.

"Everything seems to point to the university friends being the intended target: the 'us' in the messages. They all received emails and letters, plus David Farrell has been murdered. I think we're going to have to interview everyone again tomorrow.

133

Maybe one of them is hiding something. We also need to hope the technical team get lucky and identify something about the person who sent the emails."

"What about Zoe Farrell? I still haven't met her yet, but I trust your judgement..."

"She seems quite composed. At first, I wondered why she wasn't more distressed, but when you consider what she's been through with her husband's behaviour in the last few years, I think her reaction is understandable. It is hard to believe she would kill her husband, leaving their son both without a father and a mother in prison."

"True, but love can drive people to do irrational things. We've both seen it so many times."

"Yes, I know that. But, even though David Farrell has been unstable in recent years and seems to have started taking drugs again, it doesn't feel bad enough yet for her to do something as desperate as that."

Mikeš sighed. "So, what's your plan now?"

"I'm going to go back to my apartment. I think I should try to talk to Amy Poláková again. She might have a good insight into the relationship between David and Zoe."

"Be very careful, my friend. These types of women can be very manipulative. Plus, her husband is well connected."

"That's what I'm worried about."

Mikeš' phone rang and he answered.

Even with his poor grasp of the Czech language, Jonny could tell Mikeš was talking to Dr Králová. Rather than waiting, he busied himself by looking through his notebook.

Mikeš finished the call. "That was Ella. She's finished the autopsy and was calling to update me. She's still processing the fingerprints and fibres found, but there's already one very important finding. Zoe Farrell's DNA is all over the rucksack, as you would expect, but one of her fingerprints has been found on the knife handle."

Jonny looked perplexed, a frown developing across his forehead. "Hang on. Marek has only just taken DNA and fingerprint samples from Zoe Farrell. Even if he drove straight over from her apartment to the morgue, there wouldn't have been enough time to process them."

"Ella told me there was only one fingerprint on the knife. The reason she was able to identify it so quickly is that Zoe Farrell's DNA and fingerprints are already on the police database."

"Well, well," Jonny muttered. "I wasn't expecting that."

13

A True Temptress

Mikeš had needed to get back to the station to catch up with Boukal, as well as submit his own case reports. Finally alone, with the peace and quiet he'd been craving, Jonny returned to his thinking. His rumbling stomach, however, had other ideas. Knowing he had limited supplies back at his apartment, he decided to eat at the café. It hadn't been a tough decision; he knew how tasty Luka's cooking was from previous experience, and the homemade lasagne on the specials board was too tempting to ignore.

Even though it was not yet seven p.m, the pedestrian traffic in the city centre was starting to thin out as he eventually started walking back to his apartment. This was one of the benefits of living in a smaller city that Jonny really appreciated. He had become well used to the twenty-four hour hubbub in London, the city never really going to sleep. Prague on the other hand, whilst also a major capital city, didn't suffer the same level of insomnia. Yes, there were shops open all hours, where you could buy essentials at any hour of the night, as well as pubs and clubs open until the early hours, but the commuters travelling in and out of the city every day had mostly departed by five p.m during the week, leaving behind only locals and tourists.

If a new murder case of this magnitude had just begun when he was still a DCI in London, he would have been camped in his office until late with only a few hours' sleep ahead of him. His new role of consultant afforded him the relative luxury of a free evening, Mikeš taking the brunt of the paperwork and upward communications to keep his superiors in the loop. Striding home on a warm summer evening, Jonny realised properly for the first time just how lucky he was to have the best of both worlds.

If there was any possibility of a breakthrough during the evening, he would have gone back to the station with Mikeš and paced the floors waiting for news with the rest of the team. The truth was that tonight was not that type of night: it was too early in the investigation. Mikeš had issued instructions for Zoe Farrell's passport and residency papers to be confiscated, her car impounded, and a police watch placed on her apartment. A warrant had also been gained to search her apartment, including her phone and all computer equipment. The rest of the work would be administrative, Boukal and Dvořáková sifting through witness statements gathered at the metro station and preparing for the next day's interview with Zoe Farrell.

The positive match of the fingerprint on the knife had surprised Jonny, but he couldn't help feel that more would be revealed over the coming days. Without it, the only motive for murdering her estranged husband would be his drink and drug habit, as well as the potential impact on their son. Whilst he'd seen people kill for far less, it was usually when the individual felt cornered, under severe pressure, unable to see another way out. This didn't seem to be the case with Zoe; despite stress in the past, she seemed to have her life under control. The fact that her DNA and fingerprints were on the police database was irrefutable, and intriguing. I wonder what previous crime she has committed, he thought.

Strolling along the riverside road, the waves lapping at the shoreline in the dimming light, his mind wandered to what Ivana was doing. He'd purposefully not bombarded her with messages during the day, but she'd often been in his thoughts. Looking at his watch, he judged that the time was right and called her. As usual for her, she was in the middle of some drama. The washing machine wasn't spinning so all the clothes were still soaking wet after unloading. He sympathised and laughed in the right measure, missing her badly, but at the same time knowing that the path they were on was the correct one – for both of them. He left her to head off the impending domestic disaster and settled back into enjoying the magnificent view along the river on his walk back from work.

After quickly going into his apartment, discarding his jacket in the process, Jonny took the stairs up to the top floor of the building. His first ever boss had taught him to tackle any task he wasn't looking forward to head-on. Talking to Amy Poláková was one of those tasks, not because she was scary but because she clearly had a sway, one that was both striking and intimidating in equal measure.

"Honza, what a lovely surprise." Amy's head protruded around the half open door, a bare shoulder visible.

"I'm sorry," he spluttered, immediately knocked off course. "I'll come back—"

"No, no, it's fine," she replied confidently. "But, you'll need to talk to me as I'm getting ready. My hair and makeup are done, but I'm not dressed yet. I'm meeting a friend for drinks at eight, but I'm late as usual… Come in."

Her head disappeared and the door swung open. Jonny stepped into the hall hesitantly. His attention was immediately caught by the sight of Amy walking away down the hall with only a short towel wrapped around her middle, her bare feet leaving imprints on the wooden floor. He stood transfixed, unable to move, his eyes wide at the tantalising vision in front of him. The front door remained wide open. Just as she was turning the bend in the hall, the towel at her back slipped, falling away to expose her lower back and pert bottom. Everything was over in seconds, but Jonny was sure he'd seen Amy turn at the last moment, her eyes sparkling playfully, a coy smile spreading from the corner of her mouth.

Jonny stood disarmed, not sure what to do. He thought about leaving, but he couldn't bring himself to do it. However uncomfortable he felt, by what Amy was capable of doing but also how it made him feel, he knew the priority was getting information to help the murder investigation. This will only take a few minutes, he reassured himself. *I can handle it, she's just teasing me.*

"Please make yourself comfortable and have a drink," Amy shouted from down the hall.

He closed the apartment door and walked into the large living room. The room was the same as the previous evening, the only addition being a number of large cardboard boxes piled up in the corner. He saw the open drinks cabinet but decided to abstain; if there was trouble looming, he wanted to keep his wits about him.

The French doors were open so he walked onto the terrace to take in the view. The sun was setting across the river, the dark orange blaze starting to melt away into a pink glow. The view was magnificent, the additional height making it so much better than his own balcony. He lifted his face slightly, feeling the radiance of the last sun.

"I need your help with this…" Amy was suddenly standing in front of him, just inside the living room. She'd changed into a skimpy, red cocktail dress and high heels. Her hands were positioned on her breasts, holding the strapless dress in place. She turned around to reveal her naked back, the material of the dress hanging open. "Well, come on, Honza. Zip me up."

Jonny approached tentatively and stood behind her. The allure of her musky perfume engulfed his senses. He lifted his hands in preparation, carefully assessing the job in hand; he wanted to complete the job as quickly and painlessly as possible, but also not touch her bare skin in the process. Before he had the chance to grab the zip, she nestled back into him, her bare back jolting into his outstretched hands. "Come on, Honza. I'm in a rush, remember."

It was the spur he needed. He quickly grabbed the top of the zip together in one hand, making sure to hold the dress material firmly at the base of her spine in his other hand. Grabbing the zip slider, he tugged upwards in one, smooth action. He exhaled heavily in relief.

"Thank you." She twirled in front of him, holding out the hem of her dress. "What do you think?"

"It is very nice. But—"

Before he could continue, she'd leaned in and kissed him seductively on the cheek. Noticing the lipstick mark left behind, she smiled. "Silly me." She licked her finger and gently rubbed his cheek in a circular motion. "Mustn't get you in trouble with your wife."

"I'm not married."

"Interesting…" Amy fluttered her eyelids. "I'd have thought a successful, handsome detective like you would have been snapped up long ago. But, then again, you wouldn't have had so much practice at zipping up strange ladies' dresses… You know, you have very strong hands."

Jonny broke away and sat down on an armchair. He beckoned Amy towards the nearby sofa. "Mrs Poláková—"

"Amy, please. Come on, Honza, we're neighbours."

She sat down demurely on the sofa, a contented smile on her face, smoothing out the dress on her lap and stretching her legs out towards him.

Now that she was sitting directly opposite him, and at a safe distance, he was able to quickly evaluate her. The near-flawlessness of her hair, facial features, makeup and dress sense was staggering. Jonny had come across people like Amy before, where every move was made with the purpose of controlling the room and the people in it. Especially men. But, she was a professional by comparison with others he'd met before – a true temptress. She knew how strikingly beautiful she was and seemed to take her greatest pleasure from the reaction she evoked in others.

"Okay, Amy." His tone was firm, attempting to exert control over the situation. "Do you know about David Farrell? You don't seem very—"

"Yes, how awful." Her face registered a serious tone for the first time. "Michal is still at work. He's had a terrible day. You can imagine…"

"I think David has had it worse."

"Yes, poor David. He was such a lovely man. So gentle."

Jonny tilted his head to the side, considering Amy's response. "Gentle is an interesting word to use, and one I've heard from someone else today. It's not the word I'd expect people to use of someone who was addicted to alcohol and drugs."

"Honza," she began playfully, her tone light, "David was trouble, but he was still a lovely, kind man. I always liked him

141

immensely."

"What about Michal?"

"Michal loved him. And, he'd do anything for him. But, I think you already know that. I think you're testing me." She smiled sweetly, the perfect symmetry in her features throwing him momentarily off guard.

"Why did the marriage break down between Zoe and David?"

"If you want to know the truth," she answered in a matter-of-fact tone, "I'm not sure they were really suited in the first place. It took them ages to get together and nobody really understood what was going on. In my opinion, you either know straight away or you don't. Michal and I knew we were destined to be together as soon as we met."

"So, nothing significant happened to break them up? No extramarital affairs or major disagreements?"

"Not that I know of. Zoe is a lovely girl, and a friend, but she is a bit flaky: she sort of lives in her own world. I think any man would struggle to live amongst her art collection."

"But, you also have a lot of art here."

"Yes, Honza, but the paintings and statues in Zoe's apartment are dark and depressing. The art we have here is modern, bright and airy." She fanned her arm around the room as if to prove it. "Don't you agree?"

Jonny shrugged his shoulders. "Well, it's not really for me to comment. I've found myself more attracted by the architecture since I arrived in Prague."

Amy's eyes lit up. "One of our good friends is a leading architect in Prague. He runs the Planning Department in City Hall. Maybe you'd find it interesting to talk to him?"

"Thank you, but no," he asserted. "It's not really me. I prefer just to enjoy the architecture around the city rather than analyse it."

"As you wish." Amy gave him a mock disappointed look. "You're a tough nut to crack, Honza," she added with a wink.

Jonny held her gaze but did not react. "It seems that Michal took a very active part in helping Zoe deal with David's addiction."

"Michal came to David's rescue so many times I lost count. He always said it was because they were friends, but if it was me I'd have given up a long time ago: I don't have his patience. Don't get me wrong, David was a lovely guy, but there always seemed to be some trouble or another. It was like a soap opera. I left it to Michal. I didn't really pay much attention to what was going on."

"I daresay that you must have heard lots of gossip over the years—"

"What do you take me for, Honza?" Amy smiled seductively, crossing her legs whilst holding his eye.

"I just mean that being married to Michal would mean that you'd know most of what was being said." He paused to let the statement settle. "Did you hear of anyone having a particular grudge with David over the years? Especially lately."

Amy sighed. "Honza, the boys were always fighting like cats. They've known and worked closely with each other for so long. A week didn't go by without an argument of some sort. It used to get on my nerves, I lost interest a long time ago."

"What interests you then?"

"Fashion, arts, going out, having fun, and... well, me, I suppose." She chuckled and swept her hair back gently with a controlled sweep of her hand.

"You don't seem very interested in the business. I'd expect

it to be important to you… I mean, surely it funds your expensive lifestyle." Jonny repeated Amy's wave around the room.

"I think you're testing me, again. Naughty boy." She wagged her index finger at him. "Michal is the one who is important to me. I would do anything for him. He gets a fair deal out of it, I think." She ran her hands down either side of her body, from the curvy shape of her breasts to her hips, smiling suggestively at Jonny all the time.

"What about children?"

Amy snorted. "I'm still young, Honza, but to be honest I'm not sure I want any. I've seen people's lives ruined by them. They just make so much noise, don't they? We've looked after Liam a few times, but I was always pleased when Zoe came to pick him up."

"I want to ask you about yesterday," Jonny said, changing tack. "Michal said you had a walk together after the youth orchestra performance and then got a taxi back here. He said that you didn't see David after he left to pick up Liam."

Amy tutted. "Honza, I know you have to ask me these questions, but I also know you are testing me, trying to see if my story is different to Michal's. Of course we were together. We walked over Charles Bridge, stopped for a drink, and then got a taxi from near Kampa Park."

"What about later in the evening?"

"We stayed in. Michal was working as normal. I prepared a light salad for us, then had a long, hot bubble bath with a glass of champagne. Afterwards, I moisturised my skin with a new almond balm I'd bought recently, put on my sexy lingerie, and managed to entice Michal away from his papers to—"

"Okay, thanks," Jonny interrupted her, shifting in his seat uncomfortably. "I get the picture."

She lifted her left arm, looking at her diamond encrusted watch. "Honza, I'm going to be late. As much as I'm enjoying this, we're going to need to continue this another time."

He stood up and edged towards the door. Amy walked back down the hall and returned wearing a leather shoulder bag and carrying an evening jacket over her arm.

"We have more interviews lined up," he said as they stood waiting for the lift. "I may have more specific questions for you tomorrow."

"Well, you know where I am," she replied flirtatiously, fluttering her eyes.

Jonny continued looking straight ahead at the lift door. The mechanical sound of the gearings could be heard as the lift ascended to the top floor.

"I nearly forgot," Amy exclaimed. "Tomorrow night we are hosting an art exhibition in our apartment. It would be lovely if you could come along. Starts at seven thirty."

"But, one of your friends was murdered today," Jonny blurted out, unable to control his reaction.

"Honza, this event has been in the diary for over three months. About fifty guests have been invited and the featured artist is a personal friend of mine." She looked at him with pleading eyes. "All the artwork has already been delivered – that's what the boxes in the apartment are for. We can't cancel it now."

He shook his head gently, finding the information hard to comprehend. "I don't think it's my type of event," he finally said. "But, thank you for the invitation."

"Zoe and David were due to attend," she retorted quickly, trying to make amends. "Plus, all our friends will be there: Titus, Freddie, as well as their other halves. You might find out something useful for the investigation."

Jonny raised his eyebrows but didn't reply.

"Well, the invite is there. Just pop up if you fancy it. It would be nice to see you."

The bell sounded to signal the arrival of the lift.

"I'll take the stairs," he said.

Amy reached up and kissed him on the cheek again, her lips lingering near the corner of his mouth. After stepping away, she backed into the lift, smiling serenely at him. "Have a lovely evening, Honza."

14

Another Man

Tuesday, 23rd June 2010

Jonny woke early. He felt energised, inherently knowing that this day – the second full day of the investigation – was going to be crucial. Unless it was an open-and-shut case, the first day always lacked shape; the focus was on gathering background information, including meeting all the players in the real-life murder mystery show. The second day, however, was already into the business end of the investigation – the detective had to take control and drive the agenda before time ran out.

Although still early morning, daylight was already peeping around the edge of the new curtains picked out by Ivana. Checking his mobile, he saw that it was only five forty-five a.m. Still not totally at ease with the layout of the bedroom, he shuffled carefully around the bed, found his dressing gown and walked through to the kitchen to make a coffee. The air temperature was colder than he expected, but it was bearable to sit on the balcony and watch the rising sun's magic pen of light gently erase the lingering shadows of the night.

After recovering from the disconcerting call on Amy Poláková, he'd spent the previous evening going over what Zoe Farrell had told them, both after she'd been informed of her husband's murder and also during the formal interview. She'd been in control throughout, holding it together, not breaking down in the customary cocktail of emotion and tears. But, he was inclined to believe that she'd answered all his questions naturally, without any obvious deception. The only time she'd become feisty was when he'd surprised her by knowing about David's drink and drug problems. Whilst interesting and worth further probing, her reaction didn't come across as dishonest, only frustration that all the hard work she'd put in to help her husband had turned out to be fruitless. Sitting on the balcony, his hands wrapped tightly around a mug of coffee, Jonny resolved not to jump to conclusions and instead keep an open mind. The simple fact was that the discovery of Zoe's fingerprint on the murder weapon would need to be explained, one way or another. Maybe she is a psychopath after all, he thought, and my initial judgement is way off the mark.

After pottering around the apartment, using up the excess time, he set off to walk his new daily commute into the old town. He'd smiled to himself when Dvořáková had sent him an early message suggesting they meet at the café. Making sure to arrive exactly at seven forty-five a.m as arranged, he knew he'd find her already talking to Luka.

"Honza…" she called out when he entered, a healthy flush in her cheeks. "Dobré ráno. Luka was just telling me about the first time you two met."

Jonny smiled, a mixture of pride and parental responsibility rising within him.

Luka saw Jonny smiling and quickly reverted to barista. "Cappuccino, Honza?"

"Thanks, Luka. Take away, please."

"Luka was telling me that the new James Bond film has just been released," Dvořáková continued. "It's supposed to be great,

148

lots of action. I don't get much chance to go to the cinema these days, but it might be a good idea this weekend."

Jonny couldn't remove the smirk from his face. Luka continued to keep his gaze low, concentrating on filling the portafilter with freshly ground coffee.

"You know what I think," Jonny said, slowly glancing between the two of them, a serious expression etched on his face. "I think Felix would make a damn good Czech Bond."

The tense situation was instantly broken. After allowing a few seconds for the words to sink in, unsure whether Jonny was going to say anything else, Dvořáková burst out laughing. Luka initially looked lost, not sure how to react, but he soon joined in the hilarity, clearly just happy to have avoided any personal embarrassment.

***

The platform at Můstek was packed with waiting commuters. Jonny knew the station was always busy but hadn't experienced it during the morning rush hour. The Prague metro system had only three lines and Můstek provided one of only a limited number of interchanges, from the A Line to the B Line. It was also only a short distance from the main railway station that brought commuters into the centre of the city from the towns outside the capital.

Jonny and Dvořáková stood right at the end of the platform, waiting to join through the last doors of the metro train when it arrived. She'd already warned him that the arriving train would be full of office and shop workers; the numerous exits out of the station all delivered passengers onto Wenceslas Square or the adjoining streets. The process of getting on the metro train and standing where they wanted was going to be a challenge.

They couldn't have looked more conspicuous if they'd tried. Jonny was holding the handlebars of the red bike, David Farrell's helmet still hanging by its straps, the forensics team having completed their examination of it without finding anything unusual. Dvořáková stood out from the crowd in her uniform, attracting glances from other waiting passengers. She stood impassive, professional and on duty, slim and upright with her blonde hair tucked under her hat, a large A1 photo of the murder victim rolled up under one arm and a batch of smaller flyers in her other hand.

The Prague Metro Murder, as the Czech tabloids had dubbed the crime, had been all over the news the previous evening. As well as extensive information about David Farrell, his family and his role at Midakati Ltd, the coverage raised doubts about public safety given that the murder had taken place on a busy commuter metro train. The Police Commissioner had issued a statement to reassure the public, calling the murder an isolated incident. Mikeš had been indignant when he'd phoned Jonny earlier to brief him, blaming the poor press release for the bad headlines and categorically stating that he'd have managed the situation better if he'd been left alone to do his job.

The metro train arrived exactly on time, at 8.27 a.m. They needn't have worried about getting on the packed train. One look at them and the passengers parted, allowing Jonny to park the bike in the same position as they'd found it the previous day. Dvořáková took her position between the last seats in the carriage, ready to address the commuters sitting in the opposing row of seats and standing in the space at the next set of doors.

The sound of the travelling metro train was loud but Dvořáková was louder. Surprising him with the projection of her

150

voice, she explained in Czech the reason for their presence and asked for co-operation. Jonny couldn't understand much but he got the gist, Dvořáková's arm actions filling in the gaps: where David Farrell was sitting, and how he'd been found slumped forward in his seat at the end of the line. She unrolled the large photo and passed it to Jonny. He held it up high whilst she walked down the carriage handing out the leaflets.

The metro pulled into the next station, Staroměstská. Dvořáková used the opportunity to repeat her message for anyone that had struggled to hear her under the din of the wheels grating on the tracks. The doors closed and the train continued on its journey. She slowly walked back towards Jonny, acknowledging each of the seated passengers; her words and supporting nods were clearly intended to provide assurance, both about the importance of any information they had and also the confidentiality with which it would be treated.

Dvořáková repeated her request for the third time but still nobody spoke. An older lady seated in the middle of a row whispered to the woman next to her. A few passengers exchanged glances.

"Ask them if they travel on this train regularly," Jonny suggested.

Dvořáková relayed the question in Czech. The response was a sea of nods.

Seeing that the audience was warming up, Jonny suggested a follow-up, "Ask them if the man in the photo was also a regular on this train."

Dvořáková translated. The response was more positive, many people nodding, some saying, "Ano." Even Jonny knew that word – *yes*.

The older woman beckoned Dvořáková towards her. She

looked around at her fellow passengers and then made a brief statement. The short comment served as a catalyst; the reservations of the other passengers were instantly broken. A number of men and women joined in the conversation, adding a weight of noise as they clarified the information and provided perspectives of their own. Dvořáková was suddenly the conductor, encouraging and muting comments.

"Honza, they are telling me that David Farrell was a regular on this train, at least two or three times a week. And, always with his bike. Yesterday, he joined the carriage as normal at Můstek and parked his bike behind where the driver sits. But, what was unusual was that he was talking to another man."

"Another man!" Jonny exclaimed, louder than he intended. "Why haven't they come forward? They should have given this information to the police."

"Don't be too hard," Dvořáková encouraged. "They're scared."

"Excuse me, sir," one younger man began. "Most of us saw what happened, but none of us understand it. The news has frightened us. Even I considered going to work via a different route today."

The train pulled into the next station, Malostranská. A couple of new passengers boarded the train, remaining standing when they saw the police presence.

"I'm sorry," Jonny said, looking around the passengers, his eyes pleading for forgiveness. "Lucie, can you ask them if they'd seen the other man before?"

The translated question generated a chorus of denials – "Ne" – accompanied by a row of shaking heads.

"Right, that's a good start." He paused, considering how to handle the situation. "Lucie, this might be tricky but can you ask them to explain what they saw? And, please remind them that any small detail may be vital to finding out what happened."

Dvořáková spoke to the passengers again, her tone gentle and encouraging. Jonny watched as the comments flowed with pent-up emotion, the passengers pleased to be able to offload within the safety of a group environment. The overlay and speed of the multiple voices made it impossible for him to follow what was being relayed, especially as the train left the station, but he knew it was important. The train stopped at the next station, Hradčanská, some passengers departing with nods of apology.

"They are telling me that the two men were talking as if they knew each other. There was certainly no animosity. There was only one seat free, at the end of the row. Here." She pointed to the seat. "David Farrell peeled the banana he was holding, took a bite and sat down. The other man stood in front of David and carried on talking. But, David suddenly slumped forward in his seat. The man that was standing looked concerned. He shook David's shoulders but there was no response. The man tried to rouse him a few more times, but David remained leaning forward."

"Did the other man touch David before he slumped forward?" Jonny asked.

Dvořáková translated the question. The response was intense, everyone talking at the same time. Taking control, she orchestrated the voices, asking some passengers to wait whilst others spoke.

"They are adamant that the other man did not touch David Farrell up to the point that he slumped forward in his seat. However, he definitely touched him when he realised something was wrong, when David did not respond to his prompts."

"Are they sure?" Jonny repeated, keen to get total clarity on the point.

"At the time, we all thought the man sitting down was ill. But, now we think he'd been poisoned," the younger man said, repeating the statement in Czech for the benefit of his fellow passengers. A few nodded in agreement.

"With what?" Jonny posed.

"It seemed to me it was the banana," the man replied. "He took a bite and suddenly he was unresponsive. When I thought about it last night, after watching the news on TV, I couldn't conceive any other way he'd been killed. But, these are only my thoughts after hearing the news later. As I've already said, at the time I just thought the man was having some sort of attack and his friend was going to look after him."

"But, there's more," Dvořáková said to Jonny, taking back control. "They also told me that once the man realised that something was wrong, and David Farrell wasn't responding, he searched through the pockets of his jacket and side zips of his rucksack."

"Really?" Jonny looked shocked. "Did he take anything?"

Dvořáková asked the question to the seated audience but was met with a confused mixture of shrugs and shakes of the head.

"If he took anything it was very small," she stated, "because they didn't see anything in his hand."

"What did the man look like?" Jonny followed up, aware that the end of the journey was fast approaching.

The younger man got to his feet and walked towards Jonny. "The man looked like a student. He was wearing a brown leather jacket over a white shirt and jeans. He also had an old style school bag over his shoulders."

"Did he get off at the last stop, Dejvická?"

"Yes," the man confirmed. "All the passengers, including

me, got off. The man who died was still leaning forward in his seat. The other man was left on the train with him, but he clearly looked distressed."

"Thank you."

Jonny looked towards Dvořáková with raised eyebrows. "It's vital we get these passengers to identify this other man. We can try using the CCTV images. Can you please ask them if they will help us?"

The automated broadcast over the tannoy announced the approaching, last station. All the passengers stood up, ready to exit. Dvořáková cajoled them out of the doors and into a group on the platform, preparing to take their names and contact details.

Jonny retrieved the bike and pushed it off the train, shaking his head in confusion. That certainly wasn't the start to the day he was expecting.

15

Full of Surprises

"Well, I didn't expect that!" Jonny declared as he burst into the Incident Room.

Mikeš looked up fast, surprised by the melodramatic entrance. He and Boukal were sat together, huddled close, conferring over paperwork on the desk.

Jonny animatedly slapped an A4 still photo from the metro's CCTV coverage onto the table in front of them. "This man was with David Farrell when he died. He got onto the train with him at Můstek." He nodded his head slowly for effect, his mouth puckered in anxiety. "He was the last person with David Farrell's dead body before it was found by the train driver."

"Well, well…" Mikeš picked up the photo and studied it. "How do you say in English? That's a turn up for the books."

"Exactly. But, it gets worse." Jonny folded his arms. "This man in the photo is the same man who came looking for me at the café yesterday. On our way back from Dejvická, I went to check with Luka. He confirmed it's the same man."

Mikeš stared at the photo. "He looks scruffy like a student." He passed the photo to Boukal.

"I woke up in a good mood this morning, ready for the day ahead," Jonny stated gruffly. "But, this revelation has thrown me completely."

The earlier impromptu discussion with the metro passengers

on the platform had achieved success surprisingly quickly. Dvořáková had called over the uniform officers who'd been handing out leaflets to commuters at the escalators. In their bag they had a series of still images taken from the CCTV cameras from around the time the metro train had arrived at Dejvická the previous morning. Dvořáková arranged the passengers in a circle around her and slowly started to show them the images, Jonny peering in from the outside. At only the third image, the young man who'd acted as spokesperson got very excited. "That's him!" He pointed his finger at the photo. "That's the man on the metro train yesterday." Dvořáková held up the photo for everyone to see and the answer was a unanimous collective of nods.

Jonny hadn't been excited at this point, although the statement that the man looked like a student and carried an old, brown bag over his shoulder – the same as Luka's description – was starting to gnaw at him. Dvořáková wrapped up the proceedings quickly, leaving her uniform officers to deal with the return of the bike, as well as take the names and contact details from the group of passengers. She'd hurried after Jonny who was already standing on the opposite platform, impatiently waiting for the arrival of the train returning back to the city centre.

The return journey was quiet. His thoughts were whirling as he tried to unpick something solid from the confused picture that was developing. His only conclusion was that something seemed to have been happening to David Farrell. But, what? And also, how was Zoe Farrell's fingerprint on the murder weapon and this unknown man connected, if at all?

Dvořáková had followed Jonny's lead, using the travel time to scribble notes for the case file, before following him out of the Staroměstská metro station and towards the café. Luka had been pleased to see them again so soon, but his spirits were squashed when Jonny snappily refused the offer of a coffee and instead brought out the CCTV image for him to consider. Clearly knowing he was on the spot, Luka considered the photo carefully before nodding. "It's a bit grainy so I can't see the details of his face perfectly, but his hairline looks the same. Plus, the clothes and the bag are exactly the same… Yes, I'm confident it's the same person."

"Thanks, Luka," Jonny replied, his face strained. "We'd better get back to the station to see Felix. We need to find a way to get on top of this case before it runs away from us."

"Don't you even want a take away?"

"Sorry, no time. See you later." Jonny turned and opened the door, holding it for Dvořáková. She'd smiled apologetically at Luka and followed Jonny out.

Back in the Incident Room, he was starting to regret his refusal of a coffee to go. He slumped in the chair next to Mikeš, feeling sluggish, desperately in need of a kick.

"I wonder why none of the other passengers came forward before?" Boukal posed.

"I think it was a mixture of being scared, and also confusion," Jonny replied. "They all assumed at the time that David Farrell had had some type of seizure. They thought the other man – this student guy – would look after him. One of them told me he thought David had been poisoned, but he only came to this conclusion after seeing the news on TV last night."

"That's the fault of the press release," Mikeš stated, rolling his eyes. "The request for help was not clear enough." The dig at the Police Commissioner was loud and clear.

"I'm just worried we've lost vital time to find this man," Jonny grumbled.

"Maybe not…" Mikeš said, a glint of amusement in his eye.

"Why, what have you found?"

"The detective team have been researching the mysterious caller that David Farrell spoke to on Sunday night," Mikeš explained. "They took us through it at the briefing meeting this morning. Marek and I were going through it again, just to check."

Jonny eyes widened, his interest piqued.

Boukal took over the story. "One of the team tried calling the number every ten minutes yesterday afternoon but the call always went straight to voicemail, and with no message. Late yesterday, we managed to get an emergency data request signed off and the team contacted the mobile phone provider. This morning we got a response back with the identity and address of the owner of the mobile contract. Uniform officers have already been to the address, but no one answered."

"We couldn't get a warrant to enter the apartment without consent," Mikeš chipped in, "because at that time we had nothing to tie this person to a crime. The uniform officers are talking to neighbours though."

"However," Boukal took back the narrative, "by searching online using the phone number, and also looking at social media websites using his name, the team have narrowed down the search to one person – Leopold Holub, or Leo as he seems to be known. He's a freelance journalist. And, the good news is that it looks like the CCTV image the passengers identified matches with these pictures of him from social media." Boukal held up two images.

Jonny sighed heavily, mostly out of relief. "That certainly explains how he might get mistaken for a student."

"Leo Holub is Czech," Boukal added. "It seems he studied journalism in London before working in publishing there for a few years. It's not clear exactly when he went freelance, but he's living in Prague now."

"Maybe all is not lost." Mikeš winked at Jonny. "Honza, usually I'm the one losing the plot and you are calming me down. Seems like the roles are reversed today." Mikeš' pale yellow shirt and tie combination added a camomile-like calm to his mood.

"Yes, you're right." Jonny chuckled. "We shouldn't have a problem getting a warrant to search Leo Holub's apartment now. Actually, I think I'm also going to call him. We need to understand how he's connected to David Farrell. He came looking for me at the café yesterday, so maybe he'll speak to me."

"I will also talk to Lucie about extending the CCTV check of the Můstek station to see if we can determine where Leo Holub met David Farrell," Boukal stated, jumping up and scribbling a note up on the Murder Board. Whilst seeming on top of his game, his appearance had suffered as a result of the late hours worked: his tie was poorly tied, his top button undone, and his shirt was badly creased.

As if on cue, Dvořáková walked into the room carrying two coffees. "Here you go, Honza. I thought you might need one."

"Now I am feeling better," Jonny declared jokily. "Thank you, Lucie."

"We should take the opportunity to go through where we are on this investigation," Mikeš said energetically. "There's a lot happening, and, with continued interest in the case from the Commissioner, I want to make sure we all know what's going on so today turns out to be a good day."

Boukal quickly explained to Dvořáková how the journalist had been identified before starting his briefing. "Last night and this morning have been very busy, but we've achieved some progress. The second interview with Zoe Farrell is booked in for eleven a.m at the station. She's bringing a legal representative

160

with her. The Autopsy Report has been issued, and it confirms that Zoe's fingerprints were found on the knife. Photos are in the file…"

Dvořáková slid the file across the table to Jonny, opening it at the relevant section.

"Her DNA and fingerprints were also found on David Farrell's rucksack, as well as around the apartment," Boukal added.

"I'd expect to find Zoe's DNA and fingerprints all over his apartment, based upon what she told us yesterday," Jonny commented. "But, her fingerprint on the knife is definitely unexpected."

"A number of other fingerprints were found around the apartment," Boukal continued. "The forensics team are in the process of trying to identify them, but it's made more complex because a new cleaner has just started, coming in on a Monday and a Friday—"

"Zoe said it was just a Monday," Jonny stated.

"That's what the new cleaner told us David Farrell asked her to do," Boukal clarified. "Plus, David Farrell also had a plumber come in last week to unblock the kitchen sink. The one part of the autopsy findings I found interesting was that fibres found around the groin area of David Farrell's trousers, including the zip, had Zoe's DNA on them."

"How do we know he was wearing the same trousers on Sunday, when Zoe came over to his apartment?" Jonny questioned, a sceptical tone in his voice.

"We don't," Boukal answered quickly, "but it does seem to imply that David and Zoe were sexually active recently. It's certainly not the impression that Zoe gave us when we interviewed her yesterday. The old cleaner told us that David had

161

five pairs of work trousers and she used to take the dirty ones for dry cleaning every week. That would suggest that David and Zoe had a sexual liaison in the last week or so, possibly even on Sunday."

"I understand your point, Marek," Jonny said gently. "But, there are lots of couples that break up and continue to have a sexual relationship. Zoe never said she hated David, remember. Maybe deep down she was hoping they would be reconciled. We should definitely ask her about it in the interview, but if it is true surely it would indicate that they were closer than we think… more of a reason for her *not* wanting him murdered."

"I didn't think about that," Boukal admitted.

"Tell Honza about the messages," Mikeš said, clearly keen to move the meeting on.

"The technical team have been working with the IT Department at Midakati," Boukal explained, "and we now have a full catalogue of all the threatening emails received by the directors. The first message was received by Michal Polák five weeks ago, but within days all three others had received the same email message: 'ONE OF US LIED'. As Michal told us yesterday, the messages became more frequent, until last week when they started receiving one every day."

"Is there any news on where they were sent from?" Jonny prompted.

"Not yet. The technical team have been here most of the night and are still working on it. But, we do know that no other member of staff, even senior management, received the message by email or post. Also, none of the directors received an email message yesterday."

"So, the changed message of 'ONE OF US WILL DIE' was only sent by post?"

"Yes," Boukal confirmed. "We collected the letters received by Titus Arnold and Freddie Pedersen yesterday. David Farrell also had the same message: we found it in his post box. All are being checked by forensics. Interestingly, the uniform officer watching Zoe Farrell's apartment has confirmed that the post has been delivered this morning, but that a letter has still *not* arrived there."

"Why do you think a letter wasn't sent to Zoe Farrell's apartment, like before?" Mikeš queried.

"I don't know," Jonny murmured, scratching his head. "Maybe it's nothing. Zoe told us that all the letters she received were addressed to David anyway. None of the messages seem to have been addressed to the wives or partners, just the four directors."

"That's correct," Boukal confirmed. "Every email or posted message we have seen has only been addressed to either Michal Polák, David Farrell, Titus Arnold or Freddie Pedersen."

"Have the technical team checked Zoe's laptop yet?"

"Yes," Boukal confirmed. "There were no emails to the directors of Midakati, other than personal emails to her husband about Liam and other practical matters. They also couldn't find any templates for printing the messages that were sent by post, even in the folder of deleted documents."

"Interesting," Jonny commented. "Maybe Zoe had access to another computer. We need to ask her about that."

"But, Honza, Zoe Farrell must still be our prime suspect," Mikeš declared. "I mean, her fingerprint is on the knife, she was in David's apartment on Sunday evening, and she has motive because she'd just found out that he'd started taking drugs again."

"It is hard to argue against that, Felix. I'm still finding it hard to fathom why she would go to such lengths to murder her husband, but she definitely has a lot of questions to answer. I also

163

want to have a closer look through the evidence in this file before we interview her. Have we worked out why her DNA and fingerprints were already on the police database?"

"It seems that she was arrested for assault but the charge was subsequently dropped," Boukal explained. "It was during her university days, back in 1998. A student party was raided on suspicion of drugs. The case notes are thin but it seems that Zoe manhandled the arresting officers when the party was raided. She was put in a cell for a few hours, but eventually released without charge. Josef Liška was the lead detective on the raid."

"Was anyone else arrested with her?" Jonny asked.

"There is no information in the case file," Boukal confirmed. "Only that she was arrested and held for a while, but no charges were brought against her."

"Actually, Josef was asking for you, Honza," Mikeš added. "It's not about this old case, that's nothing, just another student party out of hand. No, he said he'd noticed something in the evidence retrieved from David Farrell's apartment."

"That's interesting. I'll go down to see him."

Mikeš turned to Dvořáková. "What's the update from your uniform officers, Lucie?"

"Well, sir, we haven't yet completed the review of all the CCTV footage, but so far all the information given to us by Zoe Farrell, Michal Polák, Titus Arnold and Freddie Pedersen checks out: we have images of Zoe Farrell on Wenceslas Square at 6.40 p.m, just after she left David Farrell's apartment; witnesses have confirmed that Michal Polák, Titus Arnold and their wives left The Klementinum around five p.m; the taxi companies have confirmed pick-up times; and Freddie Pedersen's movements for yesterday have been confirmed. David Farrell was also not caught on CCTV leaving his apartment on Sunday evening. This is supported by his phone signal, which doesn't move from the location of his apartment between early Sunday evening and

Monday morning, when he left for work. The only thing we've picked up that was unexpected—"

"Yes..." Mikeš encouraged.

"The organiser of the youth orchestra event said that Michal Polák and his wife, Amy, were delightful..." Mikeš sighed audibly, momentarily making Dvořáková pause. "But, David Farrell seemed agitated. Just before the first performance was due to start, Michal and David were talking alone at the side of the room. David suddenly became angry and raised his voice. Amy went over to the men and the situation calmed down quickly, but many people had turned to look at them."

"I wonder why Michal, and especially Titus, didn't mention that yesterday," Jonny commented.

"Final report from me, and not good news," Dvořáková added. "The bins at David Farrell's apartment were emptied on Monday morning. Unfortunately, there's no way of checking what was in his bin when Zoe Farrell emptied it."

Jonny shrugged. "Never mind. Thanks Lucie, great work."

A light tap on the office door made them all turn.

Boukal jumped up and opened the door. A tall, ungainly looking man was standing outside, his hair in need of a trim and, oddly for the station, wearing a casual shirt, jeans and trainers. He nervously held a piece of paper in his hand.

"This is Hynek," Boukal explained to the group, beckoning him into the room. "He leads the technical team. He usually works over at the Police Headquarters, but he and a couple of his team moved over here to help with the investigation."

"How's your English, Hynek?" Mikeš asked.

"Pretty good, sir. Much of the IT world only speaks English, so we have no choice."

"Good. Have you got something for us?"

"Yes. Firstly, I'd like to apologise for my clothes. I knew this was going to be a tough assignment... A couple of us have been

165

here all night."

"That's what I like to hear." Mikeš slapped the table, turning to Jonny with a beaming smile. "Bravo!"

"Thank you for your dedication," Jonny added.

"The first breakthrough we got was working out the IP address of the person who has been sending the emails to the directors of Midakati Ltd. Interestingly, David Farrell had also worked this out because the IP address was written down on the papers found in his apartment. He must have been a pretty smart guy to work it out himself, without access to all the additional databases we have."

"That backs up what Titus Arnold told us," Boukal declared.

"We'd been able to work out ourselves the area of Prague that the user was logging on from, but we were not able to identify the actual person or their address. Using the same data request that we used for the phone records, we approached the internet provider and they have just come back with the information."

The atmosphere in the room was heavy with anticipation.

"The person is Nikola Vaněková. She lives in Prague 7. Her address is on this paper."

"That must be Karel Vaněk's wife," Jonny exclaimed. "He's the former university friend, and director of Midakati, who left after a disagreement and subsequently committed suicide."

Mikeš looked stunned. "This case is turning out to be full of surprises!"

16

Bomb Site

The latest curveball had stunned them all into confused silence. Once Hynek had left the Incident Room, his ears ringing with thanks and praise for a job well done, they all sat looking at each other blankly. Jonny broke the impasse by pulling the case folder towards him, flicking to the catalogued list of messages sent by email and post over the previous five weeks.

Mikeš, for once, appeared lost for words. Boukal and Dvořáková held their counsel, clearly waiting for instructions on the next steps.

Jonny broke the silence. "So, we have a prime suspect in Zoe Farrell," he began slowly, keen to be precise. "Since we spoke to her yesterday, her fingerprints have been found on the murder weapon, and we have a second interview booked with her this morning. However, as of this morning, we also have a mysterious journalist, Leo Holub, who was on the metro talking to David Farrell when he died. It is also possible he stole something from the murder victim before he left the scene of the crime. But, most confusing of all is the recent revelation that the original email messages – the most likely way to determine who the 'us' is, as well as what the 'lie' is – were not sent by anyone we have yet interviewed, but instead by the wife of an ex-friend of David and the others, and ex-director of Midakati Ltd, someone who took his own life a few years ago."

"What a mess!"

"You've never spoken a truer word, Felix."

"What do we do now?"

"We must talk to Nikola Vaněková before we do anything else," Jonny replied instantly. "The working assumption has to be that this whole situation started because of the messages. Maybe the real reason is something that happened in the past, something we don't know about, but the messages have stimulated a series of actions resulting in the murder of David Farrell."

Mikeš nodded. "Seems logical, Honza."

"I suggest we don't warn her before we arrive. The element of surprise may help us get to the truth quicker."

"I also want a warrant to search her property," Mikeš added. "We need to move fast on this one."

"What about Zoe Farrell?" Boukal prompted.

"We can talk to her later," Jonny suggested. "Put the interview back to this afternoon. Hopefully we'll have better information about the messages by then."

"I'll arrange it," Dvořáková confirmed.

The others departed with chores to do, leaving Jonny alone with the ring binder of collected evidence, the tangled illustration of photos and connections on the Murder Board, and his spinning thoughts. He studied the photographs of the rucksack and knife again, taking his time with the detailed images showing the fingerprint impression. The imprint was full and firm, placed squarely in the middle of the black handle of the knife, just above the wide cross-guard. *Zoe Farrell must have known that her fingerprint would be identified.* It was hard to imagine her making such a mistake, he thought, she always seemed in control. Shaking his head in frustration, he decided to leave further

168

analysis until after they'd interviewed her again.

Picking up his mobile, he unlocked the screen and called the journalist's number. The call went straight to voicemail, no personal message.

"Hello. This is a message for Leo Holub. My name is Jonathan Fox, a consultant with the Czech Police. I believe that you have been looking for me. I also need to talk to you about David Farrell. It seems to me from the evidence so far that you are not involved in his murder. But, we need to speak as soon as possible in order to understand what happened, and also eliminate you from our enquiries. Please call me as soon as you get this message so that we can arrange a time to meet. Thank you."

Finishing the call, he saw a message from Ivana.

Hi, Honza. Washing machine fixed ☺ How are you? Miss you x

The message was simple, nothing elaborate or intimate, but it was enough to slightly disorientate him. Other than his trip back to the UK, this was the longest period they'd been apart since meeting. Whilst the adjustment to their relationship was necessary, he knew he hadn't yet acclimatised to not being close to her and seeing her smile every day. Yes, he missed her too, more even than he'd thought he would. The intense focus on the new murder case had provided a shield, protecting him against his true feelings. Right at that moment, he realised that life without her was incomprehensible. *Could I be in love?*

Ivana, I don't feel complete without you. Miss you so much x

After sending the short but heartfelt reply, typed so fast to avoid second thoughts, he closed the case file and left the office in search of another coffee.

***

Nikola Vaněková lived in perhaps the least desirable area of the city, Prague 7. Boukal's hurried research before they'd left the station had established that she had not remarried, rented the apartment she lived in, worked as a part-time teaching assistant in a local school, and had two young children. Jonny accepted the facts without reaction, but the stark difference to the fortunes of Michal Polák and her dead husband's other ex-friends didn't go unnoticed.

Jonny had taken the front passenger's seat when he and Boukal left the police station. Mikeš had again been summoned to see the Police Commissioner and they picked him up in front of the Police Headquarters. Mikeš waved away Jonny's offer of the front seat and hopped into the back. The car sped through the city streets, propelled by Boukal's driving prowess, Mikeš moaning as he bounced around on the back seat. Although still not enjoying the ride, Jonny at least felt securely strapped in. "Definitely a smoother ride in the front, Felix."

The street they parked in was bleak and without feature: dark, grey buildings lined both sides of the road, with no grass borders, just concrete pavements and pathways to the building entrances. A parade of small, local shops were visible down the street, a group of undesirable youths larking about the forecourt in front. The youths stopped when they saw them. Mikeš shouted out a warning that Jonny did not understand, but the fierce point at the car was enough to get the gist of it.

Boukal pushed the intercom and announced their arrival. A female voice confirmed she was Nikola Vaněková and buzzed them in. With no lift, they walked up the drab stairwell to the second floor.

170

A slight woman with short, black hair, cut harshly at the front and sides, greeted them at the apartment door. She wore an old, casual t-shirt and tracksuit bottoms. On first impression she seemed to be in her thirties, but her drawn face and the dark circles around her eyes gave her the appearance of someone ten years older.

Jonny stood back as Boukal introduced them. Mikeš nodded in greeting, but his face was stern.

Nikola led them through to the living area. Clothes, toys and magazines were strewn everywhere – the room looked like a bomb site. She quickly cleared the sofa and chair, throwing the collected items through the open door of the nearest bedroom.

Mikeš and Jonny sat down on the sofa. Nikola sat down in the beaten armchair, tears already welling up in her eyes.

"Mluvíte anglicky?" Mikeš asked her.

Jonny recognised his cue. "Mrs Vaněková, I am a consultant working with the Czech Police. Unfortunately, I don't speak Czech very well. Would it be possible to speak in English?"

"Yes," she replied quietly.

"Do you know that David Farrell has been murdered?"

Suddenly her face came to life, her eyes bulging in disbelief. "What?"

"Yes, he was found murdered on the metro yesterday."

Nikola wiped her eyes. "I saw that on the news. But, I didn't know it was him."

Jonny waited. His experience was telling him that now was the time to stay quiet, to let the other person speak next.

"You don't seriously think I had anything to do with it..."

"You tell me, Nikola." Jonny paused. "You've been sending threatening messages to Michal Polák, David Farrell, Titus Arnold and Freddie Pedersen for weeks now – five weeks to be precise. Have you got what you wanted?"

Nikola put her head in her hands and started to cry.

Jonny waved his index finger at Mikeš and Boukal, making it clear they should leave her.

After a few minutes she lifted her head. Her eyes were bloated, her cheeks streaming with tears. "It just wasn't fair. Michal promised me that he'd look after my family when Karel died, but then the payments stopped. He promised, Mr Fox… That's why I said he'd lied."

"So, you're telling us you had nothing to do with the murder of David Farrell?"

"Of course not. Look at me, I can hardly take care of myself and my kids. How could I possibly plan a murder?"

"Mrs Vaněková…" Mikeš intervened, waiting to get her full attention. "This is a very serious situation. Despite your claim that you were not involved in David Farrell's murder, we have to investigate the matter fully. Think about it for a moment… You sent an increasing number of threatening messages to the directors of Midakati Ltd for over five weeks, and then one of the directors is found murdered."

"I didn't do anything wrong," she wailed, again burying her head in her hands.

"We are going to need to take you with us, back to the police station in Prague 1," Mikeš confirmed. "Once there, you will be formally interviewed, and samples of your fingerprints and DNA taken. We also have a warrant to search these premises and your laptop or other computer equipment."

Boukal stepped forward and placed the warrant document next to her, on the arm of the chair. Nikola glanced at it sideways, through watery eyes, but did not pick it up.

"Nikola, are your children at school?" Jonny asked.

She nodded.

"Chief Sergeant Boukal will help co-ordinate all the necessary arrangements to make sure the children are looked after. Do you have someone he can call?"

She nodded again, her head still forward. "My sister," she muttered.

"Does she live in Prague?"

Nikola raised her head, dabbing away the tears running from her eyes. "Yes, just outside. Her phone number is on the board." She pointed to a cork noticeboard covered in children's drawings. "Aneta."

Boukal walked to the noticeboard and located the phone number. He walked into a bedroom to make the call.

Nikola slumped back into the armchair, lifting her hands to her face. "Michal is so two-faced."

Mikeš smiled at Jonny: 'I told you so' was the clear, unspoken message.

"Nikola, I have a couple of questions for you whilst we are waiting," Jonny began. "If what you are telling us turns out to be true, and you had nothing to do with David Farrell's murder, we need information quickly to understand what has happened here. There is a reason he was murdered and, at the moment, nothing is making much sense."

"What do you want to know?" Nikola barked back. "I'm probably going to get framed for something I didn't do. So, what the hell…" She opened her arms wide in anger, inviting accusations.

"Nikola, it's not like that. I just want to find out who killed David. Of course, you might still get into trouble for sending the messages, but that is not my primary concern right now. Do you understand?"

Nikola relaxed, dropping her arms. "Yes."

"We have managed to compile a list of all the emails you sent, from the first email to Michal in April this year, through to the last emails on Friday. The letters, with the same message, did not start arriving until early May. Why did you wait a few weeks before sending the messages by post?"

"They were ignoring me. So, I decided to bombard them: I started to send them more emails, almost daily, and I also started to send the letters."

"To Zoe Farrell's address as well?"

"Yes, why not? I knew she and David were living apart, but I wanted her to see the messages. I was desperate. I thought maybe Zoe would understand my position and talk to David and Michal." She suddenly became animated, waving her arms around. "Look, these people have had everything go their way. They are making loads of money, having fun, whilst we're the people who suffer. First, my poor Karel, and now me. I have nothing! I can hardly even pay the bills, let alone buy anything nice for the children. What great friends they all turned out to be…"

"I understand how you feel, I really do," Jonny replied quickly, hands up to placate her anger. "I'm not saying anyone is to blame. I just want to get to the truth."

He let silence fall on the room, allowing her time to calm down.

"Nikola, why did you not send any emails over the weekend or yesterday?"

"I was too busy: my daughter was ill. But, I sent emails to them all again this morning when I had some free time."

"We haven't seen those yet," Jonny confessed. "Had you also changed the wording of today's email messages?"

174

Nikola pulled a face, distorting her features. "What are you talking about?"

"Well, you changed the message in the last letters you posted. I was just asking if you also changed the message in the emails—"

"I don't understand what you mean."

"The message changed to 'ONE OF US WILL DIE'," he clarified.

She shook her head vigorously. "That's nothing to do with me. Even the emails I sent this morning said 'ONE OF US LIED'. Nothing else."

Jonny and Mikeš exchanged a confused glance.

"So," Jonny stated, speaking slowly, "you are telling us that you haven't sent any messages at all saying 'ONE OF US WILL DIE'?"

"Correct. You can check my laptop. I haven't sent any messages like that."

17

Interview 1 – Nikola Vaněková

The following is a transcript of the recorded interview conducted with Nikola Vaněková (NV) on Tuesday, twenty-third June 2010. The interview was held at the police station in Prague Old Town.

Present at the interview were Chief Warrant Officer Felix Mikeš (FM), Chief Sergeant Marek Boukal (MB) and Consultant Jonathan Fox (JF).

The interview was conducted in English, in agreement with the interviewee.

MB: Interview commenced at 12.37. Please state your name for the record.

NV: Nikola Vaněková.

MB: Mrs Vaněková, I would first like to confirm that arrangements have been made for your sister to pick your children up from school. One of our uniform officers is scheduled to meet her at your apartment so that she can pick up some clothes and toys for them. The school has also been notified.

NV: Will I be able to see them?

MB: That very much depends on how this interview goes. I'm sure we can organise a call to your sister later, but at the moment, I cannot promise more than this. Also, I know you have waived the right to legal representation in this interview, but if you change your mind at any time please just let us know. We will stop the interview whilst a solicitor is organised.

NV: I understand, but I haven't done anything.

MB: Finally, I can confirm that at this point you have not been charged with any offence, hence this interview is not being held under caution. The purpose of the interview is to get answers to some questions we have regarding the murder of David Farrell on Monday. Your apartment is also being searched now, under the warrant we served you earlier. Depending on the outcome of these, you may be cautioned later.

JF: Nikola, can I confirm that you are still comfortable continuing this interview in English? We can revert to Czech at any—

NV: You are clearly the smart one. I'm happy to speak English if it helps you realise that I'm innocent.

FM: Please just calm down and answer the questions. It is in everyone's interest if our questions are answered quickly.

JF: I would like to start by talking about you and your husband. I don't want to make this painful for you, but it would be very useful for us to understand the background to what happened between Karel (Vaněk) and the other directors of Midakati Ltd.

NV: Just hearing that name makes me angry. I asked Michal (Polák) to change it loads of times but he refused. He said the company name was now established and it was too risky to change it. I mean, what's the difference between Midati and Midakati?

JF: I appreciate your feelings. I understand you and Karel also met at university. Going back, what was the relationship between Karel and the others like?

NV: They were great friends. Other people we knew amazed at how close they all were. Michal was the ringleader, but all five of them used to play their part. The dynamics of their

177

friendship used to make me quite envious at times: many people never get the chance to experience something like that.

JF: Were you surprised when four of them started a business together?

NV: No. It was all they talked about from the time I met Karel. He and Michal studied on the same course and were always throwing ideas around about potential start-up companies. It was hilarious when they were drunk because the ideas used to get more and more zany.

JF: Sounds like good times.

NV: Yes, they were. When university finished, Karel was so energised. He worked crazy hours – they all did – but he loved it so much.

JF: We understand that it was Michal and Karel who eventually fell out?

NV: Yes. Michal had always been a good, loyal friend to them all. But, he always had to be in charge – that was the cost of having his friendship. Karel started to get stressed when his views on one of the early prototypes wasn't being listened to. He felt the rollout was too early, putting the product at risk. Michal overruled him and it ended up as a big fight between the two of them.

JF: With the luxury of hindsight, Michal's decision seems to have been proved right.

NV: That's not the point. They had formed the business together, and held an equal share. For Michal it was all about control. David and Titus (Arnold) were forced to choose sides – and Karel lost. He had no choice but to leave.

JF: From what we understand, the settlement when Karel left was mutually agreeable.

NV: He had no other choice. They had the company valued and

the others bought Karel's shares. Obviously, it's nothing compared to what the company is worth now...

JF: Yes, but Karel decided to leave.

NV: Mr Fox, he had no choice. If he hadn't left by agreement, he'd have been forced out eventually. And, probably with nothing. That's Michal for you!

JF: But, Karel received enough money to start another business...

NV: Not really. He put together a business plan for a new venture and used it to borrow the extra money he needed from the bank. Karel was clever, certainly as smart as Michal, David and Titus, if not smarter, and the banks could see the business plan was worth backing.

JF: So, what happened?

NV: I'm sure Karel made some mistakes, but the biggest problems were caused by Michal. He convinced some important suppliers not to work with Karel. Michal will say that he'd got exclusive contracts, but Karel knew he was being squeezed out. The only contracts he could get were poorer quality and more expensive. It became a fight, and Michal was always going to win – he always had the knack of knowing the right people in the right places.

JF: I'm assuming Karel eventually had to put the company into administration?

NV: Yes. It was a slow, painful process, and Karel became very depressed. He went to the banks with a recovery plan but none of them believed it enough to put more money in. The company formally finished in 2003 and Karel took his own life in 2006. We were broke, he couldn't see any other way out.

JF: That is an extremely sad story. It must have been difficult for you.

NV: We'd wanted children early, so when he died I was left with

179

debts, high rent on our apartment and two children under five. It was a nightmare. I eventually went back to work as a teaching assistant, part-time, but it's been a constant battle. This year, I moved to a much cheaper apartment in Prague 7, but I still hardly have enough for food at the end of the month.

JF: Don't your or Karel's parents help out?

NV: Karel's parents were traumatised by his suicide and have been very ill since. Both have been off work and don't have much money. My parents died young, in a car crash. The only people that help me when they can are my sister and my aunt, but it's not much.

JF: When we spoke earlier, at your apartment, you implied that Michal had broken a promise. You said that he'd stopped payments to you.

NV: I was in bits when Karel died. I was so angry with Michal, David and Titus, and didn't want any of them at the funeral. But, afterwards, Michal was insistent on meeting and eventually I allowed it. He told me that whatever had happened, Karel was still his friend and he had a duty to look after us. He offered to pay for my rent from the company. I didn't want to accept, but I didn't really have much choice – I was broke and it was the only way I could have stayed in the apartment I had before. Then, at the end of last year, he told me that he couldn't pay the rent any more. It was something to do with cleaning up the company finances ahead of their big plans to float on the stock market. Michal said that he wanted to carry on helping me but he couldn't. I got the impression that Freddie (Frederick Pedersen) had pushed him to stop.

JF: Did all the directors know Michal had arranged for your rent to be paid?

NV: I don't know, and to tell you the truth I didn't really care at the time. I needed the money. All of them were at least some part responsible for what happened to Karel.

JF: Did any of the wives know about the arrangement to pay your rent?

NV: Again, I don't know and don't care. They were never there to support Karel and me when things started to go bad. They only ever think about themselves, especially Amy (Poláková).

JF: And, you haven't seen any of the wives or girlfriends of the other Midakati directors over the past few years?

NV: No.

JF: Right. Let's move onto—

NV: Actually, I did bump into Zoe once down the city centre when I was shopping. Yes, I remember now. It was at the start of this year, just after I'd been forced to move out of my old apartment. Zoe and I used to get on well at university, even afterwards, but Michal had obviously got at her because she pretty much blanked me. I tried telling her how difficult it was for me but she just said that Michal and David had done everything they could. The conversation was very brief, but it was clear she wasn't interested in helping me.

JF: You haven't seen her since?

NV: No.

JF: Thank you. As I started to say, I'd like to move on to the messages that you started sending. I'm assuming that once the payments stopped, money was even tighter?

NV: As I've told you, I'm broke without that extra money, and I had to move to a cheaper apartment.

JF: So, you started sending the messages to get attention to your situation? To maybe embarrass Michal and the others into helping you with money?

[Pause]

MB: Mrs Vaněková, please answer for the tape.

NV: Yes.

JF: Why didn't you talk to them individually before you started sending the messages?

NV: I did. Come on, I'm not that stupid!

FM: Please calm down. This is a serious matter and we need clear answers to the questions.

JF: Tell us what you did.

NV: Michal phoned to tell me he'd have to stop the payments. I cried and pleaded with him. He said it had been nearly three years, but I told him that I still didn't have enough money to live on. I phoned him and sent him messages over the coming weeks, but always the same thing. I tried David as well, but he was useless and told me to speak to Michal. So, I decided the only way was to try to embarrass them.

FM: It could be construed as the start of a blackmail process.

NV: Think what you want. I never asked for money, or included any threats in the messages. I just wanted them to see their responsibility to help my family: Karel's wife and two children.

JF: Does anyone else know you were sending the messages? Maybe a close friend?

NV: No, I didn't tell anyone.

JF: Why include Freddie as well?

NV: He was Karel's friend, and is just as involved as the rest of them. I know he wasn't involved in the trouble at the business, when Karel had to leave, but he never really stepped in to try and help me. In fact, all he did was push Michal to stop making payments to me. So, in my eyes, he's as culpable as the others.

JF: Earlier you told us that you've only ever sent messages to the directors of Midakati Ltd with the message 'ONE OF US LIED'. Is that correct?

NV: Yes. You can check my laptop. On it you will find all the emails I sent, as well as a document I used for printing the messages I sent by post. I never sent any message saying 'ONE OF US WILL DIE', or whatever it was you said earlier.

JF: But, you must admit how odd it is that these messages get sent by post straight after your messages, with what looks like the same font and layout.

[Pause]

JF: Have you got any idea who would have sent these messages if it wasn't you?

NV: I have absolutely no idea. Anyway, when did these other messages start?

JF: It doesn't matter.

NV: I think I have a right to know if I'm being accused of something—

FM: We will decide what information you will be told. And, *we* are asking the questions.

MB: Mrs Vaněková, we will be checking your laptop as part of the thorough search of your apartment. Is there anything else you want to tell us at this stage, maybe about something we will find?

NV: No! I've told you everything.

MB: Can you confirm where you were on Sunday and Monday? This is to hopefully eliminate you from part of our enquiries.

NV: My daughter was ill. She woke up feeling bad on Sunday morning, with a high temperature. I had to call the doctor out, and she suggested I take her to the hospital for a checkup. My neighbour looked after my son. I didn't get back from the hospital until about nine in the evening. She was feeling better on Monday morning but I kept her off school as a precaution. My neighbour took my son to school. I only really got any time to myself today because they both went to school and today is my day off. That's why I sent the new email messages, probably about ten this morning. But, the messages were the same as before: 'ONE OF US LIED'.

JF: Last question from me. Have you ever heard of a person called Leopold or Leo Holub?

NV: He's the journalist.

JF: You know him?

NV: He called me, wanted to talk to me about Karel and Midakati. I wasn't interested. So, yes I spoke to him briefly over the phone, but I never met him.

JF: Do you know what he was interested in?

NV: We never got that far.

MB: Thank you for answering our questions, Mrs Vaněková. We have further interviews to hold today. Until the results of the search of your apartment and laptop come back, you will be held here at the station. This is standard procedure: we are allowed to hold you for up to forty-eight hours without charging you. We may also need to interview you again later. Interview terminated at 13.21.

NV: Whatever. Just do what you have to do and let me out of here. I haven't done anything wrong.

FM: Interview terminated.

18

Case Study

Despite his best efforts, Jonny had been unable to pacify Nikola Vaněková. She was still ranting at him – about Michal Polák, the other so-called 'friends', and the world in general – when he'd finally exited the interview room. Mikeš and Boukal had left immediately after the interview finished, their excuse being the need to check for updates on the case. But, Jonny had decided to hang around. The truth was that he felt sorry for her. The detective in him had also wanted to hear what else she might say in anger. He'd remained in the interview room, adding words of support and empathy as the uniform officers prepared to take her back to her cell. But, there were no further revelations. Her fury was blinkered by her husband's ex-friends, who had, in her view, cheated him and then driven him to his early death, in the process leaving her own life in pieces.

His instinct was telling him to believe her story. The rage she'd vented had been as pure as he'd experienced in many years of interviewing suspects. He also doubted that Michal and his friends had intentionally set out to hurt Karel Vaněk; they had, after all, been friends since university days. Whilst Jonny had not really liked any of the remaining directors, their actions were probably only intended to protect the company they'd built together. But, Nikola's perception of them was tainted by having to watch Karel's decline up close, and the cruel luck she'd had to subsequently suffer herself.

Sauntering down the inner stairwell of the station, his body and mind were tired. It was only lunchtime, but it felt like he'd been in the boxing ring for the full twelve rounds. What a morning! And, whilst they were slightly further forward in uncovering connections surrounding the murder of David Farrell, it still seemed like the sands were shifting under their feet.

He switched on his mobile, half-hoping for a new message from Ivana to give him a boost. Instead, he saw a message from Leo Holub.

Meet you at the café at five p.m. Come alone or I won't talk.

His immediate reaction was to go to the meeting alone, in secret, without telling anyone. Whilst he was pretty sure he wouldn't be in any danger, he knew instinctively that it wasn't the correct approach. In the past, especially during his last years in the Metropolitan Police, he'd often bent the rules to fit what he wanted: following lines of inquiry when he'd been warned off by his superiors, putting an unauthorised track on a suspect based on nothing more than a hunch, or even going into dangerous situations without backup. This singular focus had never truly backfired on him, but to plough on alone in this situation would be selfish and unprofessional – he worked for Mikeš now, and owed him the respect and loyalty to agree the course of action by consensus.

Jonny descended the stairs and found Dvořáková in the small kitchen, tucked away in the corner of the open plan floor.

"Ahoj, Honza. I was just making a coffee. Do you want one?"

"Good idea. Mind you, it'll be my fourth of the day..." He looked at his watch. "And, all before two p.m. I'll be bouncing off the walls with the caffeine."

She laughed. "Katka will be along with the sandwiches soon."

"That'll make Felix happy."

Dvořáková opened the cupboard and took down another mug. The coffee percolator continued to gurgle away, permeating the air with enticing aromas.

"Have you heard that Nikola Vaněková's story checks out?" she asked.

"I thought it might," he replied brightly, his tone encouraging her to continue.

"Hynek has analysed Nikola's laptop and all the email messages she sent were 'ONE OF US LIED', exactly as she told you. Even the messages sent this morning were like that. The IT contact at Midakati also called Hynek earlier to advise him that Michal Polák and the other directors, including David Farrell, had all received new emails. This all fits with what Nikola Vaněková told us."

"It also supports her claim that she didn't know David had been murdered," Jonny stated. "She was so busy looking after her children, she didn't have time to see anything more than the news headlines."

The coffee machine beeped. Dvořáková poured the filter coffee slowly into the mugs.

"If Nikola didn't send the other messages, who did?" Jonny's question was spoken out loud, as much to himself as Dvořáková.

"Zoe Farrell?" she suggested.

"That's the obvious conclusion," he answered, his tone flat. "I pushed Nikola quite hard about her relationship with Zoe. She admitted to bumping into her once whilst shopping recently, but claims not to have had any real contact with her over the last few years. Or the wives or partners of the other Midakati directors for that matter."

"She could be lying."

Jonny nodded slowly, sipping his coffee and pondering the possibility. "Lucie, you're the budding detective. Imagine this was a case study in your exam tomorrow. What are the key fundamentals of the murder case at this point?"

"Is this a test?" She smiled.

"Well, I did promise to write up a test question for you. But, with this case there just hasn't been the time…"

"No problem."

He grinned teasingly. "But, let's use this live investigation as your test… Why not? It's the best practice you could have, and it'll help fine-tune your investigative thinking."

She leaned her back against the work surface, mug in hand. Her face was set in concentration, deep in thought. "Well, the prime suspect is still Zoe Farrell," she began. "Her fingerprint was found on the murder weapon, after all. I know we haven't found anything on her laptop or phone to suggest she sent any of the messages, but the fingerprint is material evidence. During the upcoming interview, we need to explore possible motive, especially her relationship with David, and also opportunity, including access to a knife like that used to murder her husband."

"Good," he encouraged. "Let's now think about the last message for a minute: 'ONE OF US WILL DIE'. Who could have sent it?"

"It must be someone who knew about the original message because they've copied the style almost exactly, the only difference being they changed 'LIED' to 'WILL DIE'."

"I agree. But surely they'd have known we'd soon find out that Nikola didn't send the changed, second message?"

"Maybe it was a distraction to buy some time," she offered. "Could they be planning something else, maybe another murder?"

"That's exactly what I'm worried about," he confessed, rubbing his chin. "At least we've had Zoe Farrell under observation at her home since last night... But, if she didn't murder her husband, who else is in the current pool of potential suspects?"

"Well, Nikola could be lying, as we've already mentioned. Maybe she found another way to send the second messages, and is now trying to appear innocent. But, she's also in custody... All the directors of Midakati Ltd obviously knew about the messages, plus their wives, and maybe also Freddie Pedersen's on-off girlfriend. The senior management and IT Team at the company would possibly also have been aware of it. I think we can discount his cleaner, or the plumber that came last week." She paused, pursing her lips. "After that, it starts to get difficult because any of them could have told someone else."

Jonny nodded. "And, why kill David Farrell?"

"He was clearly a potentially unreliable character, especially with the drink and drug problem. My guess is that he was making life difficult for the murderer. This could definitely be true for Zoe Farrell, or any one of the directors at the company."

"Do you think all the directors could be in it together? To get him out of the way – either doing it themselves, or maybe organising a professional hit? He was clearly instrumental in the creation of the drone product when the business started, but maybe his presence is now more of a hindrance than an asset?"

"It has to be a possibility," she confirmed, nodding vigorously. "Perhaps we should get a warrant to search through the company documentation, including emails between the directors?"

"It's a good idea, but we'll need something more concrete than just a hunch to get a warrant. I'm sure Michal Polák would find a way to block it."

Dvořáková laughed. "You're enjoying this, aren't you?"

"It's good for me as well," he admitted. "Sometimes when you talk a case through with another person it opens new avenues to explore."

"Yes, I can see that."

"Anything else?" he prompted. "Think about it. You are in the last five minutes of the detective exam tomorrow and you're reviewing your answers. Is there something you've missed? A possibility that nobody else has thought of, another reason why David Farrell was murdered..."

The small kitchen went silent.

"The only other possibility I can think of..." Her voice trailed off, not sounding confident.

"Yes?"

"Maybe someone has used the messages, and David Farrell's murder, to try to frame Zoe Farrell. It seems very unlikely, especially given the evidence, but it must be a possibility."

"Excellent, Lucie. Well done. I also agree it is unlikely because there's no evidence that anyone has a real grudge against Zoe Farrell. And, as for the fingerprint on the knife... well, someone would have to be a magician to pull that trick off."

"Thanks, Honza. That was really useful."

"I think you'll have no problem with the exam tomorrow," he declared. "But, just remember to keep pushing yourself, make sure you've considered every possibility, no matter how unlikely."

They smiled at each other, both pleased with their

contribution.

"Now comes the hard part," he concluded with a sigh. "We've got to keep working all the leads and just hope that the murderer has made a mistake. It's never easy…"

"By the way, we've checked the CCTV from the Můstek metro station and there are clear images of David Farrell and Leo Holub entering the station together. They walk down the steps into the entrance hall, talking to each other, and seem on good terms."

"Interesting. Sounds like they knew each other."

"Also, uniform officers have been watching the journalist's apartment all day, but there haven't been any sightings. They talked to some of his neighbours who have confirmed that he was there over the weekend, but he hasn't been seen since Sunday night."

"He's laying low," Jonny stated. "But, I received a text message just now. He wants to meet me later today. I need to talk to Felix to see how he wants to handle the situation. Leo Holub was clear in his message that he wants to talk to me alone."

"That's very intriguing. But, please be careful."

"I will, Lucie, don't worry. After coming on this long journey to Prague, and discovering my mother's long-lost family, I can assure you that my number one priority is to enjoy it."

"Thanks, Uncle."

They laughed, both enjoying the personal moment in the whirlwind of a full-on murder investigation.

"The only other message for you is that Josef Liška was again looking for you."

"My next job after talking to Felix," he declared. "Let's hope he's found something to help us."

19

Access Rights

The basement was empty and eerily peaceful. Only the low hum of background music broke the unsettling silence. After entering, using the secure keypad system, Jonny stood still to allow time for his eyes to adjust to the lack of natural light. Although painted throughout in brilliant white, the only splash of colour offered by the red soft chairs, the low ceiling and stuffy air made the space unappealing for any type of extended stay.

Jonny had been downstairs on numerous occasions during his time working with the Czech Police, mostly sifting through evidence of an on-going case. But, despite over one hundred people working in the building, he'd never once come across another member of staff using the space. Anyone needing access to the police procedural manuals, or even just to borrow one of the many reference books stored on the shelves, made sure to be in and out quickly, signing the library book for the item they'd borrowed. The only permanent fixture in the lower ground floor was Josef Liška, Mikeš' ex-partner and now the gatekeeper to the evidence room and reference material.

Like every police station basement the world over, the space was used as a vault, hiding away the less glamorous or downright dirty aspects of police work. The storage of evidence was a tedious and laborious job, not one high on most police officer's desired career path. Anyone needing to visit the evidence room, including Jonny himself, was keen to check the required aspects of the case and get out of the basement and back to the sexy parts of the job as quickly as they could.

Liška had gone against the flow a few years before, choosing the sanctity of the evidence room for both personal and professional reasons. Despite a successful career, and wealth of experience working alongside Mikeš for many years, the frustrations of detective work had started to irritate him immensely. His large, bulky frame, built-up over years of excess, had also become a severe limitation to chasing criminals. He instead opted to spend his pre-retirement years alone in the basement, with just his beloved classical music collection to keep him company. Whilst seemingly being out of the way, his knowledge of how things worked, and in particular where to find something, meant he wasn't far away from being involved in almost every serious crime or murder investigation.

Jonny walked forward to the sliding glass window, the only access point for unauthorised personnel to speak to Liška. Next to the hatch was a locked security door with a multiple swipe access and keypad system.

Standing at the window, Jonny could see Liška moving slowly around the office inside, carrying a newly delivered box of evidence. After placing the box onto the correct shelf, Liška stopped and looked upwards, eyes closed, lost in the operatic music playing.

Jonny tapped on the glass gently, trying to subtly get Liška's attention. The music was too loud. He rapped on the window again, this time harder. Liška's entranced state was suddenly broken, but a beaming smile spread across his chubby face when he spotted his waiting visitor.

Liška opened the hatch. "Ahoj, Honza."

"What?" Jonny shouted, the music now overpowering with the window slid open. "Can you please turn it down?"

Liška waddled over to the music system and adjusted the volume to a tolerable level.

"Ahoj, Honza," Liška repeated.

"Ahoj, Josef. How are you, my friend?"

"Happy to see you. Not many people come to see me these days."

Jonny laughed. "I get the impression that's the way you prefer it."

"You may have a point there!"

The men laughed together.

"Josef, this is Mozart," Jonny stated, the realisation suddenly dawning on him. "I've never heard you playing any music down here that wasn't written by a Czech composer."

"Very observant, Honza. You are indeed correct, this is *Don Giovanni*. But, what you probably don't know is that the opera was premiered here in Prague, at the Estates Theatre in 1787. Yes, amazing, isn't it?"

"I never realised."

"Not many people know. But, even more amazing is the fact that the performance was postponed by two weeks because Mozart had supposedly forgotten to compose the opera's overture. The historical records show that Mozart only finished it on the evening before he himself conducted the first performance. Of course, it was a musical triumph and one of Prague's finest moments…"

"Great story. I love coming down here because I never know what new musical gem I'm going to learn."

"I've told you before, Honza, you have a lot to learn about the Czech influence on opera and classical music."

"That I do," Jonny agreed with a resigned shrug of his shoulders.

They listened attentively as Zerlina's famous aria 'Vedrai, carino' came to a close, the tender orchestral coda swirling around her pulsating heartbeat.

"Felix seems anxious about this new case," Liška finally said, turning the conversation back to practical matters. "I think it is bringing back bad memories."

"I assume you were still his partner when the previous Police Commissioner took control of the case concerning the murder of the businessman?"

"Yes, I was. The Commissioner's actions were unethical in my opinion. He was lucky to survive. But, that's what happens when you have friends in high places... Felix was deeply disturbed about it for years. In fact, I'm not sure he's ever really got over it."

"I'm worried he's going to use this case as a chance to right a wrong, or something like that."

"Don't worry, Honza." Liška shook his head dismissively. "Felix knows which side of the law he's on. He might get angry and upset, but I'm absolutely sure he'd never do anything dishonest just to correct something from the past."

"That's good to hear." Jonny paused, collecting his thoughts. "Has Felix discussed Zoe Farrell with you? She's the suspect we're due to interview again about her husband's murder. Marek dug out the old case file, from just over ten years ago, and it had your name down as lead detective. It was a drug raid on a student party, but there were no arrests."

"Yes, he did mention it, asked me to take a look at the file. My memory of that night is not very clear, mainly because no arrests were made. At the time, there was an increasing level of

195

drug use around the universities and we undertook a campaign to raid random parties we heard about. It was less about making arrests, more about scaring people, whilst also trying to educate them on the effects of drugs. You know what it's like though, the police focus soon changed to something else and we had a new target."

"Do you remember Zoe Farrell?"

"I haven't seen her photo yet, but I do remember a young woman who was quite drunk. She wouldn't listen to us and was making quite a nuisance of herself. She took it upon herself to be the spokesperson for the group, claiming we had no right to search everyone at the party. Eventually, she pushed an officer and we took her back to the station."

"Was anyone else arrested with her?"

Liška paused to think, but quickly shook his head. "I only remember one woman – she was very drunk. I'd need to have a look at the file. It might help stir my old brain cells."

Jonny laughed. "Lucie told me you'd found something in the rucksack belonging to David Farrell…"

"Yes. They sent the rucksack over to me last night, once forensics had completed their examination. Dr Králová and her team still have the murder weapon, but the rucksack and everything else in it has been sent over. You should have a look through the evidence box – I have it ready for you. I think you'll find some of the documents useful background information."

"Interesting. Thanks, Josef."

Liška turned around slowly and shuffled over to the shelves. He returned with a cardboard box and pushed it through the hatch along with a paper form. "Just sign here." He placed a pair of plastic gloves on top of the box.

Jonny signed the form and pushed it back through the

window.

"Use any of the rooms, they're all free. But, as usual, please don't leave the basement before returning the box to me."

Jonny grinned. "I wouldn't dare, Josef. I remember your saying: rules are rules."

Liška leaned forward, seemingly worried that he would be overheard. "Last week, one of the detective team took something out of an evidence box without authorisation. He claimed he was in a rush and forgot to get permission. When the box was returned, I re-checked what was inside against the contents list and it didn't match. It was a good job I found it on his desk later in the day. He's learned his lesson – and had a strong telling off – but it would have been so much worse if it had gone missing. He'd have been in massive trouble."

"We've all made mistakes like that early in our careers. Let's hope he learns from it." Jonny picked up the box. "Thanks, Josef, I'll bring it back soon."

Jonny carried the box down the short corridor and entered the first small office. The room was stark, containing only a small table and two chairs.

He put the plastic gloves on and opened the box, first taking out the itemised list of contents and placing it on the table: a clear plastic bag containing the clothes David Farrell was wearing when he was murdered and his black rucksack. The clothes had already been tested by forensics so Jonny put the plastic bag to one side. Lifting the rucksack out of the box, he proceeded to check all the smaller pockets, cross-referencing with the list. As Dr Králová had informed him at the autopsy, the pockets contained only small, personal items including sweets, a small packet of tissues and bike accessories: a portable pump and trouser clips. The first compartment contained only computer wires, a set of small screwdrivers and two USB memory sticks, as he remembered – the laptop had been taken for analysis. He juggled the USB sticks in his palm. Maybe these were what the journalist was looking for, he thought. He put them to the side of the table, his intention being to organise for them to be analysed by Hynek's technical team.

The only other items in the rucksack were the paper files in the biggest compartment, closest to the shoulder straps. He pulled out the folders and, holding them together, turned them clockwise in front of him, studying the hole created by the knife. The puncture was positioned centrally on the A4 folders, but less than ten centimetres from the top edge. Whilst the paper files were thin, each containing a set of papers, they were quite sturdy. Using the files to hold the knife in position was almost inspired, he thought. The murderer must have planned it carefully, and with prior knowledge of what David Farrell carried in his rucksack.

Pushing the box away, he placed the collection of paper files on the table. The first files contained loose papers which seemed to be personal notes: a garbled to-do list, a random scribble of words and sentences across three pages, the writing slanted at seemingly random angles, and some loosely sketched drawings. Jonny couldn't understand the purpose of the papers but it appeared to be related to the design of the company's drone product.

The next paper file contained company documents: agendas for upcoming meetings, product design proposals, and supplier contracts for review. Nothing seemed to catch his eye – just normal business papers.

The next folder was the thickest. The documents at the front were minutes of company board meetings from three years ago, stapled to a signed contract between Midakati Ltd and a company called Blackburn Mann Capital. Jonny shook his head in disdain, pleased not to have heard of them before. The contract was in English and detailed the legal terms of an investment of some kind, but the first few pages he scanned didn't make any sense to him. The magnitude of the contract was unveiled on page five, the stated investment figure of fifteen million euros printed in bold, positioned just below the hole created by the knife that killed David Farrell. The final documents in the file were printed online articles about the investment company. Whilst understanding the documents could be important, Jonny didn't understand their relevance, if any, and knew he was not going to be able to join the dots on his own. Once again, the journalist, Leo Holub, sprang into his thoughts.

The letterhead of the only paper in the last file perked his interest further. The brief letter had been sent to David Farrell by a solicitors' firm in Prague named Willis & Horak.

Dear Mr Farrell,

Further to our recent consultation, I am writing to document my legal consideration of your rights in the event that your wife decides to move abroad, in particular back closer to her family in the United Kingdom...

Jonny sighed in relief, realising he'd found the rift between David and Zoe Farrell. The timing of the find was perfect given that the second interview with Zoe was scheduled to begin in less than thirty minutes.

He slowly read the remainder of the letter. The consultation referred to by the solicitor had clearly been an initial meeting because the advice was fairly generic, and with no great insight.

Jonny noted with interest the question posed about why the married couple had started to live apart in the first place, and also the lack of any reference in the letter to David's history of drink and drug problems. It didn't appear that he'd been full and frank with the solicitor, Jonny concluded.

Liška's instinct had been right. The battle over access rights to their only child, Liam, would definitely have raised the stakes between David and Zoe. Jonny was sure that Zoe would have gained custody in the end, but the process of negotiating a legal framework, possibly including a divorce settlement, would have been messy. It was a further sign, alongside the effect of David's addictions, of an emerging motive for why Zoe Farrell might want her husband dead. Time for some tough questions.

20

Interview 2 – Zoe Farrell

The following is a transcript of the recorded interviews conducted with Zoe Farrell (ZF) on Tuesday, twenty-third June 2010. The interview was held at the police station in Prague Old Town.

Present at the interviews were Chief Warrant Officer Felix Mikeš (FM), Chief Sergeant Marek Boukal (MB), Consultant Jonathan Fox (JF) and solicitor, Brigita Svobodová (BS).

The interviews were conducted in English, in agreement with the interviewee.

Interview #1

MB: Interview commenced at 15.08. Please state your name for the record.

ZF: Zoe Farrell.

BS: Before we begin, I would like you to confirm if any charges are being brought against my client.

FM: Brigita, you already know the situation, it has been laid out very clearly. Material evidence has been discovered that links your client to the murder weapon that was used to kill her husband, David Farrell. Yesterday, and again this morning, we have been busy with the investigation. Rather than keeping your client overnight in a cell, we gained approval for her to stay in her apartment with her son, the only concessions being that her passport and residency papers were confiscated, and she was not allowed to leave without prior agreement. I think this is more than fair given the circumstances. Finally, as you know, we obtained a warrant to search your client's apartment, including her laptop, emails and phone.

BS: What do you plan for this interview?

FM: We have important questions to ask her, in particular about the murder weapon. Depending on the answers we are given, we will either charge your client, ask for an extension to detain her for longer, or release her.

MB: Mrs Farrell, please take a look at these photographs. [Pause] For the purposes of the tape, I am showing Mrs Zoe Farrell photographs of her husband's black rucksack and its contents. These were found on him when he was discovered dead yesterday morning aboard a metro train at the Dejvická station. The photographs include images of a knife found in the rucksack.

JF: Zoe, let me explain what we've found and why you are here. David was killed by the knife you can see in these photos. It was fixed into his rucksack with the blade pointing towards where his upper back would be when he was wearing it. The knife was tied securely into the back compartment by wrapping fasteners inside the rucksack around the handle. To ensure the knife was held in position, and at the right angle, the blade was pushed through the paper files David was carrying in the compartment nearest the straps.

ZF: I have never seen this knife before.

BS: Zoe, remember what I told you. Don't venture any information unless they ask you a specific question. Even then, you don't have to answer a question if we don't think it is necessary.

[Pause]

JF: As I was saying, Zoe, the knife was fixed securely into the rucksack. When David sat down in the seat on the metro train, pushing back hard on the rucksack, the blade came through the material and ruptured his heart, killing him almost instantaneously. As you would expect, a full forensic examination has been conducted on the rucksack and its contents, and I can confirm that we have found your fingerprint on the handle of the knife. In addition to this material evidence, we also have a catalogue of circumstantial information that is not helping your case. Firstly, you confirmed in yesterday's interview that you knew David always wore his rucksack, and that he rarely took it off when travelling due to an old shoulder injury. Secondly, you've also confirmed that you were at David's apartment on Sunday evening, leaving around six thirty. During the visit to David's apartment, you admitted to finding traces of cocaine in his kitchen. We also know how frustrated you were to find out that your husband's drug use had returned. It was the primary reason you and David separated in the first place, and you have since had to endure years of looking after him. And, finally, we believe that you told David you were going to move back to the UK with your son, Liam (Farrell), prompting David to seek legal advice on his rights if—

ZF: I don't know what you are talking about.

BS: I want a break to talk to my client. A fifteen minute break. Now!

MB: Interview terminated at 15.21.

Interview #2

MB: Interview commenced at 15.44. Please state your name for the record.

ZF: Zoe Farrell.

BS: After discussion with my client, we would like to make it clear for the record that, despite the wealth of evidence you claim to have, she has never seen a knife like that in the photos you showed her, nor did she have anything to do with David Farrell's murder. She went to his apartment on Sunday evening, as she told you when you interviewed her yesterday, but that was only to pick up Liam. Despite being separated from David, and having a difficult few years, she still cared for him and wanted the relationship between him and Liam to be as strong as possible. She would never want any harm to come to David, whatever her feelings about the way he lived his life.

JF: Thank you. Can I ask Zoe if she agrees with all of those words because this is a very serious point in the investigation?

ZF: Yes. I would not, and did not, do anything to hurt David.

JF: I know we pushed a lot of information at you at the start of this interview, but I hope you understand why. The reason I summarised the case against you was to see your reaction. I'm sorry if you felt ambushed. I want you to know that we are still keeping an open mind about what happened to David, and we are following up on all the evidence we have. Do you understand?

ZF: Yes.

JF: But, the evidence against you is strong and we need to talk about it. The more information you can provide, the greater chance you have of clearing your name. I don't want to go over all the ground we covered yesterday, only to ask a few specific questions about the new evidence we've uncovered since.

BS: Mr Fox, you have put my client in a very difficult position. She will co-operate with you, but I will be watching the questions very closely. If I detect, at any time, that you are trying to lead her, I will immediately bring this interview to an end.

JF: You have my word. [Pause] Zoe, here is a copy of a solicitor's letter to David concerning his rights if you moved back to the UK with Liam.

MB: For the purposes of the tape, Mr Jonathan Fox is showing Mrs Zoe Farrell a photocopy of a letter we found in David Farrell's rucksack.

JF: As you can see, the letter is dated last week. Why do you think David was taking legal advice on this matter so recently? Are you planning to move?

ZF: Mr Fox, the last three or so years have been very difficult. As I told you yesterday, my main focus during this time has been Liam, but I've also tried to help David as much as I could. As a result, I've had almost no time for myself. I initially thought David would go through a rehabilitation process and then maybe we could have another go at our marriage. It was what I wanted, both for myself and also Liam. But, as time went on, it became clear to me that it would never happen. I've been exhausted: it has been like looking after two children. The only person who has helped me is Michal (Polák), but even I know this was mostly because he needed David functioning in the business. At the start of this year, I decided that the best place for Liam would be back in the UK. I would then have my family around me to help, plus I miss home more and more now. I raised the subject of moving back to the UK with David over five years ago, when things were better between us, before we separated, but it wasn't possible with his responsibilities at the company. He always said that we would go back eventually, but only after the company had been floated and he'd got his money. But, the situation between us had changed, and was never going back to what it was. So, my conclusion was that we should formalise a divorce and I would move to the UK with Liam over the next year, before he starts reception classes at school. There was no urgency, but it was in my opinion the best option. I told David in March and he was naturally upset. We argued a lot in the following weeks. But, and this is very important, I never actually started legal action about the divorce, or told anyone else, even my parents, about moving back to the UK.

JF: Do you think this was the reason why David started drinking and taking drugs again?

BS: Mr Fox, I hope you are not implying that my client is responsible for this—

ZF: Brigita, this is important. I want to clarify the situation for the record. [Pause] Mr Fox, I tried so hard with David, but nothing helped. He was super intelligent, but what came with that was a certain brittleness, not being able to deal with life. I kept his family informed – ask his parents – and was always honest with them. It breaks my heart, but I have to do what is best for Liam. Yes, David was upset and angry, and it is probably connected to the drugs I saw on Sunday, but that was never my intention. I had made my mind up, and will still move back to the UK in due course, but I always wanted David to be as close as possible to Liam.

JF: Did you consider David to be a threat to Liam in any way?

ZF: No, not at all. David was so gentle, and Liam loved him to bits. But, I couldn't tolerate excessive alcohol or drugs being around my son. I told David this was the one non-negotiable point. Somehow we'd managed through without the situation getting really bad, and I had never felt it necessary to seek legal advice on limiting David's access to Liam.

JF: But, you would have had to see a solicitor sooner or later about the divorce and the move…

ZF: Yes, I would. But, I repeat, I haven't consulted a lawyer up to this point. I tried to manage the situation between us, with help from Michal when I needed it.

JF: That is clear for now. Going back to Sunday, how was David when you left him?

ZF: He was angry and defensive, mainly because I'd given him such a hard time about the drugs. But, he knew I was right. He sent me the message later, which I'm sure you've seen, asking me to give him another chance.

JF: Did he indicate if he was due to see anyone else that evening?

ZF: No.

JF: Can you explain how your fingerprint got on the knife?

[ZF and BS are heard consulting, but the conversation is inaudible.]

ZF: As I explained to you yesterday, I quickly searched his rucksack. I did not look closely inside, just waved my hand around inside the compartments and side pockets. I was only interested if there was any dirty washing there… or any drugs. I remember putting my right hand inside all the compartments, holding the rucksack with my left hand. I found nothing inside: no clothes, no drugs, certainly no knife.

JF: Are you sure you didn't feel anything metal or sharp?

ZF: Yes, I'm sure. But, I didn't spend a lot of time searching the rucksack.

JF: So, you don't have any explanation for how your fingerprint got onto the knife handle?

ZF: No. I must have touched it by accident. My fingerprints must be all over his apartment because I went there every week, sometimes twice a week.

JF: Are you sure you've never seen the knife in these photos before?

ZF: I am sure.

JF: Please look again. The knife is quite distinctive, especially the large cross-guard.

[Pause]

ZF: Mr Fox, I've told you already, I've never seen the knife before.

JF: So, you've never owned a knife like this as part of your collection of African artefacts?

BS: Mr Fox, you have searched Zoe's apartment. If you've found any pertinent evidence then ask my client questions about it. If not, I suggest you don't ask open questions intended to trap my client.

ZF: Mr Fox, despite what you think, I've never owned a knife, nor have I ever seen the one in the photos you showed me earlier.

JF: The forensic examination of the murder victim also found your DNA around the groin area of the trousers David was wearing. Did you—

BS: Mr Fox, you should know better than—

ZF: I'm getting fed up with this. I have answered all your questions honestly. But, now you are implying what… that David and I had sex of some kind on Sunday night, when my son was around? Just for the record, the last time that David and I had any sort of intimate liaison was back in 2007, before we separated. I think I've had enough of this…

JF: Apologies if you are offended, but we have to ask these questions. Why did you have a key to David's apartment?

ZF: David and I agreed when he moved out, in case of an emergency. He also had a key to my apartment.

JF: Who else has a key to David's apartment?

ZF: Only Michal, as far as I'm aware.

JF: Does he use it?

ZF: I have no idea. All I know is that David was happy with the arrangement.

JF: Where did you keep your key?

ZF: In my kitchen. I gave it to Chief Sergeant Boukal yesterday.

JF: Have you ever noticed it missing?

ZF: No.

JF: Do you remember anything about the police raid at the student party you attended back in June 1998? You were arrested for assaulting an officer and taken to this police station. You were held for a few hours, and samples of your DNA and fingerprints were taken.

[Long pause]

FM: Mrs Farrell, if you are innocent it will help you immensely if you answer the question.

ZF: I don't remember much, and if truth be known I've tried to forget about it. The police raided a party of university friends, looking for drugs. I was quite drunk and reacted badly because I thought the police were being heavy-handed. They took me away but released me later. It's all a bit of a blur for me really, I don't remember much.

BS: This was something that my client deeply regrets, but university days are not the basis to judge people's future behaviour. Her reputation and record in the community has been exemplary since then.

JF: But, her fingerprints taken at the police station, after the raid on the party, match the fingerprint found on the knife – the murder weapon.

BS: I think we've already covered this.

JF: Moving on, I'd like to ask you a question about Nikola Vaněková.

ZF: Nikola? Why?

JF: Well, we've found out that she was sending all the messages, the ones that said: 'ONE OF US LIED'.

ZF: Really? Why would she do that?

JF: It seems she felt that her ex-friends had turned their backs on her since her husband, Karel, committed suicide.

[Pause]

ZF: I don't really know what to say. I'm shocked. What happened to Karel was very sad, but Michal and David helped her out for as long as they could. Has this got anything to do with David being murdered?

JF: Good question, one that I was going to ask you. Can you think of any reason why Nikola sending some silly but pretty harmless messages to the directors of Midakati would lead to David being murdered?

ZF: Sorry, I have no idea. It doesn't make sense at all.

JF: The other confusing part of this is that Nikola did not send the last set of messages received by post on Monday: the messages that said 'ONE OF US WILL DIE'. Did you send them?

ZF: No, I did not.

JF: All the directors of Midakati received one by post, including David at his new apartment. But, one was not sent to your apartment. Can you think why you wouldn't receive one?

ZF: Mr Fox, as I've already told you, all the messages sent by post to my apartment were addressed to David, not to me. They had nothing to do with me.

JF: Do you have access to any computer equipment other than the laptop in your apartment and your smartphone, both of which we now have in our possession under the warrant?

ZF: No.

JF: Zoe, I know I've already asked you this, but can you think of anyone else who might have had a grudge against David?

ZF: I have thought about this, but I have no names for you. I always believed that David was well-liked.

JF: What about you? Has anyone got a grudge against you?

ZF: Not that I'm aware of.

JF: Who else knew that David never took off his rucksack? That he used to keep it on during a journey, including on the metro?

ZF: I don't know, many people I expect.

[Pause]

JF: Do you know who his drug dealer was?

ZF: Of course not.

[Pause]

JF: Have you heard of Leopold or Leo Holub?

ZF: No.

JF: Really? He was with your husband on the metro when he died.

BS: Mr Fox, you are fishing...

[Pause]

JF: Okay, here's an easy one for you. I understand you and David were supposed to attend Michal and Amy's (Poláková) art exhibition tonight. Is there any reason why that would be significant to this investigation?

ZF: I was supposed to attend. But, I wasn't going because of David. I was going because Amy invited me. If he was there, I would have spoken to him, of course, but we weren't going together. The reason I accepted the invitation is because of my friend, simple as that.

JF: Who is your friend?

ZF: Frida Nilsson.

BS: I think we are done here. You are just asking random questions now. My client has answered all your questions

211

honestly. She maintains that she has nothing to do with the murder of her husband, David Farrell. If you have further questions, we are happy to help you, but only if you clarify whether charges are to be brought against my client.

FM: We have asked all the questions we have for Mrs Farrell right now. Due to the seriousness of the material evidence against her in this murder investigation, she will now be held in custody at this police station. As you know, this is standard procedure: we are allowed to hold her for up to forty-eight hours without charging her. Depending on the further results of the investigation, as well the search of her apartment, we may also need to interview her again later.

MB: Interview terminated at 16.19.

21

Small Island

Jonny sat in the corner, pretending to be disinterested in the comings and goings of the café's customers. Whilst nonchalantly sipping his cappuccino, seemingly oblivious to what was happening around him, his trained eye was however in full surveillance mode. From his carefully selected table, he was monitoring movements at the door by utilising all the available reflective surfaces around the café, including mirrors on the wall and the front windows.

Mikeš was sat at a table around the other side of the counter, his back to the café entrance to conceal him from sight. He'd insisted on being involved in the operation to ensure Jonny's safety; nobody in the team was allowed to operate solo. But, Mikeš had also insisted on a police presence to ensure that Leo Holub was captured even if at the last minute he changed his mind about talking to the police. The agreed police operation was purposefully low-key so as not to scare off the journalist, but planned carefully with readily available backup: Boukal was positioned outside, out of view but with a clear, unobstructed view of the café entrance, and two police cars were on standby, parked in backstreets less than one hundred metres away.

Luka was nervous but trying to act as normal as possible. He'd initially been excited when told about the plan but then the reality of the situation had hit home; he'd become anxious about the role he had to play, convinced that he'd fluff his lines. Jonny tried to calm the situation by assuring Luka that Leo Holub would not be armed or dangerous, encouraging the café owner to just focus on his job: making good coffee. The only unusual demand Jonny made was that Luka temporarily lock the back door, close to the restrooms. The emergency exit door only led into the quadrant behind the buildings, but Jonny wanted to restrict access so that the journalist had just one way in and one way out.

Jonny's reaction to the latest interview with Zoe Farrell was mostly disappointment. Going in, his expectations had been low, but the stoic defence of her innocence had proved feistier than he'd anticipated. The frustration was that they'd learned nothing significantly new to follow-up. The case seemed to boil down to one inflection point: Zoe was either lying, or there was a supportable explanation for how her fingerprint got onto the handle of the knife used to murder her husband. All the other evidence was circumstantial and, whilst it would help build the case against Zoe, it wouldn't be enough on its own to prosecute her.

The only new information that registered as interesting was that Zoe Farrell was friends with Frida Nilsson. She was the artist exhibiting her latest work at Michal and Amy's apartment that evening, as well as being the alibi named by Freddie Pedersen for his movements on Sunday. Whilst Jonny wasn't looking forward to another engagement with Amy, he knew he now had to go to the exhibition. As well as being able to meet Frida, it was an opportunity to speak informally to Michal again.

Mikeš had looked stressed after the interview. He'd admitted to Jonny that the Police Commissioner was keen to wrap up the case quickly; the physical evidence of the fingerprint was considered enough for a strong prosecution case. Back in the

214

Incident Room, Mikeš had paced the limited space muttering to himself, "Something's not right." When Jonny had sought to comfort his friend, Mikeš' terse retort of, "This has got something to do with Michal Polák, I just know it", had done nothing to ease the tension. The planned rendezvous with the journalist had provided a timely distraction, getting them both out of the station and giving a good reason for delaying Mikeš' impending meeting to update the Commissioner.

The clock on the café wall ticked past 5.10 p.m. Leo Holub was late. Jonny had been expecting it and had briefed the team accordingly beforehand. He'd warned that the journalist would most likely stake out the café, ready to bolt at the first sign of the police; keeping Jonny waiting was of secondary importance to making sure he'd come to the meeting alone. Jonny knew that the journalist would wait for as long as he needed to feel comfortable, at the same time testing their resolve.

Jonny calmed his heartbeat, breathing steadily and concentrating on the bitter taste of the coffee. The task ahead didn't worry him, but he was anxious how Mikeš would react. Whilst an experienced detective, Mikeš was agitated by the additional pressure of the murder investigation, the shadow of the flawed case from years ago looming large over the present one. Whilst accepting Mikeš' decision to be involved in the operation, Jonny had been concerned about how recognisable Mikeš was. The compromise agreed was that Mikeš ditched his customary hat and cane, and sat in the corner of the café with his back to the door and counter.

The doorbell tinkled gently. An elderly couple entered, dressed in full tourist regalia, cameras proudly sticking out front. They stood in front of the counter, looking around the café with wide, inquisitive eyes. Luka gestured to a cluster of tables near the front of the café. "Please take a seat. I will come to take your order."

Mikeš hadn't moved when the couple entered. His gaze remained fixed on the back wall of the café, his posture unyielding. But, when the bell rang again almost straight away, he twitched ever so slightly, twisting his head to catch a glimpse of the new entrant out of the corner of his eye. An unsuspecting customer would never have noticed the subtle movement. But, Jonny did. So did the journalist. Before the door had even closed fully behind him, Leo Holub had spun around, jerked the door back open violently, and run back out of the café, heading right towards the river.

Jonny was out of his chair in a flash. He got to the door before Mikeš, who was struggling to get his knees free from under the table. Boukal ran over from his position to the left of the café, phone glued to his ear. "One of the police cars is coming round," he shouted as Jonny set off running down the pavement after Leo Holub.

The elderly couple rose from their table, looking scared. Only Luka's swift action to offer them a drink on the house placated their unease. They sat down compliantly, but remained poised on the edge of their seats, looking uncomfortable, ready to leave in the event of any further action.

Leo Holub had twenty metres on Jonny. Whilst clearly not a natural athlete, the journalist was young and kept moving, his shock of unruly brown hair flopping from side to side as he pumped his arms and legs to maintain the gap between them. His jacket flapped open as he scampered along, his brown satchel swinging wildly around his neck and shoulders.

Approaching the end of the street Kaprova, Jonny thought the journalist was going to duck down the Staroměstská metro

216

station, seeking anonymity amongst the crowd of evening commuters. Seeing the flash of a red tram crossing the T-junction up ahead, Leo Holub instead ran straight past the station entrance. At the junction, he darted straight into the busy road, horns blaring as cars swerved around him. Managing to get across the road unscathed, but leaving chaos in his wake, Leo Holub caught up with the number seventeen tram waiting at the stop. Jonny navigated his way across the road in pursuit, hopping as quickly as he could around the now stationary cars, only to hear the doors of the tram closing. The tram started to pull away, accelerating fast. Jonny stood in the middle of the tram tracks, breathing heavily, and watched forlornly as it sped away. Leo Holub's strained face looked back at him through the rear window of the tram's back carriage.

The approaching police siren was deafening, loudly competing with the blaring car horns from unhappy drivers stationary on the main road. As it manoeuvred its way carefully across the two lines of traffic, Jonny was not surprised to see Boukal at the wheel of the marked police car, its lights pulsing to match the blaring siren.

The police car stopped on the tram tracks and Mikeš waved for Jonny to jump in the back, next to the two uniform officers. Boukal accelerated away before the door was closed, leaving Jonny the frantic task of holding tightly onto the door handle whilst trying to wedge himself into the limited space. The burly officer sitting next to him leaned over and pulled the door close, using his greater arm leverage from the middle seat.

The car engine roared as Boukal closed in on the tram. Within a minute, they were bumper to bumper as it started slowing towards the next stop. As soon as the tram and car had stopped, Jonny jumped out and, edging his way past the departing passengers, climbed onto the back carriage of the tram via the last set of doors. The tram was an old model: two separate carriages with no connection between them. The second, back carriage, was busy, full of commuters heading home in the evening rush hour. He moved his way down the carriage steadily, holding up his police badge and scanning all the passengers, searching for Leo Holub's face amongst the crowd. Only when he'd reached the front of the second carriage did he look up and see that the journalist was now on the first carriage – he'd jumped carriages during the stop. The tram started up again, accelerating fast, moving quicker than the slow moving cars travelling in both directions alongside the river.

Jonny knew that the next stop was make or break. From the second carriage, he could see Leo Holub moving forward, down the first carriage, past passengers, towards the front of the tram. *What's he going to do?* Jonny racked his brains, appealing to his growing knowledge of the city map. *Where is the next tram stop?* He sighed in frustration, not able to place it. Whilst this route was now his daily commute to work, he'd only walked it a few times and hence was not yet familiar with all the landmarks, including the tram stops.

The tram stopped abruptly, throwing many of the standing passengers slightly off balance. Jonny held on to the door frame and was first out as soon as the doors opened. He started running, but Leo Holub was also out quickly. The journalist ran as fast he could, straight down the pavement, his satchel now slung out horizontally behind him like a cartoon character. Jonny followed, gasping for air to fill his failing lungs, his only goal to make sure that he didn't lose Leo Holub before backup arrived. Whilst the journalist was still ahead, he was slowing, losing pace by turning his head to check Jonny's progress behind him.

Within thirty metres, Leo Holub turned onto the narrow bridge running across to Slovanský ostrov, one of the small islands on the River Vltava. Jonny heaved a sigh of relief, knowing that the chase was nearly over. The only other way off the island was through a pedestrian route near a restaurant at the far end of the island and one of the police cars would be able to block it off. Leo Holub was going to be trapped.

As if to ratify the journalist's dire predicament, Boukal skidded the police car onto the bridge and parked across the narrow entrance road. The car, its lights still flashing but the siren now turned off, provided a physical barrier to prevent Leo Holub doubling-back and exiting over the bridge. Mikeš and Boukal hopped out of the car, followed by the two uniform officers from the back seats.

Jonny kept his eye on Leo Holub, now walking down the island, looking over his shoulder, whilst Mikeš bellowed instructions. The two officers immediately started preparations to block off the entry to new visitors wanting to visit the island.

The second police car arrived. Mikeš ran over and briefed the officers through the open window. The car sped off down the main road, lights on and siren blaring.

Jonny pointed down the small island when Mikeš and Boukal caught up with him. Leo Holub could be seen disappearing around the corner of the Žofín Palace, towards the Šitkov water tower.

"The other police car is driving to the visual arts centre, Manes Exhibition Hall," Mikeš relayed to Jonny. "There's a pedestrian walkway around—"

"The restaurant," Jonny finished the explanation.

Mikeš nodded, clearly impressed. "Good knowledge, Honza."

Jonny smiled, pleased with himself. "I know *my* Prague, Felix."

Mikeš slapped Jonny on the back. "Let's catch this journalist and see what he has to say."

They set off in pursuit of Leo Holub on foot, spreading out to cover the width of the small island. The surrounding water completed the tranquil setting, the stillness only broken by shrieks of enjoyment from tourists on the hired pedalos circling the island. They passed through the island gardens, either side of the palace building, the width of the island now narrowing to less than forty metres: Mikeš led from the middle with Jonny and Boukal fanning out either side of him.

At the children's playground, Jonny caught sight of the two uniform officers patrolling the pedestrian exit from the far end of the island. Both exits off the island were now blocked. Scanning the surrounding area, he saw Leo Holub leaning over the side of the railings, clearly assessing his options in the water.

"Leo, the chase is over," Jonny shouted, walking forward. "Let's just have a quiet chat... There's no need for this drama."

Jonny stepped closer; he was now only four metres away. Mikeš and Boukal were running over to join him. The journalist looked at the water again. The swans looked serene, gliding effortlessly on the surface, but the water current was strong despite the summer months.

Leo Holub sat down on the path, resigned to defeat and exhaustion.

Boukal went over and cuffed his hands behind his back. The journalist was still breathing heavily, his head down to avoid eye contact.

"Now you will have to speak to us, whether you like it or not!" Mikeš barked at him with menace.

22

Interview 1 – Leo Holub

The following is a transcript of the recorded interview conducted with Leo Holub (LH) on Tuesday, twenty-third June 2010. The interview was held at the police station in Prague Old Town.

Present at the interview were Chief Sergeant Marek Boukal (MB) and Consultant Jonathan Fox (JF).

The interview was conducted in English, in agreement with the interviewee.

MB: Interview commenced at 17.41. Please state your name for the record.

LH: Leo Holub.

MB: Before we start, I would like to confirm that you have the right to legal representation in this interview. If you change your mind during the interview, just let us know.

LH: Fine.

MB: At the moment, we just want to ask you some questions about David Farrell. You have not been charged with any offence. We will decide how to proceed at the end of this interview.

JF: Leo, why did you come looking for me at the café yesterday?

LH: I wanted to talk to you off the record.

JF: Sadly, everything related to the police is on the record. The idea is that it protects you, but at the same time also protects us. Why did you run away from the café today, when we'd agreed to meet?

LH: I was scared. I have no idea what happened to David Farrell, but I'm worried you're going to try to pin his murder on me.

JF: Leo, we need to clear up your involvement in the events of yesterday. We have no evidence you were involved in the murder of David Farrell, but we do know that you were with him on the metro yesterday morning when he died. We also know that you called him on Sunday evening. It is my belief that David had agreed to pass some information to you, possibly about the company that invested in Midakati Ltd. This is why you met him on Monday morning.

LH: You're good. You'd make an excellent journalist.

JF: I'll ignore that. I'm just trying to get to the truth, whereas most journalists seem more interested in sensationalist lies.

LH: A true man of the people…

JF: Look, you may be a cocky, young journalist who thinks your generation knows better. But, I would like to remind you that you are being formally interviewed about your involvement in the murder of a high profile businessman. If you don't take this seriously, you may end up in very deep trouble.

LH: Here comes the fit-up.

JF: Leo, stop this. Instead of thinking up clever comments, take a few moments and explain how you met David Farrell, and your contact with him up to and including Sunday evening.

[Pause]

LH: I used to work for a series of IT publications, initially in London but then also in Amsterdam. I left because I get bored: I don't like being tied down. Plus, I wanted to travel a bit. After saving up some money, I moved back to Prague two years ago and set up as a freelance journalist. I still write regular articles for the publications I used to work for, as well as researching bigger stories to sell to the online content providers and the national press around Europe.

JF: Why back to Prague?

LH: No reason, really. My mother was ill so I had to come back to the Czech Republic for a while, but I separately made the decision to move back permanently. I can easily travel from here to most places.

JF: Please continue.

LH: I talk to lots of people in the IT world every day. About six months ago, I got a sniff of a story. I was told that the company that invested in Midakati – Blackburn Mann Capital, or BMC as they're commonly known – had made false claims about their support for climate change: they've been piling money into fossil fuel projects across Africa, and also one of the other companies they'd previously invested in was responsible for aspects of the supply chain in delivering trees cut down from the Amazon forests in Brazil. I contacted BMC but they refused to comment. The information was hard to get to because there are many subsidiary companies involved, most of which were set up overseas, but over the following few months I managed to build up quite a damning picture. What I'd initially found was just the tip of the iceberg—

JF: This all sounds very interesting, but what does it have to do with Midakati?

LH: When Midakati took investment from BMC back in 2007, one of the reasons Michal Polák gave for the decision was that BMC had an impressive green agenda. You have to remember that Midakati are a successful company with products based on reusable energy: battery and solar power. In return for investing fifteen million euros in Midakati, BMC got a 20% stake in the company. I could suddenly see a big story. I already had evidence that BMC had lied about their previous and on-going investments in non-green projects. My next step was to determine whether the directors of Midakati knew this but still decided to go ahead with the investment because of the favourable terms of the deal.

JF: Did you make contact with Michal Polák?

LH: I asked for a meeting with him, but he was suspicious because I am freelance. He kept asking what the meeting was about and where the story would be featured. I lied of course. I told his assistant that I was writing a feature about the innovative design of their drone products, as well as the potential transference of the technology to other applications. After ages trying, he eventually bought it and I met him at their swanky offices. The meeting was going fine, we were getting on well. But, when I mentioned the climate change record of BMC, he immediately closed down the meeting and had me escorted out of the building.

JF: So, Michal Polák knew what you were planning to write about?

LH: I didn't exactly tell him, but I assume he guessed when I changed my line of questioning.

JF: What did you do next?

LH: I tried contacting all the other directors of Midakati, but they didn't reply. My assumption was that Michal had got to them.

JF: Including David Farrell?

LH: Yes. Then, I received a solicitor's letter through the post threatening legal action if I published anything incriminating against Midakati, or personally against the directors of the company. I'm used to these bully boy tactics, so I just carried on. I contacted the wife of the ex-director, Karel Vaněk, but she wasn't interested at all.

JF: So, how did David get interested?

LH: I just kept plugging away. Initially I kept sending him snippets of my research by post. Although I included my business card every time, he never called. Then, I got lucky. I was at an IT industry event in Budapest, where he was one of the conference speakers. I managed to bump into him, if you know what I mean, and although he was annoyed at being ambushed, he said he'd give me five minutes. I talked and he just listened: he didn't say anything. At the end of the meeting he just got up and left.

JF: When was this?

LH: Two weeks ago. Then, at the beginning of last week, he called me. He said that my intervention had caused him some concern and he'd since done some research of his own. Whilst he didn't agree with all my findings, citing certain reasons why the true facts were misrepresented, he agreed that BMC had lied.

JF: What was his motive? Surely, he'd potentially stand to lose a lot of money if the company suffered.

LH: I asked him about that. He said that money wasn't what drove him. The purity of the company and the product, especially its green agenda of being carbon neutral by the time of any flotation on the stock market, were the most important factors for him. He told me that if these were compromised he'd rather leave the company.

JF: Why did you target David?

LH: Once I'd completed further research on all the directors, it was clear to me that David was the one to target. He was active online through social media, supporting green causes and donating to charities. If any of the directors were going to turn once they found out the truth, it was him.

JF: What happened next?

LH: When he called me, the conversation was brief, but he told me to call him on Sunday evening. And, that's what I did. On

Sunday, he told me he had a raft of documents for me, briefly explaining what they were. He asked me to meet outside the Můstek metro station at eight fifteen on Monday morning. He said he'd explain more then, as well as give me a USB memory stick.

JF: One or two?

LH: He only mentioned one.

JF: Okay. We know you met him on Monday morning because we've seen you on the metro station's CCTV, plus we also have witness statements from commuters who saw you with him on the train.

LH: I am not denying it, but I have to make it totally clear that I had absolutely no idea anything was going to happen. I had nothing at all to do with his death.

JF: Just explain what happened. Step through it slowly.

LH: I was waiting for him at the station entrance on Vodičkova, as agreed. He greeted me but was very serious. Before continuing any further, he said he wanted my assurance that his name would not be mentioned in any article I wrote. I agreed. He explained that the USB stick contained documents he'd found on Midakati's company servers, documents he'd obtained from the Internet, as well as a brief document explaining where to look for the contradictions. He then told me that he'd been back over documents presented to the directors before the investment from BMC was approved, and in his words they contained 'some barefaced-lies'. He said that he was going to take what he'd found to the Midakati Board of Directors with the view to getting the investment rescinded, replacing BMC with a new investment partner. But, he made it totally clear that he didn't want any of this included in what I wrote. His plan was to get the situation corrected quickly, so that when any article came out, Midakati could comment that they had been misinformed at the time of the investment decision and had already taken corrective action.

JF: To be clear, he said to you that he was going to take on Michal Polák and the other directors over the matter?

LH: Not exactly in those words, but yes. There was no doubt in my mind that this is what he meant.

JF: Did he give you the USB stick?

LH: No. I think he was testing me. He told me to ride with him to Dejvická. We entered the metro station and descended the escalator, him in front holding his bike, then waited for the train on the platform. Whilst we were waiting, he told me that he'd raised the matter with Michal Polák at an event on Sunday. Michal had got really angry and threatened David, saying that he'd kill him—

JF: Are you sure of that?

LH: Absolutely sure. That's definitely what he told me. I just laughed, reminding him that people say that sort of thing all the time. He gave me a very grave look, and said something about Michal being willing to do anything if people tried to block him. His words were something like: he'd trample over his dead mother's grave to get his own way.

JF: Are you sure? The insinuation is very serious.

LH: It is what David Farrell told me. Clearly it is third-hand, but I'd be willing to testify in an affidavit, or something like that.

[Pause]

JF: Back to Monday morning, you got on the train together...

LH: Yes. I stood in the carriage whilst he parked his bike and took a seat. There was only one spare seat, on the end of the row, so he sat down and I positioned myself to stand in front of him. It was a light-hearted conversation, we were talking about people we both knew in the IT industry. He peeled the banana he'd been carrying in his hand, took a bite, and then sat back in the seat. I carried on talking, but he didn't respond. It was strange. I asked him a direct question, but he didn't reply. His eyes then started to glaze over, and he slumped forward in the seat. It was a weird sight because he was still holding the banana. I knew something was seriously wrong but I didn't know what to do. It looked to me as if he'd been poisoned.

JF: When David sat down, did he lean back hard on his rucksack?

LH: He must have, I suppose, because he still had the rucksack on. Otherwise, he wouldn't have been able to fit onto the seat. But, why is that important?

JF: Doesn't matter. Please continue.

LH: I tried moving him by shaking his shoulders, but he remained slumped forward. I froze, scared, not sure what to do. It all seemed to happen so fast, a blur. I was panicking…

JF: Take your time.

LH: The train was approaching Dejvická. I didn't know what to do. I'm ashamed to say that I searched the pockets of his jacket and the outer compartments of his rucksack. It was a stupid thing to do. I should have just reported the situation to the station staff at the last stop.

JF: You were looking for the USB stick?

LH: Yes. But, I didn't find it. I feel so stupid now. I didn't take anything from him, nothing at all. I waited for all the passengers to leave the train, then I also walked out and exited the metro station. I went back to my apartment, collected some things and went to stay with my girlfriend.

JF: You have made this very difficult for yourself. We could have sorted the situation out quickly if you'd have gone to a police station immediately. Your actions have delayed us getting this information for nearly two days.

228

LH: I'm sorry. I was scared. What he told me about Michal Polák totally freaked me out. I was obviously concerned about getting the blame pinned on me, but I was also worried that I'd be next. I now know it was the wrong decision, but at the time I thought it was best to lie low and try to talk to you privately. Hence why I came to the café yesterday.

JF: Are you sure there isn't anything else you need to tell us? If we find out you're withholding information for your own purposes, like writing an article, you will definitely be charged.

LH: No, I have told you everything.

JF: You will be held here at the station until we can validate what you have told us. We will then decide how to proceed, in particular whether you will face any charges. Also, I don't want any articles written on this subject until you get clearance from us. Do you understand me?

LH: Yes.

MB: After this interview, you will need to provide DNA and fingerprint samples. One of the detective team will also sit with you so you can provide all the details of your route back from the Dejvická station, your girlfriend's address, and, importantly, all the research you have collected on BMC and Midakati.

LH: Understood.

MB: Interview terminated at 18.23.

23

Too Close For Comfort

Leaving Boukal to deal with Leo Holub and the associated paperwork, Jonny headed out of the police station in haste. Next stop was the art exhibition being hosted by Amy Poláková. Whilst still harbouring some concern about her potential to embarrass him, he knew the opportunity to talk to all the main players in David Farrell's life, as well as observe the dynamics between them in a social situation, was too good to miss. He especially needed to press Michal Polák about the information provided by the journalist, as well as introduce himself to Frida Nilsson.

Amy had told him the exhibition started at seven thirty p.m. Somehow the day had disappeared in the blink of an eye and the time was fast approaching seven p.m. He was running late. His strong preference was to arrive early – having the element of surprise on his side – to observe the guest's reactions as they were introduced to the police detective hunting David Farrell's murderer. These were situations he enjoyed, and revelled in. Watching a person's eye and mouth movements closely could provide a window to their soul: the unintentional facial microexpressions exhibiting emotions such as surprise, fear or disgust. These natural reactions, along with body movements and gestural shifts, could provide valuable insight into someone's real feelings.

After scurrying through the cobbled streets of the old town and reaching the river, Jonny spotted a number two tram approaching. He managed to get across the main road in time and jumped aboard the last carriage before the doors closed. Only once he'd sat down did he realise he was following the same route as in the earlier chase after Leo Holub. He smiled wryly; how funny it was, he thought, that a normal day at work could turn out to be a hop-on hop-off tour of one of the most historic cities in the world.

The tram was fast, its progress aided at road junctions by the reduced number of cars now on the road. After striding up the stairwell of his building, two steps at a time, quickly jumping into the shower, and changing into a clean shirt and a fresh pair of trousers, he was ready by 7.40 p.m. Not bad, he thought – work late, get home early. After pulling a comb through his still wet hair once more, he put on his best jacket and left the apartment.

Although time was against him, Jonny had still managed to call Mikeš and update him. The news from the Police Commissioner was less positive: he wanted to meet with Mikeš and Jonny the following morning, and he'd stipulated that Zoe Farrell be charged with her husband's murder by four p.m latest if no mitigating evidence was uncovered in her defence. Jonny had half expected this, his faith in senior police decisions never amounting to much. The important point he took from the call was that time was running out. Whilst he had nothing concrete to support his claim, he was starting to believe, like Mikeš, that there was something they were missing – it certainly wasn't the cut and dry case it appeared to be on the surface. They needed a breakthrough, and quickly, if the investigation wasn't to be closed down soon, before they could get to the right outcome.

Amy answered the door within one ring. Jonny still had his

hand on the doorbell when her beaming smile lit up the hallway. Whilst she seemed happy to see him, Jonny could detect an element of surprise around her eyes. Good, he thought, she wasn't expecting me to come.

The awkward moment allowed him a fleeting moment to silently take in her beauty again. Everything about her makeup and outfit was immaculate. Her blonde, curly hair was pulled up high on her head, the sparkling jewellery setting off her slender neck and bare shoulders. The satin dress hugged her curves, splitting just above her knees and tapering to a finish behind her calves. She looked stunning, a perfect hostess, and it was clearly *her* evening.

"Ahoj, Honza." She tilted her head playfully. "Sorry, I wasn't expecting you. One of our other guests just pressed the buzzer outside the building. I thought it was them."

"Sorry," he faltered. "You did invite me, remember? After I thought about it, I decided you were right—"

"I'm always right. Just ask Michal." Her smile was beguiling, and immensely confident in the knowledge that no one was going to contradict her. "You know you're always welcome. It's lovely to see you. But, your hair is still wet…" She reached out and ran her fingers gently down the side of his hairline, above his right ear. "You should let me know next time. I'll come and style it for you."

Jonny stood disarmed. "Well…"

She smiled, enjoying his discomfort.

"Come on in," she pleaded, extending her arm, the implication in her tone being that he was the one holding them up. "Almost all the guests are here. I'll introduce you to everyone once I've welcomed these last few. They should be coming up in the lift now."

232

Jonny waited courteously by the door, knowing he was the outsider. Whilst he hadn't exactly gate-crashed the party, he understood how some in attendance might conclude that he'd done so.

Amy didn't seem to register any signs of conflict. In fact, she seemed pleased to be able to announce a new face to her important group of friends. As they walked around the living room, Amy introduced him to all the guests, switching between using his formal title, calling him the top detective that had solved The Old Town Square Murder, to quips such as, "He prefers to be called Honza but I call him Sherlock." She was in total control, obtaining gasps, murmurs of "Congratulations", and even chortles, all on cue as she planned. Jonny smiled cordially and shook hands, knowing that any resistance was futile – Amy had the baton and she was orchestrating the show to her own tune.

The guests represented a thin slice of Prague's high society: a selection of prominent Czech artists were in attendance; the Swedish, American and British Embassies were represented; a dignitary from the Prague Mayor's office provided the local politics angle; even an elected official from the Government Treasury department was under Amy's influence enough to attend the exhibition. The only person he wasn't introduced to was Frida Nilsson. When Jonny asked, Amy told him that she was in the restrooms and that she'd introduce them later.

The living room had been rearranged since his visits on Sunday and Monday evening. The sofas and furniture had been pushed back near the French doors, allowing a central area for guests to mingle in comfort. A long table carried perhaps the best looking canapes he'd even seen. This judgement was, however, more influenced by the sudden realisation that he hadn't eaten since lunchtime.

He walked around the perimeter of the room, studying the paintings on show. The oil landscape paintings were lightly textured, but rich in colour. He found himself standing in front of a painting of Old Town Square at dusk – his favourite time to walk the cobbled space – mesmerised by the merging twilight colours of day and night. He'd always found paintings hard to relate to, but this canvas seemed to be calling to him, demanding his attention.

A waitress approached him and handed him a flute of champagne. He took a sip, starting to relax and enjoy himself, only to turn around and see Michal Polák, Titus Arnold and his wife, and finally Freddie Pedersen all glaring at him. "Do you think this is appropriate?" Titus hissed. "David has hardly been dead a day... Anyway, I thought you had a suspect."

Jonny knew he had a choice: either to apologise in some way to pacify the situation, or try to provoke a reaction. He went for the latter. "Na zdraví," he said, lifting his glass in toast.

"Amy invited me," he added swiftly. "But, I'm keen to know who told you about our suspect. As far as I'm aware, nobody outside of the police knows this information." The fleeting, worried glances of the others towards Michal Polák told Jonny everything he needed to know.

"I think it's disrespectful," Titus' wife snarled, pulling her husband away forcibly by his upper arm.

"I'm going to see if I can help Frida," Freddie added, scampering after them.

"I'll need to formally interview both of you again tomorrow," Jonny shouted as they walked away.

Jonny was left with Michal. The silence between them hung heavily in the air. Michal seemed to raise himself up, extending

234

the frame of his body. He towered over Jonny, who himself was not short. Michal flexed his shoulders and flicked his thick mop of hair, as if preparing for a fight.

"I believe you've already met Leo Holub." Jonny fired the first salvo. "We interviewed him a few hours ago, and he gave us some very interesting information."

"He's one of those parasites that has no backbone, living off other people's misery: a lowlife. I met him because I thought he had an interesting angle, but he was just fishing – he had nothing."

"Well, David didn't think so. He met Leo yesterday morning at the metro station, ready to hand over some information on BMC, your investment partners." Jonny smiled dispassionately. "But, somehow, before David had a chance to hand over the information, he was murdered. Strange that, don't you think…?"

Michal stepped forward into the space between them. "If you want to talk to me again, I suggest you contact my solicitor." The last words were spat out in anger, and people standing close by turned to see what the commotion was.

Amy suddenly appeared by her husband's side, her smile unaffected by the increased tension in the room. "Come on, darling, I'm about to make my speech." She yanked Michal so hard he nearly toppled over, his concentration focused on locking eyes with Jonny rather than watching his feet.

She clapped her hands excitedly and waited for everyone's attention. Michal stood next to his wife in support, but his angry eyes remained fixed on Jonny across the room.

As Amy started speaking, initially welcoming her guests and thanking them for coming, Jonny scanned the friends around the room. Her tone was light and playful, as always, openly teasing some of her guests, but pulling it off without generating any offence.

Amy turned to Frida, beckoning her to step closer. "Ladies and gentlemen, Frida was already talented when I met her. But, over the last decade, her work has become more mature with age, to the point where she is now one of the most renowned artists working in the city. Michal and I are delighted and proud to be able to sponsor this event, and play a small part in her success."

Watching Frida intently, Jonny spotted a momentary narrowing of her eyes and a tightening of the muscles around her mouth. If he wasn't mistaken, the facial gesture was one of contempt: a flash of irritation or disapproval, an almost certain dislike of what her supposed friend had just said. The natural, inescapable facial expression was quickly replaced by smiles as she took over from Amy, explaining the themes of her latest collection, inviting everyone to study the paintings and ask any questions they had. Jonny was also interested to hear that all the framed pieces were available for sale.

He started to walk across the room towards Frida, when a large woman with a bouffant hairstyle accosted him. She was wearing what he would later describe to Mikeš as a meringue dress, and her high-pitched voice indicated that she'd already drunk one glass of champagne too many.

"Mr Fox, how are you finding Prague? My name is Felicity, my husband is the British Ambassador. We've been here for four years now, and we absolutely love it. Much better than Stockholm, where he was posted before – too cold! Don't get me wrong, it can still be cold in Prague over the winter, but I couldn't stand the snow for almost five months of the year. Awful! It's fine for you men, but it's a nightmare for us ladies when it comes to choosing what to wear to events like this…"

He was stuck. Subtle attempts to extricate himself from the

conversation proved futile, the monologue keeping him pinned to the side of the room. Felicity just kept talking, and talking, arms out wide to marshal any getaway moves.

Discreetly watching Frida Nilsson across the room out of the corner of his eye, he suddenly saw his chance. She was closing her conversation with the man from the Swedish Consulate and his wife, turning to look for a fresh glass of champagne.

"Excuse me, please," Jonny said to Felicity with delicate force, readying to move away.

"But, Honza, you haven't heard the rest of my story…"

"Sorry. I just need to congratulate the artist on such an excellent gallery of paintings."

Felicity huffed silently and joined the group next to them. Jonny could hear her interject into their conversation. "Have I told you that my son has been offered a place at Oxford?"

As swiftly as he could, Jonny picked up a fresh glass of champagne from a waitress' tray and walked over to Frida Nilsson. "Were you looking for one of these?"

"Thank you," she replied, accepting the offered glass. Her hair was long and blond, but that's where any comparisons with Amy stopped. Her dress was elegant but not showy, handmade to retain a bohemian influence.

"You must be Detective Fox. I'm Frida."

"Yes, I know. Congratulations on the exhibition. It looks to have been a great success. Before anyone else gets to you first, I'd like to buy the painting of Old Town Square at dusk. I've just moved in downstairs and it will be perfect for my wall."

"That's lovely. Thank you so much… And, yes, I promise you can have it."

"I came here from the UK a few months ago and the square is very special to me. Your painting captures the mystique of the

237

space perfectly."

"Thank you." Her dancing eyes and controlled smile were offset against each other: the artist loving the compliment but wanting to keep her response in check. "I only ask if I can borrow the painting sometimes, if and when I need it for a larger exhibition of my past works."

"Of course," he agreed. "It would be my pleasure."

A stalled silence descended, the next subject of conversation obvious but not easy in the surroundings.

"I suppose you also want to talk to me about David's murder."

"Well, yes. I know that our detective team have talked to you in order to establish Freddie's alibi on Sunday. And, by the way, we have been very discreet."

"Thank you."

"But, I didn't realise until about an hour ago that you were also friends with Zoe Farrell."

A confused frown developed across Frida's forehead. "I've known Zoe since university, Mr Fox. Same as Amy, and the others."

Now it was time for Jonny to look puzzled. "So, you've known each other for a long time?"

"Zoe is lovely, maybe a bit too serious at times. But, yes, our friendship goes back over ten years."

"Sorry to press you, but who do you mean by 'the others'?"

"I thought you knew." Frida angled her head as she looked at him. "I mean, you're the detective…"

"It would be helpful if you could just tell me."

"Amy, Zoe and I all shared a student house. Along with Nikola Vaněková, as you know her, and also an Australian girl, Danni Hogarth. We all stayed in Prague after university, apart from Danni. She worked here for a few years, then went travelling, moving back to Australia about five years ago."

"So, you all shared a student house together," Jonny repeated slowly, absorbing the information as he spoke. "And, three of the women in your house married men living in the house with Michal Polák. In fact, four relationships if I include you and Freddie."

"Yes. Strange, isn't it? We lived in the same street as them, and the two houses were almost inseparable in the second and third years at university."

"Inseparable is one word," he replied, pursing his lips in concentration. "Frankly, it all sounds a little incestuous to me, too close for comfort."

24

Ulterior Motive

Wednesday, 24th June 2010

He'd slept badly again, waking up numerous times during the night. The tangled interconnections of the people surrounding David and Zoe Farrell's lives, both individually and together as a married but recently separated couple, had played tricks with his mind; images of faces or words said over the past days kept popping up in his hotchpotch picture reel of dreams. At one point, only an hour after first falling off to sleep, he'd woken with a jolt in the belief that Amy Poláková was standing behind him, ready to run styling gel through his hair and give him the fresh, new look she'd promised.

This was however nothing new. During his career in the Metropolitan Police, he'd always slept intermittently at best during murder investigations. The distress of the victim's loved ones played on his sensibilities, his normal disposition only returning once the case was solved. He felt personal responsibility for bringing the perpetrator to justice – it wasn't just a job to him.

Sitting up in bed at two a.m with a soothing herbal tea, he'd been tempted to go into the police station and sit in front of the Murder Board. But, somehow, sleep had eventually caught him. When he woke with the six thirty a.m alarm, he'd found a scribbled note to himself on the bedside cabinet, something he was hardly conscious of writing in the middle of the night. The note luckily was clearer than his now clouded thoughts: 'Find how Zoe's fingerprint got on the knife or charge her'.

He'd worked with many police officers who'd been able to find a way to detach themselves from personal involvement in the crime, seeing an investigation as merely part of their job. Jonny had always been different and knew it was too late to change. During the long night, the image that kept coming to him behind his closed eyelids was that of little Liam Farrell looking lost. Jonny knew what was playing on his mind – he needed to be sure that Zoe Farrell was guilty if she was to be charged with murder. The thought of leaving Liam without a parent throughout the rest of his childhood was hard to bear, and any doubt at all would burn a hole in him for the rest of his days.

The other truth was that his telephone conversation with Ivana the previous evening was also playing on his mind.

The atmosphere at the art exhibition had been tense after Jonny had finished talking to Frida Nilsson. Amy had managed to contain any lasting damage to the evening, skilfully circling around her guests with effervescence, keeping them occupied with funny stories, offers of more canapes and top-ups of champagne. Jonny marvelled at her ability to work the room as hostess, keeping everyone smiling. Eventually though, the piercing stares across the room became too much. He made his excuses to Amy, and said goodbye to Felicity and a few others he'd spoken to. His final act was to thank Frida again, at the same time pressing his business card into her palm to seal the deal on the painting.

Back in his own apartment, he'd suddenly realised how ravenously hungry he was: the canapes had been tasty but had hardly touched the border of his appetite. He ordered a delivery pizza, put on Bob Dylan's *Together Through Life* album, and sat in his new favourite chair with a malt whiskey. The opening track of 'Beyond Here Lies Nothin'' usually soothed his nerves, putting all his worries into perspective. But, not this evening. He'd quickly found himself out of his seat, pacing the room. He knew he needed someone to offload to. He was also missing Ivana.

"Honza, I'm in bed. You're calling a bit late."

"Sorry. I just wanted to talk to you. I've had a bit of a bad day…"

"I thought every day was a bad day when you're working a big case."

Jonny sighed. "You're probably right." He'd sat back down on the reclining chair, his body starting to relax at last.

"I don't know why you do it. Remember, Honza, you only live your life once. Maybe you should try something else." Her voice went up an octave, suddenly infused by a good idea. "You could try painting."

He laughed. "You always make me smile, even when you're telling me off."

"I'll take that as a compliment, Mr Detective."

"There's just this poor, little boy," he began, his tone serious. "His father has been murdered and his mother is the prime suspect. But, it doesn't feel right to me. It's, I don't know… too neat. Felix and I both sense it, but I'm concerned we're not going to have enough time to unravel what has really happened."

"Yes, you will," Ivana replied firmly. "Your job may drive me crazy at times, but I'm proud of you. I know you'll do the right thing, and also do it as best you can. It's one of the reasons why I love you."

242

Jonny jolted forward in the chair, almost dropping his glass. *What did she just say?*

Before he'd a chance to respond, Ivana was talking again, firmly in control. "But, whatever you do, don't be late for your name day celebration tomorrow night. Remember, seven p.m at the Hloupý Honza. I've organised something special with Jerry."

"Okay," he stuttered, still reeling from her previous statement.

"If you're late, there will be big trouble!"

"Good night, Ivana. Sweet dreams."

"You too, Honza. Dobrou noc a sladké sny."

He'd rocked back in the chair after finishing the call. *Love.* That's definitely what she said. An irrepressible smile overtook him as he realised that he felt the same. He didn't know how to express it, do it proper justice with words, he only knew that he'd never felt this way about anyone else before. He'd wondered before whether it was the mystery of falling in love in a foreign city that was luring him in, playing to the romantic fool inside, but this time apart, and the move to a more serious stage in their relationship, had only heightened his feelings for Ivana.

Now walking along the river towards the station in the fresh morning air, he started to doubt whether she'd meant it the way he'd heard it. Her English was excellent, but she often got the wording incorrect. The perfect example was her use of 'upstairs' to describe to him if something was in a top cupboard, usually when cooking together in her kitchen. When he'd first queried what she meant, she'd only waved it away as nonsense, explaining that Czech people used 'up' or 'upwards' in many contexts: she was just confused. But, he'd noticed that she'd kept on saying the same thing – her little foible, she explained – despite him correcting her. Was it possible, he considered, that

243

she'd also used 'why I love you' out of context? He sighed heavily, sure only that he had a poor track record in matters of the heart.

Despite there being plenty of cars on the road at the early hour, 7.20 a.m by his watch, he cut a solitary figure walking the river path. The lapping waves and shimmering low sunlight on the river surface added rhythm to his long stride as he watched the city skyline break out from its shadows. I must have the best commute to work in the world, he thought, resolving to put thoughts about what Ivana meant out of his mind and just enjoy the ride – wherever she was going to lead him.

His mobile started ringing, startling him.

"Honza, where are you?" Mikeš barked before Jonny could even speak.

"Good morning, Felix," he replied sarcastically.

Mikeš could be heard tutting on the other end. "Marek and I are outside your building, but you're not answering the intercom."

"That's because I'm walking alongside the river, near the Dancing House—"

"Stay right there. We'll pick you up." The line went dead.

The unmarked, black Skoda Superb pulled up alongside him within three minutes. Jonny opened the back door and got in, only to see Dr Králová also sitting on the back seat.

"Don't worry, Honza, I won't bite," she mocked him on seeing his surprised face.

"Sorry. Good morning, all."

Mikeš and Boukal greeted him from the front seats. Jonny could see that Mikeš was wearing a summery pink shirt and flowery tie combination to complement his usual tweed suit.

"Felix kindly picked me up this morning," Králová

explained. "Marek is dropping me off at the hospital if that's okay with you."

"Of course, Ella. It's nice to see you."

"And, Happy Name Day," she added, her wishes quickly echoed by Mikeš and Boukal.

"Thank you."

"Are you having a big celebration tonight?" she enquired.

"No. Ivana has something planned at the pub, but it will be small. The main priority is to get this murder investigation closed."

Boukal steered the car away from the kerb, into the growing rush hour traffic. Jonny clipped in his seat belt, half-expecting the car to roar in acceleration. But, to his total surprise, Boukal had metamorphosed into a chauffeur, setting off at a sedate pace and avoiding any unexpected jerky movements. Jonny smiled, knowing that this was all due to Králová's presence – under Mikeš' strict instructions, of course – but was nevertheless happy to accept the resulting smooth ride.

"Actually, I do have an ulterior motive for hijacking a ride. I called Felix last night and told him that I'd found something interesting…"

Mikeš turned from the front passenger seat, nodding knowingly at Jonny.

"Firstly, I want to give you a summary of what I've been doing since the autopsy," she stated, controlling the pace of the narrative. "We've completed a thorough forensic examination of David Farrell's apartment. The fingerprints we've found belong to Zoe Farrell, as you know, her son, Liam, Michal Polák, the new and old cleaners, plus the plumber, who Marek managed to track down. Same for the DNA fibres we found."

"I asked Ella to take another look at Michal Polák's DNA

and fingerprints," Mikeš blurted out, interrupting her flow.

She glared at him, pausing for dramatic effect. "I reviewed again where Michal Polák's DNA and fingerprints were found, but I didn't find anything suspicious. They were found mostly in the living room, but all in places you would expect for a visitor: on the front door, on the leather sofa etc. But, I couldn't find anything linking Michal Polák to David Farrell's rucksack, including the murder weapon, or the clothes the victim was wearing on Monday morning."

Jonny's forehead was creased in confusion, unclear where the briefing was going, and especially why Mikeš looked so interested.

"There is one set of DNA and fingerprints we found at the apartment that we've been unable to account for. The fingerprints appear mostly in the kitchen, but also in the bathroom and living room, as well as DNA on the outside of the rucksack. We've checked against all the DNA and fingerprints you've taken as part of the investigation, including Leo Holub and the other directors of Midakati Ltd, and also against the police database, but there's no positive identification. I had the DNA and fingerprint checks repeated to be sure, but still nothing."

"There could be a simple explanation," Jonny offered. "David's drug dealer may have visited him over the weekend. He or she could have moved around the apartment and touched David's rucksack for some reason."

"That's very possible," she agreed. "Maybe we'll never know. The only other DNA we found on the rucksack belonged to David Farrell's old cleaner – she must have moved the rucksack when cleaning his apartment. But, the conclusion at this stage is the same: the only DNA and fingerprints found on the murder weapon *and* the rucksack belong to Zoe Farrell."

246

"You double-checked?"

"Yes. I had to make sure. The samples we collected match with the police database. There is no doubt."

"We've checked David Farrell's phone records thoroughly," Boukal said, eyes fixed ahead on the road, "but unfortunately not found any link to an unidentified person such as a drug dealer."

"David would have been very discreet," Jonny stated. "He would have known the potential damage to his career. Plus, Zoe Farrell was watching him like a hawk." He sighed heavily. "Anyway, I'm not sure this is going to get us anywhere..."

"We haven't yet taken DNA and fingerprint samples from the wives and girlfriends of the directors," Mikeš commented, his voice full of early morning enthusiasm. "We still need to check Amy Poláková, Elena Arnold and Frida Nilsson."

"That's true," Jonny confirmed. "And, we should do so for completeness. But, I really don't see what it is going to achieve. We might identify the mysterious fingerprints at David Farrell's apartment, including on his rucksack, but it will not explain how Zoe Farrell's DNA and fingerprints are all over the rucksack *and* the murder weapon. And, to be honest, if we can't explain that she probably is guilty and should be charged with her husband's murder."

"Go on, tell him," Mikeš enthused, his grin more akin to an excited young boy in a sweet shop.

Králová shook her head in mock irritation.

Jonny looked expectantly between Mikeš and Králová.

"Firstly, I want to cover off the various letters received, including the envelopes which were kept. The fingerprint checks showed nothing unusual. Each letter had the fingerprint of the recipient, as you'd expect, but no other common fingerprint was found. There were plenty of unidentifiable fingerprints on the

247

envelopes but this is because the letters would have been handled by multiple people during the post sorting process."

"I didn't expect anything else," Jonny noted. "The person who sent the second messages wouldn't have been sloppy enough to leave a print on the envelope of each of the last letters."

"Secondly, there's the contents of the murder victim's rucksack and the clothes he was wearing when he was found. These were analysed and then sent over to the evidence room, as you know. We still have the knife just in case any further tests are required."

Jonny looked between Mikeš and Králová again, not understanding where the drawn-out explanation was going.

"The only other bits of evidence we have at the morgue are the loose papers and the empty envelope that you found in David Farrell's apartment. Copies of the papers have already been sent to the technical team. We'd also dusted them all for fingerprints but found nothing unusual, only David Farrell's fingerprints. Early last evening, however, I decided to have a closer look at the empty envelope because I remember you saying that it was sealed when you found it."

Jonny nodded his head. "I opened it carefully with a pen, but it was empty."

"Well, I put the envelope under the microscope and found two fine hairs inside – hairs from a child's head, to be precise. I despatched one of my team over to Zoe Farrell's apartment and he came back with the hairbrush from Liam Farrell's bedroom. You've guessed it, the hair samples match."

"There was definitely nothing else in that envelope," Jonny confirmed. "The only rational explanation must be that David Farrell suspected that he wasn't Liam's father, and had collected the hairs for a paternity test."

Mikeš was grinning from ear to ear.

"Exactly as I thought," Králová confirmed. "We know that Liam is Zoe Farrell's son from the medical records we have. So, I decided to run a paternity test for all the directors of Midakati Ltd, including David Farrell, and—"

"Let me guess..." Jonny glanced at Mikeš who was still beaming. "Michal Polák is the father."

It was Králová's turn to nod.

25

The Bigger Picture

Mikeš was still beaming when Boukal pulled up in front of the hospital. After promising to email over the results of the paternity tests, Dr Králová wished everyone a good day and got out of the car.

Boukal accelerated away, freed from his constraining chauffeur role. Back in racing driver mode, he effortlessly steered the car at speed around the narrow streets of the old town, his almost relentless honking of the car horn the only competition for the squeal of the tyres on the cobble stones. The silent journey was concluded within minutes. He opened the fenced entrance gate of the police station with the key fob and parked in the reserved parking space.

"Honza, I thought you'd be pleased," Mikeš said eagerly, turning in the passenger seat.

"I am, in a way," Jonny replied, his facial expression defying his words. "It definitely provides us with ammunition to put pressure on Michal Polák. And, we might have discovered the real reason why he was so keen to assist Zoe Farrell in looking after David when he started having problems with alcohol and drugs. We might even be able to use this new information to uncover the true nature of how Michal has been manipulating his so-called friend over all these years, using David's creative mind for his own, selfish, purpose, of growing the business."

"Exactly."

"The trouble is…" Jonny started, but his words dried up.

"What?"

"Unless we find out some startlingly crucial new piece of evidence, this revelation about who Liam's real father is only adds weight, in my opinion, to Zoe's motive for killing her estranged husband. Think about it for a moment. David Farrell suspects that Liam is not his son and is ready to organise a paternity test, in the process opening a Pandora's box of allegations that could threaten Zoe's custody of Liam. Maybe David doesn't know who Liam's real father is, maybe he can guess… I don't think it really matters. Zoe's life with her son, including her move back to the UK, is suddenly in jeopardy. Her motive to get rid of David before he can reveal the secret, supported by the physical evidence of the fingerprint on the murder weapon, is now even stronger… and almost certainly enough to prosecute her."

Mikeš' beaming smile faded.

Boukal cleared his throat, preparing to say something. "But, Honza, why would Zoe Farrell kill him in this way, when she must have known we'd find out?"

"I don't know, Marek. Maybe she thought she was being clever, believing the murder would be pinned on Nikola Vaněková because of the messages she was sending. Or, maybe she just panicked and didn't think her plan through fully, resulting in the fatal error of leaving her fingerprints and DNA all over the rucksack and the knife. Whatever happened, it seems highly likely she's lying to us. I mean, if she can lie about who Liam's father is, she's surely capable of lying about anything."

Mikeš scowled. He turned forward in his seat and looked forlornly out of the front windscreen.

"Of course," Jonny continued, "we still have to follow all the leads we have in the time left on the case. But, I'm sad to say, this new information must make it highly likely that Zoe Farrell murdered her husband."

Mikeš had clearly heard enough. He jumped out of the car, stabbing his cane hard into the tarmac surface, and slammed the door behind him.

***

Dvořáková was alone in the Incident Room when Jonny and Boukal arrived.

"Ahoj, Lucie." Jonny looked at his watch: still not even seven forty-five a.m. "Another early bird, I see."

"Ahoj, Honza. I wanted to get in early to make sure the case files are in order, and then brief my team, because I'm obviously off this afternoon…"

"Ah, yes, the big day – the detective exam. Feeling confident?"

"I didn't get much sleep, I was reviewing past papers until late. But, yes, I feel ready."

"That's great." Jonny smiled at her. "You're going to smash it, I just know it."

"Thank you. And, Happy Name Day."

A perplexed expression crept over Jonny's face. "I wasn't expecting so many people to know it was my name day. It's not even eight a.m yet and four people, including you, have already wished me a happy day."

Dvořáková laughed gently. "It's a big thing in the Czech Republic, second only to your birthday. And, as name days go, 'Honza' is perhaps the most famous. Every Czech person knows

252

someone call Jan, or John or Jonathan, all nicknamed Honza like you, and so a name day celebration isn't far away."

Mikeš strolled into the room, placing his hat and cane deliberately down on one of the free tables. Jonny was expecting some short of outburst, judging by the way he'd stormed off in the car park.

"Felix, I'm sorry if I was overly negative—"

Mikeš put his hand up to placate Jonny, stopping him mid-sentence.

"It's me that must apologise. I've been so fixated on Michal Polák that I lost sight of the bigger picture… in fact, maybe the real purpose of the investigation. Whilst I would love it if he was personally responsible for what has happened, I believe the rationale for your analysis of the current position is exactly right. I have just been into the restrooms and shouted at myself in the mirror. I can assure you it will not happen again."

Boukal lowered his gaze, clearly not sure how to react to his boss' unusual act of contrition.

Jonny stepped over and put his arm around Mikeš' shoulders; he knew from past experience that admitting to errors of judgement was a strength of character not found in many people.

"Sir," Dvořáková piped up, her voice edged with nervousness. "I just want to say that I've learned so much from working in this team. Without your guidance, plus help from Honza and Marek, my knowledge of policing would be limited to what is written in the manuals. You have not only given me insight into what is needed to be a top detective, you've also shown me how to behave and maintain the high standards needed to be proud of yourself. Thank you."

The room went silent, everyone absorbing her bold

statement.

Dvořáková blushed. "I'm sorry, sir. I just felt that I had to say that… I hope you don't mind."

Mikeš smiled warmly and shook her hand. "Thank you, sergeant."

"What a team you have here, Felix," Jonny remarked.

"Yes, yes," Mikeš blustered, "but we'd better get back to this case. Time is short. Let's go through where we are so we can wrap it up with the right result…" He turned to Jonny. "Whatever that result may be."

Jonny brought Dvořáková up to speed with Králová's revelation about the paternity test whilst Boukal jumped up to the Murder Board, marker pen in hand.

Standing up at the front, Boukal's appearance could only be described as scruffy: his recently new suit was starting to look more crumpled, his tie also slightly askew. Jonny made a mental note to have a quiet word with his protégé once the storm had passed, to make the point about maintaining high standards even, or maybe especially so, when an investigation was in full flow and the schedule was intense.

"Based upon the revelation of the paternity test," Boukal began, "I presume we need to book interviews with both Michal Polák and Zoe Farrell." He started scribbling on the board.

"Yes," Jonny confirmed. "But, let's take Zoe first. She is the prime suspect, after all. And, the more information we have to make Michal feel uncomfortable, the better."

"I'll organise them," Dvořáková offered.

"And, as Felix has suggested, we should take DNA and fingerprint samples from the other wives or girlfriends of the Midakati directors: Amy Poláková, Elena Arnold and Frida Nilsson," Jonny confirmed. "I'm not sure it will tell us much, but

254

it would be wrong if we didn't do so."

Mikeš nodded his agreement.

"We've finished the search of Zoe Farrell's apartment," Dvořáková stated. "The full report is in the file. We didn't find anything unusual. She did keep all the receipts from the artwork she bought and sold, probably to prove the authenticity of the items. Marek and I went through these records last night and there's no reference to a knife or anything like that. There was also nothing in her phone messages, emails or financial statements linking her to such a purchase. Hynek even checked the browser history on her laptop but no strange websites have been visited recently."

"Good to know," Jonny agreed, "but she could have had the knife a long time and only recently decided to use it. The only person that would maybe know about it is dead – her husband."

"Or, Michal Polák," Mikeš suggested, a childish glint in his eye.

Jonny laughed. "That's not a bad thought, Felix. It doesn't mean he murdered David Farrell, but maybe he was a conspirator to the murder. Something to test him on later in the interview."

"Can we check again through all the emails, messages and calls between Zoe and Michal?" Mikeš requested. "I want to see if there is any scheming between them, or any pattern of contact." A big smile spread across his face, clearly pleased to be back in the game.

"The phone records for Zoe Farrell show us that she called Michal Polák at 8.12 p.m on Sunday, when she got back from her husband's apartment," Dvořáková reported. "But, she did tell us about this call in the interview yesterday. We also know that she didn't make any other calls on Sunday evening. She also didn't go out because the signal of her mobile remained at her apartment from when she returned home about seven p.m on Sunday evening. And, checking back over the past couple of months, there does not appear to be a pattern of regular calls between Zoe Farrell and Michal Polák. In fact, there's only a couple of calls over the previous two weeks."

"Well, keep looking," Mikeš instructed.

"Hynek has also confirmed that there appears to have been no contact between Leo Holub and Zoe Farrell," Boukal stated. "This supports what the journalist has already told us. We've also searched Leo Holub's apartment and found nothing unusual."

"Great work," Mikeš boomed.

"Hynek has also reviewed the two USB memory sticks found in David Farrell's rucksack. One of them contained online documents about the investment company, Blackburn Mann Capital. The other stick contained nothing relevant to the case, just backups of technical documents David Farrell was working on when he was murdered." Boukal held up a ring binder. "All the documents on the USB stick have been printed and put in this file, along with the research that Leo Holub has given us."

"I'm not going to read them all," Jonny said, pulling a face. "Too much legal jargon for me! But, it'll be useful to show them to Titus Arnold and Freddie Pedersen to get their reaction. I don't know how it fits in, if at all, but we need to use everything we have to try and get to the truth, even if it turns out that Zoe Farrell killed her husband after all."

"By the way, after the interview with Leo Holub yesterday, I contacted Michal Polák's assistant, Olga," Dvořáková informed them. "I wanted to know his movements today because I thought you'd want to interview him here at the station. She told me that Michal is out of the office this morning, but due back this afternoon. Titus Arnold and Freddie Pedersen, however, are due to be in head office all day."

"Perfect," Jonny said smiling to himself.

"Why?" Mikeš enquired.

"We can organise the interview with Michal for this afternoon, here at the station. And, this morning I can go to see Titus Arnold and Freddie Pedersen unannounced."

"Don't forget we have a meeting with the Commissioner at midday."

"I won't be long," Jonny assured him. "But, I want to surprise them, see how they react."

"You love an ambush, don't you, Honza." Mikeš chuckled.

"A face can say a thousand words," Jonny retorted, laughing as well. "Talking of facial reactions, I'm sure that Frida Nilsson was unhappy with Amy Poláková's speech at the art exhibition last night. Amy was her usual, charming self, trying to claim some involvement in Frida's success. On the surface, it all seemed fine, and I'm sure nobody else noticed, but Frida's face definitely showed a momentary dislike for her so-called long term friend."

"What do you make of the new information that everyone seems to have known each other from university?" Mikeš asked. "It is very unusual."

"I agree. Frida gave me some good background, particularly about Michal and Amy. It seems that they were the first to meet, in the first year, and cajoled everyone into sharing respective boys' and girls' student houses. Frida said it was fun most of the time, but Amy in particular was very bossy, trying to organise almost every activity they did together. Frida used the words 'king' and 'queen' to describe the way Michal and Amy acted sometimes. I also asked her about the student party in 1998, where Zoe Farrell was arrested and subsequently released without charge, but she said she was back in Sweden for the early part of the summer holidays. She said she remembered something being discussed afterwards, but couldn't recall any details and claimed it wasn't a big deal."

"Do you think it's relevant to the case?" Mikeš asked.

Jonny shrugged. "Not sure. But, we have to keep poking around. I did get the phone number of Danni Hogarth, the last woman from the house, who now lives in Australia. I might call her." He looked at his watch. "I also want to ask Josef Liška if he remembered anything else about Zoe's arrest after I spoke to him yesterday."

The room went silent, their individual minds exploring potentially untapped avenues of the investigation. Boukal stood at the whiteboard, his pen at the ready, but no further thoughts were forthcoming. Jonny's shrug of the shoulders seemed to bring the analysis of the case to a halt.

"Sir," Boukal addressed Mikeš, "shall we release Nikola Vaněková?"

"Yes, but confiscate her passport and identity card. I also want her to sign in at her local police station at nine a.m and five p.m each day."

"Before you do release her, I'd like to ask her a question," Jonny said.

"Your choice," Mikeš said, his tone flat. "I'm not talking to that woman again. She's crazy!"

Jonny laughed and patted Mikeš on the shoulder. "Better get going, lots to do…"

"Yes, let's get this painful case sorted today," Mikeš concurred. "And, one last thing…" He turned to Dvořáková. "Good luck today, Lucie."

"Thank you, sir."

26

Them and Us

The other sergeant working in the police station – Dvořáková's peer – was Oskar Beránek. Like Mikeš and Liška, Beránek was fast approaching retirement age and carried a formidable reputation. His wizened face, whilst carrying scars of battle from his extensive service, had a grandfatherly appeal, but the potency of his wide stance and cold stare were not as welcoming and mostly put off other station staff from asking for his help or advice.

Beránek was the Duty Sergeant, responsible for the smooth running of the police station. This included the booking in and care of all detainees, whether held for a few hours to sober up after a heavy night out, or overnight if charged or suspected of involvement in a serious crime. His proud claim was that nobody had committed suicide on his watch, whether at his current police station or the others he'd worked at during his nearly forty years on the job.

Unlike Dvořáková, who still had headroom in her career, her dream being to reach the rank of Chief Warrant Officer, Beránek had long ago realised his ceiling. Whilst content to settle for what he'd achieved professionally, he didn't settle for any drop in standards and took his responsibilities very seriously. Probably too seriously. His armed forces background shone through in his immaculate uniform and shiny shoes – each and every day, without fail. Anyone working in the station who heard his jangling keys approaching subconsciously looked down at their shoes or adjusted their tie. He was an old school copper, not to be messed with.

The UK Police had been packed with similar characters when Jonny had joined up at the tender age of twenty: people to look up to but also fear at the same time. When Mikeš had taken Jonny under his wing, signing him up to the consultant role after the fanfare of the Old Town Square Murder, Beránek had been the only dissenter. Whilst not openly voicing his objections to Jonny's face, he'd made his views widely known. Boukal and Dvořáková had reported back discreetly, but Mikeš hadn't acted upon the information, believing that his old stablemate would come round eventually. After hearing word of the mild protest, and knowing Beránek's importance to the fabric of the station, Jonny had requested a meeting. The meeting hadn't been a disaster, but it also couldn't be claimed a total success, the language barrier proving too big a gap to close. So, the mutually unspoken middle ground was that Beránek was polite to Jonny whenever they came across each other in the station, but their rapport never moved past the terse and formal.

Expecting a frosty reception, Jonny asked Dvořáková to accompany him downstairs to the cells. "Oskar isn't my biggest fan," he explained as they descended the stairwell. "He doesn't believe Felix's team need any outside help. Especially not from a foreigner."

Dvořáková shook her head in frustration. "I respect him and what he's achieved, especially his high standards, but he's got a blinkered approach. He wouldn't accept the difference you've made even if it was staring him right in the face."

Jonny stopped at the entrance to the cells. "But, we both need

260

to keep him on our side, right?"

"Very true, Honza." She sighed. "He just drives me mad sometimes, quoting rules and regulations at me all the time."

"The trials and tribulations of a budding detective…" Jonny chuckled. "It's something you're going to face a lot as you climb the ladder. Especially as a successful woman. Whilst many will appreciate your success, knowing that you deserve it, some will resent it and keep quoting the minutiae of the job at you in order to remind you about them. It's best to think of it as a backhanded compliment."

"I suppose you're right." Her face didn't seem as convinced as her words. "How do you want to play this?"

"He won't talk to me," Jonny asserted. "Can you tell him that Felix is preparing an order to release Nikola Vaněková, but has agreed that I can speak to her informally before she is allowed to leave? Tell him I just want a quick word with her in her cell. And, of course, if she objects or asks for a solicitor at any time, I will respect her request and stop the conversation."

"Sounds fair enough to me."

Dvořáková punched in the entry code, pushed open the door and marched up to reception. Beránek stood up and leaned on the counter, his arms spread wide in authority. He barked an order at a female uniform officer sitting at a desk behind and she scurried away to the filing system lining the rear wall.

Jonny's greeting was hardly registered as Beránek and Dvořáková entered into a staccato conversation, the request met with a firm shaking of Beránek's head. He picked up the internal telephone and made a call before she could plead her case. Jonny was struggling to follow the words spoken, but understood enough to know that Beránek was calling Mikeš to question the reasoning behind the unusual request.

Slamming down the phone, he sighed in disapproval. "Pět minut!"

"We have five minutes," Dvořáková explained to Jonny.

Beránek stomped down the short corridor, stopping outside cell number three, Jonny and Dvořáková following at a respectful distance. He slid the viewer aside and peered in, before unlocking the cell and pushing open the heavy door.

Nikola Vaněková sat hunched on the bed, hugging her knees. Beránek spoke to her in Czech and then retreated, repeating the limit of five minutes as he departed.

Jonny edged into the cell. Dvořáková remained standing at the door.

"Hi, Nikola. I'm pleased to say that you will soon be released, probably within the next hour. A police officer will drive you home."

Nikola remained mute, shrugging her shoulders half-heartedly in response.

He decided to try again. "I'm sure your children will be pleased to see you…"

"What do you want, Mr Fox?"

"I just want to ask you a question. You have no obligation to answer me, but I think you might be able to help me with the investigation into the murder of David Farrell. And, if you want a legal representative present—"

She stopped him mid-sentence with a forceful shake of her head.

"Look, I'm sorry if you feel you've been mistreated," Jonny continued. "And, I sympathise with your situation, I really do. But, you have to look at it from our perspective. You sent the original messages to Michal Polák and the other directors of Midakati, and, without realising it, you seem to have sparked a chain of events that has resulted in one of your original group of friends being murdered."

She didn't respond.

Jonny waited.

Nikola eventually lifted her head, jutting out her chin proudly. "Mr Fox, I've had time to reflect in here, and I've made peace with the fact that none of my old friends care about me and my children. It is very sad, but it's true. And, now it's time to move on…" She looked directly into his eyes. "Ask your question, Mr Fox. Then, I will be free from them all, and will never have to think about them ever again."

"Thank you." He sat down on the only chair in the cell, moving it closer to the bed.

The cell was stark. Apart from the low bed and the chair, the room was devoid of any furniture. The dull, white walls and the in-built central light provided the only brightness to the three square metres, the small, barred window failing miserably to provide any natural light.

"My question is similar to the one I asked you in the interview yesterday. But, at that point, although I knew that you and Karel met at university, I didn't realise that you had shared a student house with Zoe Farrell, Amy Poláková, Frida Nilsson, and also Danni Hogarth."

Nikola stayed silent, staring intently at him with a tired, drawn expression.

"I know the messages were aimed at Michal Polák and the other directors, but was there any other special significance to using 'us' in the emails and letters you sent?"

She lowered her head and laughed, the stifled noise a mixture of her pent-up anger and a pithy cackle. Jonny waited until she stopped. Finally, she raised her head, exposing the tears rolling down her cheeks.

"It was all driven by Michal and Amy," she spluttered, recovering her composure. "Of course, we all went along with it, so we have to take our own share of the blame… but they were the instigators. They planned everything together, and we fell in line: they said we're going to a party, we went out together; they said let's play this drinking game, we played that game; they set the schedule for choosing the music; they organised the kitty for buying the alcohol; they even planned the chores in the two houses. Whatever they said, we did!" She wiped her eyes. "It sounds terrible now, but at the time it was so much fun. We were all away from home for the first time and it was lovely to have so many friends. We were like a close family supporting each other, and none of us had ever experienced that togetherness before. It was amazing."

"I feel there's a 'but' coming…" Jonny prompted.

"Amy started using the term 'us' at the beginning of the second year and it sort of stuck. We would toast 'To us!', and it was always 'Us against them'. *Us, us, us.* The motto was that we were a unique group, and that we were going to support each other for the rest of our lives. Unlike other so-called 'real friends', we were really going to stick together, support each other through thick and thin, especially if something bad happened to one of us. But…"

He waited whilst she blew her nose noisily.

"But, it all meant nothing. Nothing at all. The first time anyone disagreed with one of them – when Karel questioned Michal's decisions in the business – we were cut off. And, the opposition was so tough that it pushed Karel into taking his own life. The token offer to pay my rent for a few years was only because of their guilt. But, it didn't last long." She again looked

264

Jonny directly in the eye. "The 'Them and us' was really a threat. You were either following, in which case you were part of 'us', or you were an outsider, one of 'them', discarded with no further interest. So, our so-called special group was, in fact, really no different from all the other shits in this world."

Jonny waited whilst she wiped away the tears rolling down her cheeks.

"Thank you, Nikola. I have just one more question… Back in June 1998, Zoe got arrested and taken to this police station. A student party was raided but it seems that she was drunk and got physical with a police officer. Do you remember it? In particular, given what you've told me about the group of friends, I was wondering if Michal and Amy were involved in it."

"I only know what Zoe told me, and that wasn't much. She was mostly embarrassed about it. I told her to just forget it. I think Michal helped her sort it out somehow but I don't know any more than that."

Beránek was standing at the cell door, next to Dvořáková.

Jonny rose from the chair, leaving her crying softly on the bed. He stopped at the cell door and turned to face her. "Nikola, you can do it without these people, I know you can. Stay strong." She looked up and he could detect a glimmer of steely determination in her eyes.

Jonny and Dvořáková left the cell. Beránek locked up, checked through the viewer again, and followed them down the corridor.

Arriving back at reception, Jonny was surprised to see Boukal and Liška in discussion, hunched over a piece of paper on the top of the counter. Beránek walked behind reception and resumed his position of authority. Whilst his position was stern, there was however the hint of a smirk on his face.

"Ahoj, Honza," Liška began. "Oskar called me and asked me to come up. I was talking to him yesterday about the student party raid back in June 1998. My mind's a bit foggy because we just made a few arrests and dropped them off here. I might have better recollection if we'd have brought charges, but as you know they were all released without caution. Oskar, however, claims he can remember everyone he's ever checked into the cells."

Liška translated for Beránek, who stubbed his index finger into his chest. "I remember," he managed in a heavy accent.

"So," Liška continued, "I asked Marek to bring down headshots of the people involved in this current murder investigation." He pointed to the paper on the counter.

"I also managed to find a photo of Danni Hogarth from her social media," Boukal added.

Beránek spoke in Czech, for Liška to translate, "He says that he was on duty that evening. One of his team took the DNA and fingerprint samples, but he oversaw the process of booking them in, including putting them in the cells."

"That's great," Jonny remarked, nodding respectfully towards Beránek.

They all huddled around the photos on top of the counter, Dvořáková squeezing in next to Jonny.

"I suppose Zoe Farrell is in one of the cells now?" Jonny asked.

"Number two," Boukal answered.

"Does Oskar remember her from that night back in 1998?"

Liška relayed the question. "Ano," Beránek answered. Boukal put a tick next to the headshot of Zoe Farrell.

"Does he remember any of the others from that night?"

Liška translated. Beránek put his finger on the photo of Michal Polák. Then Amy Poláková. And, finally, Danni Hogarth.

Boukal ticked the relevant photos.

"Is he sure?" Jonny asked, careful to get his tone right. "Definitely nobody else was arrested?"

Beránek turned and picked up a large ledger from the desk behind the counter. He opened the ledger at a marked page and placed it on the counter top. He ran his fingers down the column of names. "Zoe Henderson, Michal Polák, Amy Russell, and Danni Hogarth," he read out slowly, struggling with the pronunciation of the non-Czech names.

"This is the book used to log everyone who is detained in the cells," Liška explained.

"We know that Henderson is Zoe Farrell's maiden name," Boukal stated. "Looks like Russell is Amy Poláková's maiden name, but we'll need to check."

"That is very impressive," Jonny remarked. Liška translated. Beránek smiled, pleased with the compliment.

Beránek started speaking rapidly in Czech, directed to Jonny. "He says that he's been based here for twenty years, and can find the correct ledger for any day within an hour," Liška translated.

"Josef," Jonny addressed Liška, "can you please ask Oskar if he remembers anything else about the four people who were detained? Did anything unusual happen?"

The question was relayed and Beránek answered in Czech. "He says that the man, Michal Polák, was in control of himself, not too drunk," Liška explained. "He was the only one who could speak Czech, and he tried to reason with Oskar so that he was held and the women were released. Obviously, Oskar ignored him and they processed all four of them before putting them in individual cells. All the women were drunk and made a big scene. Zoe Henderson was the worst, very drunk, and didn't stop

267

talking, threatening the police officers on duty."

"Anything else?"

Beránek waved his arms around in animated fashion, whilst talking to Liška.

"He says that Amy Russell was trying to charm all the policemen on duty, feeling their arm muscles and squeezing their thighs. She was loving all the attention, and wouldn't stop laughing, even when she was finally put in a cell."

"That sounds like Amy," Jonny concurred, rolling his eyes.

27

Raised Voices

Jonny left the cells with a spring in his step. His upbeat mood was less to do with the proof of who'd been arrested along with Zoe Farrell at the student party raid: the evidence presented had only confirmed his own suspicions, and did little to change the material facts of the murder case. No, he was pleased because he'd managed to crack the one remaining lukewarm relationship within the hierarchy of the police station.

His glowing praise for Oskar Beránek's memory and excellent record keeping had been genuine. Jonny had worked with many excellent sergeants, some real sticklers for detail, but he doubted if any of them would have been able to recall an everyday occurrence over ten years ago. The two men parted with an earnest handshake and enhanced mutual respect, Beránek's normally serious face softened with the fulsome compliment.

"Happy Name Day, Honza," Liška said to Jonny.

"Thank you, Josef."

"Všechno nejlepší k svátku," Beránek echoed. "See you soon."

"Dekuji."

Jonny headed back up the stairwell, Dvořáková and Boukal following behind. "See you soon..." he repeated to himself in a low voice. He stopped on the second floor landing. "Lucie, what do you think Oskar meant by that?"

Dvořáková shrugged her shoulders, exchanging a blank look with Boukal. "He could mean anything, I suppose. I mean, his English is not very good. Maybe he just wants you to pop down to see him sometimes, like you do with Liška. You have a new friend…"

"Yes, maybe." Jonny looked between them, something not quite adding up.

Jonny hadn't been surprised by the outcome of Beránek's paper-based identity parade, the sergeant's memory substantiated by the decade-old ledger. After what Nikola Vaněková had told him, he'd expected Michal and Amy to not be far from the action – ringleaders in the extreme. The interesting ingredient in the mix was Danni Hogarth. Jonny resolved to call her during the morning, when the ten hour difference in the clocks would mean it was still an acceptable time of the evening in Melbourne, Australia.

The evidence still pointed to Zoe Farrell either being stone-cold guilty, committing the murder single-handedly, or Michal Polák was pulling the strings in some way. *Maybe Felix was right all along.* But, Jonny knew there was still nothing material to suggest duplicity between them. The interesting omission from the arrest sheet was David Farrell. The 'gentle soul', as some had described him, was murdered for a reason. But, why? Was he too clever for his own good, finding out about Liam, and unwittingly provoking his wife into killing him? Or, had he been the innocent pawn in his supposed friend's sinister game over many years?

With Boukal busily preparing for the next interview with Zoe Farrell, and Dvořáková tying up loose ends before heading off for her exam, one of the detective team was set the task of driving Jonny to the Midakati head office. He'd come across the detective a few times during the recent investigations, but whilst affable and competent, he seemed to lack any drive or ambition. After being wished 'Happy Name Day' for the umpteenth time, Jonny engaged in the stilted small talk for five minutes before they eventually settled into a comfortable silence. At least the drive was smoother, with less heart-stopping moments than when Boukal was at the wheel.

The reception area of Midakati's head office was subdued compared to his last visit: fewer people milling around, less smiles on employee's faces, even the brightly painted walls seemed duller. The modern breakout area was empty, the large photo and book of condolences for David Farrell dominating the space, making it unwelcoming for a coffee break or informal meeting with a colleague.

Jonny approached the receptionist, carrying a large, padded envelope in his hand, and asked for Titus Arnold and Freddie Pedersen. When he explained it was police business, holding out his badge for scrutiny, she looked scared and made a quick call.

"Please have a seat. Olga will come down to see you."

"I will wait here. Thank you."

Jonny swivelled around, his back to reception, and used the time to mentally calculate his approach. He knew that Michal Polák's assistant was going to try to block him from entering, but he'd faced enough of these situations over his career to know the touchpoints that would open the door.

Olga appeared within minutes. She was young, in her late twenties, and smartly dressed. Being empowered as the CEO's eyes and ears gave her an air of confidence, evident in her practised, confident stride across the marbled floor from the lifts. But, Jonny could see blemishes in her stern expression, her eyes being held too tight in concentration. This was a task she was clearly dreading, one definitely not part of her job description.

"Mr Fox, I'm sorry but Titus and Freddie are not available to speak to you."

"No problem, I'll wait."

"I've spoken to Michal and he told me—"

"I understand you need to do your job, but do not – I repeat, do not – try to get in the way of a police investigation," Jonny stated flatly. "I would not recommend it for your clearly good record as a citizen of this city, nor for your future career prospects for that matter."

Olga looked directly at him, giving nothing away.

"One of my team is in contact with Michal's solicitor and a formal interview with him is being organised for this afternoon, at the police station in Prague 1." He paused, letting her absorb the information. "I need to talk to Titus and Freddie. If they do not talk to me, either here or down the station, they will be arrested for not complying with a police investigation. And, that includes anyone else who stands in the way of this request."

Her eyes flared in alarm, clearly considering the limited options available to her.

"Follow me please," she managed, her voice having lost some of its previous composure.

They ascended to the top floor in the lift. Olga showed him into Michal Polák's office. Closing the door, she scampered off into one of the other offices in the director's suite. Jonny could hear raised voices as either Titus or Freddie, or both, objected to her actions. He was pleased to hear her firm voice answering back, making her own case as he expected her to do.

The office door was pushed open forcefully. Titus entered, followed by Freddie.

"This is most irregular—" Titus began, his voice raised.

"This, I think you'll find, is a murder investigation," Jonny corrected him, pointing firmly to the sofa opposite him.

He waited, letting them sit down at their own speed.

"If you are angry with me about last night, then so be it... I was just doing my job, plus I was invited by Amy." Jonny looked between them, searching their eyes. "New, valuable information has come to light this morning which I need to talk to you about. It will take twenty minutes maximum. I hope we can talk here, in the privacy of the office, because it will speed up finding out what really happened to David. But, if you really oppose it, I have a car outside and we can transport you immediately to the police station—"

"Just ask your questions." Freddie crossed his arms. "Let's get this over and done with."

"Thank you." Jonny paused for effect. "On Sunday, Michal and David were heard arguing at The Klementinum, before the youth orchestra performance—"

"Mr Fox, they were always arguing," Titus interjected quickly. "Hardly a day went by without some sort of feud. It was normal behaviour for them."

"Yes, but do you know what they were arguing about?"

Titus and Freddie shared a look, but remained silent.

"I'll tell you. After being contacted by a freelance journalist, David had discovered that your investment partner, Blackburn Mann Capital, or BMC, had lied in its proposal to the Midakati directors at the time of the investment decision back in 2007. The lies relate to BMC's claims about its past record on environmental issues, or climate change."

"I don't believe you!" Titus blurted out, the lilt of his American accent noticeable in his anger.

Jonny opened the envelope he was carrying and fanned the papers out on the low table between them. "These are copies of the documents we recovered from David's rucksack when he was found murdered. As you can see, they are printed copies of documents presented to the Board of Directors, plus minutes of meetings from the time of the investment decision. David has highlighted key passages with a marker pen. We know that David had also prepared a USB memory stick for a journalist that had contacted him about this matter. The memory stick contained online articles David had found to disprove BMC's previous claims. David told Michal about these on Sunday, and that is why they argued. David was planning to raise them with the other directors – by this, I mean you – with the intention of forcing a change of investment partner."

"Wow," Titus said, falling back into the sofa. "He didn't say anything to me about this. I didn't have a clue."

Freddie silently flicked through the papers on the table. "It looks like David had something," he said finally, "but I'd obviously need to examine these in more detail. However, I'm not sure this on its own would be enough to prove that BMC didn't disclose the required information. We'd probably need to get a legal opinion."

"The journalist told us," Jonny began explaining, "that David was incensed that an investment company with a poor green record should be shareholders in a company – your company – that is claiming to be the leading product designers of energy-efficient drones. If this got out, it could have a detrimental impact on your plans to grow and then float the business."

Titus and Freddie shared another look.

"As Freddie has said, we'd need to get this checked over, but it definitely would need to be acted upon if true. We'd certainly need to head off any adverse publicity."

"So, my first question to you," Jonny started, "and please

274

don't get defensive, is did your CEO, Michal Polák, have any incentive for signing the contract with BMC?"

"You think Michal murdered David?" Titus exclaimed.

"I'm not suggesting anything. Just answer the question."

"Michal has known the guys at BMC for years, and he introduced them to us. But, we went through a detailed selection process…" Titus rubbed his face with his hands. "I am shocked, but I still can't believe Michal would have done anything untoward for his own gain."

Titus looked towards Freddie, who shook his head. "No incentive was declared when the investment decision was made. I know because it was pretty much my first job after joining the company as Chief Financial Officer. But, like Titus, I've never had any reason to question Michal's motives."

"Thank you," Jonny said sincerely. "We might need to raise a warrant and go through the company documentation. I trust I can rely on your support, purely so that we can clarify the truth of what happened."

Titus nodded his agreement.

"I will help in any way I can," Freddie added, "but I can assure you that the company documentation is in order. I know it inside out. If anything dubious has happened in relation to this investment, the evidence you are going to need to find is not here."

"Did Michal spend a lot of time with the owners of the investment company?" Jonny probed.

"Michal was close with Walter Blackburn," Titus explained. "He's the main man. The other partner, Rupert Mann, is quieter, stays in the background."

"Can you explain what you mean by 'close'?"

"Walter is based in Paris but travels all around Europe.

Michal had introduced him to a lot of people in Prague—"

"Like whom?"

"Other businesses, politicians, the usual movers and shakers," Titus confirmed. "Michal knows a lot of important people."

"Yes, I am aware," Jonny retorted, his tone harsh.

"They used to go on holiday together as well," Freddie added.

"That gives me enough of an idea. Thank you."

"I'm not saying there was anything inappropriate going on," Freddie quickly added. "Michal has enough money himself."

"Yes, but some people never have enough money, do they?" Jonny left the accusation hanging in the air.

Titus and Freddie stayed silent. Jonny collected up the papers, shuffled them together and slid them back into the envelope.

"Next subject, do either of you remember a student party back in June 1998, whilst you were all at university? The police raided the party and arrested a few people, including Zoe Farrell."

"Michal mentioned this to me yesterday—" Titus began.

"What reason did he give for mentioning it to you?"

Titus shrugged. "Not sure. He said he thought that's how Zoe Farrell's fingerprints were on the police database."

"He told me the same," Freddie confirmed.

"But, it doesn't really matter because I don't remember the party at all." Titus shrugged. "Maybe I wasn't there, I don't know, but I have no recollection of a drugs raid. I think Freddie's the same…"

"That's right," Freddie stated. "It would have been the end of the university year and many people went travelling or back

276

home for the summer. I vaguely remember something about the police being mentioned, but it wasn't a big thing. We were students, stuff like that was happening all the time… It was also a long time ago."

"Are you sure?" Jonny prompted. "Michal never talked about it?"

Titus shook his head in denial. Freddie pursed his lips in vagueness.

"Right. The last thing I need to ask you about is the relationship between Michal and Zoe Farrell."

"What are you talking about?" Titus was angry again. "You seem to have a vendetta against Michal—"

"Titus, I can assure you that I'm not the slightest bit interested in Michal. I am only interested in the truth. We are talking to him at the police station this afternoon, but I can confirm that we have definitive proof that Michal and Zoe had a sexual relationship."

Titus and Freddie shared another look.

Jonny waited, leaving the space for one of them to talk.

"I don't know what to say," Titus stuttered. "I've known both of them since the first year at university, about thirteen years ago, and I had no idea."

"I was away for a number of years," Freddie added, "but I would never have guessed."

"Your shock is evident," Jonny clarified. "But, didn't Zoe work for Midakati in the early years?"

"Yes," Titus confirmed, "she worked for me. It was probably three or four years in total, up until 2007, when David started having his problems."

"What was her role in the company?"

"She had gained some experience in Press Relations at a

277

large, multi-national company in Prague, so we asked her to set up the PR function for Midakati. She was good, a natural. Obviously, she knew everyone in the business, so she understood the culture and what we were trying to achieve. We worked closely together in the early years, formulating the right language to get the business sector interested in the drone products we were developing."

"Did she work closely with Michal?"

"She used to travel with Michal quite extensively. They attended events all around Europe, and a few times even in the US, both to explore the competition in the early days and also to promote our early prototype when it was ready…" Titus' voice trailed away, the enormity of what he'd said hitting him.

"So, David never said anything to you about Michal and Zoe? Not even a hint?"

Titus shook his head, raising his palm to his forehead in exasperation.

"This is all new to me, Mr Fox," Freddie confirmed. "But, it sounds like you have the answer you were looking for."

28

Interview 3 – Zoe Farrell

The following is a transcript of the recorded interview conducted with Zoe Farrell (ZF) on Wednesday, twenty-fourth June 2010. The interview was held at the police station in Prague Old Town.

Present at the interview were Chief Warrant Officer Felix Mikeš (FM), Chief Sergeant Marek Boukal (MB), Consultant Jonathan Fox (JF) and solicitor, Brigita Svobodová (BS).

The interview was conducted in English, in agreement with the interviewee.

MB: Interview commenced at 11.02. Please state your name for the record.

ZF: Zoe Farrell.

BS: Because of the confusion at the start of the last interview, I would like to have it clarified why you have asked for another interview with my client. She has been forthcoming in answering all your questions so far, and has made it crystal clear that she had no involvement in the murder of her husband, David Farrell. I also want to know if you plan to charge her, because if not—

JF: If you would permit me five minutes, I will explain the current situation and our dilemma in this murder investigation.

BS: Agreed. But, no fishing with general questions looking to trap my client.

JF: The situation is grave, Zoe. And, I'll be honest, at this stage we need your help. Otherwise, you're going to be charged with your husband's murder later today. The problem is that the only fingerprint found on the murder weapon belongs to you. In addition, your fingerprints and DNA are all over David's rucksack. And, despite dedicating virtually all our police resources to this case, and diligently following up every potential lead, we have not been able to uncover any weakness in this material evidence. The Czech equivalent of the UK Crown Prosecution Service is currently reviewing the case, but my expectation is that this evidence will be considered sufficient to charge you with murder.

[Pause]

JF: I know it is painful to go over old ground, but we need to talk again about what happened on Sunday, when you went to David's apartment. We already have your version of events recorded in a previous interview, and therefore we don't really need to go over it again. But, Chief Warrant Officer Mikeš and I want to give you the opportunity to consider them again, to see if you can recall anything else relevant to the investigation.

[ZF and BS are heard consulting, but the conversation is inaudible.]

BS: My client is happy to talk again about Sunday.

JF: Yesterday, you told us that you went to David's apartment at six o'clock to pick up your son, Liam (Farrell). Can you describe again, in your own words, what happened, up to the point when you found traces of cocaine in the kitchen and then confronted David?

ZF: Before I talk about going to David's apartment on Sunday, I want to tell you about something that happened earlier in the day. With all the stress of the last couple of days, I don't think I've explained myself very well. It might just explain the reason I was so stressed about the drugs.

JF: Take your time, Zoe.

ZF: David had been getting increasingly stressed in the past few weeks. I couldn't really put my finger on why, but I knew him very well and could see that something was wrong. Remember that I'd also found the credit card in his kitchen a few weeks before. The weekend before, I'd asked him if he was okay but he said it was nothing, that he was just busy at work. When he arrived on Sunday, I could see that he wasn't good. He was anxious, fidgety, you know. I recognised the symptoms immediately. When I asked him if he was okay, he said that he'd had to rush over from The Klementinum, and that he'd had an argument with Michal (Polák). I made him a coffee and he started to relax, playing with Liam. My concern was that he wasn't in a fit state to take Liam out for the day. Eventually he calmed down, but now I've thought about it, I'm convinced that David bought his cocaine on his way over from The Klementinum.

JF: Do you know who his drug dealer was?

ZF: No. I quizzed Liam discreetly when we got back to our apartment on Sunday evening. Liam said they went to the park, then went to the toy shop, grabbed a burger and went straight back to David's apartment. Liam is a clever boy and would remember if his dad met someone he didn't know. That's why I think David bought the drugs before he picked Liam up.

JF: David could have had the cocaine already.

ZF: Yes, I suppose so. But, you didn't see David when he arrived at our apartment. He was wired. My guess is that he'd already taken some of what he'd just bought.

JF: Did David mention anything recently about the investment company that invested in Midakati in 2007 – Blackburn Mann Capital, or BMC? Or, maybe he mentioned a journalist called Leo

281

Holub?

ZF: No. I don't remember David saying anything about them.

JF: So, you don't know anyone from BMC, or Leo Holub?

ZF: No. I was introduced to someone from BMC by Michal a few years ago, at an event, but I can't even remember his name.

JF: Walter Blackburn?

ZF: It sounds familiar, but sorry, I can't remember.

JF: So, you had some suspicions when David came to pick up Liam, and were worried…

ZF: Yes.

JF: Can you explain again what happened from when you arrived at David's apartment?

ZF: As I've told you, I arrived at six on the dot, and everything seemed fine: David and Liam were playing with Liam's new toy in the living room. Because I was on alert, I quickly dashed around the apartment before David could cover up anything. That's when I found the traces of cocaine in the kitchen. I immediately went back to the living room and searched his rucksack. Yesterday, I told you that I searched the rucksack quickly, mainly because I didn't want to seem like I was trying to control David's life. In truth, I searched the rucksack more thoroughly than I said. I picked up the rucksack, opened every compartment and put my hand inside. I didn't pull the pockets open and look inside, but I pushed my hand around and felt inside. I didn't find any drugs. But, I also didn't feel anything like a knife. The more I've thought about it, the more I'm convinced the knife wasn't there – I'm sure I'd have felt it when I was swishing my hand around inside the compartments.

JF: Zoe, that's useful clarification, but it still doesn't explain how the knife got into the rucksack, and also how your fingerprint got onto the handle of the knife.

ZF: I'm sorry, I have no explanation for that. All I know is that it had nothing to do with me. I have never seen that knife before – the one you showed me photos of yesterday – and I had nothing to do with what happened to David.

JF: And, you called Michal when you got back to your apartment?

ZF: Yes.

JF: Can you explain why you did this, and what you agreed?

ZF: When David first started having troubles, Michal and I agreed to talk regularly. He was so helpful, I'm not sure what I'd have done without him. And, being truthful, I'm not sure David would have been able to continue in his role at Midakati without Michal's loyal support. Michal was obviously disappointed when I told him what I'd found on Sunday – the cocaine in the kitchen – and he said that he'd talk to him at the office on Monday. We didn't agree anything particular because we didn't have enough information, but I told Michal I was worried.

JF: Michal didn't tell us you'd called him. He said he'd called David later, about nine, but told us it was just to agree some things for the week ahead.

ZF: I don't know anything about that. I haven't spoken to Michal since I called him on Sunday evening.

JF: So, you definitely didn't agree anything else with Michal?

ZF: No.

JF: Were you and Michal close?

ZF: I've obviously known him and Amy for years. We were closer during university days, and in the years straight after, but we are all still friends now.

JF: Nikola Vaněková has a very different view on that…

BS: Mr Fox, what someone else thinks is hardly relevant to this interview with my client.

[Pause]

JF: Zoe, your belief that David bought drugs on Sunday afternoon is relevant, and we will follow up on this lead. But, and this is really important, you have given us no new information that provides an explanation for how your fingerprint got onto the murder weapon.

ZF: I know nothing about the knife, and I had nothing to do with David's murder – I would never hurt him.

[Pause]

JF: There is something else we want to ask you about. This morning, we discovered something important to the investigation, something you haven't disclosed to us. It concerns Liam.

ZF: Liam? What about him?

JF: Who is Liam's father?

ZF: David.

JF: That's not true. When we searched David's apartment we found a sealed envelope. I initially thought it was empty, but our forensics team found two hairs inside which we have matched with Liam's hair. My immediate reaction was that David had doubts over whether Liam was his son. So, we did a paternity test and it confirmed that David is not Liam's father. We then widened the test, only to find that Michal Polák is Liam's biological father.

BS: What sort of ambush is this? Mr Fox, you should be ashamed of yourself—

FM: Ms Svobodová, you can think what you want. We have confirmed medical proof to support the information Mr Fox has just provided. It is fact. And, what we now want to know is why Zoe has lied to us about this.

MB: For the purposes of the tape, I am showing Mrs Zoe Farrell two paternity test results, along with translations in English. The paternity tests show results for whether the person tested is the father of Liam Farrell: one for David Farrell which is negative, the other for Michal Polák which is positive.

[Long pause]

ZF: I didn't know.

JF: Zoe, you must tell us the truth. This is important. You must see how this looks from our perspective.

[Pause]

ZF: I honestly didn't know. Or, maybe the reality is that I didn't want to know. The truth is that Michal and I got drunk at a conference we attended together in late 2006. David had just started getting depressed, and I was quite upset. We drank too much, and at the end of the night one thing led to another... It was a mistake.

JF: Your approach to this is quite hard to believe. You had sex with your husband's long term friend and boss, and don't even worry that he might have been the one who got you pregnant.

ZF: You make it sound so callous. Michal told me that he and Amy had tried for a baby for a while, but there was a problem with his sperm count. Plus, whilst David was starting to have some issues, our sex life was still good. I suppose I was just happy to be pregnant. I certainly wouldn't have had an abortion under any circumstances. I just hoped that David was Liam's father.

JF: David must have started to suspect – he had collected Liam's hairs in an envelope. Whilst I can't prove to you that he was planning a paternity test, it would seem a pretty reasonable assumption.

ZF: He never mentioned anything to me.

JF: Really? Liam is a big child, and Michal is also very tall.

ZF: Sure, but my father is also tall. I had no reason to suspect that

285

David wasn't Liam's father.

JF: But, something must have happened for David to become suspicious… Help us out here, Zoe.

ZF: I'm sorry, I can't think of anything. He never said anything to me.

JF: Does anybody else know about what happened between you and Michal?

ZF: No. Michal and I promised not to tell anyone else. And, it never happened again. At first, I didn't think Michal would honour the promise, but he's never actually talked about it with me since. It's like it didn't happen. And, as I've already said, he had been so helpful to David and to me. We couldn't have got through David's problems without his assistance.

JF: It's all a bit hard to believe, if I'm honest.

ZF: It's the truth.

JF: Okay, let me play this back to you. You are part of a group of friends from university that, unusually, pair off so that three couples get married and one couple have an on-off relationship for years. You marry David, who is the creative genius behind a successful new business. David struggles with the pressures of work, suffers from depression, turning to drugs and alcohol. You and his friend, and boss, Michal, become his support team, helping him through his troubles. But, as a result, your marriage to David breaks down and he moves out. However, you have already had a sexual relationship with Michal. Whilst you claim you only had sex once, Michal turns out to be the father of your son, Liam. One Monday morning, the day after you find out that David has started taking drugs again, he is found murdered on the metro, stabbed in the heart by a knife jammed into his rucksack. After the murder, we find out that David suspected he was not Liam's father, and also that he had sought legal advice

286

on his options because you wanted to move back to the UK with Liam. But, he is murdered before he can action the paternity test, or take any legal action. And, final thing, your fingerprint is found on the murder weapon – the knife – along with your fingerprints and DNA on David's rucksack.

FM: Mrs Farrell, was Michal Polák involved in the murder?

BS: I want this interview stopped… Now!

[Long pause]

ZF: The only thing I am going to say is that I had nothing at all to do with David's murder. I still loved him.

MB: Interview terminated at 11.44.

29

Explosive Recipe

Jonny had only been to the Prague Police Headquarters once before. The Old Town Square Murder had caused quite a splash in the media, the murder victim being a tourist only serving to heighten the longevity of the story's newsworthiness. The Police Commissioner had wanted an informal meeting, over a glass of wine, to congratulate Mikeš and Jonny, as well as seal the deal on his proposed new consultant role.

This meeting felt different. Firstly, they were still in the midst of a high profile murder investigation: the pressure was on, there was no time for congratulatory drinks or back slapping. Also, there was the intriguing, and potentially awkward, link between the Commissioner and Michal Polák. Jonny knew from experience that these types of relationship rarely helped an investigation, creating potential problems for an impassioned detective asking too many questions.

They were also going to be late. Mikeš didn't seem bothered, however, insisting they walk. Jonny had the strong sense that he was heading into the eye of the storm: the concoction of Michal Polák and his octopus-like style of controlling people, the rising stress levels, and the bad memories of Mikeš' past case serving to create an explosive recipe. At the same time, he knew he was virtually powerless to head off any trouble: his consultant role was crime solving, and his knowledge of city politics was virtually zero.

Walking in silence, Mikeš led them out of the old town, skirting around Náměstí Republiky before crossing the river on Štefánikův most. The busy bridge seemed unmoved by the hurly-burly happening atop and around it, the heavy traffic travelling in both directions in and out of the city centre. Whilst the air was not cold, the summer feel was being challenged by the dense clouds gathering overhead. The river, not to be left out, seemed to sense the opportunity for some fun, using its choppy, cold waters to help whip up a fresher breeze. Both men pulled in their jackets against the wind, Mikeš holding onto his hat as they paced purposefully across the bridge.

Once on the other side of the river, they crossed the main road and ascended into the leafy summer park overlooking the city, Letenské sady. The contrast to the hostility of the bridge was stark, the winding paths and tall trees softening the hard edge of the bustling city. Mikeš strode into the centre of the park, the landscape opening up to offer a panoramic view back across Prague old town.

Mikeš abruptly stopped, waving his arm suggestively across the picture postcard before them. "You know, Honza, I'm starting to wonder whether it's time for me to retire." He sighed heavily. "I've loved this job. Almost every minute of it. But now... I don't know, something seems to have changed..." His voice trailed off, unable or unwilling to describe his inner torment.

Both men looked out over the city, standing shoulder to shoulder, Mikeš leaning forward with his hands on the top of his cane.

"Felix, only *you* will know when the time is right." Jonny turned to look at Mikeš' side profile. "And, whatever you decide, I will support you. But, don't decide anything now. Put it to the back of your mind, and let's close down this investigation. Once it's over, take some time. See how you feel then."

They stood in silence.

Mikeš turned to face Jonny. "Wise words, my friend, wise words. Thank you."

They shook hands earnestly, attracting the attention of tourists and locals walking in the park.

"Come on, let's get this over with." Mikeš turned and marched off, swinging his cane to the rhythm in his limbs. Jonny scampered after him, struggling to keep up with the increased pace.

The remainder of the walk took them uphill into Holešovice, past an eclectic grouping of coffee shops, trendy bars and specialist antique shops, eventually reaching Prague's National Gallery at Veletržní palác. The Police Headquarters loomed large as they approached, the beige 1980s featureless building uncannily resembling almost any government establishment from any capital city from across the world.

Mikeš booked them in at the front desk, before navigating them through security and up the wide stairs to the first floor. The celebrated detective was known to everyone, attracting informal greetings, handshakes and waves. Jonny's face was unfamiliar in head office so he played the straight partner, not drawing attention to himself, only nodding his silent acknowledgement when the inclusive greeting was intended for both of them.

They were twelve minutes late and impatiently waved straight in by the Police Commissioner's assistant. The office was spacious but dreary, dominated by the dark wooden furniture and beige walls. The blind on the window blocked most of the available natural light, the dust in the air catching the few shafts escaping through the broken slats. Only the slim glass cabinet in the corner offered any brightness, a selection of silver shields and trophies gleaming proudly.

The Commissioner sat behind his large desk, his sparkling blue uniform setting the prim tone, matching the tidy desk, unruffled bookcases and perfectly positioned family photos dotted around the furniture. Tall, and sitting upright in his chair, his posture was clearly crafted to provide an air of separateness. His peaked police cap sat portentously on the desk along with the gold name plate: 'Lieutenant Bernard Zima'.

Seeing his guests enter, Zima stood and shook hands with Mikeš.

"Sir, you remember Jonathan Fox…"

"Of course. Thank you for coming in, Jonathan. Felix tells me so many good things. We are lucky to have you."

"Thank you, sir."

Zima beckoned to the available chairs.

Jonny had never enjoyed these meetings, but he knew his role. In his experience, it was important to be courteous, respect rank, provide the update required, and then get out as quickly as possible. Whilst he wouldn't want the top job in a million years, he still found it troubling how the succession of people that got the job seemed to have been created from the same mold.

"Sir," Mikeš began, a forceful edge to his tone, "we all call him Honza around the station. It was my idea but it's sort of stuck."

"In that case, may I wish you a Happy Name Day." Zima beamed his practiced smile. "But, if you don't mind, I'll call you Jonathan."

"I've been called lots of things, sir… Just ask my ex-wife."

Zima paused, processing the information. "I like that. The British sense of humour is famous, but many Czech people do

291

not know how to take it."

"After working with Honza for three months, my English has improved and I find his jokes very funny." Mikeš smiled smugly.

An uncomfortable silence settled on the room. Jonny waited, knowing that it wasn't his role to lead; the history between Mikeš and his superior was personal to them.

"So, we still have Zoe Farrell in custody?" Zima posed, his formal tone indicating he was keen to move on to business.

"Yes, sir," Mikeš answered curtly. "This morning discovered that Michal Polák is the father of her son, Liam. We have just interviewed her again. She claims that she did not know. She says that she got drunk one evening at a conference she was attending with Michal, and one thing led to another... It also seems that David Farrell had started to suspect – we found hairs from his son's head in an envelope. We don't yet know how or when he was going to conduct a paternity test, but—"

"That's all very interesting," Zima interrupted, "but is there anything to explain how Zoe Farrell's fingerprint was on the murder weapon?"

"Well, no, not yet. We have an interview booked with Michal at three p.m."

Zima turned his shoulders away from Mikeš. "Jonathan, what do you think?"

Jonny paused before starting his summation, knowing that it was vital for the case, as well as potentially his future with the Czech Police. The ghostly image of Liam Farrell passed across his vision. "Zoe Farrell has been our prime suspect since we found her fingerprint on the knife in the rucksack. Despite interviewing lots of witnesses and suspects, as well as following all the leads we've uncovered, there is still no reason to call into

292

doubt the validity of the evidence against her. And, although my knowledge of the Czech legal system is limited, I believe that the combination of material and circumstantial evidence we have gathered passes the evidence threshold. The additional new find that Michal Polák is the father of her child only adds weight to her motive, namely that David Farrell found out about his wife's secret, plus her intention to take Liam back to the UK, and threatened her, forcing her to kill him to keep him quiet. But…"

"Yes, Jonathan…" Zima encouraged.

Mikeš was staring at Jonny, riveted and clearly slightly nervous about where Jonny was going next.

"Well, the thing I'm struggling with is that we've now interviewed Zoe Farrell four times in total, but at no time have I suspected her of lying. She has a slightly detached demeanour, seemingly unaffected by the stress and emotion of the situation – she hasn't cried once, or got really angry – but she is straightforward in her answers, with no hesitation, and has remained in control throughout."

"Couldn't she just be a good liar?"

"Yes, sir. But, her reaction when we told her about the paternity test was genuine surprise. Getting pregnant from her one-off fling with Michal was clearly a possibility, but Zoe seems to have discounted it and put it to the back of her mind. I know she works in PR, so she'll be used to manipulating the truth to a degree, but there is nothing in her background or previous behaviour to indicate that she's a compulsive liar." Jonny hesitated, glancing at Mikeš. "In summary, sir, if it wasn't for the fingerprint on the murder weapon, I would be inclined to believe her story."

Zima looked between Mikeš and Jonny, taking his time before responding.

"So, what do you suggest?"

"The only option I can see," Jonny began, "is to delay charging Zoe Farrell until we can—"

"That's not an option," Zima interjected, cutting across him. "This case is very high profile: the media are still all over us. If we have enough evidence, we *must* charge Zoe Farrell with the murder." He nodded vigorously to support his verdict. "If any other evidence turns up, we can supply it to the prosecution team, but in the meantime we have other serious crime cases in need of our resources."

Silence descended on the room again.

Zima turned to Mikeš. "Felix, please close down the case and hand it over to the legal team. According to the case list I looked at this morning, we have some important open cases."

"None as important as this case," Mikeš replied too quickly. "Sir."

"Felix, my decision is final. Please close the investigation down, as I have requested. We have solved the murder. That's all we can do. And, congratulations on another excellent job." Zima nodded his acknowledgement to Mikeš, and then to Jonny.

"Sir," Jonny ventured tentatively, "I completely understand and respect your decision. But, for the completeness of the file, can I ask you a couple of questions about Michal Polák? You seem to know him and his wife, Amy, so it would be useful to help frame the case given that he is now linked with the evidence against Zoe Farrell. We want to be prepared in the event that we get challenged."

Mikeš sat back in his seat, smiling to himself.

"I don't see why not." Zima looked at his watch. "But, I have to leave in five minutes."

"Thank you, sir. Could you first describe how you know

294

him?" Jonny asked. "In general terms, of course. We are only interested in the connections he has."

"I met Michal at a city function about five years ago, and I suppose I've got to know him quite well. Of course, I'm careful not to be seen with him too often: tongues can be very loose around this city. We've had lunch a few times, but mostly I see him, and Amy, at functions. They both do invaluable work in the community. I admire what he has done with his business, building a reputable company that Prague should be proud of."

"Have you been to their apartment, perhaps to an art exhibition like the one I attended last night?"

"No. I understand what people see in art, but it's not really for me."

Jonny smiled in understanding, belying his true feelings. "Have you ever met Walter Blackburn?"

"Yes, I have. Very charming. I think I met him at a charity concert about two years ago."

"This is a bit delicate, but have you ever heard any stories of incentives being offered for favours? Perhaps holidays, or the use of properties abroad, for assistance in business deals?"

"No, not at all." Zima leaned forward in his chair. "That would be quite irregular. And, wrong."

"Thank you, sir. Sorry I had to ask, but your answers are duly noted. I will make sure the summary is written up clearly."

Zima smiled at Mikeš, clearly pleased with his contribution.

"Did Michal ever tell you about the student party in June 1998?" Jonny continued. "He was arrested and brought to the cells, but was never charged."

Zima laughed. "Yes, he did tell me. Quite funny. Something like this has happened to us all at some point in our youth. But, he wasn't charged, so it doesn't exist in the public domain – he doesn't have a criminal record."

"Thank you. Final question from me, sir. Has Michal Polák ever approached you personally for help with any police-related matter? Perhaps something trivial that may have got lost in the busy schedule of the department?"

"No. I can categorically say that Michal has never asked me to intervene on his or anyone else's behalf. He's an honourable man, and I know he wouldn't ask me for anything like that. And, even if he did, I wouldn't entertain the idea." Zima puffed out his chest. "Jonathan, the people of this great city expect my independence in this job, and I would never let them down."

Jonny knew he'd reached the end of the line: he had no further questions, and could see no way to keep the conversation going, probing deeper into the Commissioner's relationship with Michal Polák.

Zima looked at his watch again. "I appreciate that this new information, namely that Michal is the father of the accused's child, will need to be documented. But, we need to tread very carefully now because, through his lawyer, he has raised a formal complaint about police harassment—"

"That's ridiculous!" Mikeš shouted, unable to control his emotions.

"Felix, please calm down." Zima put on his reading glasses slowly and picked up a paper from his desk. "This only arrived thirty minutes ago. It cites unnecessary attention on Michal himself, his family, and also the Midakati business, when we have a prime suspect in custody."

"Sir, how did they find out about Zoe Farrell?" Jonny asked. "They knew last night, when I attended the exhibition of Frida Nilsson's latest paintings. And—"

"It doesn't matter now. The media are reporting that we're

296

holding Zoe Farrell for questioning, so there's hardly a case to answer." Zima consulted the paper and peered at Jonny over his glasses. "Actually, your attendance at the art exhibition is cited in the complaint—"

"But, sir, I was invited by Amy Poláková," Jonny pleaded.

Zima paused for effect. "Your unannounced visit to Michal's apartment to interview his wife on Monday is also mentioned, as well as your demand to interview the other Midakati directors this morning, when Michal was out of the office, I understand."

"Sir, Honza was just doing his job," Mikeš asserted.

"I know that, and none of this is a serious problem to me." Zima took off his glasses and lined them up neatly with the papers and hat on the desk. "Michal is making a point with the complaint. And, I must admit that I do have some sympathy for him. If we do have a prime suspect, which we do, why should we be disrupting *his* personal life, and also *his* business? This is a difficult situation for everyone, but I do not want this to come to the situation where the press pick up on a story that the police have been intimidating an innocent party—"

"I'm sorry to cut across you, sir," Jonny ventured carefully, "but there is still the small matter that Michal Polák is the father of Liam Farrell. This cannot just be dismissed."

"And, I'm not suggesting it should be. But, in the circumstances, I think a written statement will suffice. We already have the transcript from today's interview with Zoe Farrell, and whilst I haven't seen it yet, from what you told me earlier it seems there is nothing to contradict or question the material evidence we have on file. If the statement from Michal includes an admission to the one-off liaison, shall we say, with Zoe, but also clarifies that he did not know that Liam was his son, then we have all the edges smoothed on the case and, I believe, the case can be closed down."

Zima sat back in his chair, smiling, his arms crossed.

"So, to be clear," he continued, "Zoe Farrell will be charged as soon as you get back to the station. And, Felix, you will organise a statement from Michal Polák over the next few days. But, and this is important, I do not want any further interviews with Michal, his wife, or anyone at Midakati, unless I give clearance first."

30

Deceiving Appearance

Mikeš couldn't control himself. He looked towards Jonny with a frown of resignation, sighed noisily, and rose slowly from his chair. Towering over the seated Commissioner, he appeared threatening but also fragile at the same time; his normal bright eyes were darting around his field of vision uncontrollably, set loose by the inner rage clearly burning up inside him.

"Felix, this is the best outcome." Zima leaned forward and put his elbows on the desk, his gesture intended to accentuate the statement. "And, I want to repeat again, it was excellent work by you and your team, catching the murderer so quickly."

"I'm sorry, sir, but I disagree." Mikeš picked up his hat and cane. "It is not good police work."

Mikeš turned and stormed out of the office. The door banged hard into the wall.

"Jonathan, I'm sorry you had to witness that."

"Sir, I owe a lot to Felix for the opportunity he gave me. He is one of the best detectives I've worked with." Jonny stood up. "I support Felix wholeheartedly, and I agree with his sentiments. It does feel like Michal Polák is controlling this process, rather than just letting the investigation take its natural course."

"I can assure you it's not like that. I have to take hard decisions sometimes, for the best of the Police Department and everyone involved. This is maybe one of those decisions. But, I hope that over time you and Felix will come to see it as a correct decision."

"I hope so too, sir. I know Felix is feeling a touch of déjà vu. He thinks this case has the hallmarks of a previous case that was closed down too early in his opinion."

"Yes, I know the case," Zima accepted. "I was younger, like him, at the time of that case. But, having looked at it again, I really don't think there is any comparison between the two cases."

Jonny shrugged; he'd said what he wanted to say but had no information to challenge the Commissioner's view.

Zima held out his hand. "Look after Felix. He's a good man."

"I will, sir."

They shook hands and Jonny left, closing the door behind him.

Jonny found Mikeš smoking a cigarette outside the side entrance of the building. "I didn't know you smoked, Felix."

"I don't." Mikeš took a drag and blew out smoke expertly. "I used to smoke, like many Czech people, but stopped thirteen years ago. That meeting has stressed me out though. I pinched one from a sergeant that used to work for me."

"Well, don't get hooked again. This case, and what the Commissioner has decided, isn't worth it."

Mikeš threw the half-finished cigarette on the floor and screwed it flat with his shoe. "He's wrong not to let us interview Michal Polák again." Mikeš tapped his cane hard onto the concrete step. "The investigation cannot be considered complete: a statement from him is insufficient. The decision that Zima has made is solely to protect Polák, nothing else. That man should be forced to face what he's done."

"The trouble is that we can't prove he's actually done

anything… other than get Zoe Farrell pregnant, of course. I assume that Marek and Lucie haven't been able to find any pattern of contact between Michal Polák and Zoe…"

Mikeš winced and looked down, the answer clear.

"Well then, unless a person close to him tells us something incriminating, or Michal himself makes a mistake – which seems very unlikely – then we're stuck where we are." Jonny sighed. "Maybe Michal Polák is just an incredibly controlling and irritating man, but is innocent of any wrongdoing…"

Mikeš turned to Jonny, pulling the peak of his wide-brimmed hat down to partially cover his eyes. "I just can't help feeling that we've been played. This all started when we were summoned to Polák's apartment through his relationship with the Commissioner. And, at the end, he's spared an interview that would possibly embarrass him. And, he gets away with it, how do you say, scot-free!"

Jonny chuckled at Mikeš' use of one of the English phrases he'd taught him.

"Felix, perhaps you should have a holiday. You could do with some time to relax, help get it out of your system. Take Ella somewhere exotic for a summer holiday, away from the city."

Mikeš' face remained impassive, but he nodded his head slightly in acknowledgement of the suggestion. "That may not be such a bad idea."

***

Jonny sat quietly in the corner of the café, gazing out of the steamed up window. He'd headed straight for the table on entering, seeing Luka busy serving another customer. This behaviour wasn't unusual in itself: the café was his refuge of

301

sorts, and Luka knew his coffee order. What was unusual was his stillness. During an investigation, he usually got to his table and immediately started reading through papers or his notebook, attempting to make the most of the peace and quiet. Not today – there were no notes to consult, motives to mull over, or even interviews to prepare for. So, he sat still and let everything come to him: the sound of the coffee machine hissing, the tinkle of the doorbell as customers entered or left, and people hurrying past the café window on their way to a meeting or heading home early.

Whilst not exactly dejected, he felt flat and listless. The day had turned out the way he'd feared it might; whatever the truth behind Zoe Farrell's relationship with her husband and Michal Polák, she was going to be charged with murder. The final interview had given her the last chance to clear her name, but she'd been unable to do so. The nagging doubt was that she was innocent, but Jonny had no more leads to follow, or time left on the investigation to continue seeking cracks in the solid evidence that was stacked against her.

He grimaced, the image of Liam Farrell once again creeping up on his consciousness. That poor boy: a mother to be charged with murder, the person he called 'Dad' now dead, and his real father discovered to be one of his father's best friends. And, all of it none of his doing. *What a mess.*

The solitary walk from the Police Headquarters had been soothing. He'd declined the lift arranged by Mikeš back to the police station in Prague 1, instead opting to allow the beauty of the city's rolling landscape to pull his mind away from the frustrations of the case. The blustery wind had cleared the worst of the earlier clouds before rain could fall. Patchy blue sky and sun were now jostling with the thinning cloud cover to reclaim back the summer day. At the start of the Čechův most bridge, he

302

stopped to look across the river at the city centre. The river curved away from him to his left and right, providing the deceiving appearance of the old town seemingly trapped on an island. He chuckled to himself, enjoying how the city still had enough wonders up its proverbial sleeve to continually surprise and enchant him.

Another text message from Ivana reminding him not to be late for his celebration dinner – the fourth such message of the day – had made him smile. Usually the one slow in answering, she was clearly feeling the responsibility of organising a special event. Jonny's expectation was another one of the pub landlord's specialities from his late grandmother's recipe book. He only hoped that Ivana hadn't buckled to pressure from Mikeš and organised dinner for four. He tapped out a reply to ease her concerns.

I wouldn't dare be late! Case closed early so plenty of time on my hands. Love H x

Seeing a uniformed policeman walk past the café window, Jonny's thoughts turned to the Commissioner. He'd never really connected with any of the senior officers he'd worked for, believing that they'd all, in some way or another, sold their souls to the necessary evil of police politics: maintaining a good image, improving crime clearance rates, and securing the on-going funding of the police force. Whilst history was driving Mikeš' anger at Michal Polák's seeming untouchability, Jonny himself felt only cold. He'd been expecting Zima's decision in some form or another, and believed that any Commissioner he'd known in the past would have come to the same conclusion.

"Happy Name Day," Luka said, placing the cappuccino on the table and jolting Jonny from his daydreaming.

"Not you as well." Jonny laughed. "More people have

remembered my name day here than remembered my last birthday back in the UK."

"Well, it's a big thing in most European countries, including my home country, Croatia. Usually we give presents as well, so this coffee is on the house."

"Thank you, Luka."

"Lucie will be taking her detective exam now," Luka said, his voice slightly anxious.

Jonny looked at his watch. "Yes, you're right." He looked up at Luka. "You like her, don't you?"

Luka hopped hesitantly from foot to foot. "She's a nice lady. I hope we can go out soon, once her exams are over. Let's see…"

"Good luck to you both. I hope it works out."

The doorbell announced a new customer. "Thanks, Honza. I appreciate that." Luka walked back towards the counter.

Jonny's phone beeped. Anticipating another message from Ivana, he opened the message quickly.

Hi Mr Fox. You didn't call. I'm still up for another thirty mins or so. Danni Hogarth

"Shit." Jonny had left Danni Hogarth a voicemail earlier to introduce himself and request a telephone call at a convenient time. She had then responded by message, suggesting a time to speak, but he'd forgotten with the strain of the day.

"Danni Hogarth."

"Hello, Ms Hogarth, it's Jonathan Fox. Please accept my apologies. My day has been a bit hectic, and I well… Sorry, I forgot."

"No worries. And, please call me Danni."

"Thank you, Danni. Have you heard the news about what's happened here in Prague?"

"Yes, truly awful. I always liked David. He was a top guy."

"Can I ask how you found out?"

"Well, we're all connected on social media so I've seen all the messages in the last few days. But, it was Amy who initially called me. She also told me about the messages that were being sent."

"Amy?"

"Yes. We were the closest of all the girls in the student house at uni: both of us were loud and outgoing. We were also on the same biology course. It's difficult to keep in contact when I'm halfway round the world now, but Amy is pretty good at keeping in touch. She's the only one I speak to really."

"I wanted to talk to you to understand a little bit more about the dynamics amongst the group of friends at university. I thought you might have a different perspective. Is that okay with you?"

"I heard that Zoe has been arrested. Did she really kill David?"

Jonny sighed. "I can't really say too much. But, the evidence against her is quite compelling."

"I can't believe it!" Danni stalled. "She was always the prim and proper one. Very British, if you know what I mean."

"I understand. But, she and David did have quite a lot of problems…"

"Yes, but she was never the type to get excited, or overreact. She was always the calm and collected one. Never ruffled. Also, quite righteous in a way."

"I know what you mean. But, there was the event back in June 1998 when a group of you were arrested and brought to the police station in Prague 1."

Danni laughed. "Mr Fox, that was just a stupid situation that got out of hand – it was nothing. I think there were a few joints

305

doing the rounds at the party, but there were definitely no heavy drugs there. I've no idea why the police raided that particular party. Zoe took it upon herself to stand up to the police officers who arrived, but unfortunately she was a bit too drunk and started being abusive to them."

"Yes, that's what I've been told. But, how did it end up with you, Amy and Michal also being arrested?"

"We wouldn't let them take Zoe alone, so they had to take all of us. Michal was being serious as usual, trying to negotiate with the police officers. But, Amy and I knew they had nothing on any of us and would have to let us go eventually. So, we flirted with the policemen, tried to make it embarrassing for them."

"One of our police officers who was there remembers Amy laughing a lot…"

"I think we both were. I remember her kissing one of the policemen, leaving a bright red lipstick mark on his cheek. We were having a real laugh: they were in a total spin. I remember her telling the officer that he was going to get in trouble for that, just before they marched her off to a cell. We were all let out a few hours later. Zoe was still angry and wanted to make a complaint, but we calmed her down and took her home."

"I've interviewed almost all the friends in your group at university. The way the young men and women from the different houses paired off and stayed together was quite unusual. But, Michal and Amy seemed the definite ringleaders. There seemed a strong emphasis on 'us' in the rules for the group. What can you tell me about that?"

"Being honest, it was the part of the whole group thing that I didn't like," Danni said earnestly. "I'm more of a free spirit – you know, live and let live – but there was an element of control about everything that Michal in particular, but also Amy, did. I love her to bits, and spoke to her about it, but she seemed to like being top girl a bit too much for my liking. Even after university it was there, both of them trying to control what people did at the weekend. Michal was also in his element setting up the business with David, Titus and Karel… It was one of the reasons I went off travelling."

"What did the 'us' mean to people in the group? How did you interpret it?"

Danni sighed. "It was supposed to represent the togetherness of the group: loyalty, supporting each other, honesty and truthfulness, plus also faithfulness, I suppose."

"Faithfulness?"

"We were all young and pairing off, but the agreed rule was that we should respect the relationships and the people in them. So, there was no getting off with each other in secret. If anyone was unhappy, they had to break up their relationship before dating anyone else in the group."

"It all sounds very mature—"

"Stupid you mean," Danni replied bitterly. "Of the ten people across the two student houses, only Titus and I were not in a relationship and it used to get on our nerves. Sometimes it was like a Mr & Mrs game show. We were only twenty years old. I used to hate it."

"Did anything bad or unusual ever happen, relating to that or any of the other rules?" Jonny probed.

"No, I don't remember anything. Freddie and Frida had a bit of an on-off relationship that caused a few problems – she is quite highly strung – but it was actually calm most of the time. A bit too calm, really. I wanted a bit more of a party…"

"Thank you, that's useful. I'm not sure it is going to change the outcome of the investigation, but it certainly helps provide background history for the case file."

"It's Liam I feel sorry for." Danni could be heard sniffing at the end of the line. "I've not been back to Prague for over five years, so I've never met him. But, I've seen the photos. He looks like a lovely boy, but now… It's just awful."

"I'm glad you say that, Danni. Do you know what saddens me most about this whole case?" Jonny composed himself, the emotion climbing inside him. "You are the only one of the friends to have said anything like this. About Liam, I mean. Everyone else seems to be thinking only about themselves."

31

No Secrets Here

The heat of the summer sun had won the battle of the skies, burning off the cloud to reveal a concave ceiling of dazzling blue. Despite the remaining wispy trail of hazy cloud, city workers and tourists could sense the change in the weather and started to strip off their jackets and thin jumpers. The spread of smiles and chatter amongst people walking the city centre streets was conspicuous as they began making plans for the warm midsummer evening ahead.

Emerging from the café, Jonny also took off his jacket and swung it over his shoulder. A smile was harder to muster. The telephone conversation with Danni Hogarth, as well as a quick call to update Mikeš, had done little to lighten his mood. He kept telling himself that the investigation was over, with the bonus of a successful outcome: evidence had been gained for a prosecution, the suspect had been caught quickly, and the Commissioner was pleased. But, something was still bugging him, and he couldn't shake it off.

The lack of satisfaction with the premature closure of the case centred on Michal Polák. The man's ability to weasel out of further scrutiny was admirable in one way, but, sadly, not unexpected; many people with power and/or money managed to slip through the net due to their influence. Jonny's real frustration was that it prevented him getting to the truth, or at least closer to it.

Jonny also knew that a bit more time on the investigation offered no guarantee of getting a different result. Despite believing that Michal Polák should face further questioning, he still couldn't imagine Michal risking everything – his marriage, potentially even the business – to be with Zoe and their son by killing David. It didn't make sense. For starters, Michal and Amy seemed inseparable. In addition, Zoe and David were already separated, so if Michal knew about Liam and wanted to be with Zoe, he could have manipulated the situation if he'd have really wanted to. But, it wasn't even clear if Michal knew that Liam was his son… Jonny sighed heavily in frustration as he sauntered down towards the river; he hated loose ends.

Deciding to walk back to his apartment, Jonny tapped the side of his head gently to shake away his spinning thoughts. He'd been over it in his mind what seemed like a thousand times, but there was still nothing to cling to, nothing to prise an opening. Many murders were simple and happened without planning, gripped by the emotion of an unexpected event. Perhaps Zoe had been incensed by David's behaviour, the extent of which she wasn't revealing, and had simply used the stir caused by the threatening messages to hatch a bungled plan to murder him. Raising his face to the warmth of the pervading sun, he resolved to put the case to the back of his mind. After all, it was his first name day celebration in the Czech Republic and he wanted to make the evening special. He was also looking forward to seeing Ivana; he'd missed her more over the past few days than he'd ever imagined he would.

The path alongside the river was almost deserted, most people still being at work. Only a few mothers pushing buggies and a toddler feeding the ducks interrupted the slapping of the

310

river's waves. Seeing the young children brought his thoughts to Charlotte. She was coming to visit him in three weeks, once her exams were over. The trip was important to both of them: celebrating her hard work, establishing Prague as his new home, and resetting their relationship to reflect her status as a young woman. He knew he needed to draw up a plan soon, booking some restaurants and a few places to visit.

As he approached the main entrance to his building, fumbling for his keys, he heard a woman's voice behind him. "Honza!" Turning around, he saw Amy Poláková struggling out of a taxi, a multitude of designer bags in each hand.

He was stunned, disarmed, as seemed to be the case every time their paths met. *Why is this happening to me?* Of all the people he could meet, on today of all days—

"Come on, Honza, help me with these bags. My arms are dropping off!" She stood impatiently, a big smirk on her face, holding the bags out from her body as if she was in the middle of a photoshoot. Her bobbing blonde hair had been curled for her trip out shopping, bouncing on the shoulders of her silky, pink summer dress.

He was tempted to ignore her, quickly find his keys, disappear through the main entrance to the building, and run up the stairs to the sanctity of his apartment. But, he couldn't do it. The gentleman inside him wasn't going to allow such unscrupulous behaviour. He sighed resignedly, moving towards her with his arms stretched out to help.

The flurry of muddled arms – him taking the bags, her giving, but all in a jumbled fashion – brought them up close, almost face-to-face. She started laughing, pulling back her handbag and cardigan, before bringing their messy dance to a halt. With his face starting to blush, he secured his grip on the remaining bags with his spare fingers and stepped back as quickly as he could to a safe distance.

"Thank you, Honza." She laughed again, stepping forward to give him a kiss on the cheek. With his hands now full of bags, he was defenceless to her actions, unable to move backwards or sideways out of the way. "My detective hero."

She stepped around him and opened the main door. "Come on…"

There was no other option. He stumbled into the building with the swinging bags, through the door she was holding open, and followed mutely as she led the way across the foyer to the lift.

"Michal and I have a wedding at the weekend. Very lavish. I've just bought myself an amazing, new dress. Fits me perfectly." She put her hand up to the side of her mouth to indicate the secret. "Of course, I had to buy a matching hat, bag and shoes as well… But, don't tell Michal."

Jonny had no idea how to react so stayed silent.

"You made quite an impression last night," she quickly added. "And, clever you for buying that painting of Old Town Square. I was thinking of buying it myself but you got there first. Frida was very pleased."

"It's still my favourite place in Prague," he replied, conscious that he should say something. "The colours she captured in the painting are captivating."

The lift door opened and they squeezed in, bags jutting out all around them.

"Yes, Frida is so clever. Most of the paintings in our living room are hers. She seems to be able to bring any scene to life. Amazingly vivid colours, as you say. I can stand and look at her paintings for ages."

The lift arrived at the top floor. Amy stepped out and headed across the landing to the apartment door. Jonny shuffled his way out of the lift sideways, bags still in hand. She opened the door and pushed it wide open. "Just drop them down here in the hallway. I'll go and put the coffee machine on."

"Amy!" Jonny surprised himself with his tone of voice. "I don't think I'm Michal's favourite person right now. The Police Commissioner has told us all, Felix included, to refrain from contacting either of you. The interview that was scheduled for this afternoon has been cancelled…" He paused, realising he was talking too much. "Anyway, I think it's better if I don't come in."

"What nonsense," she snapped, shaking her head in disbelief. "Michal is home. I'll get him."

"Amy. No! Please…"

She was gone, heading into the apartment, leaving him standing outside the apartment with all the shopping bags still in his hands.

He could hear voices from inside the apartment, but couldn't detect any stirring of an argument. Amy reappeared at the door with Michal standing behind her. His face was neutral – the experienced negotiator. He wore almost the same outfit of designer shirt and chinos that Jonny had seen him in every time they'd met.

"Honza, I've just told Michal that we need to bring an end to this hostility. After all, we are all living in the same apartment block. I don't think any of us want to forever be avoiding each other." She looked between Jonny and Michal, both of whom remained silent. "Honza was just doing his job, which I assume has the side effect of creating a few enemies when he's asking tough questions. Whilst Michal, my darling husband, is deeply saddened by the death of one of his friends, and Zoe's arrest for

313

David's murder."

The silence was claustrophobic, the ceiling of the top floor hemming them in. "Come on, boys," Amy pleaded, reaching her hands out in settlement.

Jonny decided to go first, looking directly at Michal. "My involvement in this was, and is still, purely professional. If you felt wrongly accused of something then I can only apologise. As Amy has just said, as a detective I have to poke around and it can sometimes leave a sour taste. But, well, that's my job, I suppose…"

Michal glanced at Amy, who made a circling hand gesture encouraging him to get on with it. "Apology accepted," he said finally. "Please come in."

Jonny cleared his throat to gain their attention before they could move. "We have one small problem," he said. "The Commissioner decided to cancel the interview planned for this afternoon and asked for us to leave you alone, at least until you need to make a statement later."

Michal waved away the objection. "I'll call the Commissioner. I'll leave him a voicemail to say that Amy and I have invited you up – our choice. You call Felix to say that you've been invited up. That should cover all the bases."

Amy turned and walked into the apartment. Michal stepped forward onto the landing, collected the bags with his long arms, before following her inside.

Jonny called Mikeš but it went straight to voicemail. "Ahoj, Felix. Bit of a strange one. I've got back to my apartment building and bumped into Amy Poláková. She and Michal have invited me up to their apartment for a coffee, the intention being to smooth out any misunderstandings. Michal is also going to let the Commissioner know. Just thought I'd keep you in the picture.

I'll call you later, once we're finished. Wish me luck…"

He stepped into the apartment and closed the door.

"Have a seat, we'll be with you in a minute," Michal shouted out from down the corridor – the same corridor that a half-naked Amy had swept down, her towel dropping seductively, only two days before.

The living room had been transformed back to its habitual state; nobody would have guessed that the room had hosted thirty or so guests for canapes and champagne the previous evening. Walking between the large sofas, he noticed a side table had been cleared and now hosted two framed photos, fronted by three burning tea light candles: a professionally taken photograph of David, Zoe and Liam, from when Liam was still a baby, and a snap of Michal and Amy out with them all on a walk in the countryside. Next to the framed photos was a small, red toy car.

Michal walked into the room and saw Jonny looking at the shrine. "Amy created it. She always knows exactly what to do. We bought the car for Liam the last time we babysat for him, but Zoe forgot to take it home with her."

Michal indicated towards the opposite sofa and the men sat down facing each other.

"David was a genius. Yes, that's the only way to describe him. I am all business process – logical, you know – but he would come out with some amazing things: real left-field. Obviously, some of his ideas were rubbish, but others were just absolutely brilliant. You had to see it to believe it."

Jonny remained silent, sensing that the confession wasn't finished.

"I tried everything to keep them together: David and Zoe, I mean. But, it was impossible. We both loved them very much, and…" Michal lowered his head for a moment. "I just don't know

315

what happened."

"I think…" Jonny stuttered, keen to find the right words. "I think that's why Felix and I pushed so hard. Despite the evidence we uncovered against Zoe, we find it quite hard to believe."

"I do understand. But, a fingerprint on the murder weapon is pretty conclusive, isn't it?"

Jonny looked directly at Michal, feeling his temper rising. "How did you get that information?"

"It probably doesn't matter now, does it?" Michal shrugged. "Facts are facts, after all."

"I don't want to cause another fight, but this is the other reason why Felix and I feel riled. Imagine trying your best to get to the truth about a murder, with no preconceptions, only to find out that key information is being leaked. It's just not right in my opinion."

Michal looked up and rubbed his chin. "I can see that. And, I apologise if I've put you and Felix in a difficult position. But, and this is really important, I only asked because I want justice. The friend I shared a student house and then a business with, for something like thirteen years, has been murdered. I know I had nothing to do with it, so I just used every connection I have to get some information on who did do it."

Amy breezed in carrying a tray of cups, her presence immediately brightening up the room. "So, how are you two boys getting along?" She placed the tray on a side table, and handed a cup and saucer to Jonny, then to Michal.

"My relationship with the police wasn't always so close," Michal continued. "I know you've been asking about the time that Amy, Zoe and I were arrested—"

"And Danni," Jonny corrected him.

"Yes, of course, Danni was there as well." Michal smiled at

316

Amy, who was passing around a jug of warm milk. "Arresting us was an abomination in my opinion. They held us all in the cells for hours, even the girls, and took our fingerprint and DNA samples. We'd done nothing wrong at all."

"It's okay, darling." Amy patted Michal's forearm. "It's all in the past now."

"Yes, but it was wrong. Bernard laughs at me—"

"The Police Commissioner?" Jonny clarified.

"Yes. I've told him these type of practices should never have been allowed to happen. I was outraged for years: I hate injustice. Three years ago, I even put in a legal request for our fingerprints and DNA to be removed from the police database."

"You and Amy?"

"Yes. They had to do it because we weren't charged. I told Zoe she should do it as well but I don't think she did anything about it. She didn't seem overly concerned, one way or the other."

Jonny sipped his coffee and remained silent.

"I also know from Titus and Freddie," Michal began, "that you were asking about BMC and Walter Blackburn. On this point…" He glanced at Amy. "On this point, David had a valid argument. I never did anything intentionally, but I think I was swooned by the big investment and perhaps didn't look closely enough at the detail of BMC's background."

"It is not really for me to say," Jonny replied, his tone softer. "All I would say is that maybe it's your opportunity to reward David's legacy by righting a wrong. I suggest you speak to Leo Holub though, because he has a lot of information and if he goes to print without your input it could be quite damning for your business."

Michal nodded, his appreciation clear to see. "Thank you."

317

"How's the coffee, Honza?" Amy asked, her smile radiant. "I get the coffee beans from a small, specialist coffee shop just off Wenceslas Square."

"I really like it. Lovely aroma."

"When we met at the door you said something about needing to complete a statement," Michal enquired.

"Yes, that's right. You will probably be asked for a statement in the next few days."

"But, why?" Michal's frown showed evident confusion.

"It's because of new evidence that came to light this morning."

"What new evidence?"

"I'm sorry but I can't say."

"Come on, Honza," Michal commented casually. "There are no secrets here. Amy and I share everything. Just tell us."

"I don't think I can."

"The so-called evidence must be related to me, otherwise I wouldn't need to make a statement. We're going to find out anyway, so just tell us now."

Jonny paused to assess the situation. The seconds seemed to tick by slowly. I will be telling the truth, he thought, and I have a valid reason for being here. *They're going to find out anyway.*

"Come on, Honza, tell us," Michal insisted. "Amy won't mind."

Amy was beaming her usual smile. "Of course, I won't mind. Nothing fazes me."

Jonny looked slowly between the two of them. *How will they react?*

"Michal, you are Liam's father."

The world seemed to stop. A deathly silence fell on the room. The first thing Jonny saw was a flying cup and saucer, the released coffee falling towards the wooden floor. Through the crockery, seemingly suspended in mid-air, came a whirl of limbs, Michal jumping over the low table and heading straight at him.

Michal landed on Jonny before he could move. His own cup and saucer fell onto the sofa, the undrunk coffee spilling onto his shirt. Jonny put his hands up to protect his face as uncontrolled fists rained down on his head. A punch connected. Using his training, Jonny centred his posture and used all his energy to push outwards, sending Michal flying across the table, back towards the opposite sofa.

"Honza, stop!"

Michal was crumpled up on the wooden floor, moaning under his twisted legs. Amy knelt over him, protecting him from further damage.

"You have just attacked a Czech police officer," Jonny managed between deep breaths, "and I will be filing a report to the Police Commissioner. I suggest you get yourself a very good lawyer."

32

Miscarriage of Justice

Now, he was in trouble. And, not just with the Police Commissioner. Ivana was not going to be happy at all with him turning up for his special dinner with a swollen eye; an evening he'd been looking forward to all week now had the potential to go badly wrong.

Standing in front of the bathroom mirror, Jonny turned his face to examine his eye. No angle helped: the eye was swelling, and starting to discolour on the edge of his eyelid. He hunted through the makeup that Ivana had left in the cabinet but found nothing to help cover the blemish. There was no way out of it, he was going to have to admit that he'd been involved in a fight.

Michal Polák's reaction had been almost primal. The controlled ambience, manufactured by Amy to restore the peace between them, had been punctured the instant Jonny had uttered the truth about Liam Farrell. The attack was without control, self-consciousness, or thought for the consequences; Michal's sole intent had been to hurt back the man who he saw as the symbol of all the hurt befallen on himself, his wife, and his circle of friends. The whirl of arms and legs had been uncoordinated and easily rebuffed, but somehow Michal's long arms had breached Jonny's defences, his fist catching the delicate area around the corner of his left eye.

Thankfully, Amy had remained calm. Once Michal had

recovered, sitting upright on the wooden floor, she'd stood commandingly between them. When she was satisfied that her husband wasn't seriously hurt, she'd turned towards Jonny. He was expecting a shouting match, or at least a barrage of abuse, but her voice remained surprisingly calm and assured when she finally spoke, "Honza, I think you should go."

"I did warn you… But, Michal insisted."

She'd remained impassive, looking at him blankly, her eyes cold. "What does it matter?" Her face suddenly showed the world of pain underneath the usual, false pretence of happiness and smiles. "Please, just go."

"I will. But, I want you to know that I didn't mean to hurt anyone. What I said is true. I thought Michal knew."

Jonny had closed the top floor apartment door and trudged down the stairs to the third floor. Despite what he'd said to Amy, Michal's reaction had told him everything he needed to know – Michal didn't know he was Liam's father. So, both Zoe and Michal probably didn't know, he thought, their drunken liaison one night at a conference being an unspoken secret that they'd pushed to the back of their respective minds. But, as Amy had said, what did it matter? The material evidence was against Zoe. Even if Michal was involved in some way, and Zoe was protecting him, there didn't seem to be any way to prove it.

Back in his own apartment, Jonny had sat down heavily at his dining table, not knowing whether to write a resignation letter or a record of the events that had just happened. He knew his consultancy role was in jeopardy: whilst there was a trail of voicemails to prove he'd been invited up to Michal and Amy's apartment, there was only his word against theirs about what had subsequently unfolded, especially the scuffle. The result, whether he tried to dispute it or not, was that Jonny had antagonised a

321

person known to and liked by the Commissioner, a high profile businessman in Prague, one who had also made a complaint about police harassment during the investigation. Jonny sighed, knowing how every Police Commissioner he'd worked for didn't like unresolved, messy situations, and how appealing a scapegoat always was to clear up the mess.

Feeling the love for his role with the Czech Police, and especially the loyalty and trust shown in him by Mikeš, Jonny set about documenting every action and word spoken, with approximate timings, from his first interaction with Amy outside the building. Forty minutes and five sides of A4 paper later, he had his version of events. After signing and dating his statement, he'd sat back in the dining chair and only then noticed the pulsing around his eye.

***

The Hloupý Honza pub was quiet, so quiet that it looked closed. If he wasn't a detective, he almost certainly wouldn't have sensed that something was off. It was his training. Like it or not, he had an in-built detector that knew what to expect, and an alarm went off loudly in his head if even the slightest detail was suspicious.

He'd left his apartment in plenty of time and strolled uphill to Prague 2, cutting across one of the local parks, Havlíčkovy sady. The weather had delivered on its promise, the evening still warm and muggy. His thoughts had been filled with Michal Polák and his worsening black eye, when he'd suddenly stopped across the road from the corner pub. Something seemed wrong. The lights outside the pub were on, illuminating the colourful signage, but the window blinds were pulled down and the lights inside were off.

His first reaction was to check his phone. There was no message from Ivana since the last reminder earlier in the day. He scrolled up the messages: the Hloupý Honza, Wednesday, seven p.m – it was all correct.

After looking up and down the street to survey the scene, he crossed the cobbled road surface cautiously. He crept along one side of the corner building, careful not to make a sound, peering through the windows where the blinds were not fully pulled down. Returning to the front entrance, he inspected the other side of the building. Nothing.

Taking his phone back out, he called Ivana but the call went straight to voicemail.

He pushed at the door. It wasn't locked. Taking one more look in both directions, up and down the street, he edged the door open. "Jerry?" he called out. The landlord didn't answer. He was now inside the pub, standing opposite the familiar, and usually welcoming bar. But, instead of the regular happy, friendly faces, he couldn't see anything – the bar area was submerged in complete darkness. The only light was a faint glow through the door leading to the kitchen.

"Hello… Is anyone there?" Silence, apart from the slight echo of his own voice.

He jumped, stepping back defensively: a faint rustling sound to the left of the bar. He stared hard into the darkness but couldn't make out anything, just the outline of the closest table and chairs. *What the hell is going on?*

All the lights suddenly came on. His natural instinct was to crouch down, putting one hand up to protect his eyes. The other hand was outstretched, ready to fight off any attackers. But, then came the cheering: a mixture of "Surprise", "Překvapení", and shouts of "Honza". He cowered back towards the door, his heart

323

beating hard, seeing about thirty people coming towards him from both sides of the bar. Jerry and his loyal barmaid, Monika, jumped up from their hidden positions behind the bar counter.

Ivana was first to get to him, wrapping her arms around him and planting a big kiss on his lips. "Happy Name Day, Honza."

Next up was his Czech family. His eyes lit up to see his half-sister, Lenka, her husband, Miloš, and beside them their daughter, Lucie – Sergeant Dvořáková, in uniform, straight from her exam. "Wow," was all Jonny could manage before he was engulfed in hugs and best wishes. "Thank you."

A sudden realisation wrestled him back to reality. He grabbed Dvořáková's arms in anticipation. "Lucie, how was the exam?"

"It wasn't as bad as I thought it was going to be," she replied, quickly translating the exchange for her parents.

Jonny wasn't going to let her off that easy. "Do you think you've passed?"

She blushed slightly. "I think so. Let's just say I'll be very disappointed if I haven't."

Jonny smiled, clapping his hands together in delight. "I knew it." He kissed Dvořáková on the cheek.

Mikeš and Králová were next up, followed by Boukal. After accepting their handshakes and best wishes, he scanned the faces in the now illuminated room. Almost everyone he knew in Prague was there: Luka, Liška, most of Mikeš' detective team, his new friend Duty Sergeant Beránek, various uniform officers from Dvořáková's team, and Ivana's close friend, Barbora. The locals from the Hloupý Honza trailed behind, including Štefan and his faithful dog, Viky.

"What happened to your eye?" Ivana blurted out, pulling his face towards her for a closer examination.

He shrugged innocently. "I had a little altercation."

"A fight? Honza!" She shook her head. "I'll get some ice." She moved away towards the bar.

Mikeš stepped forward, moving in to study the damage. "Michal Polák?"

Jonny rolled his eyes and nodded.

"Well, I hope you gave him a good smacking. He deserves it."

Jonny laughed. "Smacking?"

"Just a word I've picked up from working closely with you." Mikeš winked.

"Actually, I need to confess something to you—"

Before Jonny had the chance to finish, he was whisked through the crowd. Ivana plonked him down on a chair and applied a compact of ice to his eye. "Honza, how could you?"

"It's the half-Czech side of me," he joked – his usual excuse for doing something wrong.

"I'm just glad you're okay."

"I am now." He smiled as sweetly as he could. "I've missed you so much."

She kissed him long and seductively whilst still applying pressure to his eye.

"Thank you for this…" He waved his arm around the pub. "I've never had a surprise birthday party, or anything like it… So many people."

"Well, there are a lot of people in this city that love you already." She shrugged. "Plus, it was your first name day, so I thought I'd try to make it special."

"Thank you, Ivana."

"Prosím."

"How did you manage to pull it off?"

"Easy really, but I had to ask the celebrity detective to help me."

She moved the ice pack. "Ouch," he moaned.

"It serves you right." She kissed him again. "Mikeš placed a plain clothes detective in a car down the road, in the direction we thought you'd walk. He radioed ahead when you arrived, and we turned all the pub lights off."

"You are more cunning than I thought. I can see that I'm going to have to keep an eye on you."

The next thirty minutes were a whirl as he spoke to everyone who had come to celebrate with him. The presents were a surprise: the Czech people shook his hand formally, wished him the best of health and happiness, and handed over a small gift of chocolate, a bottle of beer or wine. Mikeš, Králová and Boukal had clubbed together to gift him a voucher for a Beer Spa in Prague. He was overwhelmed by the generosity of their friendship. Whereas when he'd first arrived in Prague, he'd felt embraced by people because he was a novelty – the celebrated foreign detective – he couldn't now deny that he was here because people wanted him to be here. It had been a curious transition, but perhaps the most rewarding of his life.

Once the party was in full swing, and the beer flowing, he found himself at the bar with Mikeš, Boukal and Dvořáková.

"Just before I left the station, I discovered something about Michal Polák and Amy Poláková," Boukal said, his eyes bright with excitement.

"I'm not sure it will make any difference, Marek," Mikeš muttered. "That man is squeaky clean."

"After you told me about your meeting with the Commissioner, I checked the police database," Boukal continued, unabashed. "We have Zoe Farrell's DNA and fingerprints on the system, as you know, logged under her maiden name, Zoe Henderson. We also have Danni Hogarth's. But, there are no previous records of DNA or fingerprints for Michal Polák or Amy Poláková. Or rather, Amy Russell as she was known in 1998."

"Yes, I know about this," Jonny replied, indicating towards his eye. "Michal told me earlier that he never trusted the police after the incident at the student party. He called the arrest a disgrace. He said that three years ago he submitted a legal request to have his and Amy's DNA and fingerprints removed from the police database. And, it looks from what Marek has found out that he was successful. It's not a surprise really: he's now a successful businessman and doesn't want that event on his record when they were never actually charged with an offence."

Mikeš tutted. "That man will use every means available to him to maintain his clean image. It's odd though that the Commissioner didn't say anything about it."

"Maybe he didn't know, or didn't remember..." Jonny shrugged his shoulders in indifference. "It's a fairly standard practice in the UK now, certainly nothing unusual. People don't want their details held on the police database if they've never been cautioned. But, it does explain why the case file for Zoe Farrell's initial arrest was confusing – some records on the police database from that night had to be deleted."

"So, you think Michal Polák had nothing to do with the murder of David Farrell?" Boukal proposed.

Jonny sighed, glancing at Mikeš. "When I told him about the result of the paternity test, he couldn't control himself." He pointed to his blackening eye again. "His reaction seemed genuine to me. I really think he believed I was making it up just to annoy him."

Mikeš tutted again, rolling his eyes disparagingly.

"He also admitted to mistakes with the due diligence on the investment company," Jonny added, "and seems committed to sorting them out in David Farrell's memory."

"Maybe he will, maybe he won't." Mikeš shrugged, displaying his lack of interest.

"There is something odd about the relationship between Michal and Amy though," Jonny mused. "I've known it from the start, but I still can't put my finger on it."

Realising that the atmosphere was becoming a bit solemn for such a happy occasion, Jonny turned to Dvořáková. "So, Lucie, tell us about the exam. Did you have a question about an old investigation, like we were discussing?"

"Sort of, but it was different. They presented a case that led to a miscarriage of justice: the defendant got off on appeal, and the police were criticised for mistakes made during the investigation."

"That's an interesting approach," Jonny replied. "Quite clever actually. It makes the aspiring detective think about what potential mistakes can lead to."

"It took a while to get my head around it. We had to analyse the investigation and identify the failures, explaining the correct procedures that should have been followed. The defence lawyers managed to prove that the material evidence used in the initial prosecution case was incorrect and hadn't been verified against all available data. There were even suggestions that the evidence had been tampered with, possibly by the police…"

She stopped mid-sentence, seeing Jonny step back and run his hand through his hair. He put his hands to his face, his eyes wide in alarm.

"Are you all right, Honza?" Dvořáková asked, looking

328

concerned.

"What is it, Honza?" Mikeš stepped forward and put his hand on Jonny's shoulder.

He remained silent, attempting to capture and process his thoughts, blood draining from his face as realisation of the truth came to him.

"That's it," he finally muttered, turning to look at Mikeš. "I think I know what's happened. Zoe Farrell didn't kill her husband!"

33

Murder Show

Thursday, 25th June 2010

Jonny didn't sleep at all. Despite a long, traumatic day on the investigation, being centre of attention at the celebration, a few too many beers, and being seductively led to bed by Ivana, he hadn't been the least bit tired. His brain was fizzing with overactive neurons, going back over his synopsis of the murder case, analysing each element repeatedly, to test and retest his supposition.

When his six a.m alarm sounded, he'd curled up next to Ivana's bare back and kissed her gently on the head through her splayed hair. "Ivana, I have to go." Her sleepy reply was inaudible. After kissing her again, this time on the shoulder, he pulled the duvet up to her neck as she buried her head into the pillow. Sliding out of bed, he'd quietly opened the wardrobe to get a clean shirt and underwear that Ivana had wisely insisted he leave at her apartment, and tiptoed into the en-suite.

The party had been difficult for him. As soon as he'd realised the mistake they'd made, his inclination was to rush off and attempt to correct it. But, he knew he had responsibilities: to Ivana, his family, and to everyone else who'd come to celebrate with him. He also couldn't envisage any way to tell Ivana that he needed to leave the party – a party she'd organised – and get away with it. Realising the delicacy of the situation, Mikeš had pulled Jonny over to the side of the bar and made him run through his suspicions. Their huddle appeared to other guests like two good friends sharing a personal moment, but their tête-à-tête was in fact a rapid analysis of the case and an evaluation of potential next steps. Jonny was hesitant: he wanted to stay, but he also felt the pull of justice tugging his arm. Mikeš had eventually won through, convincing Jonny that a few hours wasn't going to make a big difference, so they agreed a plan and rejoined the party. Jonny's only way to push the case to the back of his mind was to throw himself into the celebration, hugging Ivana and raising a toast to thank everyone for coming.

Sitting in the Incident Room, the morning still in its infancy, he stared up at the slow ticking hands of the clock on the wall. He knew he was early, but he'd wanted to be there first: to wait for the answers to either prove or undermine his hypothesis. After all, he'd started the ball rolling in this direction. He felt confident he was right, but he wanted to be ready to face the consequences if he turned out to be wrong. One thing was guaranteed: the Police Commissioner wasn't going to be pleased if Jonny's hunch caused a flurry of unnecessary action and all for nothing. Definitely not after he found out about Jonny's fight with Michal Polák!

First to arrive was Dvořáková, carrying two mugs of coffee. As ever, she looked fresh, unaffected by a busy full-time job, the stresses of revising for an important exam, and attending a party the evening before. "You look at bit rough, Honza," she said, a playful sparkle in her eyes. "Too much celebrating last night?"

"I just need this resolved," he bemoaned, ignoring her banter. "I feel responsible… I should have seen it before."

"Honza, stop it." Her facial expression changed into serious

331

mode. "If you're right, you may have saved Zoe Farrell from serving a prison sentence for a crime she didn't commit. If you're wrong, then she deserves everything she gets. I'm not privy to all that you and Felix were discussing last night, but I do know you're doing this to get to the truth. That's all anyone can ask."

He grimaced, unconvinced, pulling the mug towards him. "Thank you for the coffee."

"You know, one thing I've learnt over these past few months is how emotionally attached you have to be to a case in order to be a successful detective." She sat down opposite him, reaching across the table for his hand. "You and Felix are the same. You both feel the pain, and it seems to invade you, driving you on to consider every angle until justice is done. It's a very special quality, you know."

They exchanged a long, reflective look across the table.

"Painful, though." He sipped the coffee.

"Honza, I'll be pleased if I become even half the detective you are," she insisted. "And, I'm proud of you... All your family and friends are."

The hint of a smile emerged. "Thank you, Lucie."

Any calm was broken by Mikeš' flamboyant entry. "Good morning, all," he called out loudly, taking his hat off with a flourish and placing it on a table with his cane. He sat down next to Jonny. "This is all very dramatic!" The sunny disposition of his wide, energetic grin and orange shirt/tie combination counterbalanced Jonny's pensive mood.

Boukal came through the open door moments later, laden down with papers and bags, looking like he'd already completed a full day's work. His suit, shirt and tie looked even more dishevelled than the previous day, the tail of his white shirt visible below the hem of his jacket. Rather than taking his usual position at the Murder Board, Boukal sat down heavily on the seat next to Dvořáková and plonked all his luggage on the table.

Sensing everyone looking at him, Boukal breathed heavily and began his update. "Last night after the party, I came back here and went back through the files again. When you told us you thought Zoe Farrell was innocent, I was worried someone might have dumped the DNA and fingerprint samples I took from her on Monday. Because we'd already matched her DNA and fingerprints with samples on the police database, the samples I took weren't in theory needed any longer, and I thought one of the team might have thrown them away. But, thankfully, they were still in the file." He sighed in relief. "This morning, to make sure, I went to the cells downstairs and took new samples from Zoe. She was a bit shocked to see me so early, and had lots of questions as you'd expect, but I just said that we'd update her later."

"Great work, Marek," Jonny remarked.

"I also picked up Dr Králová in the car, gave her both samples with the associated paperwork, and then dropped her off at the hospital." He took a deep breath. "And then, back here…"

"Did she say how long it will take?" Mikeš asked.

"Not long, but she did say that she was going to double-check the results, and compare against the original tests, to be absolutely sure."

"And the CCTV?" Mikeš looked at Dvořáková.

"They are going through the CCTV from Monday morning now, sir. Unfortunately, I don't know how long it will take, but there is only a limited time period to be checked. We have two officers working on it."

Mikeš turned to Jonny. "Honza, I think you should give us a run-through of your theory whilst we're waiting. I'm obviously

333

aware of the highlights you told me last night, but Marek and Lucie only know that you believe Zoe Farrell to be innocent. We need to get it totally clear because, if you're right, we're going to need to act fast, including briefing the Commissioner."

Jonny breathed in deeply to compose himself. After taking another sip of coffee, he put his hands on the table. "There were a couple of things bugging me throughout this murder investigation. The first was that we were being played. Felix, as you kept saying, it all started from when we were summoned to visit Michal and Amy on Sunday evening. The focus at that point was the menacing messages sent to the directors of Midakati Limited. But, it immediately changed when David Farrell was found murdered on the metro on Monday morning." Jonny sighed. "All of our attention was on Michal Polák. He was the leader of the male friends from university, and CEO of the business; nothing happened without his say-so. He had powerful connections, both in the business world, and amongst the city's elite – including the Police Commissioner. He also had a beautiful wife on his arm. His influence was clear for all to see. We were blinded by it, and were almost trying to convince ourselves that he was involved in some way. This was exacerbated when we found out that he was Liam Farrell's real father. But, whilst Michal was definitely ruling over the business, the director's lives, and influencing the high and mighty of the city, his wife was running this particular murder show."

"Amy?" Boukal exclaimed, unable to supress his surprise. "Really? She seems a bit of a dreamer to me, just interested in cocktail parties and socialising with the rich and the famous."

Jonny shook his head firmly. "She gives the impression of being an airhead, not caring much, but in fact she's the calculating one. She's actually a very clever woman and knows

334

exactly what she's doing. The more I dug deeper into the history of the group of friends, including talking to Danni Hogarth yesterday, the more I realised how much the friends were controlled by Michal and Amy: they were told where to go out, set schedules for cleaning the student houses, even given rules about how to conduct their relationships. Whilst Michal definitely likes to be in charge, Amy enjoys the control of the situation: exerting power over her friends."

Jonny paused to take another sip. The atmosphere was tense.

"The second thing bugging me was the friends' lack of real empathy with Zoe and David Farrell's situation. This includes Titus Arnold, Freddie Pedersen, even Frida Nilsson. And that, in my opinion, is because they are all a little bit scared. Only Danni Hogarth spoke the truth. An example is the sad situation to befall Nikola Vaněková, especially her husband's suicide. The other friends turned their backs on her, and nobody challenged Michal on how he treated her. I also remember Amy telling me that she'd do anything for Michal. I thought it was an odd choice of words at the time, but now I believe it had a sinister edge to it. I bet if we dig deeper, we'd find many more instances where Michal and Amy's control of their so-called friends was more like bullying."

Mikeš shook his head in obvious dismay. "Why do normal people maintain friendships with these type of controlling individuals?"

"Probably the same reason that women stay with abusive partners," Jonny proposed with a shrug. "These people wrap the others up in rules, promises, anything to bind them in and make it hard for them to leave."

"Madness," Mikeš blurted out.

The group fell into a silent state of disbelief.

"The third thing involved children," Jonny continued.

335

"When I interviewed Amy on Monday evening, she told me she didn't want children. But, then we find out that Michal is Liam's real father. Zoe told us in the last interview that Amy and Michal had had problems conceiving, Michal having told her that he had a low sperm count. I initially missed it, but this must be unlikely if Liam was conceived when Michal had sex with Zoe just one time. I now believe that Amy can't have children, or, at the very least, there's a serious problem with her having children. It is the one part of Michal and Amy's supposedly perfect pairing that is… well, not perfect. I just know that Amy would have wanted to be the first woman in the group to have a few beautiful, bouncing children. But, it clearly wasn't possible. I also believe that the envelope containing Liam's hairs was Amy's big mistake. I believe she knew somehow that Michal was Liam's father – maybe just through their physical similarities – and used it to get close to David. But, she meant to take the envelope away, not leave it at his apartment. She was physically shocked when I told Michal about Liam yesterday. Her mask came off for the first time, and you could see the sadness in her eyes. I'd expected her to be angry with me, but she just seemed sad and tired. I didn't realise the significance when it happened, but now it all seems to make sense." Jonny scoffed, lifting his hand to his swollen eyelid. "Maybe the black eye was worth it, after all."

The door opened quickly, shaking the concentration in the room.

"Ella!" Mikeš exclaimed, seeing his ex-wife. "Come in, sit down." He was out of his seat in a flash, arranging the chairs so she could sit down next to him.

"Stop fussing, Felix," Králová flapped, clearly not enjoying the overzealous attention. "I can sit down by myself!" She took a seat at the end of the table.

336

All eyes were now on Králová: she not only had control over Mikeš, but she also held the vital information to prove Jonny's suspicions about Zoe Farrell. She opened a paper folder and slowly pulled out some loose papers. The silence was almost deafening.

"I first checked the DNA and fingerprint samples taken from Zoe Farrell on Monday against the samples Marek took from her this morning. The good news is that they are a match." Králová scanned the faces around the table. "I then checked them against the police database, and there was no match. So, the DNA and fingerprint samples that we assumed were Zoe Farrell's are, in fact, *not* hers. This means that the fingerprint on the knife, the murder weapon, is *not* Zoe Farrell's."

Jonny sat back in his seat, letting out a massive sigh of relief.

"Your hunch was right, Honza," Mikeš bellowed, slapping Jonny on the back.

"Also," Králová continued quickly, seizing back control, "Zoe Farrell's correct fingerprint and DNA samples match the unidentified samples found in the murder victim's apartment, including on the rucksack."

"So, she was telling the truth," Jonny stated, his tone flat. "She started tidying up David's apartment on Sunday, saw the cocaine, and then searched his rucksack. The question is, does the DNA and fingerprint on the murder weapon belong to Amy?"

"I'm sorry but I can't help you with that," Králová answered. "The DNA and fingerprint samples we thought were Zoe Farrell's do not match with anyone else on the police database. Plus, there are no samples for Amy Poláková on the database, even under her maiden name."

A gentle rap on the door glass made everyone turn their heads. Seeing a female uniform officer standing outside,

Dvořáková got up and opened the door. "This is Sergeant Novotná," she explained. "She has been studying the CCTV with one of her colleagues."

"Welcome to the party, Judita," Mikeš boomed, revelling in the drama. "I'm hearing great things about you from Lucie. What have you got for us?"

Novotná handed out a series of printed images to everyone around the table, but remained standing to brief them. "Sir, we have checked the CCTV footage from the cameras positioned around the street Jungmannova, where David Farrell lived, between seven and eight a.m on Monday morning. The first two images show Amy Poláková approaching the street – she is picked up on two different cameras moving in the direction of the apartment at 7.09 a.m. Then, at 7.32 a.m she is picked up again by the same cameras, but this time she is moving in the opposite direction, away from the apartment."

"Thank you, Judita," Mikeš said. "Great job."

She bowed respectfully and exited the room.

"Amy is wearing her running gear, exactly as I thought she'd be," Jonny stated. "She is wearing a small shoulder bag in these images, but she must have dumped it on her way back." He paused to shake his head in disbelief. "So, she hangs around in the hallway of my building about eight a.m, ready to accidentally bump into me, and tells me that she's heading out for a run. Whereas, in fact, she'd already run the three kilometres or so into the city centre to David Farrell's apartment, and also run back again. She must have left straight after Michal departed for work and got back quickly enough to catch me and hand over the envelope received in the post."

"An envelope that *she* sent," Dvořáková suggested, "in order to frame Zoe Farrell?"

338

"Yes. When the directors started to receive the threatening messages, she saw an opportunity to sort out all her problems. By framing Zoe Farrell for David's murder she would put a stop to his erratic behaviour having a negative impact on Michal and the business. In addition, because Zoe would be in prison for a long time, she thought Michal would eventually be able to use their perfect couple status to apply for custody of Liam, using all their connections in Prague to block any opposition by Zoe's family."

"But, how did she plant or tamper with the DNA and fingerprints?" Boukal questioned, a confused frown on his forehead.

"The simple answer is that she didn't." Jonny leaned forward, scanning the faces around the table. "Back in June 1998, when the student party was raided, Amy must have switched her and Zoe's DNA and fingerprint samples. At the time, there was nothing sinister in it. She was just having fun, giving the police officers on duty the run around."

"Really?" Boukal exclaimed. "Lucie and I know how tough Oskar Beránek is about his team following procedures. It's hard to imagine anyone being able to force one of his officers into making an error like that."

Boukal looked at Dvořáková for support. She nodded her agreement to the statement.

"Well, the first thing to remember is that this happened twelve years ago," Jonny explained. "I'm sure the controls weren't nearly as strong as they are today. I have no idea how it happened, but I do know how manipulative Amy can be. I've seen her in action."

"Oskar talks a good game," Mikeš interjected, "but it was very different in the '90s."

"Anyway, Amy must have switched the DNA and fingerprint

339

samples somehow. When she remembered this, added to the fact that Michal had made the request to have both their DNA and fingerprint samples deleted from the police database, she had the start of a plan. If she could murder David and leave what would be detected as Zoe's fingerprint on the murder weapon, the material evidence would be enough to convict Zoe. Of course, Amy had to make sure that we didn't take her DNA or fingerprints during the investigation. That's why we've had all these games to push us off the scent: using the Commissioner to get updates so she was always ahead of the curve, running me in circles, and finally getting Michal to file the harassment complaint. We thought Michal was the mastermind, but Amy was really pulling the strings."

"But, why did she send the second message at all?" This time it was Mikeš who was confused. "Surely, it wasn't necessary."

"It was just more circumstantial evidence to frame Zoe. I'm not sure if Amy knew that Nikola Vaněková was sending the 'ONE OF US LIED' messages or not – maybe she guessed – but her plan wasn't reliant on it. She just tried to make sure Zoe was accused of sending the second message, even if it couldn't be proved. In truth, it was all part of her game, delivering the envelope to me and getting us running around. I bet if we search her laptop we will find a template for the second message – 'ONE OF US WILL DIE' – although she will have definitely deleted it."

"Hynek will find it," Boukal confirmed, nodding confidently.

"So, the plan was all set," Jonny continued unabated. "Amy had switched the DNA and fingerprint samples in 1998, and importantly nobody knew. She had the opportunity once the first messages started being received. Then she got friendly with

340

David, starting to whisper in his ear. I can't be sure what she told him, but I reckon it was about Zoe wanting to move back to the UK, and then sowing doubts about him being Liam's father. At some point, maybe at the orchestra performance on Sunday, she organised to drop in early on Monday morning to set the ball moving with the paternity test. That's why she had the envelope. Whilst she was there, she fixed the knife into David's rucksack in order to kill him. She positioned the knife very carefully, using her familiarity with the human body, and also knowing how he always sat down with his rucksack on. She made sure to leave a juicy fingerprint on the knife before running back home to bump into me. But, she forgot to take back the envelope with Liam's hair in – her big mistake. Obviously, it was going to come out sooner or later that Michal was Liam's father, but at this point she didn't want us to be aware that there was any doubt."

"I doubt we'll find out how she got the knife," Boukal added. "It's proving hard to trace."

"Maybe we'll get lucky and find a receipt when we search her laptop." Jonny shrugged. "But, if Amy's DNA and fingerprints match the knife and the rucksack, then I think, along with the CCTV footage and the other circumstantial information, there should be enough to charge her with David Farrell's murder."

Králová suddenly started clapping. "Bravo, Honza. If I wasn't sitting here, I'd find it hard to believe. You really are as good as Felix told me."

"Thank you, Ella."

"Yes, bravo," Mikeš echoed, grinning from ear to ear.

Jonny leaned back in his chair once more and ran his hands through his hair. "I'm just relieved." He sighed. "The most important point is that Zoe Farrell can be released, and reunited with her son. But, now we have to find Amy to prove the rest. Until then, it's just conjecture."

He turned to look at Mikeš who was still smirking next to him. "You look very happy, Felix."

"Well, first of all, I think you've just solved a complex and high profile murder. Secondly, you've proved the Commissioner wrong. And thirdly, you've also severely damaged the reputation of that slimeball, Michal Polák – exactly what he deserves!"

34

The Discarded Image

It was time for the second stage of the plan. The first hurdle was to obtain a warrant, and for that they needed clearance from the Police Commissioner.

Mikeš was energised, holding court at the table, enjoying the extended audience. "Remember, everything has to be done by the book – no mistakes. If we don't follow the correct procedures, the Commissioner could have second thoughts given the complaint that has already been filed. Plus, Michal Polák's lawyer will deploy any means available to stall us from searching their apartment, or taking Amy's DNA and fingerprint samples."

Boukal and Dvořáková hurried out of the Incident Room to brief their staff and prepare the necessary paperwork.

Dr Králová stepped over to Mikeš and kissed him on the cheek. "Good luck, dear."

She turned to Jonny. "As for you, Honza, I'm not sure what else to say really… truly inspiring. Once you've caught her, I insist on a dinner for the four of us – with Ivana. I will not accept any excuses. And, *I'm* paying."

Jonny and Mikeš looked at each other and chuckled: a brief moment of jollity before the heat of battle.

"Ella, thank you," Jonny replied. "Ivana really enjoyed meeting you last night at the party. We'd be delighted to come to dinner with you and Felix."

Mikeš dug Jonny in the ribs. "Told you."

Once Králová had departed, Jonny gently manoeuvred Mikeš back into a chair and sat facing him. "Felix, despite the success of the morning so far, there's something important I need to talk to you about." Jonny paused to ensure he had Mikeš' full attention. "The fact is that we made a mistake. We should have made sure that the DNA and fingerprint samples we took from Zoe Farrell on Monday were tested, instead of just relying on the police database. I know we've caught the situation, saving a potential mistrial controversy, but the fact is that we still made a mistake."

"Yes, but—"

"The second point is that I went against the Commissioner's wishes, antagonising Michal Polák, so much so that he attacked me."

Mikeš moved to interrupt again, but Jonny's raised palm stopped him.

"I know you need to call the Commissioner now. I just want to say that if further complaints have been raised against me, or if he wants the case reviewed, I'm willing to resign. I don't want any accusations of malpractice coming back on you, and especially not on the blossoming careers of Marek and Lucie."

Mikeš laughed loudly. "Don't be stupid, Honza. You're worth a thousand of that man, and he knows it. Everything you've done has been focused on seeking out justice. If he decides to pick on you because of this, he'll have to pick on me as well. Maybe we'll both have to resign… But, somehow, I very much doubt it."

Jonny busied himself whilst Mikeš made the call: he sent a wake-up message to Ivana, and another to thank his half-sister for coming to the party. Mikeš' raised voice reverberated in his head but he forced himself not to listen to the words.

"Done," Mikeš finally said, a big smile on his face. "I'm definitely not the Commissioner's favourite person, but then again I never was." He laughed. "The warrant has been approved but he wants me to phone Michal."

Boukal burst into the room. "Sorry to interrupt, but I wanted to let you know that Amy Poláková is not answering their landline number. We've been calling almost constantly for fifteen minutes. Unfortunately, we don't have a mobile number for her."

"Never mind, I'm calling Michal Polák now," Mikeš stated, his control of the situation clear. "And, Marek, get the car ready."

Jonny wanted to listen to this conversation: it mattered to the outcome of the investigation.

The telephone call progressed in a smooth, if formal, fashion, until Mikeš raised his voice. "Mr Polák, you can call me whatever names you want. The same goes for Jonathan Fox. But, yes, yes... Listen... It means nothing to me because I've just had a warrant approved to search your apartment, and also to take Amy's DNA and fingerprint samples... Yes, the Commissioner does know about it. He's actually the one who approved it... Don't try playing games with me! I suggest you meet us at your apartment in twenty minutes. And, make sure your wife is at home when we get there."

Mikeš was still smarting as the Skoda Superb zoomed around the cobbled streets of the old town towards Prague 4. The gearstick and clutch were working overdrive under Boukal's artistry, the car veering from side to side as it was expertly steered around the slowing cars. Every few minutes, Mikeš muttered something in Czech, clearly disgruntled, but otherwise he was silent: in the zone, focused, ready for the task ahead.

The truth was that Jonny didn't like Michal Polák either;

he'd never liked these type of controlling, smarmy individuals who thought themselves better than everyone else. But, as he held tightly onto the door strap in the back seat, he had to concede that Mikeš' hatred of the man was on another level. Whatever the real reason, it seemed to be immovable, and personal. Jonny had also been fixated on people at certain times during his long police career in the UK, usually elusive criminals, but he knew this type of obsession never ended well. He could only hope that the conclusion of the investigation would bring Mikeš release from his unhealthy preoccupation.

Michal Polák's Bentley entered the car park outside the building at the same time as the Skoda. He got out of the car, slammed the door hard, and strode towards Mikeš shouting a barrage of staccato abuse, his face reddening with anger.

A marked police car arrived. Two uniform officers got out of the car and joined the group, clearly sensing that a potential situation might be developing. Mikeš stopped them in their tracks, his hand signal indicating that everything was under control.

"This will be the end of your long, distinguished career," Michal shouted bitterly. "I can promise you that!"

"Inside!" Mikeš barked back.

Michal puffed out his cheeks in irritation, and strode angrily off towards the main entrance of the building, the others following behind. He quickly opened the door, leaving it hanging ajar, and stormed off to the lift. "You're finished," he shouted back towards Mikeš before the lift doors closed.

Jonny, Mikeš and Boukal climbed the five flights of stairs, past Jonny's own apartment, and up to the top floor. The uniform officers followed a respectable distance behind. The apartment door was open. Leaving the uniform officers on patrol outside, they stepped tentatively inside, guardedly checking down the hall towards the bedrooms. The living room was also empty, but they could hear the banging of cupboards in an adjoining room.

The layout of the main room was so familiar to Jonny: the arrangement of the sofas, the art on the walls, the draw towards the terrace and the panoramic view over the city. The realisation suddenly dawned on him that he'd been inside the apartment on five successive days. The missing piece was Amy: the space seemed cold and stark without her flirtatious hold.

Michal strode down the hall and stopped in the middle of the room. His stance was intentionally menacing, clearly demonstrating his disdain for the detectives. Whilst he looked like a successful businessman in his designer suit and open-neck shirt, his facial features were the opposite of cool and collected: his neck and face were blotchy under the stress, his nose flared in fury. "Where's Amy?" he demanded.

Jonny decided to take the lead, hoping to head off an inflamed confrontation. "We were about to ask you the same question. Have you called her?"

"Yes. She's not answering. Her mobile's going straight to voicemail... I've also tried some of her friends, but nobody's heard from her today."

"Was she going out today?"

"How should I know?" Michal snorted. "She's probably gone shopping."

"Look, Michal, this is serious. We have a warrant here to search these premises. You can either comply with the order, making it easier for everyone, or else we remove you from the apartment and conduct our own search." Jonny nodded towards the hall. "What's it going to be?"

Boukal stepped forward and handed the warrant to Michal.

"Why are you looking for Amy? She hasn't done anything."

"I am not at liberty to say at the moment. We just need to find her and ask her some questions."

Michal lowered his head and shook it slowly.

"How was Amy when you left this morning?" Jonny persisted. "Did she say anything that might indicate where she's gone?"

"I left just before seven, as usual," Michal answered snappily. "Amy was still in bed."

"And, last night?"

"Well, obviously, you put a bit of a dampener on the evening, but we talked it through afterwards and she seemed fine—"

"Michal, I don't want to cause another fight, but don't you think it's a bit strange that your wife isn't upset after finding out that you are the father of your friend's child?"

"That's because I told her it was a lie."

"It isn't." Jonny looked Michal directly in the eye, not flinching. "We know you had sex with Zoe once, at a conference – she has confirmed it. We also have a paternity test result to prove you are Liam's father. You can have a copy of the test, if you like."

Boukal stepped forward and handed over a second paper. Michal took this one more graciously, and studied it closely.

"Michal, I think there's a good chance that Amy already knew about Liam. Are you sure she didn't say anything to you that would indicate where she might be going today?"

Michal rubbed his forehead vigorously. "She said she was thinking about going to see her family, to get away from all the stress for a bit." His face brightened. "But, she hadn't booked anything yet. She said she'd look for flights at the weekend."

"Where do her family live?"

348

"Her parents live in Seattle."

Jonny stepped forward. "Right, Michal, this is important. Can you quickly go and check if her passport is where it would normally be, and also if any clothes or personal items have been taken."

Michal obediently walked off, down the hall. They could again hear the sound of banging drawers and cupboard doors from the bedroom area, followed by returning steps on the wooden floor.

"Her passport's gone," he said slowly, a shock of surprise in his eyes. "And, her small travel case is missing. I know because we bought matching cases last year. We keep them at the bottom of the wardrobe."

"Marek," Mikeš began, "call Lucie back at base and ask her to check all flights from Prague Airport for the rest of the day. It sounds like she's heading for the US, but she could have booked a flight to another European city to get a better connection."

Jonny sidled up to Michal. "I know this is difficult for you, but we need to find Amy quickly. It's the only way to sort out this situation. Have you noticed anything else missing?"

"Her wardrobe door's open and it looks like some clothes are missing." Michal's voice had lost its strength. "But, no, nothing else seems to be missing."

"Can you please have one more look around?" Jonny requested.

Michal sighed but trudged off to the kitchen area.

Boukal moved to the corner of the room, talking on his mobile.

"We'd better get to the airport quickly," Mikeš stated, his tone serious.

"Just give me five minutes, Felix. Something doesn't add up.

I can't believe that after all the trouble of trying to frame Zoe for David's murder, Amy would just jump on a plane and run away. I know she made a mistake with the paternity test, but how can she be sure that we've worked it out?"

Michal walked back past them, heading towards the bedrooms again.

Jonny started to walk slowly around the room. He scanned Amy's precious art collection on the walls, and the furniture, but all seemed in order. The coffee table was scattered with papers and magazines. He rifled through them quickly, but found nothing. Lifting his head, his eyeline met the side table next to the sofa. He froze. Something was wrong. The shrine created by Amy was still there, the unlit candles in front of the photo frames. But, whilst there were still two frames on the table, only one of the frames now contained a photograph – the print that was in the other frame the day before had been taken out. And, the toy car was missing.

Michal stumbled back into the room, panting slightly. "I haven't found anything," he said apologetically.

Jonny pointed at the side table. "Michal, a photograph is missing from its frame. I'm sure there were photographs in both frames yesterday."

Michal scratched his head. "I think it was a photo of Amy and me out for a walk with David, Zoe and Liam. Yes, that's right... I was holding up Liam, with Amy on one side, and Zoe and David on the other... But, where could it have gone?"

"The toy car is also missing," Jonny added.

Michal opened his mouth to speak, but no words came. A confused frown started to develop across his forehead.

Jonny stepped forward and picked up the frames, one by one. Whilst inspecting the now empty frame, he spotted something on the floor behind the table. Bending down, he saw it was a damaged photograph laying upside down on the wooden floor. Picking it up and turning it over in his hand, he saw that the photograph had been torn, leaving only the discarded image of Zoe and David standing next to each other.

"Liam!" Jonny exclaimed. "That's it."

35

Runaway Murderer

The car screeched past the entrance to the park, lights flashing, into the quiet street where Zoe Farrell lived. The few pedestrians stopped to stare. There were no available parking spaces, so Boukal double-parked the car on the one-way street and they all jumped out.

Michal Polák opened the rear door. "Back in the car!" Mikeš growled. "Stay there until we get back."

Once Jonny had discovered the missing toy car and the torn photo – the significance of the missing portion being irrefutable – Michal had wanted to accompany them. Mikeš had strongly resisted, his distaste for the man visible in the pained expression on his face. But, Jonny had insisted. His whispered assessment that Michal might be useful to lure Amy away from a dangerous situation, especially if Liam was involved, had trumped Mikeš' objections.

A hurried recap of the situation in the apartment had established the relevant facts: Amy Poláková held an American passport, had a shared bank account and credit cards with her husband as well as in her own name, plus she was travelling with a fabric, designer travelling case suitable for taking onboard a flight. The information had been relayed to Dvořáková, co-ordinating activities from the station, who was instructed to put out a broadcast to all mobile units in the vicinity of Prague, and full alerts to the airport and main train stations in the city. A forensics team were also called in to search Michal and Amy's apartment as soon as possible, although her laptop couldn't be located and was assumed to have been taken with her.

The atmosphere in the car had been tense, cloaked by a stony silence. Mikeš had remained mute, facing forward throughout. Michal kept trying to call Amy without success. Only Boukal broke the stillness at one point, updating them on what was ahead of them. "Liam Farrell has been looked after by a close neighbour since Tuesday: I believe she has a child the same age as Liam. But, Zoe's parents are flying into Prague today, and were due to be taking over babysitting duties."

Now standing on the building steps, the tranquil setting didn't manage to offset the seriousness of the house call. Jonny was anxious, his disquiet being that Amy had got there before them and used all her charms to prise Liam away. He sighed heavily, bracing himself, as the birds swooped between the trees in the park across the road, enjoying the beginnings of the expected dry, summer day.

Boukal negotiated the intercom system and they took the lift to the top floor, where Zoe Farrell lived. The neighbour was standing at the open door of the apartment across the landing, a worried expression on her face. Mikeš took over, introducing himself, showing his badge and asking questions. Jonny's heart sank; he was hoping for the boisterous noise of a couple of children playing together, but all he could hear was a single child's voice, "Mami."

"We're too late." Mikeš sighed heavily. "Amy has been here. She told the lady that Zoe was going to be released today—"

"So, she guessed," Jonny stated flatly. "She knew that I'd work it out, realise her mistake."

"Seems so. Amy said she'd come to pick up Liam so she could take him to meet his mother when she was released. She left here about an hour ago."

"Did she give any hint about where she was going?" Jonny prompted, using his hands to encourage Mikeš to ask the neighbour quickly.

"No, she didn't," the neighbour answered. "Sorry, I speak a little English, but it's not perfect."

"Okay, thanks. So, she didn't say anything that was even a bit odd?"

"Not really. I know Amy a little bit through Zoe. She also knows Liam well. She seemed excited, told Liam they were going on a little trip to get his mummy. I was just so pleased to hear the news, I didn't really think about it. Amy said they'd be back by early evening latest."

"Did she take anything of Liam's with her? Any personal belongings?"

"She said that she needed Liam's identity card for the police documentation. She initially asked for his passport, but I don't think he has one. It seemed an odd request, but she was very insistent. I'm sorry if I did the wrong thing…" She wiped away the tears forming in her eyes. "I used the key that Zoe gave me and got Liam's identity card from her apartment."

"Don't worry at all," Jonny replied, maintaining a calm voice. "Amy can be very persuasive. We will find Liam."

A young boy of about three years old appeared at the door, immediately grabbing hold of his mother's leg when he saw the three visitors.

After a few, brief comforting words, they were back in the lift and running outside to the car.

"To the airport," Jonny bellowed. Boukal put the car into

gear and sped off at high speed.

Mikeš turned around in his front passenger seat. "Are you sure, Honza? If all she has is Liam's identity card, how will she get through the airline checks? He's only three: she'd need to have approved authorisation from his parents."

Michal was following the exchange between the two detectives, his eyes wide in alarm.

Jonny sighed, knowing this was a big moment. At this point, he was starting to regret that Mikeš had talked him into staying at the party instead of arresting Amy immediately. He'd always believed it was better to act quickly and deal with the aftermath later, including in this scenario the probable stink that would have been caused by the Police Commissioner and Michal.

"Felix, I'm not sure to be honest. I just know how manipulative Amy can be…" He felt his eyes struggling to focus under the strain. "If she's implemented such a convoluted plan up until now, she's capable of forging an authorisation form, possibly with a faked signature for either Zoe or David." He paused for thought, puckering his lips in concentration. "But, I cannot see Amy driving a car to the border, or taking a train. She's used to luxury… No, I'm convinced she's going to try to get a flight if she can."

"I trust your intuition on this one," Mikeš said firmly. "It's the best hope we have. Will you liaise with Lucie? I'll make contact with the airport."

Jonny nodded respectfully, recognising the trust that Mikeš was placing in him.

Michal started to ask a question but Jonny rebuffed him with an open palm. "You just keep trying to call your wife. Leave the rest to us."

Jonny took out his own phone and called Dvořáková. "Ahoj,

Lucie. Amy has taken Liam."

"Damn. What do you think she's planning?"

"I think she's heading for the airport. Do you have any news on today's flights?"

"There are no direct flights to the US from Prague, but we're currently working through the possible connections by flying first to another European city."

"Lucie, you need to extend the search to all flights. Even if Amy wants to get to the US, she's not going to be able to just change somewhere and fly on: Liam doesn't have a passport and she'll need to arrange the visas. My guess is that she's just trying to get out of the country. We need to check all the flights, anywhere she might be able to get to with Liam's identity card and a faked parental consent."

"Right, I'm on it."

"And, Lucie…" Jonny's head started buzzing with an idea. "Could you get to the airport quickly?"

"Yes, I suppose so," she stammered. "Judita is very capable of organising everything this end. Why?"

"It's just that Amy hasn't met you. She's met Felix, Marek and I, and would recognise us if we approach her. If you were in plain clothes, maybe with your hair down, she wouldn't think you were with the police. I don't know if it'll work, but it's worth a try."

Dvořáková laughed. "I only took my detective exam yesterday…"

"We both know you passed." He chuckled. "And, don't worry, I'll tell Felix it was my idea."

"Okay. Better get ready. I'll get a lift with the uniform officers heading to the airport as backup."

Jonny was suddenly thrown across the back seat, landing

356

shoulder to shoulder with a sullen-looking Michal. Boukal was in his element at the wheel, throwing the chassis around like a rally car. They crossed the river on Hlávkův most, negotiated the standing queue of cars on Bubenská by driving down the opposite side of the highway into a swerving onrush of cars, and drove straight across the roundabout at Dejvická, reserved only for trams and buses.

The normal journey of forty minutes at best took only twenty minutes. Jonny didn't see much; even when he did open his eyes, the passing buildings, and then green spaces, were just a blur. He focused on stilling his mind, blanking out everything around him, his sole purpose being to apprehend Amy – and bring Liam home safely.

At Terminal One, Boukal turned off the siren and circumvented the barrier by riding the kerb. Mikeš held his police badge out of the passenger window. Two armed airport police gathered around the car. Mikeš again instructed Michal to stay in the car, and led them all into the terminal building, straight into the heart of the departures lounge. Mikeš briefed the armed officers in Czech.

"Honza, I've given them a description of Amy and Liam and asked them to check with all the airline desks."

"But, the flights here only go to non-schengen countries. I know because this is where I flew back to the UK." Jonny scratched his head anxiously. "I know a Czech national can technically travel on just their identity card within Europe, but I'd be surprised if Amy would risk a non-schengen country with Liam. If it's not a problem here, I'm sure it would be a problem at the other end." Jonny looked directly at Mikeš. "Tell the airport officers to check with passport control for completeness, but I really think we should go straight to Terminal Two."

Mikeš called back one of the armed officers and updated him. He turned to Boukal. "Marek, drive the car round. Honza and I are going to run to Terminal Two."

Jonny didn't expect that. "What?"

"Come on!"

Mikeš set off hard, holding his badge out ahead of him. They dashed past the Terminal One arrivals gate, forcing the people waiting to jump out of the way. Jonny was puffing hard. He managed a quick glance across to see Mikeš smiling back at him. He couldn't smile, he had to concentrate on his feet: step, step, step... The long corridor seemed endless. They finally reached the stairs and ascended into the departures lounge of Terminal Two.

Jonny put his hands on his knees, wheezing.

Seemingly unaffected by the run, Mikeš beckoned over two different armed officers and started briefing them. Boukal arrived. A couple of airport security staff ran over to join them. Suddenly they were fanning out, asking staff at the check-in desks.

Jonny decided to head towards security. Three staff were manning the entrance, checking boarding passes. He showed his police badge. "I'm a consultant working with the Czech Police. Have you seen an attractive woman in her thirties – medium length, blonde hair – come through with a young boy? She would have been pulling an expensive travel case."

The security officer shook his head. "No, sorry."

The other two security officers gathered around and Jonny repeated the question. Same answer.

Mikeš arrived beside him. They barged their way through the queue of people waiting for the security check, police badges held high. Mikeš took control, using his loud voice to ask the same question in Czech to all the security staff as he worked his way down the open lanes. All the responses were negative.

Jonny's mobile rang. "Jonathan Fox."

"Mr Fox, it's Judita from the police station."

"Ahoj, Judita."

"Sir, we've checked through all the flights from Prague today, and neither Amy Poláková nor Liam Farrell are booked on any of them. Hynek has been leading the computer search so we're sure it's correct. He's even checked against Amy's maiden name."

"He's checked every flight?"

"Yes, sir. We double-checked but found nothing. There are also no reports from any of the train stations. Finally, Hynek has checked Amy's bank accounts and credit card, including the ones shared with Michal Polák, but there have been no flight purchases on it today or in recent days."

"Damn!" Realising his faux pas, Jonny quickly added, "Judita, great work. Sorry. Thank you for the update. Please keep checking in with the train stations. Let me know if you or Hynek spot anything unusual."

Jonny walked out into the main area of the large departures lounge, feeling a bit dizzy. *What now?* Could Amy be so conniving, he thought, to purposefully plan an escape plan that was against her usual nature? Out of the corner of his eye, he noticed Michal stumbling through the crowd. He looked lost, squinting up at the departures board. Jonny caught up with him. "Michal, does Amy have her own money?"

"How do you mean?"

"Well, you run the Midakati business. Amy doesn't work as far as I know, but does she have income from anything else?"

"Her father is very wealthy. He's a Deputy Attorney General

in the Northwest. Lovely family, massive house—"

"Felix!" Jonny hollered.

Mikeš ran over, his lip curling when he saw Michal with Jonny. Dvořáková arrived at the same time, running over from a lift.

"I've got it wrong," Jonny confessed. "We need to get to Terminal Three. I think Amy has organised a private jet through her father."

Mikeš called Boukal over and they all headed to the lift. They descended one floor in apprehensive silence, and ran outside, swerving to avoid arriving passengers. Dvořáková shouted out instructions to her uniform officers standing next to the parked cars and jumped into the back seat of the Skoda next to Jonny.

Michal had followed them out of the building and was left looking aghast on the pavement as the car sped off, siren and lights flashing.

Mikeš took out his pocket watch to check the time before making a call. His voice was unfaltering, providing clear and decisive instructions over the sound of screeching tyres as Boukal swung the car out of the main airport, onto the back roads.

"Honza, you were right," Mikeš reported. "Amy and Liam are in the terminal building, waiting to board their jet. I've told the airport staff that all planes are grounded until I get there, but that no announcements should be made."

"I've never been to Terminal Three before," Jonny shouted above the engine noise. "What's the layout?"

"It's like an airfield," Mikeš shouted back. "A few planes, a simple check in, no questions asked…"

"Sounds like Amy… I should have guessed."

Jonny held on to the door strap, as normal, but was able to

360

look at Dvořáková properly for the first time. He'd seen her a few times recently in civvies, but it was still a surprise to see her not wearing her uniform on a police operation. Her attire was formal: a knee-length skirt and jacket, paired with a simple blouse, and strappy shoes with a heel. Her hair was free from her usual bun, hanging loose to her shoulders.

She saw him assessing her outfit. "I'm sorry, it's all I had available. I leave some evening clothes in my locker for the odd occasion I go out straight from work."

"No, it's perfect. You look official enough to be working for a private airline."

Jonny shifted forward in his seat to address everyone. "When we get close, I think we should approach with caution. Turn the siren and lights off, and drive slowly up to the departures area. Amy won't be armed, but we don't want her panicking and trying to do something stupid. Liam's safety has to be the main priority."

"Agreed," Mikeš shouted back over the roar of the engine.

"I think Lucie should go in, pretending to be a manager for the terminal, checking that Amy is being looked after. She'll love the attention… We can hang back, guarding all the exits out of the building. Lucie can keep her talking and, when the time is right, get between her and Liam. Then, we'll enter to arrest her." Jonny looked at Dvořáková. "Are you happy with that, Lucie?"

"Yes, sir."

The car approached the entrance barrier, lights and siren turned off. Mikeš spoke to the security guard and explained the plan. Boukal drove on at a sedate pace, stopping the car thirty metres short of the terminal building.

"I want eye contact from us to Lucie at all times," Mikeš said to Jonny. "Marek can patrol the back of the terminal building."

"Agreed."

Jonny and Dvořáková waited at the main door to the small terminal building. Jonny carefully peered through the window. Amy was sat in the waiting area with Liam sitting beside her. Otherwise, the room was empty of passengers. Amy looked more like a film star than a runaway murderer: her hair had been set in perfect curls, her colourful summer dress as radiant as the weather, and the finishing touch of a thin, silk scarf tied around her neck added the touch of a bygone movie era.

"Amy and Liam are in there," he whispered. "The only other person I can see is a woman sitting in the corner. Probably airline staff."

After waiting a few more minutes in silence, Jonny looked through the window again, careful to keep his head back out of view. Mikeš was on the other side of the building, standing up close to the wall but visible at an angle through the opposite window. The door for boarding was next to the window. The men exchanged nods.

"Right, we're set," Jonny whispered. "Play it by the book, Lucie. I don't want you taking any chances."

She smiled, placing her hand reassuringly on his forearm.

She patted down her skirt and entered the building. Jonny stuck out a leg to stop the door from closing fully. Now he could see inside and hear the conversation.

"Hello, Madam. My name is Lucie, the Airline Liaison Manager. I believe your flight is almost ready to board, so I just wanted to take the opportunity to wish you a safe and comfortable flight."

Jonny waited for the reaction – the pause seemed to last an age.

"Thank you, Lucie," Amy finally replied.

"I hope you have been well looked after. Has everything been to your satisfaction?"

"Yes. Liam and I are having fun, aren't we?"

Jonny could see Amy pull Liam close and ruffle his hair. Liam was holding the toy car in his hand.

"Mind you," Amy continued, "the terminal is pretty basic. I was expecting something a bit more lavish. Maybe it would be a good idea to invest in some comfortable seating and decorate the walls. And, personally I'd recommend some champagne for guests."

"You're not the first person to say that," Lucie concurred. "We have plans to modernise the terminal but I'm not sure it will be that lavish."

The two women laughed together.

"And, you, young man, are behaving very well." Dvořáková bent down. "Have you been given a lollipop?"

Liam's eyes lit up in excitement.

"I think we have some behind the counter over here..." She held out her hand. Liam took it and she led him across the room.

Jonny kicked the door open and burst into the room. Mikeš entered from the other door. Amy saw Jonny, and immediately rushed towards Liam. Dvořáková was ready, pushing Liam behind her, using her other hand to keep Amy at bay. Amy swung her arms, pulling at Dvořáková's jacket sleeve. "Let him go..."

Jonny grabbed Amy and wrestled her away. Mikeš took Amy's other arm, and together they pulled her back into a seat. Amy kicked out and caught Jonny on the shin. He winced.

Boukal was next on the scene. He quickly took out his handcuffs and clasped Amy's hands behind her back. "Amy Poláková, I am arresting you for the murder of David Farrell..."

Jonny turned away to see Dvořáková comforting Liam, who

363

was crying. She'd cleverly turned around to shield Liam from seeing what was happening behind her. "Liam, everything will be okay. We'll drive you back to see your mummy now."

"You bastard, Honza."

He turned to see Amy foaming at the mouth, her eyes full of hatred for him.

Dvořáková led Liam away, out of the main door.

"Liam should be with me and Michal. He is *our* son."

"Amy, that's simply not true. Liam should be with Zoe – she's his mother."

"I'm a better mother than she'll ever be."

"I very much doubt that," he answered. "A good mother would never put her child through something like this."

"Honza, you don't realise how hard Michal and I have worked to help everyone over the years. Nikola and Karel were useless. Titus and Freddie aren't much better. Frida thinks she's great but she's just a prima donna. They'd all be nowhere without us! And, as for David and Zoe, well, they weren't even fit to be parents."

"Yes, but at least they all still have their dignity, and will not be imprisoned for murder."

Jonny smiled smugly at her, maintaining eye contact, as Boukal raised her from her seat and led her forcibly out of the terminal building.

36

Catalytic Action

Liam's face lit up when he saw his mother. Finally overcome by emotion, tears rolled down Zoe's face as she bent down and wrapped her arms around her returned son.

Jonny and Dvořáková stood aside and waited, both just happy to be part of the moment. "Thank you," Zoe mouthed.

Liam broke free from his mother's hug and looked at her earnestly. "Mummy, Lucie said I've been very brave. Can I have pizza for being a good boy?" Zoe wiped the tears from her cheek. "Of course you can." She kissed him. "Pizza is his favourite," she explained through a wide smile.

She stood up, holding Liam in her arms. "Sorry, please come in." She walked into the apartment, leaving Jonny to close the door behind them.

"When we were in the car, Liam was telling me about his toys," Dvořáková said to Zoe. "Would it be possible for him to show me? I'd really like to see them."

"Yes, yes…" Liam shrieked in excitement, attempting to wriggle free of his mother's grasp. He grabbed Dvořáková's hand and pulled her down the hallway towards his bedroom.

Zoe indicated that Jonny should sit in the armchair. She sat down on the sofa opposite him. "When I was being released, one of your detectives explained to me what happened," she started. "He also explained your role in sorting it all out. I just want to say thank you. I can't imagine what would have happened to Liam if you hadn't saved the situation."

"Zoe, I'm just sorry that you and Liam had to go through this ordeal. I should have seen what Amy was doing earlier—"

"Mr Fox, that woman has been trying to control all of our lives for years. Michal is a nice guy, but he let her get away with whatever she wanted. You are perhaps the first person to really stand up to her, and finally put a stop to it. So, whilst I was very angry with you before, I'm not now... Don't feel bad. You were the only one to realise the tangled web of lies that she has been spinning. Without that, I may have been rotting in jail for years. And, Liam would be... I don't even want to think about it."

The tears returned. She wiped her eyes with a tissue.

"Do you have enough evidence to prosecute her?" she finally asked.

"I believe we will have. We obviously still need to compare Amy's DNA and fingerprints against the forensic data we have for the murder weapon, as well as the rucksack David was wearing on Monday morning. The search of her apartment, and in particular her laptop, also has to be completed. Amy is definitely guilty, otherwise she wouldn't have been trying to run away with Liam. But, right now, the most important thing is to build a compelling case, with as much material evidence as possible, so that she ends up in prison for a very long time."

"What will happen to Michal?"

Jonny scanned her face looking for clues to the intention behind the question.

"It really depends on what we find," he replied, keeping his words and tone neutral. "At this stage, I don't believe that he was involved at all. However, if we find out that he was an accessory in any way – knowingly hiding something to protect his wife –

then he may face his own charges."

A silence fell between them. He waited, sensing that she wanted to say something.

"I don't know what I'm going to do…" she finally said, her voice wavering.

"I presume you mean about Michal being Liam's real father," Jonny stated, finishing her statement. "I'm sorry, but it wouldn't really be right for me to give you advice on this matter. All I will say is that Liam must be your main priority. Depending on what happens to Michal, you will need to talk to him at some point, but perhaps this is a situation that needs some time to heal first."

Zoe nodded, wiping away her tears.

Liam's laughter could be heard from the bedroom.

"He's a lovely boy," Jonny commented.

"Yes. He's my world."

Jonny and Zoe smiled at each other.

"I'm definitely going back to the UK though," she blurted out. "A fresh start." She nodded her head firmly, confirming her statement.

"That makes sense."

Dvořáková walked back into the room, holding Liam's hand. "Thank you, Liam, I really enjoyed that." She winked at Zoe.

Liam ran into his mother's arms. Zoe cuddled him tightly, kissing the top of his head.

"I think it's time for us to go," Jonny stated, rising from the chair. "But, I'd like to ask you to do something, Zoe."

She looked at him inquisitively.

"Would you give Nikola Vaněková a call? Not right now, but maybe in a few days. I just think you both might need a friendly face right now. I don't know all the history, but she's also had a tough time. You were friends at university. Maybe you can be a support for each other again."

The crease of a smile appeared at the corner of Zoe's mouth. "I will. Thank you, Mr Fox."

Jonny couldn't remember feeling so content with his day's efforts for a long, long while. Apprehending a murderer, and in the process solving a complex case, was always a great feeling, but the cherry on the cake was safely reuniting loved ones. Seeing Liam well on his way to recovery, back in his mother's arms, had restored his faith in the fight for good over evil, and provided reaffirmation of why he did the job. Yes, this day would stay with him for the rest of his life.

Dvořáková's role had been critical to Liam's wellbeing. In the firing line properly for the first time, asked to bait a suspect, she'd excelled in creating an opportunity to seize Amy, but had had the foresight to shield Liam from danger and exposure to the angry confrontation. Although Zoe had directed her thanks to Jonny as the lead detective, she'd also clearly noticed the exceptional care given to her son. At the apartment door, Zoe stepped forward and embraced Dvořáková, squeezing her close in a final release. "Thank you," she whispered.

"Mummy, can Lucie come to tea one day?"

Zoe dabbed her eyes. "Lucie is probably very busy. The police have to work very hard, Liam. But, if she wants to come over to see you, she can come whenever she wants."

Dvořáková bent down and tickled Liam's tummy. "I tell you what. If you are a good boy for your mummy, I will come over to see you in a few weeks. How about that?"

Liam nodded vigorously, smiling up at his mother.

The quietness in the car on the way back to the station was due to tired reflection. Jonny sat in the back of the marked police car, Dvořáková having taken her place in the front seat alongside one of her uniform officers.

"Honza, was it really what I said about the case study in the exam that made you realise Amy had switched the DNA and fingerprint samples?" Dvořáková had turned in her seat to address him. "You know, the question about the miscarriage of justice?"

Jonny laughed. "You do have an inquisitive mind, Lucie."

"I just want to learn."

"Well, the first thing to say is that every case is different. But, often it's the timing of when you come across the information." He chuckled to himself. "The closest parallel I can think of is a thousand piece jigsaw puzzle."

Dvořáková looked confused.

"Well, think about it. How many times do you pick up a piece and not recognise anything to connect it to? It happens a few times as you work on building up the picture. But, then you suddenly have enough pieces already in place and you can see where it fits."

"Yes, I know what you mean."

"A murder case throws out lots of information, but it doesn't appear in a logical order. You have to keep a clear picture in your head at all times, otherwise you'll miss an important, connecting piece."

"So, when I mentioned failures in evidence, it made you question the validity of Zoe's DNA and fingerprint samples?"

"I suppose I'd always found it hard to believe that she wanted David dead. But, I'd accepted the material evidence as fact, and taken my job to be explaining how it was connected to the murder. After all, who questions what the Forensic Pathologist says? Or, for that matter, what's on the police

369

database?"

She nodded her head in acceptance of the point.

"But, when you started to talk about your exam," he continued, "I remembered that we hadn't actually tested the DNA or fingerprint samples we'd taken from Zoe on Monday. Of course, by then, I also had other information to wrap around it: I knew what Amy was really like, how manipulative she could be; I knew more about the evening when the student party was raided, especially how Amy was laughing when she was put in a cell; plus Danni Hogarth had told me how she and Amy had studied biology, giving Amy the knowledge of the human body she would have needed to position the knife in the rucksack. None of these bits of information were enough on their own, but with the information about Michal being Liam's father – her one mistake – I suddenly had the outline of the puzzle."

"So, if I'd have taken my exam on Tuesday you may not have had enough information to put everything together?"

"That's very possible." He laughed. "It's all in the timing. We may have got there another way, but I fear we may have been too late to stop Amy snatching Liam. Plus, there would have been a right mess when it was discovered that the material evidence being used to hold Zoe in custody was incorrect."

Dvořáková shook her head. "Amy is one conniving bitch, isn't she?"

Jonny laughed loudly. "You're right there!" He shook his head in disbelief. "She nearly had me wrapped around her little finger as well, but I thankfully managed to see what she was doing before it was too late."

37

In a Box

The second floor of the police station was awash with noise as they climbed the final steps of the stairwell; the celebration had started without them.

Seeing Jonny and Dvořáková walking across the open plan office, Mikeš stepped out from the crowd and started clapping. "Bravo!" The gathered team of detectives and uniform officers joined in with the usual rhythmical clapping, the sound rising and falling in crescendos.

Mikeš held out his hand to greet them. "Top work, detectives!" he roared.

Jonny shook Mikeš' outstretched hand. "Thank you, Felix."

"Sir," Dvořáková began, her eyes searching Mikeš' face for clues. "You just said *detectives…*"

"Yes, I know." He smiled at her, a teasing twinkle in his eyes. "I've just been informed that you passed your exam. Congratulations, Lucie."

Dvořáková looked at Jonny, her eyes now sparkling with excitement. Momentarily forgetting herself, she threw herself at him. He caught her, swinging her in celebration. "Congratulations, Lucie. Nobody deserves it more than you."

She suddenly realised her indiscretion and stepped back, facing Mikeš. "Thank you, sir." She stood upright and held out her hand formally. They shook hands to seal the news.

"Give me a few weeks to sort out the reorganisation, but

you'll make a great addition to the detective team. Judita seems very capable of taking over, with a little support and guidance from you, of course."

"Yes, sir." Dvořáková glanced at Jonny again, a wide grin on her face.

"Any news from forensics?" Jonny asked.

"Ella phoned me five minutes ago. Amy's fingerprints are a match to the murder weapon. Plus, Hynek has found the template for the second message sent by post; the document had been deleted from Amy's laptop but he managed to recover it." Mikeš clapped his hands. "Come now, it's a double celebration. Sadly, there's no alcohol because it's still lunchtime. But, Katka has made some of her special sandwiches, and we even have some cake."

Jonny threw himself into his second party in as many days. This one was more relaxed, knowing the case had been settled, with the perpetrator heading to a court hearing in a few days' time.

Boukal sidled up to Jonny, looking slightly pensive. "I want to thank you, Honza."

"What for, Marek?"

"I've been worried all day that my mistake would get me in trouble."

"I don't understand…" Jonny searched Boukal's concerned frown. "What mistake?"

"Well, I'm sure it says in the procedures manual that all DNA and fingerprint samples should be sent to forensics for checking. The purpose of the rule is to stop situations like this occurring."

Jonny tutted. "Marek, stop it. I'm sure we'll review the case after this, but don't go beating yourself up. All the decisions taken on the investigation were ratified by either me or Felix. Plus, Oskar Beránek's team are likely to face the most criticism if there is any – they let the samples be switched in the first place."

Boukal's face brightened. "This case has been a learning point for me. I think I've been coasting for a while, pleased with my progress. I never thought for one minute that Zoe wasn't guilty. I believed the evidence implicitly, even the suggestion that Zoe and David were still in a sexual relationship."

"You mean the DNA samples on David's trousers?" Jonny sighed. "Yes, well that was Amy playing games with us. I've no idea what she did to David, but it threw all of us off the scent for a while – *not* just you."

"Yes, I suppose so."

"But, Marek, your point is a good one, and also timely. I've noticed that your standards of dress have slipped again, and it can be a sign of complacency. Let's meet tomorrow to make sure you're looking good for when you pick up your bravery award from the Commissioner. We can also have lunch next week. You are a very good detective, and Felix respects you. Don't forget that."

Hush suddenly descended on the office. Jonny turned his head to see the Police Commissioner advancing across the floor.

"Jonathan, congratulations on solving the case."

"Thank you, sir."

Mikeš arrived at Jonny's side. The others in the party group stepped back to give the senior police officers privacy, using the excuse to get a drink or another sandwich.

"It's hard to believe that Amy would be capable of such a crime," Zima stated.

"She nearly had us all deceived…" Jonny left the words hanging.

"And, what about Michal?"

"We've brought him in for questioning," Mikeš confirmed. "He's in an interview room now."

"It seems unlikely he was involved," Zima suggested.

373

"Let's see," Mikeš answered flatly. "This case has had more than its fair share of surprises. At this stage, I'm just going to interview him with an open mind."

Zima nodded. "Of course, there will have to be an internal inquiry. The complaint from Michal Polák is on the record, and we have to investigate how Michal and his wife were spoken to yesterday evening when I'd given strict instructions that they were not to be contacted—"

"Yes, but—" Mikeš started.

Jonny stopped both men by pulling out the five page statement from the inside pocket of his jacket. "Sir, this is my written account of what happened. It includes mention of the voicemail I left on Felix's mobile, and also the call that Michal told me he made to you. I realise that it doesn't look good on the surface, but I only spoke to them by invitation, and all I said to them was true. The visit to their apartment last night was also the stimulus for me to understand what had really happened. So, I can categorically say that it was worth it."

Mikeš smiled smugly. "That's right. Plus, we have enough evidence to charge Michal Polák with assaulting a police officer."

"Yes, well," Zima stuttered, "I just want to make sure that we have no loose ends, so to speak. Now, let me say my thanks to the rest of the team."

Zima shook hands and wandered off, extending his gratitude to the gathered detectives and uniform officers.

Jonny put his arm around Mikeš' shoulders. "So, Felix, have you given any more thought to retirement?"

Mikeš laughed loudly. "You must be joking, Honza. They'll have to carry me out of this place in a box."

38

Love is in the Air

Sunday, 28th June 2010

The appealing aroma of the cooking roast wafted through the apartment, escaping out of the wide open French doors. The daylight was just beginning to fade, the burning sun of the scorching midsummer's day starting its descent into the horizon.

"Are you sure you don't need any help?" Ivana called out.

A clatter of noise came from the kitchen area as Jonny placed a roasting tray quickly back into the oven, steam escaping around him. "I think we're on schedule. Should be ready in about an hour."

"What time are Lenka and Miloš arriving?"

"Soon. I said six thirty. Time for a drink on the terrace before we eat."

"And, definitely no Lucie?"

"No. She called earlier to apologise. It's the only day that Luka could get off from the café, so they're going to the cinema and then something to eat."

"Sounds like love is in the air," Ivana remarked, smiling to herself.

"I think you're right," he replied whimsically.

He picked up the glasses of white wine from the kitchen island and walked over to the middle of the room. "Na zdraví."

He kissed her lightly and they sipped the wine.

They turned to look at the wall. The oil painting hung alone, dominating the space, screaming out for attention. The thick, silver frame focused the eye towards the bold brushstrokes and vibrant colouration of the twilight sky over Old Town Square.

"I love the way the colours change throughout the day," Ivana said. "This morning the painting seemed full of blues and pinks, but by evening it's changed, the dark purple and turquoise coming through."

"I know, that's what I told Frida. She's captured the essence of space and light perfectly."

They fell silent, each drawn to their own aspect of the canvas.

"You know, you definitely have an eye for art. And architecture. Maybe you missed your vocation in life…"

Jonny laughed. "I could draw a bit in school, but otherwise art was a mystery to me – it didn't seem to make any sense. I tried playing the guitar but could hardly string two notes together."

"But, you could be a late developer. I've already told you, you should try painting."

"I don't know about that," he scoffed. "I think I'll just enjoy the finished results – I'll leave the creative side to the people better qualified than me. Much less stress."

She scowled at him, her disparaging look abundantly clear.

Sensing her disappointment, he decided to change the subject. "So, is my eye for art another reason why you love me?" He bit his lip in anticipation of her reaction.

She turned to face him. "So, you heard that…"

He nodded. "I'm a detective. It's my job."

"Guilty as charged," she said mockingly, raising her arms high, the wine sloshing around in the glass.

376

He smiled. "Well, I have a confession of my own to make."

Recognising the seriousness in his tone, she lowered her arms. Cupping the wine glass with both hands, she looked deep into his eyes.

He glanced down momentarily, concentrating on forming the right words. *I should have planned this.* Emotional situations had never been his strong point.

She waited, the crease of a smile developing at the corner of her mouth.

Here goes, he thought.

"Well, I've now had three months to gather my evidence…" He smiled nervously. "And, I can report that there are many things I love about you."

She smiled, waiting for him to continue.

"Firstly, it's the way you move… I don't know, it's like you are floating over the ground, swishing the hem of your summer dress as you go. I just stand there mesmerised, watching you walk off."

Ivana let out a short laugh, her eyes sparkling at the compliment.

"Also," he continued, encouraged by her positive reaction, "when we're having dinner across the table and you shake your head, your large earrings sparkle in the light, creating a sort of hypnotic effect… I'm convinced it's some sort of magical power you've got."

They laughed together.

"Then, of course, there's your eyes—"

"Honza, shhh… I get it." She lifted herself up on tiptoes and kissed him hard, their lips squashing together in an unrehears/ manner. He pulled her into him with his spare arm, not wan/ to let her go.

They parted, both smiling self-consciously; the moment had passed but they each retained its indelible mark.

They turned back to the spell of the painting.

"It could be worth a lot of money in years to come," she commented, after a long, contented silence.

"Maybe. But, I'll never sell it. It means too much already."